Acclaim for

DAVID MALOUF'S

The Great World

"Malouf is a first-rate writer—a sensitive historian of the spirit, an expert mapper of the fluctuating topographies of souls—and he has composed, in *The Great World*, a passionate, penetrating and remarkably powerful book about nothing less than what it means to be human."   — *Wall Street Journal*

"*The Great World*...reveals a writer with great imaginative powers and a gift for acute psychological characterization."
— *Boston Globe*

"At once an absorbing page-turner and a thought-provoking examination of friendship, family and fate."
— *New York Newsday*

"An engrossing book where the characters take on lives of their own...masterful."   — *San Francisco Chronicle*

D0150286

DAVID MALOUF

The Great World

David Malouf is internationally renowned as one
of Australia's finest contemporary writers. His
other novels include *Johnno, An Imaginary Life,
Harland's Half Acre*, and *Remembering Babylon*. In
1991 he received the Commonwealth Writers' Prize
and the Prix Femina Etranger for *The Great World*.
He divides his time between Australia and Tuscany.

VINTAGE

INTERNATIONAL

The Great World

The Great World

a novel by

David Malouf

Vintage International

VINTAGE BOOKS

A DIVISION OF RANDOM HOUSE, INC.

NEW YORK

FIRST VINTAGE INTERNATIONAL EDITION,
OCTOBER 1993

Copyright © 1990 by David Malouf

Library of Congress Cataloging-in-Publication Data
Malouf, David, 1934–
The great world: a novel / David Malouf.
p.   cm.
ISBN 0-679-74836-9
I. Title.
[PR9619.3.M265G74   1993]
823 — dc20   93-15510
CIP

Manufactured in the United States of America
10 9 8 7 6 5 4 3 2 1

Part One

1

People are not always kind, but the kind thing to say of Jenny was that she was simple.

Children whose mothers were cooking and found they were short of something, breadcrumbs or a kilo of flour, would set up a wail at the thought of having to go down to Keen's and fetch it. 'Aw no, mum! Why me? It's Brett's turn. Make Brett do it!'

It wasn't the walk they objected to, though it was far enough, down the hill and off the main road to the river, or even the interruption to their favourite programme on TV. It was the odd feeling you got when you stood on the doorstep with the bead curtain still clattering behind you and saw the old woman half-sprawled on the counter there, breathing like a big fish that had just been hauled out of the river and stranded. Sometimes she was asleep. You would have to poke a finger into the wool of her cardigan and she would start up and look around in a wild sort of way, then, when she saw that she knew you, give a wet smile.

But simple was the wrong word for her, or so smaller kids thought, because the real thing about Jenny, as she flopped about with her thick arms and shuffly slippers, was that she was likely to say things, and do things too, that you weren't expecting and could make neither head nor tail of.

They felt too a kind of doubt she raised about the order of things. She was ancient, over sixty, but grown-ups treated her as if she was six. You could tell that from the way they spoke to her.

Real children looked at Jenny Keen and she was neither a nice old lady nor a stranded fish, neither a grown-up nor another bigger kid. So what was simple about her?

She was slumped now with one elbow on the flaking sill, looking out across the yard, past the clothesline and the rotting pepper tree, to where her brother was sitting at the edge of the river, just where the bank shelved to the stream.

3

The river was wide, this side of it sunlit, the other in shadow. Digger had a line out and every now and then he jiggled it, but he wasn't fishing. When Digger does something he gets absorbed. The whole of him under the old felt hat is drawn to such a pitch of concentration you can feel it, *she* can, even at a distance; it can be frightening. What he was concentrating on now was the other feller's talk. The line was a bluff to make the talk or the listening easier.

She made a face. She pushed her tongue up under her lip and squinted. She rubbed the back of her head where the hair was hacked off short as a man's. 'C'mon Dig,' she said out loud. 'Givvus a break.'

The two men sat apart but had their heads together, you could see that: Digger in an old sweater that was loose at the elbows and had a couple of good-sized holes in it that she meant to mend; the other feller, Vic, in a smart-looking overcoat. He was the same age as Digger but looked younger because he took care of himself. He was always very well turned out. He sat now with his shoes, which were new and well polished, set down very carefully in the dirt. She noticed the shoes because each time he came they were different, he must have a dozen pairs.

She narrowed her eyes, trying to get the gist of what they were talking about – it was the third time he had been here this week. She couldn't actually hear anything, not at this distance, but if she really put her mind to it she could sometimes pick something up. Not always. But after a minute or two, with nothing coming through, she made a huffing sound, got up, went in behind the shelves of the store into the kitchen, and took a peek at the oven.

This was more like it. Scones. Scones were her long suit. They were coming on nicely.

She went back, leaned her elbows on the linoleum of the counter, and was just beginning to get comfortable when she saw that two magpies had flapped down and were perched now on the clothesline, shifting their heads from side to side in an abrupt, interested way and keeping watch. It was the end of any consolation she might have got out of the scones.

She had a war on with the magpies. She had lots of wars, but this was her fiercest and most continuous.

Big black-and-white brutes with sharp little eyes and even sharper beaks, she hated them, and wondered really what they had been put in the world for except to be a torment to smaller creatures. They strutted

4

about as if they owned the place and were just waiting to take over. As if they had been given control of it; to spy and patrol up and down and peck and punish. Black and white, like bloody nuns.

If she put out the baking-dish, for instance, where she'd just cut up the last of a bread pudding, they would all swoop down, a dozen or more, all jostling, and the little birds, the wrens and finches, would be too scared to come near. 'Get away,' she'd yell, and kick out with her boots. 'This isn't for you.'

But she couldn't be there all the time. She had housework to do and the shop to watch. They'd parade about then as if the yard was theirs, yodelling, muttering their magpie rosary. They'd sit on one of the clothesline stumps and shift their heads, following her every move. If she went out with a basketful of washing they'd go for her head, swoop and dive-bomb her the way they came down flapping and took the eyes out of baby lambs.

It was a war that had been going on for years. It was on a daily basis. Sometimes she won, sometimes they did. But there was only one of her and heaps of them, and they kept coming.

Occasionally an old feller would fall victim to one of the feral cats; or he'd choke on a lump of bread, or a kid with a slingshot would get him. But before you knew it September would be round and there would be babies again, except that these babies were as big as adults and just as fierce, but black, they were born black. So there was no way in the world that you could win.

She had a war on with cats as well, the ferals, but she had inherited that one. It wasn't personal. She kept it on out of loyalty to her mother, to stop the lazy buggers from lying down and sunning themselves in the flowerbeds and flattening the plants, though there were no plants much any more, just a few straggly gerbera, a rosebush or two and a patch of mint. It was partly to make up to her mother for letting the garden go that she kept after the cats.

They were huge. When they stretched out in their matted black or grey fur they were like old felt rugs with just the red of an eye in them, that could suddenly come alive and snarl or show a claw. 'Garn,' she'd tell them, 'don't try that on me!' Every now and then, out of habit, she would slosh a bucket of mop-water at them.

These were her open wars. The others she had to be cunning about.

The young fellers and their girls, for instance, who came into the shop just to tease and make a nuisance of themselves, picking things up and putting them down again just to aggravate. She had to stop herself from yelling at them, telling them off. 'Look youse, if yer gunna buy that tinna jam just buy it, don't stand there chuckin' it about.' But if you did that there would be trouble. For one thing, they were customers, and for another they were dangerous. They had spiked hair, green some of them, and the girls were all in black like widows, and they had earrings, even the boys did, and tattoos. 'How much is this?' one of them would ask while another one got off with a Picnic bar or a packet of crisps. 'See ya,' they'd call, letting the door slam, and she would shout after them 'Drop dead!' – but under her breath.

Her fourth war, which she also had to wage in silence, was with this feller Vic. It went back years.

'So waddazee want?' she had demanded when he first turned up. 'Who *is* 'e?'

Dumb, that was. She knew no better in those days. That wasn't the way to find out.

'A bit of a chat.' That's all Digger would tell her. ''E's a mate.'

A mate! Men had mates. She had never even had a friend. All she had ever had was Digger, and that's just what she had against *him*, this Vic. He butted in. He got between them. He took Digger off.

The first time he turned up she thought he was a ghost, he was that washed-out looking. As pale as potatoes.

'Who are you?' she challenged.

He was standing there in an old army coat that fell to his ankles, all chapped and unshaven, with a short back and sides and his blondy hair sticking up in peaks. You could have blown him over with just a puff. She was younger then. Pity she hadn't done it and got him out of the way once and for all, and saved herself the next forty years. He would have gone over like ninepins.

'I'm Vic,' he said, as if he expected her to know.

If he wasn't a ghost she didn't know him from Adam.

She looked at him hard and saw that for all his being such a tuppence worth of God-help-us he was pretty keen on himself. 'Digger about?' he asked, casting little looks around and ignoring her.

'Of course 'e's about,' she snapped. ''E's off somewhere.' She jerked her head towards the river, not to be too specific (let him do his own finding), and stood with her hands shoved down into the pockets of her cardigan and watched him trudge off with his ears sticking out and

6

the coat hanging from his thin shoulders. She knew where Digger was, all right. He was out the back.

'So waddazee want?' she demanded when Digger appeared at last and saw him mooching about there under the she-oaks. She wasn't going to be fobbed off with this business about mates. 'What's 'e after?'

Digger's face clouded and he was a long time replying. 'Nothing much,' he said, his eyes away there. He didn't seem all that anxious to go down and meet him.

'Listen, Dig,' she had said, lowering her voice, 'I could get ridduv 'im.'

'No,' Digger said after a minute. 'He's all right. He's a mate.'

He went down across the yard, ducking under the line, that was low on its props, to where the fellow in the coat had turned and could see him. He looked so forlorn there, for all his tallness, that she might have felt sorry for him; but she had sensed something in him, first thing at the door, that made her wary. He was stronger than he let on.

She watched them face one another.

They stood a long way apart. Digger was nodding his head and she could tell from the pitch of his shoulders what his eyes would be like; he was an open book, Digger. Then he moved, touched this Vic very lightly on the shoulder and they turned away together under the she-oaks.

She couldn't tell at that distance whether they were talking or just sitting in silence.

If it was talk it had the tense, quivering quality of long silence.

She was a pretty good judge of silence. If you lived with Digger you had to be.

Since then he had been turning up on a regular basis every three or four months – till these last weeks.

It was always the same. Digger afterwards would be as silent as the grave; he couldn't be reached, you couldn't get through to him. She'd flop about like a wounded bird, not knowing what to say or do that would bring him back to the table or into the house even, he'd got so far off. She would try to be quiet with the dishes, but each time her hands let her down and they would clash and bang. When he laid his knife and fork down and went out, she would watch him wandering about there in the moonlight, walking up and down under the clothesline, lost in himself.

7

Digger had other visitors, also mates, but they didn't affect him the way Vic did, and they didn't come so often. That's what she had against him.

Ern, one was called. Another was a jolly, one-armed fellow called Douggy Bramson. He was the one she felt easiest with. For one thing, he had a bit of conversation and wasn't afraid to share it with you, he enjoyed a joke. Then there was the sleeve tucked up neatly with a pin; it aroused a soft feeling in her. Something missing. She tried not to look at it but couldn't help herself. Douggy understood that and didn't mind. Once, when he caught her at it, he winked.

Douggy kept poultry out at Regent's Park, near Parramatta. He always turned up with a dressed chook.

They were Digger's mates from away back. She knew that much because old times was what they talked about while they downed a pot of tea and a couple of pikelets. Hovering about behind them, fetching butter or strawberry jam, she would pick up snatches of what they had to say: names, odd bits of stories. She tried to keep the names in her head in case one day the men who owned them turned up, but they never did.

Mac was one name. Jack Gard was another. Jack Gard had eaten forty-two boiled eggs once at a show up near Tenterfield, and Ern told this story pretty well every time he came. He laughed each time as if the story was new and the others hadn't heard it, and said, 'Can you credit that? Forty-two bloody hard-boiled eggs at a single go. Waddaya think a' that, eh Missus?'

He was noisy, Ern, but Douggy was the one who asked for more pikelets and told her how good they were.

Once or twice what they talked of was the great world.

Occasionally, too, the name that came up was Vic's. She pricked her ears up then, eager to hear some bit of information about him that Digger hadn't told; but they had none, or only what she knew already: that he was a big noise out there.

'Seen Vic lately?' they'd say, 'Vic Curran? – Oh, 'e's been down again, has 'e, t' see ya? Good.'

They knew nothing more than she did. They were fishing for information. They waited, so did she, for Digger to come across with something, but he never did.

He could drive you wild, Digger, with his secrets and his silences. She had learned to live with it. Sitting quietly together over a cup of tea, around nine say with the table cleared and Digger working on some bit of a thing he was fixing, leaning close up to it with his glasses on the end of his nose while she got on with her knitting, she would find his voice in her head, and so clear that she automatically answered it. But when she looked up he was lost in his work. He hadn't spoken. Or if he had it was without thinking.

Still, there were times when he did speak up, and abruptly enough to startle her. 'You and me and Billy –' he would say with the hint of a laugh in his voice, and she would jump right out of her skin.

'What?' she'd say. 'What Billy?'

There *was* a Billy, only she didn't think Digger knew about him. Billy the Rigger. Once, years back, she had gone off to Brisbane with him.

'*You* know.'

'Do I?'

'I told you. Our brother Billy.'

'Oh. *Him.*'

He would have a story then, one of the little incidents of their childhood that he recalled and she did not, though she was three years older. Involving a tyre their father had rigged up under the pepper tree as a swing – he would have been two years old then, could he really remember these things? – or a shoebox full of silkworms, and as he described it she would begin to hear again the rustling of them and see the fat little creatures, all silvery but with darker feet, lifting their heads as they munched and moved about among the leaves; feel the breath too of a smaller kid on the back of her neck. Was that Billy?

She could have turned her head then and seen him, but she had to protect herself; she didn't want him to become too real. If he did she would only miss him when he was gone again or he'd start growing up and become a nuisance. If she let that snuffling little kid with the stream of snot in his nose (which she would not turn and wipe) start growing, he'd end up being sixty years old and right here with them. Then she'd be in a pickle. More sheets to wash, another couple of potatoes to peel, another smelly towel beside the tub, more snores and sniffles. He'd butt in.

'What'd *he* die of?' she would ask, to get it over and done with. It was kinder in the long run. 'Was Billy diftheria?'

Kind and quick. She wished she'd done that with Vic, ages ago, but Billy was easy, he was dead.

The trouble with Digger was, he remembered too much. Give him long enough and he'd remember *everything*.

2

Newcomers to the Crossing, calling on Digger to discuss a bit of work they needed doing, a sundeck extended or a new roof, took it for granted that he had got his name from the war. He was lean-jawed and leathery, said little, was never without a fag in the corner of his mouth and a spare one, newly rolled, behind his ear.

In fact he had been Digger from birth, or very nearly. They had called him that, with no special foresight, before there was any hint of a new war he might be growing up for.

Albert was the name his mother had picked out for him, meaning to call him Bert. But to the father, from the very first, he was another man about the house, a little offsider and mate.

'Right, dig,' he would tell the boy when he was barely old enough to understand, 'we're gunna take a look at this greasetrap. Are ya with me? Geez! Not so sweet, eh?' Or: 'C'mon, digger, we better be makin' tracks or the ol' lady'll rouse on us. We wouldn' wanna be in 'er bad books.' The name became Digger and stuck. After a time even the mother used it, since that was what he answered to, but she regretted Albert.

She had thought of him as Albert, Bert, all the months she was carrying him; had had conversations with him under that name, and believed later, he was such a knowing little thing, that he must remember this and the secrets she had confided to him. But once he was born the father's needs prevailed. He became Digger and that was that.

Their first little girl, Jenny, was slow. The second, May, was already gone before Digger was born. So was the third, Pearl, who survived just long enough to become another absence to tug the mother's heart. She had been banking on Bert.

Back home in England, in the orphanage where she grew up, she had had a brother called Bert. He was the only thing she had that was in any way her own. A stocky, dark little fellow, two years younger than herself, she had fussed over him and come to believe he couldn't get on without her.

Because he had no memory of their real home, or of their mother, she had set out to give him one, to impress upon him by constant telling and retelling all she could remember of their dark little room and the life they had lived there. There wasn't much, but some detail, she hoped, a yellow dress their mother had worn, a picture she recalled of two long-haired cows in a mist, might take life in him and become memories of his own. She owed it to him. To their Ma as well.

But when she sat him down on a form opposite, their knees touching, she could recall very little and he was too young to listen. What she found herself doing was searching his face for some resemblance that would link them and make solid a vision of their mother's pale, pinched features that had already gone ghostly for her. She was assuring herself that she was not alone in the world. Her intensity at these moments scared him. He would hide to avoid her.

Her last sight of him was in a line of other boys, all big-eyed and bony-kneed, shuffling about in the cold, on the stone steps that led up to the schoolroom. She stood below in a made-over dress and with a little bundle they had given her. She was eleven and was going out to begin her working life. In service.

His dark face above the curve of the banister rail was the last she would ever see of him. He was on tiptoe, frowning. Then he raised his hand and waved. When she went back three years later he had gone to be apprenticed in Liverpool.

So when what she knew was proved at last and she had a boy, she had fought for him, from the first day searching his face for some likeness to his namesake, Albert, Bert, and for some hint that her own family, about whom she knew nothing, had come through. But in the end she had given in. Her heart got the better of her. She knew what loneliness was, and how this man she had married, this boy, longed for a form of companionship that she could not give him or which he was not able to accept. Digger, she told herself, wasn't so much a name as an assurance that he would have it at last. She could not deny him that. But before she knew it Digger *was* a name. The child answered to no other. Albert, Bert, the gesture she had made to a past that was beyond recall, was just the name in a register that he would never use.

He wasn't the last. A year later there was Bill, then James, then Leslie, but by then Albert was used up. And they didn't survive anyway, these boys, any more than the girls had. In the end there were just the two children, Digger and Jenny.

Billy Keen had run off to France when he was fifteen. By the time he got home again, a survivor of Pozières and Villers Bretonneux, he had already, at just eighteen, had the one great adventure of his life. Though married and more or less settled as chief ferryman at the Crossing, he continued to live in spirit, since he was barely out of his lively boyhood, at that intensified pitch of daring, terror and pure high-jinks that would forever be his measure of what a man's life should be when he is at full stretch. Anything else was a tameness he could not endure.

History had conspired, for a time, to set him in a world where risk, up to the very edge of extinction, was a point of honour, and animal energy had scope. It was his natural element. After that, life at the Crossing seemed to him like daily punishment. He hated the regularity of it, the timetable the ferry ran on, the six-minute crossing, then the same time back, his having to be home, and already washed and brushed up, for dinner at twelve and for tea at six, the fuss about knives and forks and the state of his socks. It meant nothing to him that Keens had been at the Crossing for a hundred years and that the place bore his name. He was too young, he felt, for the responsibilities that were put upon him by a household that had arrived from nowhere, had simply crept up on him (that's how he saw it) while he was dreaming at the wheel. *She* was the trouble, the girl he'd got.

He had met her the first week he was back. She was a barmaid in a city pub. He had taken one look at her and told himself: 'She'll do.'

He said this thoughtlessly, because he was eighteen, wanted a girl of his own and didn't know any better. He was home now, and the next thing to do was get married. It was what blokes *did*. What else was there? He knew nothing about her except that she was lively, had newly arrived in the place and had a soft mouth with just a touch of colour to it. He had spent three years dreaming of that colour. She ruled the rough clientele of the pub, which was a waterside pub at The Rocks, in an easy, no-nonsense way that impressed him. You could play up to her but there was a line, and she soon let you know if you tried to cross it. He was amused by that.

She knew what he was after. He was no different in that from the rest. But there was something in him that appealed to her. He was like a cricket, very chirpy and always on the dare. His military bravado took the civilian form of impudence, especially where girls were concerned. He would look you straight in the eye with so much confidence in his own attractions that she was tempted to laugh outright. 'Yes, it's me,' the look said. 'I'm a bit of all right, eh?' He would wink then and you could see the utter satisfaction he felt in himself. 'Well, that oughta do it.'

In fact he was wrong. It wasn't that that did it. She could take with a good deal of salt the sort of swagger, of inexperience too, that made him feel she could be caught (girls are easy) just like that. 'Not me, m'lad,' she told him with a look of her own, and set her jaw.

But she too was eager to get out of her present life and be settled. It was what she had come all these miles for. And something he had said, just in passing, had caught her ear. The place he came from bore his name. Back home in England that meant something, an ancestral house or manor, or a sizeable farm at least. Family names on a map were solid; they rooted you in things that could be measured, so many acres. So what, she wondered, was Keen's Crossing? It wouldn't be a manor of course. She knew what country she was in; she wasn't quite a fool. But it must be *something*. She was a practical girl and added it to the immediate and more touching fact of his ears.

It would have surprised Billy Keen, and might have reduced him a little, if he had realised that what had fetched her was not the line he ran, not at all, but the giveaway reddening of his ears. What he had awakened in her, though she didn't know it yet, was the mother she would be in less than a year if she took him. His ears made such perfect shells.

In fact they were deceived, both of them. What she took for boyishness in him was a lightness he would not outgrow. He was strong-willed and stubborn, in fact. He would not be led. As for what amused him so much, her competence – the ease with which she managed men and change and glasses and all sorts of daring backchat – he did not like it much when it was applied daily to *him*. She was competent all right. Ambitious too. And when she got hold of a thing she hung on to it.

She would remember the journey to Keen's Crossing for the rest of her life, perhaps because she was to make it just the once. Every detail of it remained new for her.

Years later, towards the end, on a windy day in August, she would climb the bluff behind the Crossing and be astonished to see that

Sydney, a place she thought of as worlds away, further even in some ways than England, had all the time been visible, just thirty miles from where she was. She could have gone up there and looked at it any day of her life. Its outer suburbs by then were already climbing the far side of the ridge.

But it wasn't in fact the same city she had come to and left more than thirty years ago. That had been a big country town with arms of the harbour breaking into it at every turn, open trams bucketing about and sparking on their poles, wagons with heavy carthorses loaded with barrels and barefoot boys shouting headlines at every corner; a shabby place, all steep hills and with ships of one sort or another, or masts at least, at the bottom of every street. What she saw now, from a distance of half a lifetime, was skyscrapers.

The thirty-mile journey by train, and then sulky, had taken all day. At first through suburbs that were all new brick bungalows and gardens dense with pin oaks and rhododendron; then, with the last of the streetlamps, market gardens tended by Chinese. At last they had come out on to a plateau under a scud of clouds. Stretches of low flowering scrub lay on either side, broken by platforms of rock. When they left the little isolated station and made their way down to the river, the Hawkesbury, the road (a highway they called it) took bend after bend, and the trees, which were both above and below them, were of a kind she had never seen before, giants with feathery tops in bunches, and trunks and limbs of a naked pink or white, incredibly twisted and deeply creased at the joints with folds like fat. Ridged outcropping ledges tilted and thrust out at angles, and there was a smell of animal droppings, dark and heavy, mixed with the crush of ferns. She soon saw how different it was from England, and how wrong, how romantic, her expectations had been.

They turned off the highway, took a less frequented road which was also a highway, and came down to where the store occupied its elbow of dust in an arc of the river. The ferry was idling at the bank.

'Well,' he said, 'this is it. Waddaya think?'

She didn't. She had given up thinking miles back and had sworn then that she would never come this way again. Whatever it was, she would accept and make the most of. Thirteen thousand miles, plus thirty, was enough.

The road they were on came to a halt at the ferry, then took up again on the other side, where it went all the way, he told her, to Gosford,

Woy Woy, Maitland: he spoke these names as if they offered the possibility of escape. But she had never heard of any of them, and told herself she could do without them. Sydney, too. She would stick to what she had got.

It wasn't much. Whatever modest grandeur or continuity she had imagined, and had hoped in her ignorance to find in a settled-looking house and garden, had to be taken up from the landscape. It was wild, but once she stopped thinking in the old terms and opened her eyes and let it work on her, she was struck by the stillness of it, the space it gave you to breathe.

It wasn't what she had wanted – how could it be when she hadn't even known such a place could exist? – and she wasn't sure, either, that she had the qualities to deal with it, since she had been preparing most of her life for something else. But *something* in her wanted it, now that it was here. Something new in her, that the place itself would deal with.

She committed herself immediately, come what might, to *that*, and made a mission of it.

Newly come home and not too happy about it, Billy watched her closely, seated on a log and sweating, knocking away flies. 'You're not disappointed?' he asked.

She was the one who had wanted to come here. If only to take a look. He had banked on her being put off by the dreariness of the place. They would look and go back to town. Sydney was what he wanted.

Her look of fierce resignation was the first indication he got that she might not be what he had taken her for. She strode about looking, asking questions. He fell deeper into gloom. She *liked* it. She was making plans.

The river was wide between granite bluffs that were all yellow-orange in the sunset and forested with the same weird, fleshy trees they had come down through. But there was a pepper tree in front of the store and, behind, Scotch firs. Very gloomy they looked too, compared with the lightness and airiness of the bush trees; familiar, yes, but that was just what she didn't like about them. Still, it was through them that she saw what the others might be.

No sign of a garden. Not even a geranium in a tub.

Not much of a house either. Just the gabled store, all weatherboard, unpainted for ages she thought and a lot of it gone to ruin, with, at the back, three pokey rooms.

What Billy couldn't know, following behind her and feeling more and more uneasy, was that it was more than she had ever had in her life before. It was all to be *made*, and what she made would be hers.

The store was boarded up. 'Well,' she thought, 'we can reopen it.' The house was filled with rubbish except for one room. Billy's brother Pete lived there, or rather, camped in a space he had made by pushing the rubbish it contained into the corners of it. He immediately offered to give the place up to them, and his job at the ferry to Billy if he wanted it. He couldn't wait to get away.

She had looked forward to this brother, hoping to learn from him some of the things that Billy didn't know or couldn't be bothered to tell. Having got a relation at last she was determined to make the most of him. She had seen herself making meals, looking after his clothes, in exchange for which there would be confidences.

But one look at Pete was enough. He and Billy might have been strangers for all they had to say to one another; and when she followed him to the woodpile, and tried to draw him out, he was scared out of his wits. He leaned on the axe and muttered, so awkward and shy she thought he might choke. He had none of Billy's lightness. Billy stood at the door of the shack and laughed.

Pete had been living in the house as if he had come upon it by chance, and Billy came back to it, she saw, in the same spirit. The house, all this, meant nothing to them. For the remainder of the week, which he endured only to collect his wages, Pete avoided her, then was gone and they heard no more of him.

This carelessness about things she held sacred astonished her. The place after all bore their name; the house was the one they had grown up in, even if it was given over now to the bush rats whose nests were everywhere, and to big spiders with egg-sacks under their bellies, and woodlice and centipedes. Rolling her sleeves up she got the three rooms cleared and clean again, but Billy scarcely noticed and did nothing to help. He was happiest camping in one room like Pete, wearing the same filthy shirt he had worn all week and splashing his face with two fingers of water from a pail. He was, she saw now, a kind of savage, as resentful as a ten-year-old of any suggestion that he should wash his neck, or his feet at least, before he came to bed.

There were few relics in the place of any former habitation, but rummaging about one day in the bottom of a cupboard she found a stack of photographs, dusted them off, set them on the rickety sideboard and spent the rest of the morning studying them for some clue to this family she had married into – what it was that might go into her children, when she had them – and for some clue to *him*. When he came in she questioned him.

'Oh, that's Merle,' he said lightly of a big girl, lumpish and worn-looking, whom she had taken at first for the mother. He stood easing his braces over his shoulder and peering.

'Yair. That's Merle. She lives up Lismore way. Or Casino. *I* dunno.' Prompted, he named the others.

'That's Jess. Geez, what a tartar!'

'Where's *she*?' she demanded.

'*I* dunno. Married. Out west somewhere, I dunno. She's no loss.'

Eric had gone to work on the railways. 'Funny feller, Eric,' he laughed. 'A bit touched.'

Leslie?

'Went ta Queensland, oh, ages ago. Just ran off. You shoulda heard dad roar! I was on'y a nipper.'

He told all this with only the most casual interest and with none of the little details that might have made any of it real. They had gone. He didn't expect to see them again and didn't care, one way or the other. Should he?

Her parents-in-law, the mother and father of this scattered brood, appeared on their wedding day; he in a tight-looking suit with a stiff collar, a grim-faced working man who didn't know where to put his hands; she in a cup-shaped chair in front of him, her skirt spread and at her elbow a pedestal and urn.

She tried to find something in them, stunned to immobility as they were by the occasion, that would explain why every one of their children had gone off without a backward glance, or, so far as she could see, a twinge of regret. What brutality was it in the father? What empty-headedness or ignorance or dull indifference in the mother? What failure to hang on to things, or even to see, if Pete and Billy were an example, that there was anything to be held.

'Yairs,' he said. 'That's dad.'

He frowned, rubbed his chin with the heel of his hand, sounding resentful.

He took the photograph and peered at it. 'Yairs,' he said, 'that's me *mother*,' as if what she had been demanding of him was the identity of the woman at his father's side, rather than some living detail of her. 'When she was young.'

It was all he had to say, and she looked at him now and wondered what it was that had bruised all feeling out of him. Or had he never had any?

She had thought at first that he was simply lackadaisical, unwilling to be bothered, and had put this down to his youth. But the truth was that he did not care and wondered why *she* did. He looked at her in genuine puzzlement and was hurt, then irritated, but a moment later was all brightness and affection, whisking her about on the scrubbing boards, full of fun and boyish roughness and urging her to go to bed when it was still daylight.

'What is it?' he asked when they did lie down together. 'You're the one who wanted to come. I thought you liked it here.'

'That's your father's family,' she would tell Digger and Jenny. There was a vehemence to her voice that amounted to savagery, though she tried to hide it.

'This is your grandma. And this is your father's dad, your grandpa,' and so on for each of the uncles and aunts. She was determined that they should have a family and was giving them all she had to show. It infuriated her that she had never seen any one of these people except Pete.

They might have dropped out of the world the moment their likeness was taken, for all the evidence they had left in the house, or anywhere else for that matter. No toys ever turned up. Not even a peg-doll or a home-made top. Even in the yard when she broke the soil for her garden. Not one of them had ever carved his name on a bit of furniture, or scribbled drawings on a wall, or left height marks on a door. Billy, unless urged, never mentioned any one of them, and had no tales of his childhood to tell. He might never have had one. He was born with the war.

Her own family, she was convinced, would not have given in so easily to extinction. She sent letter after letter to the orphanage in an attempt to find Bert.

It was in defiance of this almost criminal indifference in their father's people that she began to inculcate in Digger, and in Jenny too so far as she was capable of it, her own view of things, which was fanatical. She had been famished all her life for what these people, these Keens – Billy among them – tossed away like the merest trash. She wouldn't let *her* kids grow up like that.

The Crossing first: *Keen's* Crossing.

They belonged here for all time now, it was marked with their name. They could see it on a map if they liked: a dotted line leading away from the highway; at the end of it a dot marking the store; beside that, in italics, *Keen's Crossing.* To turn your back and walk away from it was a crime. Against yourself first of all. Then against what had been trusted to you. Then against the place itself, and if you didn't know what *that* was, then just open your eyes and look around you.

Family next. That too was a kind of place, a place in time. Turn your back and walk away from that and you lost all hold on the line of things. The line was blood. Turn your back on your family and you drained the blood from your heart.

She painted a fierce picture, and Digger at least was terrified of her. It was a religion she was preaching, her own, and she was its implacable embodiment.

One more thing. At the orphanage they had got a good dose of preaching. She had been unimpressed by most of it, but one thing struck her and she had incorporated it into her own system. It was this: what you got in the next life was neither more nor less than what you had gathered and made something of in this one. So if you went through life with nothing, nothing was what you got in the next life as well. It was a harsh law but it chimed with something in her nature and she had taken it literally.

Her vision was of a room with curtains, furniture, the smiling faces of children round a table piled high with food (including pineapples), and with good cutlery laid out and glass and plates such as she had seen in the houses she worked in. A German roller in a cage would be trilling away and ducking its head in a bath and shaking off brilliant drops. In drawers, if you opened them, would be aprons, teatowels, napkins, all neatly folded, and silver serviette rings with initials; plus sugar tongs and grape scissors, embossed.

She saw all this very clearly, though as yet she possessed not a single one of these things. She had nothing at all. Every least bit of it however was already there, just waiting to be gathered, and would go to the making of her life; and when she was dead she would sit grandly content and justified in the midst of it, her children and grandchildren about her and each item at last in its place, even the meanest redeemed out of ordinariness and alive again in the eternal, yet recognisably and tangibly itself.

⌐She tried to pass this vision on to Digger and Jenny as a way of explaining to them why it was that she hung on to things. She did succeed with Digger, but he took the idea and interpreted it in his own way. His vision too was literal, and it was a good while before she saw that it was not at all like her own. She had made him a priest all right, but of his own religion.⌐

It was in this spirit of making and gathering, this dedication to the religion of *getting*, that she set about reviving the store.

She had a head for figures, orders, invoices and such, and took no more nonsense from the travellers who turned up with samples than she had from the drinkers at the pub she had worked in. When the store was ready she got to work on the house. From the David Jones catalogue she chose curtains and wallpaper; then later, a utility set for them to eat off, Wood's Ware, not cheap Japanese, and a set of celluloid serviette rings with initials.

Billy watched all this with suspicion. Her orderliness made him uneasy, and her tendency, as he thought of it, to put on the dog — maintaining a bit of decency was how she would have put it — enraged him. He had married a plump little girl with blonde curls and a bit of colour to her mouth, and had ended up with a woman who could run things. She tried to run him.

He submitted at first. Anything for a quiet life, that was his motto; women were odd, you had to humour them. But when she tried to rule him he rebelled. He didn't want to be cleaned up and made respectable, it didn't suit him. He hated the neat little curtains she hung, the amount of washing she put out and the new poles he had to cut for her lines, the floors he couldn't walk on in his hobnailed boots, and all the other evidence of what hampered and restricted him, this domestication she expected him to be *grateful* for.

Wasn't she making a home for *him*? That was the song she sang. Well, he could do without, he didn't want it. He resented all these little wants she had, that were in fact criticisms of the way *he* preferred to live. He even resented, at last, the success she made of the store, because of the strength it gave her. It put him in the shade. *He* could support them. He didn't need her to do it, and to show him up with how clever she was, and with manners she had picked up from people who were not their kind and that he had no time for and no wish to imitate, and all the palaver as well that went with them. Like serviette

21

rings! She cast a gloom over him with the life she was making. So did the Crossing. He hated it, always had. Her passion for it was exaggerated. He took it as another form of rebuke to him, another criticism. Everything he wanted, everything that gave his spirit scope and made his blood beat, she forbade or cast scorn on.

He set himself against her. He wouldn't have done; he was easygoing by nature, and at the start he had been genuinely fond of her, had wanted her to have whatever it was that made her happy. But she had set herself against *him*.

He would sit out on a stump and curse when he was supposed to be chopping firewood for her copper, deliberately dawdled over jobs he could have finished with one hand tied behind his back, not to give her the satisfaction of having him always on call. He stayed out with the boys when she was expecting him on the dot for tea, and complained bitterly to his mates, when he had had a drink or two, of the haste with which he had put himself in harness. What a fool! At twenty-one his life was finished.

Back there in the trenches, even if you ran the risk of extinction, and maybe most of all then, you were alive. He had known the full power of his own presence, breath and balls and fingers and the small hairs at the back of his neck. It had spoiled him, that glimpse of what a man might be. The life he was living now was nothing. Maybe it would be different if he had someone who knew what he was on about when he wanted to talk.

Then Digger came along, and he had someone at last that he could be himself with, a mate; an ally too against the world that she was mistress of, that took no account of a man's world because it had no use for it, only for the dumb, animal side of a man, work, and the bit of pleasure he would be allowed in the getting of a kid. All they wanted beyond that was to make a dummy of you, with a lot of rubbish about clean collars and toenails that didn't do damage to the sheets, and serviette rings and God knows what other useless lah-de-dah lady's business.

These were some of the things he raved about when he had Digger alone. But when the anger left him at last he had other things to pass on to the boy.

They were inseparable from the start. As a toddler with his nappy sagging and their dog Ralphie at his heels, he trotted in the father's footsteps or squatted beside him with a toy hammer in his hand, imitating the father's muttered curses and his way of holding his head to one side and sucking in his cheeks as he got set to belt a nail.

He was good with his hands, Billy Keen. Everyone knew that. He could knock up anything you liked, a table or a medicine chest, dovetails and all; or hang a door or fix a roof. He was good with machines, too. Machines, people said, would talk to him, start purring and singing the moment he laid a hand on them. It was a gift. Digger had it too, or by intuition had picked it up from him.

Machines were alive to Digger in the same way Ralphie was; and he was so close to Ralphie that it had taken him ages, when he was little, to see that they were of different species. The mother, who could not always be on the watch – she had Jenny as well as the shop and house to care for – was forever having to snatch Ralphie's feeding dish from him. 'Leave that, you little grub,' she would tell him, 'that's Ralphie's. Here, spit that out right now.' In a storm once he had crawled into Ralphie's kennel, out under the pepper tree, while thunder rolled, lightning blasted and the whole yard turned to mud. He had never felt so safe or warm. In dreams sometimes he found himself back in the dark, animal smell of the kennel, with Ralphie's warmth against him, and felt he had arrived at a place where he knew at last where he really was, had rediscovered, in the individual grains of dirt he was pushing into his mouth, what it meant to be on the earth. It was the same way with machines. He understood the workings of them as if they were continuous in some way with his own nature. They purred for him, they sang, as they did for his father. There were no words for this.

At barely ten, a scrawny kid, tough and hard-heeled, with a skin so pale you could see sunlight through it, he would relieve his father at the wheel of the ferry, feeling the huge power in his arms as the barge, with its load of vehicles, swung out into midstream. His father, leaning back against the machinery and blowing smoke, would direct him.

'One day,' he told himself, 'this job will be mine.' He had no thought but to follow in his father's footsteps.

He watched his father, picking up from him mannerisms he thought of as being essential to the man, and acquiring thus a set of gestures that were not individual to the father at all. Billy Keen, as a lad of fifteen, unsure of himself and eager to be recognised as a man, had picked them up from older fellows in the army in France. So at seven Digger had already the loose slouch that is the soldier's stance when he is off-duty or between moves. He would sit on one heel and narrow his eyes at the distance before there was any distance much to be seen.

The mother saw all this and began to regret the mistake she had made in letting go of him. She had thought then that she could afford to; there would be others. But the others all died on her, and though Jenny was a soft-mouthed, good-natured little thing, you couldn't depend on her. Digger, in fact, had been her only chance.

And the miracle was that for all his loyalty to the father she hadn't lost him after all; that was the sweetness of him. He stuck to the father, but he stuck to her as well. They were bonded. They had their own codes and passwords, that others did not recognise, even when they were at the same table. They talked in silence. And one of the things they talked about was the others, the ones who were gone now, all but Jenny, but whose invisible presence she still clung to because they clung to her. They hung on to her skirts when she was out at the clothesline wrestling with sheets. They moaned and whimpered from corners, spat out mouthfuls of porridge and chewed crusts, sat in the sooty stove-alcove and banged on saucepans with spoons. And Digger, who had barely known them you might have thought, not only saw them there but could speak to them and give you details out of their brief existence that even she had forgotten. He was extraordinary, Digger, in what he saw.

It was his ability to call up these little ghosts, and so clearly and in such detail that it broke your heart, that constituted the bond between them and made her believe that his memory might go back further still: to the time when, in her loneliness, she had talked to him in the womb.

So she too had her triumph. Let them be mates, or whatever it is these men are together! Let them! He is bound to *me*.

She was hard on him, she had to be. She couldn't be certain to what extent he had inherited his father's weakness. She believed he would see this one day and be grateful to her.

Given the choice (but who has a *choice*?) she might have let him off. There was a part of her nature in which nothing would have pleased her more than to be one of the serene mothers you read about in books. But what good would that do him, or her either?

The rages she got into scared her. She did not know at times, when she struck out at him, cuffing his ear or sending a stinging blow across his cheek, what it was in him that made her so angry, except that there were occasions when his simply being there was enough to do it, the soft look he wore, the vagueness of him. She was afraid he would go his father's way. But she was equally afraid of his brightness, his curiosity. These too might draw him away.

For all the skill he had with his hands, it was his mind he lived in, and there was no way of fathoming *that*. There were too many things in there, even if they were facts, that had no weight in the world; that's what she saw and had to warn him of. If he clung to them he would drift.

The father wasn't blind.

'You mustn' let yer mother put you off, Digger. I mean, women don't know everything, you know, though they reckon they do. It's a different world, their world. A hard one, I admit. Yer mother's got a hard life. That's me, partly.' He gave a laugh as if he were in the end quite proud of it. 'On'y we don't tell 'em everything we do, you know what I mean? All the bits of fun we have, or what we're thinkin' sometimes. They wouldn't understand. Yer mother now. I don't want t' speak badly of 'er, she's a good woman in most ways. But she's a worrier. Yer better off – you know – keeping some things t' yerself, you know what I mean? I mean they got *their* world, son, and we got *ours*, an' the two are chalk an' cheese, you can't trade 'em. Yer mother wants to hang on t' you. She wants to spare you from life. I don't blame 'er fer that. It's understandable. She doesn't want to lose you. On'y you can't go on tryin' to live her way forever. Dig – it's just not possible. One day, one way 'r another, you'll have to go out into a man's world. Believe me, son, yer mother won't help you then. I seen all that. Fellers cryin' out fer their mothers in no man's land, with half their head shot away or their guts spillin' out. They could cry as long as they liked but I never seen no mother turn up. It was a man's world you was in. It was other men you had to rely on. Stretcher-bearers, if you were lucky, otherwise just yer mates. That's the truth, Digger. That's what yer mother won't tell yer.'

These conversations took place on Sunday mornings when Digger and his father, with Ralphie trotting behind, went out with a 202 to get something for the pot.

Not far from the Crossing was a bit of a branch line that had once served a mining village back in the hills. It ran for twelve miles through cuttings, round sheer hillsides, and was little more now than a playground for kids who liked to walk its rails like a tightrope with outstretched arms, and a scavenging place where men would come with a crowbar to tear up sleepers or gather coals.

Digger loved the line, as they called it. So did Ralphie, who would leap off down the bank on the scent of something, a feral cat, maybe a rabbit, while they called after him 'Skitchum, Ralphie. You skitchum!' The walk, the stopping and starting, the intervals given over to getting a bird and bagging it, imposed a rhythm on these outings that was good for storytelling but also for talk. They were not always so chatty as they were out here. They could work side by side for hours sometimes without exchanging a single word.

The stories were the same ones over and over, and Digger never tired of them. In their daring close-shaves and feats of bravado he got glimpses, quick ones, into his father's other nature, the one that was under restraint here, the necessary restraint of the family man. In that other dimension, he was a boy not much older than Digger himself, light-footed, eager for the world, full of energy and pluck. They were of an age there, and here too once the stories got going.

'It wasn't all bad, Digger. There was a good bitta fun to be had if you looked out fer it. Always is. But a lotta the time it *was* bad, and some of it was hell. The cold fer instance. Wicked it was, you can't imagine. But you'd be surprised what blokes c'n put up with. When you really get down to it. Well, I was one a' the lucky ones.' He said this fiercely and went silent, and his mouth was so grim that Digger, watching him, wondered if he really believed it.

His stories always involved the same characters and Digger got to know the men's names as if he had known *them*. They were the men, he guessed, that his father was closest to, even now; closer certainly than to any of his drinking cronies at the pub, or fellows they exchanged a word with here and there at the ferry – regulars – or when they went into town to find some machine part they needed.

Wally Barnes was one. Digger saw him, for maybe the hundredth time, go sideways off the duckboards. Saw his eyes turned up white, filling with mud; his mouth already full as the weight of his boots, his pack – his own weight too, he was a big fellow – took him down. Felt at the end of his arms the tug of the fifteen stone, and would close his eyes and with a jerk, as his father had, for the hundredth time, break his grip.

Billy Keen told these horror stories in a voice that scared even himself, as if no amount of telling would ever get him used to the fact that they had happened, and he had once been part of them. He lifted his head and looked about the still place they were in, which was all sunspikes and glitters, almost soundless except for the flutter of a grasshopper's wings, as if it was this that he needed to be convinced was present and real.

Digger too felt a chill go over him; and the father, seeing it, would feel sorry for the boy, for having dragged him so deep into things.

'Well,' he would say, 'at least you won't have to face that, Dig, not that. It won't happen again. Can't. We finished it once 'n fer all. It can't happen twice – not that sort a' thing.'

'Can't it?' Digger asked himself. 'Is there a rule?'

He looked at his father's youthful shoulders, the jaunty way he stepped over the sleepers, and thought: 'Well anyway, he come through it. I reckon I will.'

He did not think this in a superior way. For all his mother's criticisms, which she did not hesitate to present the moment she had him alone, he knew his father's qualities and admired them. He took no part in their war.

'I'd watch out if I was you,' she warned him. They would be out under the pepper tree where he was helping her hang out, shifting the props, or it might be Friday nights in the back of the shop where she was making up deliveries, weighing out salt, flour, rice, tea in brown paper packets, while he read to her from the order book and packed each thing as she handed them to him in a butter-box. 'You'll catch *his* disease if you don't watch out. You'll be a dreamer like him.'

'Is Dad a dreamer?'

He wouldn't have said so. Action was what his father was in love with.

'What else would you call it?'

She plonked another bag on the scales, settled the half-pound weight, and poured in another dozen grains. She was precise about these things.

He took the bag from her, folded the top down and settled it in the box.

What she was really warning him of was the difference between what she called reality, or duty, or fate – she had different names for it on different occasions – and a hunger he had, and which his father had too, for something that began where her reality, however clear and

27

graspable it was, left off. Something he knew existed because he had already got glimpses of it, from his father; from fellows too who talked to him at the open doors of their cars during the six-minute ferry crossing; from books; from the pictures he had been to; and from some physical stirring as well in his own belly.

What it had to do with was the sheer size of the world, and the infinite number of events and facts and objects it was filled with. Things you could touch and smell, but other things too that were just thoughts; which were real enough, and could even be put into words and turned this way and that, but you couldn't see them.

There was no set of scales in existence that could measure all that, and no number of little paper bags would be enough to contain it, but your head could. That's what he had seen. Your head. Which was the same shape as the world, and really was the world, only on an infinitely small scale; an inch to a million as on the globe he loved to look at, where the tip of your finger could cover an area of thousands of square miles, and whole cities with millions of people in them, but only because in your head you could *see* this. Didn't she know these things? Didn't she want to know them or want him to? He saw the scared look on her face.

'Don't worry, Mum,' he could have assured her. 'I'll be all right.'

But that wasn't really the point, and he knew it. So what he said, putting his arm round her waist and hugging her, was, 'Don't worry, Mum, I won't leave you.'

'It's not me I was thinking of,' she told him, and pushed him off. 'You know that.'

'Who then?'

'You know.'

He did, too. She meant Jenny. But more than that, the Crossing. But what she really meant you couldn't put a name to. It was so powerful that when she summoned it up he could accept and bow his whole life before it, yet at the same time he wanted to break and run.

Jenny.

There was no moment he could recall when this sister of his, this big soft girl who was three years older, with her milky breath and bubbly lips, had not been at his side.

When he was very little she liked to look after him.

'Now you watch Digger,' the mother would tell her, 'there's a good

28

girl,' and just to be safe, so as not to lose sight of him, she would haul him on to her knee and hold him so tight he would go breathless.

'No, love, I said *watch* baby, don't squeeze him like that. He's a baby. He won't go away.'

But she had seen others and *they* had gone away. She kept hold of him, and if she didn't, and he began to crawl off, she would go running on her stumpy legs to their mother: 'Digger! Digger's under the dunny! Digger's eating dirt! Digger's getting *away*!'

But by the time he could talk Digger knew that he was the younger only in years. Whatever they pretended, he had on all occasions to look after *her*. To be an interpreter between her and a world that would always go too fast for her or come to her in forms she could not comprehend.

The fact that there had been others, and that in one way or another they had failed to live on, was a warning, and accounted, he saw, for the fear with which their mother guarded them, and for her intense possessiveness.

He resented these others. She would never let him forget them; never a day went by without her evoking one or other of them, May or Pearl or James or Leslie.

Pearl was just a name to him, a small dissatisfied spirit that each time he went to his mother's breast was already there, fighting him off. May, just weeks before he was born, had pulled a kerosene tin of boiling water off the stove. Her howls, he suspected, were often in their mother's ears, even when she was trying to keep her temper and talk quietly to him. She was their mother's favourite, the daughter whose company she had longed for, since Jenny was not able to provide it. She had never trusted herself after what happened to May. She had become over-cautious, terrified of the capacity of even the most ordinary objects to turn murderous on you, and the house was full of them.

Of the others, the three boys, only Billy had been round long enough to be quite real. Digger had nursed and petted the others, but Billy had been old enough to follow him round the yard, and they had played together, all three. Billy had had time to develop features and his own smell in the room where they slept, all in the one bed; a voice, demands, little oddnesses that took your heart or raised in you an antagonism that reinforced your separateness and for that reason stuck.

Billy had wandered off into the river. The river after that had a new meaning to them, the sound of it at night, the cold touch of it when you reached a hand in. It was no longer just a boundary that let you say which side you were on, or the broad stretch of sunlight in motion that their father, and later Digger too at times, sent the ferry out on. Even dropping a line into it became a different act.

'Watcha doin'?' Jenny had asked him once when she saw the line trailing. 'Are you gunna find Billy?'

She often said things you had thought of but never quite come up with, and when you did, bit off.

These deaths made the house more crowded than it might otherwise have been, but also emptier, exerting a pressure all round that forced him and Jenny, who, as his mother told him over and over had only one another, into a space that was too narrow and which he felt at times was another sort of coffin. Their having survived imposed a heavy responsibility on them: of living not just for themselves but for the others as well, and in this way letting them get another go at the world, a second breath. Since Jenny was limited, and always would be, the main weight was on him.

'It's not me, Digger,' his mother would insist when he bucked at the unfairness of it. 'How many times do I have to tell you? Do you think I would want to put a thing like that on you? It's not me. It's life!'

'C'mon, Dig, Digger, tell us somefing.'

In the beginning he told her everything he knew. His voice, velvety in the dark of their little room, was what made the world real to her. A lot of what he told was made up. She could not tell the difference.

'For God's sake, Digger!'

Hearing his voice rise as it often did to a point of dangerous excitement, their mother had come from her sewing, stopped a moment in the shade of the door, and heard him. The moment he saw her he knew how angry she would be. But he couldn't help himself. Coming to the edge of some extraordinary possibility, he would let himself claim it, put it into words; if he didn't, the force of it, huge and expanding in his head, might make him go flying off from the centre of himself. What he did now, shamefaced at being caught, was explode in giggles.

'Jenny, love,' she said, 'be a good girl and see if the postman's been.'

'He hasn't,' Jenny said. 'I been listnin'.'

'Don't you answer me, Miss,' the mother spat. 'If I say go, you do it. Quick smart!'

'You little bugger,' she said when Jenny was out of earshot, but her anger had died before the shamefaced look of him. 'How can you do that, Digger? Scaring the poor kid. What gets into you? You know what she's like. I should box your ears.'

Instead she reached out and touched the corner of his mouth with her thumb as if there were a crumb there. Sobered, he looked up at her. He never knew what she was after. She was so unpredictable.

She drew her hand away. She had been reassuring herself yet again that he wasn't simply a child of her wishing. She could not imagine sometimes where he had sprung from. He wasn't like her, or like his father either, not really. He was like no one she had ever known. Tell him something once and it was there forever. He remembered things she didn't even know she knew till he recalled them to her. 'You remember, Mum. You remember,' he would insist, and he was right, she did. Talk, facts, happenings from away back, the names of things, whole pages of any book he had read. Where did it all go in the skinny arms and legs (she thought of it as other mothers might think of food), all this knowledge he picked up and swallowed.

One night, hearing him reading aloud to his sister long after they had been told to go to bed, she had burst in in a fury.

'Digger, I've told you a thousand –'

But there was no lamp alight, no book. He was reciting the pages off, sentence by sentence, out of his head. He looked up at her, all innocence. He was nine years old.

She had known then that it was too late, that she could not hold him. It was already *in* there, the world she wanted to keep away from him, and expanding at a rate she could not control. She did not know enough to keep up with him.

He came at times like a small child, hugging her waist and hanging on. 'None of that,' she would tell him. 'You're all kidstakes. That's all that is.'

She believed he would leave her, but she never said it outright. She was protecting herself against loss.

'No I won't,' he would have assured her, 'how could I leave? Ever?'

He meant it and he did not.

*

31

'Tellus somefing, Digger,' Jenny would whisper in the dark of their little room. 'They're asleep, they won't hear.'

He no longer told her everything, but he did tell her some things.

People he saw on his deliveries, for instance, like the Breens: Mrs Breen in her old felt slippers, who always gave him ginger ale in a peanut-butter glass, sitting him down at the kitchen table, then sitting down herself, right opposite, and watching him drink.

Mrs Breen had Eddie, a big fellow nearly twenty who was a mongol. All the time he was there Eddie would be hanging about in the hallway outside. Sometimes he would poke his head round the corner and grin. 'Hullo Digger,' he'd call, too loud. Other times he would be scowling, as if he begrudged Digger his mother's attention and the mouthful of sweet soft-drink he was getting. Once, when Digger looked up, Eddie had his dick out and was playing with it. He looked quickly at Mrs Breen and she pretended not to notice, or she really didn't notice, she was too intent on *him*. As if there was something miraculous in his just being able to drink a glass of ginger ale without spilling it.

Then there were fellers he met at the ferry, commercial travellers some of them, and the stories they had to tell, including jokes; and things he got from older boys down at the river, where there was a deep pool and you could swing out over the swirling blackness on a rope. Later, when he ventured to the pictures at the School of Arts, and to dances where he hung around outside with the older blokes, smoking, swapping yarns, there was news of visits some of these fellows had made to Sydney or to the Riverina to pick fruit.

He would slip away to these dances, or to the picture shows, in secret. Not much more than fourteen, he would wait till he thought the others were asleep, then, getting up softly in the dark, pull his pants on, and with his shirt and boots in his hand creep away to finish dressing in the yard.

'Where y' off to, Digger?' she would whisper, sometimes, in her sleep.

'Sshh. I'll tellya t'morrer.'

Beginning softly in the dark, he would tell her things. He would start in a whisper, but quite soon he would get excited, break into giggles, or his voice would crack in squeaky shouts.

'Shuddup in there, get ta sleep,' their father would shout through the wall, 'or I'll bloody come in an' make yer.'

Then, after a moment, their mother's voice:

'Go t' sleep now, Digger, you can tell that t'morrow. It'll keep.'

3

'So,' Digger said, 'how'm I doin'? Still on top?'

Vic grinned. 'You're doing OK. Want a statement?'

'Nah! I'll trust ya.'

Exchanges of this sort between them had become ritual in these last weeks. They were jest. There were subjects still that they steered clear of, where they would have felt shy and constrained with one another, but there was no lack of trust between them.

Vic, elbows on knees, looked past Digger to the river and its dancing swarm, bits of winged life in millions whose bodies at moments caught the light and made a second river up there, as if the first had thrown off a lighter variant of itself, all living particles, with the freedom to hover, prop, dance on the spot, while the other, earthbound, could do nothing but flow on. Occasionally the oily surface broke. A pair of jaws rose up and snapped down a dozen of those lives, or a hundred – whatever it could get. He watched Digger jiggle the handline.

'Waddabout you?' Digger asked.

'I don't know, I think I'm winning. But they're crafty buggers. I can't be sure.'

'They still after you then?'

'Yes,' Vic said. He had caught the hint of scepticism in Digger's tone. 'They're still after me.'

Digger pretended to be occupied with the line. After a moment, falling back on an older game between them, he said: 'I don't know why you don't pull out while the going's good. I would. I don't know how you put up with it.'

There was at times, Vic thought, something prim and old-womanish about Digger. 'These are just the sort of things,' he thought, 'that mothers must say. Looking just like that, too. Half-horrified, half-impressed.' This side of Digger was a source of amusement to him.

'And young Alex?'

Young Alex, as they called him, was Vic's nephew, though in fact he was no longer young. He was forty-three.

Vic frowned. 'Oh, he's against me, I think.' He made it sound a matter of no concern. 'Only I can't be sure of that, either. He doesn't give much away.'

No, Digger thought, I bet he doesn't.

'If they get me this time,' Vic said, and Digger looked up, caught out by something he hadn't heard before, 'I'll chuck the towel in. Do you believe that?'

Is he serious? Digger thought. But Vic had already covered himself.

'Maybe I should just do that anyway,' he said. 'Chuck it in and come up here.'

He laughed at that, and after a moment Digger did too. It was so improbable.

Their lives were as different as any two lives could be that still touched and crossed and could at moments like this move quietly as one.

'You've left us f' dead,' Digger used to tease him in the early days. The mockery was of the gentlest sort, but Vic was sensitive on the point of loyalty and would look hurt.

'What do you mean? Because I'm makin' a bit of money? That doesn't make any difference.'

But as time went on he stopped protesting. It did make a difference; not so much the money as the level he moved at, the moves he made there, and the amount of interest people took in him.

'I see you've been in the papers again,' Digger would say, and Vic, though he was pleased Digger had seen it – he was still hungry for admiration, he could never have enough of it – would make a face. 'Oh, the papers,' he'd say. 'You can't take any notice of the papers.' And to make up a little for the gap between them, he began to tell Digger stories, frank, light-hearted ones, of his activities out there among the cannibals, laying it on pretty thick at times and delighting in Digger's expressions of disbelief, of disapproval too, often enough, and playing when he could for sympathy.

'Well, I'm glad it's you and not me,' Digger would tell him, letting them both off the hook. 'I dunno how you stand it. I couldn't do it. Not for quids.'

Digger in fact was being disingenuous. He knew Vic. You could trust him with your life. On the other hand, you couldn't trust him with tuppence. He had been surprised at first that some fellow he knew, and knew well, should be getting on in the world. But he saw after a time that this was naive. The very qualities he knew in Vic, both sides, took another form out there and were just what was needed. That told you something about the world, and Digger, in his own way, took note of it, but he didn't let on to Vic what he had seen.

'I stand it,' Vic would say, 'because I've got to. I've got no option.' What he meant was that change, risk, action, were essential to him.

He was inclined to look about, when he came up here, and ask how Digger stood it. It was a world, up here, that had no need of you. Everything you looked at or touched, the long strips of bark that peeled back to show glossy colours, the squiggles on a trunk that were little lives, birdcalls that came out of the scrub, ker-*whip*, ker-*whip* – all these gave you the same message. Come on in if you like, but you might as well not for all the difference it will make.

It could be a comfort, that, for an hour or two. It took you out of yourself. But any more and he felt ghostly.

What he needed was things that told him he *was* here. Lucky for him the world was full of them.

But three weeks ago he had changed all this. He had come to Digger and asked a favour of him.

For a day or two after the idea first struck him he had held back. Not because he was afraid Digger would refuse him. He knew he wouldn't. But because by asking it he was disturbing a balance that had existed between them, sometimes shakily, for more than forty years. He hesitated. Then, just as he knew he would, he went ahead and did it just the same.

'Listen, mate,' he had begun, a little shy now that he had come to the point, 'you know I wouldn't involve you in anything that wasn't strictly above board. But the fact is, Digger, I've got a favour to ask you. I wouldn't if there was anyone else.'

'What is it?' Digger said straight out. He was surprised. They didn't ask favours of one another. He wondered what it could be that was not covered already by the friendship between them.

The note of distress in his voice unnerved Vic, but he was in now and what he had said was true: there was no one else. Quickly he laid the thing out, sticking to the plainest terms. Digger heard him through.

'But what use would I be?' he said at last. 'I don't know anything about *shares*.'

'You wouldn't have to. You wouldn't even know it was happening.

36

All we'd be using, Digger,' and he paused a moment before he could get it out, 'is your name.' He went on quickly to cover the embarrassment of it. Digger was looking more and more uneasy. He was actually wringing his hands.

'You see, we need someone who isn't known, who couldn't be traced – or not easily. It's a matter of timing – to get it all done before it turns up in the records. Oh, there's nothing illegal to it. It's a bit *clever*, that's all. You know what these business fellers are like. You see, the law says I can only buy one and a half per cent of the shares every six months, even if it *is* my company. It's a silly law, but there you are, it's the law. So I need someone else to do it. *I* put up the money – well, not money exactly, collateral, you know what that is, other companies that I can borrow against. All *you* would have to do is sign a few papers. Albert, isn't it?'

'Yes,' Digger said bleakly, 'Albert.' The unfamiliarity of it was at this moment a relief.

'You see, mate, someone's after me, I don't know who. It could be anyone. Alex, even. All I know is, they've started to move. So what I've got to do is get in before them. Get the cash together, wait for the right moment, then before the others can do it, zap! we go in and make a bid for the whole show. Or as much of it, anyway, as will give me the whip hand.'

He was sweating. The boldness and danger of it excited him, but there were things too that he needed to keep back. It might scare Digger if he knew the scale of what he had in mind. For instance, the sums that would be involved.

'The thing is, to get it all over and done with in the shortest possible time. Forty days, that's the maximum. So you see, Digger, it won't be for long.' He could see how pinched Digger looked. He was sorry for that. 'I'm up against it,' he said simply. 'I wouldn't ask if I had the option. You're the only one.'

Digger worked his Adam's apple. The trouble was, he had no point from which he could judge all this, no knowledge, no experience, and there was no one he could ask. Was there an element of madness in it that anyone who *knew* about these things would see straight off?

'I'm not imagining things,' Vic said in an aggrieved tone, 'if that's what you're thinking. I know it sounds dramatic. Paranoia, is that what you're thinking? Honestly, Digger, this is the way these things are *done*. It may seem mad to you, but don't you think I know what I'm doing? This is a game I play every day of the week. Believe me, I'm good at it.'

So Digger had been drawn in, and in the weeks that followed several prime targets, companies, that is, that were vulnerable to take-over, began to pass through his hands, all as Vic had promised, with no trouble on his part; without his even knowing for the most part what had occurred. It was a phantom existence he was living out there.

The companies — Morton Holdings, Cathedral Steel and Concrete, J. & R. Randall were the largest, but there were smaller ones as well — consisted of warehouses in three states, factories, offices with desks and filing cabinets and typewriters and computers, cafeterias, fleets of vans, stacks of cardboard boxes or steel girders; but all Digger saw were papers. And even the papers, it seemed, were just promises, negotiable items of trust, no more to be associated with actual notes or coins than the name Albert Keen was with the man who was signing for him.

Digger was astonished by what was revealed to him, the glimpse he got behind the scenes into a world he had thought till now was unshakeably solid.

'But I told you it was a game,' Vic told him. 'Didn't you believe me?'

The magic for him lay in the very thing that Digger found so unsettling, the extent to which the structure he was erecting, for all its being underwritten out there by so much that was real and touchable, was a secret one, visible only to himself, Digger, his advisers and a few collaborators who were in the know. But it was solid enough. 'There's banks in this, Digger,' he would whisper, when he saw that Digger had doubts, and he would name them. But Digger, instead of being consoled, was terrified. Men drew their wages, their families put clothes on their backs and bread into their mouths, bought TV sets and video recorders; buildings went up; produce was shifted; a whole society breathed and ate and slept — but the basis of it all was no more than air, no more than promises, trust.

Vic laughed. 'But what else could it be?' he asked, as if Digger were a child. And Digger was scared by that, too. By common agreement they fell into the habit of talking as little as possible of all this, and then only in the lightest terms.

'Agh,' he said now, hauling his tackle in, 'this is a mug's game. Let's see if Jenny's got a cuppa tea,' and he made to move, but Vic stopped him.

'Not yet, eh? Let's wait a bit. It's early enough.'

Digger was surprised but made no objection. He stowed his line, leaned back, and they settled and sat in silence. There was nothing unusual in it – they could spend long periods just sitting; but he was uneasy just the same. It was the third time in a week that Vic had just turned up like this.

'I'm on tenterhooks,' he had confessed the first time, 'about this bit of business we've got on. This last bit. You don't mind, do you?' He was worried about the market. 'I want t' get all this finalised,' he said, 'a bit sooner than we thought. The market's too high. In fact that's good for us, it's what we need. Only I don't trust it.'

But they had none of that sort of talk today. It was something else.

Vic, his boots set down carefully in the dirt, his back hard against a she-oak, felt the silence swell; out over the swarming river, but back too into the clearing where the store was and beyond into the trackless scrub. But the real expansion was in him. Sitting quietly now with his head back, he saw from outside him, above and at a distance, these two old blokes sitting at ease beside a river, and it seemed miraculous to him that one of them, against all the odds, should be himself. Miraculous, too – there was no other word for it – that this breath should be here for him to catch hold of, and that this moment, just after four on an autumn afternoon in 1987, should have been waiting up ahead for them to reach it; like the leaves here that threw shadows on his hands, and had also been growing slowly towards it, and having arrived now, were turning over with a sound that was just perceptible if you listened, a little shush and scratch against the stillness.

'Listen, Digger,' and Digger was disturbed for the second time by something new in his voice, 'do you remember a cove called Anson?'

Digger sucked his cheeks in and looked out at the river. After a little he said: 'Anson, yes. John Archibald.'

Vic let out a long breath. 'Yes,' he said, 'that'd be him,' though in fact he had never till now heard these other names. He could not have explained, even to Digger, the ease he felt at having them spoken.

He was a jackaroo from up Singleton way, twenty, maybe twenty-one or -two. Claimed to have played half-back for one of the state teams but was almost certainly lying. 'What year was that, mate?' one of the others had challenged. Vic remembered the lie.

One day early on, sitting in the sun in just their shorts, they had played a game of draughts. They were seated on either side of an upturned drum, he couldn't remember where, but the heat was intense and the sunlight blinding. Changi. Or it might have been earlier, on the ship going up.

Blue eyes. Hair bleached to unruly straw. Rough, very cocky, and dead sure when they sat down that he would win.

'Only I was surer,' Vic thought, and could feel even at this distance the little spurt of triumph, the joy in his own good fortune and skill, as the move came up and he took it, 'Ha, I've got ya!'

The look of utter astonishment on Anson's face – that too had been such a pleasure to him. The feller couldn't believe it. Couldn't hide his irritation either. He had been so certain he would win.

They were in different mobs and had nothing to do with one another after that, even when they found themselves in the same camp up on the line. Then one day, in a period when they were working sixteen hours at a stretch and were half dead on their feet, in a trance most of them, so sick and brutalised they hardly knew where they were, he had been sitting over his bit of midday rice, and in glancing up for some reason – no reason, in fact – had seen Anson squatting just yards away at the side of the track.

There was no modesty among them, they were past all that; but he looked away, and then, after a moment, looked back again, just as Anson, with a worried frown half-turned to glance behind him (they all did that) and inspect what he had done. Vic saw it too, and their eyes met.

They were mostly indifferent to one another by now, too preoccupied with their own terrors to care how the next man felt. But they all knew what a white turd signified. Cholera. It was a sentence of death.

He meant nothing to him, that fellow; but he had thought he would never forget his look – or the stab of panic he felt in his own bowels – as that bit of intelligence passed between them.

He had forgotten it, of course, in time. As he had forgotten so many other things. Till just this week it had come back to him as if no time at all had gone by, just seconds. The man, moving back into himself, got to his feet and stood there, his fingers working clumsily to adjust his shorts.

The man, the *man* – but what was he called? It seemed shameful to Vic that he could not remember, though in fact they had only spoken the once. He worried his way through the alphabet, finding other names that he had also forgotten, but not that one. Then he took his mind off it and it was there.

What he had been struck by, after that first glance of panicky recognition, was the mildness with which Anson stood watching his own fingers deal with his shorts; with the ordinary but quite tricky business of hooking them up so they wouldn't fall. He had felt a kind of awe at the futility of it, as if a cold hand had been laid on him, too. He was amazed (but there was horror in it too) at the distance Anson had come since their draughts game. There was no truculence in him, none at all. With a kind of dumb patience he stood tying the rag-ends together, then turned and moved away.

But what he thought now was something different: that it had taken him forty years to accept the hard facts of existence, whereas that fellow Anson had got there in just months.

Digger sat quiet.

Anson. He came early on the list. After Amos, Reginald James. He could have gone on if Vic had required it. To Aspie, Ball, Barclay, Baynes, Beeston . . .

There were nine more after that. Then Curran.

4

Great events do not always cast a shadow before them. In Malaya in 1941 the Japanese Imperial Army arrived on rickety bikes. It didn't look like the first part of a triumph or a moment from history.

You saw them pedalling up the track between the rubber trees, rifles slung across their backs, glasses ablaze, rubber boots and leggings working up and down. Very spindly, the bikes looked. The riders sweated in their heavy gear. You took aim, squeezed gently, and the whole enterprise went haywire, the rider waving his arms about as if he believed there was something up there, the hem of a garment or the big toe of one of his ancestors, that he could grab hold of to hoist himself aloft. He scrabbled for it. Meanwhile the wheels went spinning, gravity insisted, and rider and machine slewed off into the ditch. It was comic.

But their own men died and they pulled back. Big guns lifted, rained down shells. The heat and the noise grew terrific. The narrow streets of Chinatown hurled themselves skyward. Walls ripped, flew upward and came down again as lumps of plaster and dust. Locals, Chinese mostly, ran this way and that in the oily darkness with cashboxes or rolled carpets or children in their arms, or chickens or sewing-machines or little screaming piglets. Or they trotted by with half a household on their shoulders, all the chair legs pointing upward, and fell down with fire running along their backs and the load smashed and scattered, or got up and hobbled on again among the armoured cars and the field ambulances and the walking wounded that were streaming in over the causeway to the island fortress.

That was Sunday. On the Sunday night, fellows who had been fighting hard the day before in rubber plantations on the island, or hand-to-hand on factory sites, Digger among them, were at ease at last, preparing themselves for the next stage of proceedings by darning their socks, rolling them neatly, and pushing them down the side of their packs. When all was shipshape, they counted their coins, cleaned their fingernails, and jabbing into a tin of condensed milk, sucked comfort from a metal tit.

All around, at campfires and in places off in the dark, trading had started up again: a packet of cigarette papers and two frenchies for a fountain-pen; an ounce of tobacco for a tin of the best gramophone needles, steel, with a record of Paderewski's Minuet in G thrown in.

It was as if the whole division had been constituted and shipped north for no other purpose than to ensure the movement, from one continent to another, of a million articles of no great worth or use that might otherwise have sat gathering dust in a country store, or mouldering away in a suitcase under a bed. An underground economy unknown to statistics, it was in progress at every instant here, between fights, between mouthfuls of coconut milk or bully beef, through fences, across the space between bunks. It went on even at the borehole, while the two men were engaged on that other unofficial business of easing their bowels.

Transactions. Deals. They took up so much energy, engendered so much feeling, you might have thought they were the one true essential of a fighting man's life, of tenacious, disorderly *civilian* life inside the official military one, exposing in pocket form the real motives of all this international activity, compared with which all talk of freedom and honour and patriotic pride and the saving of civilisation was the merest mind-fogging gibberish.

It was a hot night thick with cloud and the pall of rubber godowns that were blazing along the docks. Firelit shadows were in play as men went about the tasks of settling and making camp. The voices in the stillness were of fellows stirring pots, playing mah-jong or blackjack, or swapping lazy obscenities.

Others, newcomers mostly but some old hands as well, were still talking about the big fight they would be in, tomorrow or the day after, that would finish the little buggers off.

Such talk was bullshit. Those who had really done any fighting – Digger, for instance, and Mac and Doug – would have nothing to do with it. The heaviness that hung over the island was not just weather, or smoke from the storehouse of the Empire going up in flames. The rumour was (it was only a whisper as yet, men were afraid to let it out) that the commanders were already negotiating.

By eleven o'clock it was official. In a meeting with the Japanese commander, General Yamashita, the commander of the Allied Forces, General Percival, had signed an unconditional surrender, to be effective from 10 p.m. Japanese time.

So all their watches were wrong – that too. They were on Jap time now, and would be for as long as it lasted. They had, without knowing it, lost their status as soldiers, and some other qualifications as well, and been prisoners of war for the last two hours.

On the Monday they began marching, fifty thousand of them it was said, into captivity, though all it meant as yet was to move twelve miles to the other end of the island; a mass of men so huge that you couldn't conceive of it, Digger couldn't, till you came to a slope and looked back and saw the dense massed columns passing away into ghostliness in the haze.

They took everything they could carry. The army had taught them that much. What you had you hung on to: rations, equipment, an old tobacco tin, spare sweaters and socks. But also cheap watches traded or knocked off from the Chinese, propelling pencils, fly-swats, bronze Buddhas, copies of *Gone with the Wind* and *Moby Dick* and Edgar Wallace, bolts of shantung and Thai silk, inkwells, packs of cards, flasks of Johnny Walker Red Label whisky. Each man was weighed down with twenty to forty pounds of it and staggering; his shirt pockets stuffed, and such lighter articles as bottle-openers, pen-knives, screwdrivers, metal cups and water-bottles dangling from the straps of his pack or his belt-loops or from a thong round his neck. They looked less like the remnants of a military enterprise, even a failed one, than the medicine men of an advanced cargo cult, or a horde of Syrian pedlars about to be unleashed on all the country towns of New South Wales. They tottered, they clanked with relics, the accumulated paraphernalia (anything that could be upended and slung across a shoulder, or unscrewed or wrenched off) of a world that had exploded in fragments around them, and would have now, in the spirit of improvisation, to be reconstructed elsewhere – on the move if that's what it came to. But they were experts at that. They were Australians. A good many of them had been training for it all their lives.

These miscellaneous oddments, the detachable parts and symbols of civilised life, were all they had now to reassure themselves of where they had come from and what they were. What was contained in a set of surgeons' knives or a pair of pliers and a coil of wire – and in a way that was very nearly mystical – was the superior status, guaranteed, of those who had invented them and knew their use. Civilisation? That's *us*. Look at this.

But as the day wore on, and the twelve miles became a martyrdom of raw feet, raw shoulders, thighs chafed with sweat, and the sun beat down shadeless and blinding, the weight would not balance, not even against an unknown future. By nightfall even the dullest and most stubborn of them had learned something, and what he had learned could be picked up, weighed, turned over and a price put upon it, by the thousands of scavengers who moved along with them, snapping up whatever they cast aside or dropped, and would be laid out that night under lamps in shanty shops – as proof of what till now had been barely graspable: an extraordinary surrender of power, made once on paper and once in a form you could actually see and lay your hands on; in the world of commodities. What a break-up! Idlers surveying this windfall were bug-eyed with amazement at the sheer scope of it. A quartz inkwell, look, without a single chip!

It was a general stripping. In it, whether they knew it or not, they had been making decisions on which their lives would depend. Everything a man had grasped about human nature (including his own), and the unpredictability of things, was in the choice between a six-bob alarm clock and a pair of scuffed but serviceable boots.

At a point back there they had stepped, each one of them, across a line where the weight of each thing in the world, even the smallest, had been added to; but they themselves were lighter.

Sitting among so many in the sweltering dark, Digger rested against his pack, boots off at last, socks peeled painfully from the blistered flesh.

They were in an open encampment at the eastern end of the island. Changi, the place was called.

The unit was scattered. They had started off in good order, but men had kept falling behind, some to bargain with one another or with the natives who ran alongside, grinning, pointing to things that had caught their eye and shouting offers, others because they had gone sick or lame, or been poleaxed by the sun. Many of them were still straggling in, and on all sides the company sergeants were at work, shouting roll calls of their men.

Twelve days ago Mac had been wounded, not too badly, in the

45

thigh. For most of the march, Digger on one side, Doug on the other, they had half-carried him. He lay now with one arm across his eyes, as white as chalk. Digger worried and fussed.

Doug, who could never sit still for more than two minutes at a time, was out scavenging. That was the excuse. What he was really doing was walking up and down in jubilation at the scene.

He was in his element. The sanctified irregularity and disorder of it, the mixing in of Australians and British and Dutch and native troops, the great braying noise they made far off into the night, all this was tonic to him. He danced up and down among the various groups – he was a big fellow but very light on his feet – chiacking, greeting acquaintances, dipping down every now and again to share a word or two with this one or that, and to draw out the bullshit artists among them who were already sketching glorious futures for themselves among the guerrillas, or boasting of what they would have done if they'd been given the chance. He came back with a packet of Ardaths and a swag of gleeful tales to tell.

'I tellya,' he told them, 'this is gunna be a little Chicago, you mark my word. You'll see now what human nature is.'

This last was a crack at Mac. Human nature was a term Mac was strong on; he and Doug did not see eye to eye on it, or on much else, really. Their affection was based on passionate difference. He threw it out now in the hope that it might stir Mac up.

Like most men who have never had a day off work, Doug was uncomfortable with illness. His belief was that if he could only stir Mac up a bit, and lift his spirits, he would be himself again.

'Word is,' he told them, 'that we're gunna give in our gear. Wouldn' you know? So that the bloody officers can be turned out like gentlemen and impress the Nips. Walkin' shoes for all officers, two pairs apiece. Commandeered if fellers aren't willing to give 'em up. Shoes are goin' pretty cheap out there. Blokes are gettin' rid of 'em fer anything they can get, smokes, watches, silk stockin's. Silk stockin's are pretty safe.' He laughed. 'I'd settle fer smokes, meself. You watch. Smokes, bully, condensed milk, that'll be the currency. A good pair a' boots. It always comes down to the same things in the long run, belly, dick or feet. There won't be too much dick in it this time, I reckon. It'll be bellies, you watch, an' feet.'

He shook out the pack of Ardaths, offered one to Digger, then passed it across to Mac. He raised his head and looked out over the

46

great mob of them that was scattered over the flat ground. All the nonsense had gone out of him.

'They're mugs, most a' these blokes,' he said sorrowfully. 'Wouldn' know their arseholes from the back end of a rabbit warren. It's pathetic. Half of 'em are still puking up their mother's milk.'

Mac had lighted up and had his head back, drawing in smoke.

'How's it going, chief?' Doug said, settling beside him. 'A bit rugged, eh?' He looked quickly at Digger, then away.

They were spread out over a low area without definition, except that somewhere, away in the darkness, you could smell the sea. No fences, no wire, no sign of Nips. There was movement, a kind of restlessness as of a huge animal stretched out on the ground there, the sound of its breathing, a muffled roar. But everything, their movements, their voices when they spoke, had a subdued air, as if they were under surveillance and the Nips were there after all, but out of sight.

They were in the open, without protection, contained only by the gentlemen's agreement some Englishman had made in their name. It was eerie, that.

'What's up, Dig?'

Mac, who often knew what Digger was thinking, looked back over his shoulder. His expression was quizzical.

'Nothin',' Digger said. 'Just thinkin'.'

'Farewell the plumed troop, eh? And the big wars that make ambition virtue.' Mac's voice was hoarse and full of weariness, but there was some of his old humour in it. He could see they were concerned about him and was making an effort.

Doug, who got embarrassed when things took a literary turn, drew on the last of his fag and sent it in a fiery arc across the dark.

'Farewell the neighing steed,' Digger recited, taking up where Mac had left off, and in a voice that had none of the roughness of his ordinary speech, 'and the shrill trump, the spirit-stirring drum, the ear-piercing fife, the royal banner, and all quality, pride, pomp, and circumstance of glorious war.'

He came to an end, and looked up, a little shy but not at all self-conscious. They often played this game.

Mac was grinning, genuinely delighted.

He was an older fellow, thirty-eight. Back home he was on the trams. He lived at Bondi Junction with his sister-in-law, Iris, who worked in a cake shop (he had told Digger all this), and was what

Doug called a black-stump philosopher, full of all sorts of wild arguments and theories and extravagant optimisms that wouldn't have worked in Paradise, let alone where they were now. His pack was crammed with books, and every week at home he bought at least a dozen of them from barrows or second-hand bookshops down George Street. His room at home was stacked to the ceiling with them.

'He never fails, this boy,' he said now, inviting Doug to admire the phenomenon. 'Amazing, eh?'

Digger shook his head. It was nothing, a trick, that's all.

Doug was about to offer his own ironical comment when another voice broke in: 'Hey, I know that.'

It was Doug's mate, if you could call him that, Vic.

'Good fer you, son,' Doug said drily. The others, Digger and Mac, exchanged glances.

He was a big, solidly-built fellow, not yet twenty, who had recently attached himself to them and was proving hard to shake off. Originally, like Doug, from a mining village up Newcastle way, he saw this as a bond between them and made a good deal of it. He was just out of school and had, so far as Digger could see, no experience of any kind. He tried to hide it by speaking rough and making a big man of himself. Digger couldn't stand him. Mac didn't think much of him either.

It was Doug he had set his sights on, but for some reason it was the others he played up to, and this made them like him even less. But when they complained about him, Doug, who was all generosity, would shrug his shoulders and say: 'Oh, Vic's all right.' Still, this didn't prevent him from teasing the fellow.

'Go on,' he'd say with mock astonishment when Vic came out with some bit of self-promotion by which he hoped they might be impressed.

He did, too, regularly, and sank himself.

'Here,' he said now, 'I brought you something.' It was a little tin of Ideal milk.

Doug took it and turned it over in his hand. 'What's this for?' he said. 'Somebody got a birthday?'

Vic's neck burned. It wasn't *for* anything. It was something he had picked up for them, that's all. He waited for Doug to accept the thing and get it out of the way.

'Ta,' Doug said at last, and set the tin down, a bit too prominently, on his pack. Vic took this as an invitation to settle on the grass among them.

'So,' he said, 'here we are, eh? How long d'ya reckon this'll last?'

'I dunno.' Doug offered him the pack of Ardaths. 'Long as the war, could be. How long d'you reckon?'

'Well,' Vic said, 'I heard they want to exchange us. Right away, one bloke says.'

'Go on! – You hear that, Mac? – What would they exchange us for?'

'Wool, I heard. They want wool.'

Doug laughed outright. 'They'll need a lotta bloody sheep in exchange fer this lot,' he said, looking out over the mob of them. 'So howdaya reckon they'll do it – by weight? I'll be oright, they'll do pretty well outa me. You too. But waddabout Digger? Hardly be worth tradin' a mingy little bugger like that. Waddaya weigh, Digger?'

'Eight eight,' Digger laughed.

'I can just see it,' Doug said. 'It'd be like the bloody day a' judgement. I don't know whether I could be in *that*.'

'Well,' Vic said uncomfortably, 'it's on'y a rumour anyway. You know, ya hear all sorts a' things. I don't suppose it'll happen.'

'No,' Doug said, 'I don't think so either. You can breathe again, Dig, we've scrapped that plan.'

Vic watched the exchange of smiles between them. He wasn't a fool. He caught Digger's eye on him. Scornful. Digger was the one he would have trouble with. He looked like nothing, there was nothing you would notice about him; but of the three he was the one who considered longest, said least, and would be the hardest to win.

'I wish he'd bugger off,' Digger was thinking. 'Can't he see we don't want him? He spoils things.'

He was one of a large number of replacements who had only recently arrived on the island.

Three weeks before, they were still being seasick on the way up from Perth, or, in baggy shorts and boots, their shoulders blistering, had been leaning far out over the rails to sight flying fish. They had been recruited and shipped straight here, it being the intention of the service chiefs to train them on the spot. Their kit and a week's rifle practice on the range at Bukit Timar was the sum total of what made them soldiers.

The voyage, the adventure of leaving Australia, the tales they brought with them, heard from old-timers in country pubs and on the job in timberyards and sales rooms, or from uncles while the women were washing up after Sunday dinner, had raised them to a pitch of heroic impatience, a keenness untempered by any contact with army regulations or the rigours of drill. All fired up and ready for conflict, they had walked down the gang plank into *this*. Captivity.

Vic had taken the turn of events as a personal affront. Since ten o'clock on Sunday night, all the qualities he knew to be in him were out of fashion. He was among men here who had already been toughened by experience, even those of them, like Digger, who were no older than himself. They might think they had the right to despise him, for no other reason than that he was young, raw, and had had no chance to show himself. But he couldn't put up with that. He knew what he was.

He squatted on his heels looking easy – he was a pleasant-looking fellow, his hands hanging loosely over his thighs, his slouch hat across his back. But he was never easy. There was always some little irritation that pricked at him. Very aware of slights, he stayed alert and watchful.

Doug, meanwhile, had found a new topic to rave over.

'They reckon Gordon Bennett's missing,' he said. 'Have you heard that? Pissed off home in his own little rowboat and left the rest of us up the creek. Be just like 'im, eh?'

He had a poor view of anyone in authority; officers, bosses, little jumped-up clerks behind a desk who hum and ha and make you feel like shit before they'll stamp anything for you; all of them eager to lick an arse or kick one according to whether it's above or below them; all of them determined, like the bloody second lieutenants here who would soon be strutting about in their shoes, to hang on to every last little sign of privilege.

'Typical,' Doug said, and spat.

'Well, I don't know,' Vic said. He had always to be saying something. 'D'ya reckon one of our blokes would? I mean, I know 'e's a general and that, but would 'e?'

Doug said nothing, just sat there with his eyebrows raised and looked at him. The silence was too much for Vic.

'Well, would you?'

Doug laughed. 'Are you barmy? Of course I wouldn't. But I'm a bloody footslogger, I can't just piss off home. Haven't got a bloody rowboat for one thing. Neither can Mac here, or Digger. Neither can you. But who's t' say what I might do if I was a general? Or you either – well, not *you* maybe, but I wouldn't like to swear what I mightn't do if I had half the chance.'

Vic frowned. He didn't care much for the line the talk was taking. 'Anyway,' he said, 'it's just a rumour, really. Like that wool business, eh? The place is full of 'em.' There was a beat of silence. 'So,' he said, 'here we are, eh?'

Doug looked about, and the sigh he gave was theatrical. 'I dunno,' he said. 'How did I get inta this? I was always such a careful bloke. Never put me foot down on cracks – not even when I was a grown-up. Changed me socks twice a week, never went out with fast women or stepped under ladders or broke mirrors, or let 'em give me a ticket with a thirteen in it. Ya can't be more careful than that. If I saw a Chinaman I'd rush right up, you know, and jus' tip 'im, like, then duck away, fer luck. An' after all that I was mug enough to join up. I ask you, what makes us do it? Are we rational beings or aren't we? Oh Gawd, I thought, they'll send me to the *real* war. Greece maybe, Egypt, I don't want that. But they sent me up here. I 'ad Digger 'n Mac with me. I thought, "This is all right. Tropic nights. Taxi dancers ten cents a go. Chinamen all over. You'll be all right here, Douggy. This'll do." An' now look what's happened. I ask you, honestly, is there any logic to it? Do any of us know what we're doing, even when we're bloody doin' it? Is anyone weighin' it all up in a pan? – and I don't jus' mean so they can trade me for my bloody weight in wool!' He laughed. 'Still, if it does come t' that – we oughta start buildin' you up, Digger –'

'I'm all right,' Digger said, laughing.

'Here, mate.' He scooped his big hand down, swept up the tin of Ideal milk and flipped it to Digger in a quick pass. 'You get that down ya,' he said. 'You don't mind, do ya Vic? Digger's our local flyweight –'

'Feather,' Digger put in, to be accurate.

'No one in this mob can touch him.'

'Oh?' said Vic. You could see the little flicker of challenge and interest. He was surprised. Digger was such a mild fellow.

'On'y 'e wouldn't be worth a ball a' nine-ply if they took up that wool business. Wouldn' hardly make a cover for a coat-hanger or the left side of a kiddie's cardigan. Sorry, mate,' he told Digger, 'but you're in trouble. Here, gimme that!'

He took the can, spiked it twice with his jack-knife and flipped it back. 'Ta, Vic,' he said, on Digger's behalf.

Digger took a good swig.

5

Digger's reputation as a fighter had been established their first week in camp. He had gone three rounds with a state amateur champion, then fought for the unit in the battalion titles. It was Doug who put him up to it. He didn't let on to them, or not at first, that he was a professional.

For eighteen months before he joined up he had been working the country shows with a boxing troupe, in a street of gaudy sideshows and circus freaks that included a pin-headed Chinaman, a strong man who also ate swords and swallowed fire, a couple of daredevil motorbike riders (a husband and wife team who three times nightly faced the Ring of Death), a fat lady and the Human Torso, a fellow who was just a head and shoulders on a mobile tray. Digger's job had been to stand among the crowd and, if no other mug did it, offer himself up to go a round or two with one of the troupe.

He had always been a follower of fairs. The sound of a merry-go-round and the wheezy music it pumped out, the sight of a dozen men in shorts and blue singlets with sledgehammers and guy-ropes raising a tent, turning a bit of waste ground into a carnival site, was enough to draw him away from any message he was on. More than once he had got a good box on the ears for slipping under the canvas and getting in late for tea, or for hanging around outside to hear the spruikers and coming home with a mouthful of nonsense (he could learn off the most intricate patter in just minutes) that filled Jenny with a wailing desire to experience these wonders for herself.

He loved the lights strung from pole to pole, red and blue and orange, casting weird shadows where the warm breeze struck them, the smell of animal shit, the satin and spangles the showies wore, which could be grimy when you got up close, but under the lights, and in the glow that was created by the spruikers' empowering descriptions, took you right out of yourself.

Toddlers swung up high on their fathers' shoulders would be dazed or crowing. Noisy youths with slicked-down hair and a fag in their mouth would be lining up to fire at a row of ducks or to swing a hammer and ring a bell, their girls, all permed and lipsticked, looking on and pretending they weren't bored. Only later, with a kewpie doll or alarm clock or plaster dog under their arm, would these girls find something at last that really touched them. Looking out from the vantage point of a rough normality they would feel a pricking fear run up their arms at the sight of the pin-headed Chinaman drinking tea from a dolly's cup, or a poddy-calf sad-eyed and huggable on its six legs.

Digger, who had been haunting such places since he was ten years old, would move about in an excited trance, taking in the noise, the sweat, the colour, the cruelties. And always at the centre of it all, not quite a freak-show but drawing to itself some of the loose emotion the freak-shows generated, was the tent with the boxers; half a dozen fellows, not all of them young, but all dark – half-castes or Islanders – lined up on a board in front of a painted flap.

The flap showed two boxers, taller than the real ones, shaping up. On a separate platform to one side was a spruiker to stir the mob. Already gloved and booted, in silk shorts and dressing-gowns that proclaimed their fighting names in letters of gold, the coons would be dancing about just at head level, jabbing the air, hissing through their nostrils, looking terrible.

They were there as a challenge. To question the toughness and assumed manhood of the farmhands and counter-jumpers who stood about with a girl on their arm and a stick of sugarcane or a cornet of fairy-floss in their fist, asking themselves, but secretly, if they measured up. Mugs, they were.

Telling it over later to Mac and Doug, Digger would laugh, a little shamefaced before these new friends of the role he had played, but carried away by the sheer fun of it. He would do a take-off of one of those muscle-bound farm-boys standing with his arms bared and his mouth open, breathing through his nose; or the others who cat-called and chiacked, too fly themselves to step into a pounding, but quite willing to urge on their mates.

There was, after all, something very stark and simple in it that appealed to fellows whose fathers and grandfathers had cleared the country, fought off blacks, made themselves a reputation in a war. It was over, all that. Life now was a tame affair of scrounging for a living and worrying always how to pay the rent and feed the kids, or, worse still, of lining up for a hand-out; and with the vague suspicion always that you had been let down and betrayed — only who by? — and a gnawing resentment in you that needed something out there you could nail and take a poke at.

What was on offer here was a real fight: amateur against professional, white against black, an ordinary man's muscle and skill, a dairyman's or meat worker's, against forces that had to be pushed back every now and then, flattened and shown their place, or you wouldn't know what you were worth. Those were the terms.

Partly it was what the spruiker put into their heads with his quickfire clever patter. But mostly, and especially after a few beers, it was the sight of the coons themselves looking so flash up there in their leather gloves and their maroon or green silk gowns with the stitched-on lettering. You could smell them. For all the showy material of their get-up they were just abos, coons.

It was a put-up job. That's what the mugs didn't realise. But once it got going there was enough bitterness on both sides to make it real. Blood, that's what the mob wanted. To see one of the coons get laid out with a cut lip, or, if the mood took them, to see some swaggering lair, a local bully, get done over by a black. The crowd was unpredictable. It could switch sides just like that.

Most of the challengers in fact were no match for the fast-footed members of the troupe, even those of them who had seen better days and were soft-headed with grog or from the beatings they had taken in real fights. They were professionals and knew all the dodges. They had been in this game, most of them, since they first learned to shape up, and were wily and tough. All the challenger had was brute strength, his hatred of flash niggers, and the wish to impress the girl he was with or his mates.

Digger's job, standing in his shirt-sleeves in the warm night air, while the music of the merry-go-round rose and fell and beetles hurled themselves at raw bulbs, was to make himself one of the crowd, a country kid like the rest (which he was of course), and to appeal to the spirit of emulation or savagery in them.

'That big bloke don't look so tough,' he would remark to one of his neighbours, 'waddaya reckon?' and he would begin to urge this or that man on. Only if no one else would be in it would he step forward himself.

'You sure about this?' the spruiker would ask as he climbed the stairs to the platform. 'Yer mother knows about it, does she? You *are* sixteen? – Nice lookin' bloke, isn't 'e girls? Shame about that nose. Well then, son, yer on! The rest is *your* lookout.'

The first time, carried away by the noise and excitement and the certainty of his own skill, he had just gone up like any other mug and got floored. But he went two rounds and was good. The crowd liked his clean looks, his keenness, and the manager, seeing the possibilities in him – he was slight and boyish but surprisingly tough – had come out while he was washing up and offered him a job. He was to do, for three pounds a week, what he had just done for the heck of it; only from now on it would be play-acting. He would live with the troupe, travel with them from town to town, and be part of the show. What did he think of it? He jumped at the offer.

It wasn't just the three pounds, though that too was a consideration when so many thousands were out of work, or the chance to be one of the show folk, or the prospect at last of seeing the world. It was the chance it offered (he touched on this very lightly, hardly confessing it even to himself) of stepping aside from what fate, or his mother, who claimed to be its agent, had set up for him. Of getting *away*.

He kept the news to himself for a day or two and made his plans. Then he told his father.

'Good on yer, mate,' his father said, delighted to see Digger show a bit of fight and to be part of a conspiracy. 'Don't you worry, I'll cover for ya. You get away while the going's good. Wish it was me!'

He was young and took things lightly, including the bruises. It was an education. He had eighteen months of it and saw every town from Albury right through the west and up the coast as far as Bundaberg. Bought himself boots, a kangaroo-hide belt, a couple of flash shirts, and soon got to know the other showies on a neighbourly basis.

The fat lady had started off in a pet shop in Vienna, selling larks: they put their eyes out, she told Digger, to make them sing. The Human Torso was an accountant. But there was a market out there whose values prevailed, so they had decided, with only a little urging on the part of a manager, to cash in on their advantages and put themselves on show.

The fat lady read cheap romances, in French, and had a little gramophone in her wagon on which she played gypsy music. She gave a lot of attention to her nails. She did in fact have very pretty hands, which were the most diminutive part of her, except for her ears. She kept a black velvet glove on her dressing table that was stuffed up to the size of a real hand and covered with rings; but she had too much refinement herself to wear more than two at any one time. Her favourite film star was Edward G. Robinson, whose features, heavy with menace and the promise of soft violence, looked down in a dozen poses from her dressing mirror. Her only female pin-up was Hedy Lamarr. 'She's from Vienna,' she told Digger. 'Like me.'

The Human Torso was a gambler. He spent all day, wherever they were, poring over the racing sheets and drinking Beenleigh rum. He had a system. The rumour was that he had thousands of pounds stashed away in banks all over the country in different names. An American by birth, he was a loud-mouthed coarse fellow, but when you caught him sober he wasn't. He lent Digger a book by Theodore Dreiser, told him Europe was finished and that all the world's troubles were the fault of the Jews.

They were happy days in spite of the misery of the times. He did not mind living as he did.

The war came and his father went to it, changing his age again but putting it down this time. They had a drink together in Sydney.

'You should be in this, Dig,' his father told him, looking smart in the uniform of the Light Horse.

But Digger did not think so. Living with the blacks had made him see things in another way: from the side and a bit skew, but with a humorous scepticism, as they did. He wasn't one of them, he knew that; but after a time they were as open with him as if he was. 'You're all right, Digger,' his mate Slinger told him, but you could never be sure with Slinger that he wasn't having you on. 'Maybe yer a blackfeller on the *other* side a' yer skin.'

Then one day in Newcastle, when he was just hanging about looking at shop windows and considering the picture ads, he came upon a mob of fellows who were in a line to join up. A recruiting platform had been set up right in the street, flags and all, English and Australian. Men in their shirt-sleeves, and in suits too, some of them, were moving one behind another towards it. At the back of the line a fellow was putting on a turn to keep the others amused, and Digger stopped a moment to listen to him. The other men laughed, but self-consciously, and looked at one another, a bit leery of the line he was taking. He talked like a Communist.

He was a big fellow in a woollen shirt, a blusterer, but for all that there was a kind of lightness to him. If he danced you felt he would be very light on his feet, and his talk was a kind of dancing. He played up to his audience, keeping them always in tow, and after a time his play began to take in Digger as well. When Digger laughed outright once the fellow turned to him and said, as if they had known one another all their lives, 'Givvus a fag, mate, willya?' Digger stepped from the wall where he had been leaning, gave him the fag he had been rolling and rolled another. 'Ta,' the man said, dipping his head, when Digger was ready, to take a light. 'Bramson's the name. Doug.'

The others stood watching, not knowing what to make of it and hanging still on his words. He knew it and held off.

After that Digger too stood openly listening. It was all nonsense really – Digger was reminded of Farrah, the spruiker; just the sort of thing to pass the time while the line shuffled on. 'This feller could talk right through a world war,' Digger thought. 'The time'd pass pretty easy, too.'

At last he turned to Digger and said: 'You in this line, mate?'

'What?'

'Are you joinin' up or just considerin'?'

Digger was nonplussed. He hadn't been doing either, in fact, just passing the time. He looked at the pavement, ground the butt in with his heel, then glanced up under his brows, but Doug had already turned away. The question had been put, that's all, offhand. It wasn't a test.

But, standing in line with these men, he felt something. The warmth of being, in the easiest way, one of a mob, as on nights back home when he had stood round a burning log outside a dance-hall, smoking, yarning, listening to bits of local gossip, or to jokes that might have needed explaining if you didn't know the lingo. That's what he'd missed these last months. Suddenly he felt homesick. There was an easy pitch to it that was different from the one he had been living at.

The coons were touchy. He was in their world and they accepted him, but only provisionally; and there were times when he felt he would never really understand them, not even Slinger. He had never faced the indignities they had, the humiliations. He had no idea in the end what kept them going.

These fellows he did know. They were the same ones he stood among each night playing his part. He could join them now and they wouldn't see any difference in him – he *hoped* they wouldn't; unless he had picked something up from Slinger and the others that he didn't know about; a way of leaning maybe, or holding his shoulders, a smell, but he didn't *think* he had. He felt a need suddenly to be taken back, to share whatever it was these men were letting themselves in for, to be relieved of putting on an act. He turned himself inside out again and came out white.

The others hadn't noticed anything. Their attention was all on Doug. He was the star here.

As Doug went on with his patter new chaps kept coming and falling in behind, till at last it was Doug's turn to step up and sign on, and after that, Digger's.

'Listen,' Digger told Slinger that night, 'you won't believe this. I joined up.'

It was after the show. They were pouring scoops of cold water over one another's shoulders, dousing down in a rigged-up showering place behind the camp.

Slinger was an Islander, a big shy fellow, over six feet, a heavyweight. He paused now with the scoop of water, then slowly let it pour over his head.

'Done it this arvo,' Digger said. 'I was a mug, eh?' He took the scoop and dipped it.

'Shit, Digger.' Slinger looked genuinely upset. Digger was pleased by that. 'Whatt'd ya do *that* for?'

Something in Slinger's voice made him think of his mother, but it was only when he sat down later to drop her a line that he saw how she would see it: that what he was doing was taking himself further away.

He sobered. The water running over his chest was cold.

'Must of been a mug all along,' he offered.

'Yair,' Slinger said, 'you must of. An' I thought we'd learned you something.'

6

'Chilly, eh? Once the sun's gone.'

Digger looked up, startled. He had been miles away, years; feeling the shock of cold water as it poured over his head, plastering his hair down over his eyes, all his white skin goosepimpling, his cock and balls shrivelling up as he danced on the boards of their rough and ready washing place and reached for a bit of towel they were sharing.

Vic shifted his gaze to the river. 'What about that cup of tea you mentioned?'

Watching them come up the path towards the store Jenny began to fluster. This was the third time he'd been in here in not much more than a week. He'd never done that before. He was after Digger for something and Digger was worried. She'd heard him at night through the wall, tossing and turning, but he wouldn't let on to her what it was.

That last time, Thursday, he'd turned up with a present. He was always bringing her presents. It was his way of getting round her. He'd been trying it for years. He never learned.

In the early days it had been little things. A plastic hair-clip in the shape of a bow, it was once. Pink. Another time scent, 'Evening in Paris'. 'Ta,' she'd say, and put the thing aside. She wouldn't even look at it. She didn't want anything from *him*. He'd put some sort of a spell on the thing, that's what she thought, and if she used it, put it on, the hair-clip for instance, he'd have her just where he wanted.

Later the presents got bigger and came with a lot of packaging. 'Here,' he'd say, offering to help. 'I can *do* it,' she'd tell him fiercely, shoving him off. She was only opening the thing to be polite.

A jaffle-iron, that one was. Useless! Then a pressure cooker that scared the wits out of her and which he was probably hoping would blow her to buggery. Then a special pan for doing poached eggs, which Digger never ate anyway. Then a tin-opener you stuck to the wall. He came in all ready with a screwdriver and in two minutes flat had it fixed to the wall beside her sink. 'Here, I'll show you how it works,' he said, and opened a half-tin of apricots – what a waste! – when she'd already made a bread-and-butter pudding.

They were always things that were no bloody use, or that *she* couldn't use anyway without a lot of showing.

'Honest,' he complained once, 'you're a hard woman to please.'

Yair, mister, you bet I am.

But once her heart almost stopped. He turned up with a little kid, a little blond fellow of maybe five or six, in jeans and a coat with buttons on it in the shape of wooden barrels. He had blue eyes and his front teeth were missing. She held her breath. What was *he* for?

He sat very quiet, swinging his legs, which did not quite reach the ground, and every minute or so would lean forward and peer down over his knees, as if he expected, since he last looked, that he might have grown a bit. Or maybe he was just fond of his boots. He was very pleased with himself.

And why shouldn't he be? Someone, his mother probably, had got him up for a proper outing. Everything about him was neatly buttoned and tied, his hair combed, nails clean. He was perfect except for his teeth. She could have whipped him up in her arms and half squeezed the breath out of him. But little kids scare easily, she knew that from experience. She didn't want to put him off. At last she got round him with a lolly.

She offered it and he looked sideways at Vic, who was busy talking, to see if he should accept, and when Vic nodded, put his hand out, undid the wrapper and popped it into his mouth. Then looked in dismay at his sticky hands. He was a very neat little fellow.

She took the wrapper from him and ran off into the house to get a flannel, but when she got back he was licking his fingers like a cat. What amazed her was the pinkness of his tongue. She laughed, just to see it, and squeezing up to him on the bench, said, 'Hey, what's your best colour? Mine's yellow. What's your best cartoon?'

He looked at her then, a little crease appeared on his brow, and he shifted on the seat, closer to his father. She'd lost him.

So all the years he'd been coming it was something different, the present he brought, and he was different too. Meatier.

Digger was the one he was after, but she was the one he tried to get around. She knew that and kept an eye on him. She wasn't that much of a dill.

And each time the car he came in was different too. Bigger, a new one each time. He would drive up to where the track turned down sharp towards the store, park it there under the firs, then walk.

Sometimes, after they had had a bit of a talk, he and Digger would go back to the car and look it over. Walk round and round it, opening the bonnet, putting their heads in. Then Digger would get into the driver's seat behind the wheel, the engine would turn over, and she would hold her breath, expecting them to take off. But all they did was let it run a little. They never went anywhere. They would sit in the car then and talk.

When they got out and were down the river again, she'd go and have a bit of a look for herself. She didn't open the bonnet. Just stuck her head in the front window on the driver's side and smelled the leather, and looked at the numbers and that on the dashboard.

There was a mystery about cars – they were men's business, cars – that she had never fathomed. It had to do with going places.

Men didn't like to stay put. She knew that from her father. From Digger too. You could see it in the way they got their hands round that wheel. Some power came right up through them when the motor started and they used their foot to make it roar. They were already on the way.

That's why Vic let Digger do it. He was letting him in on the mystery. When they looked under the bonnet they were examining the source of it. When he got Digger into the driver's seat and let him start the engine up he was offering him the chance to get away.

Unhappily she walked round the thing, looked at the tyres and kicked the back one hard. It had air in it, but if it hit a nail for instance it could go flat. She considered using a pin, only they'd know who did it.

The big shiny machine, always well polished and each time bigger, parked there at the entrance to the track, was a warning he set. It was meant to show her the power he had: what it was, out there, that he was in touch with, and that Digger might have too if he went away. Big, it was. All metal and shining. With an engine in it that roared and could take you off fast. Anywhere.

Once they came up on her when she was still looking.

'Let me take you for a spin,' Vic offered, but she was too smart to fall for that one.

He was grinning at her. Crafty bugger!

'No thanks,' she told him, and stomped off.

She did think she had him once. Just this once he arrived in a car driven by a chauffeur and was in a real state – she had never seen that before. She watched him and Digger walk up and down, then went off quickly to see what the chauffeur was up to.

He was sitting in the front seat with his cap off and his eyes shut, a good-looking young feller, sleeping.

But when she got up close he wasn't sleeping at all. He had like little buttons in his ears and was tapping his fingers, with their bitten-down nails, on the steering-wheel.

Well, she knew what that was. Digger had one. Vic had given it to him. Only Digger's had a metal band that went over his head, under his hat. He would sit out on the porch and be there for hours sometimes while she raged up and down looking for excuses to break in.

He had an old genoa-velvet lounge out there and a mulga-wood smoker's stand with a tray, and he would sit for hours with that *thing*, that Walkman in his lap, plugged in. You had to shout to get him to come in for tea, and even then he didn't always hear; he was too absorbed. She would have to go out and signal, do a slow dance, and he would look up puzzled, as if he was so far off that he couldn't make out who it was galumping about on the horizon there and signalling to him.

He wore the phones to spare her the dirges he listened to, she knew that, but she resented them just the same, and suspected Vic of giving Digger the thing as another way of taking him off. Digger was a walkover. Anything mechanical he couldn't resist.

She would have liked to listen in one time, just to see if the music *told* you anything, gave you a clue. It was classical, of course, but who knows? – she might have got something out of it. But all she caught when she got close was a high tinny sound, like some animal, a calf or a nanny-goat wearing a bell, that had strayed off and was wandering along a boundary fence somewhere trying to get through.

What she did know was that once Digger was plugged in to the thing all communication between them was cut. He was off in a world of his own, like the kids that turned up in the store on Sunday afternoons, shuffling about to the noise in their heads, and when she spoke to them shouting as if *she* was the one that had deafened herself. So she knew that far-off look on the chauffeur's face.

She lowered her head to the back window and he didn't even see her. He was smiling, his head on the back of the seat, his eyes closed. His cap, which was black with a shiny peak, was on the shelf above the dashboard. He was tapping his fingers on the wheel. She could smell the leather in there.

Suddenly he jerked upright, his eyes open just a foot from hers. 'Jesus!' he said. She had scared the pants off him.

Later, watching from the house, she saw him get out of the car and take off his jacket. All he had on underneath was braces. He walked down to the river and sat. He picked up bits of bark and tossed them into the stream, watching them whirl and slip away. Over and over he did it. At last she went down to him.

'I bet you could do with a cuppa,' she said, as lightly as she could manage. She wasn't used to young fellers. She scared them.

He looked up at her. He was so bored with waiting.

'I don't mind,' he said, and gave a bit of a grin.

'An' a pikelet, eh?'

'I don't mind,' he said.

'And jam.'

He looked at her again and there was a flicker of doubt in him. She always went too far. 'Come on then,' she said quickly.

She sat him at the kitchen table and recalled vaguely that she had planned this a long time ago, only on that occasion it had been a little kid. Could this be him grown up?

'Hey,' she said, as she set a plate in front of him. 'You oughta put bitter allers on 'em.' She was referring to his nails, which were bitten to the quick.

'What?' he said.

'Bitter allers. It's 'orrible – but then you wouldn't bite 'em.'

He flushed and put his hands away under the table. He was a good-looking feller but with eyes that kept darting about. He was unsure of her, or maybe it was of himself.

She tried a few questions. 'Hey,' he said to show how clever he was, 'you're on the pump!' He laughed. But once he'd shown that he knew what she was up to, he was quite happy to rattle away.

Brad, he was called. He had been Mr Curran's driver for two years. Before that he'd been a courier and before that worked in a motorbike shop. He'd struck it lucky this time. Vic Curran was a good sort of bloke to work for, very strict mind you, but fair, and he had stacks. 'Stacks,' the fellow said, taking another dob of cream, and his eyes lit up in a way she found unpleasant. He was greedy.

'Got a terrific house out Turramurra,' he said, 'I wouldn' mind livin' in it. I got this nice little flat now, North Sydney, two rooms. Costs me ninety-eight dollars a week – that's cheap! But I wouldn' mind livin' in a place like that. I will too, one day . . .'

He would have gone on like this, but she got impatient. This wasn't the sort of thing she was after.

'You're stupid,' she said viciously, and the young man, his mouth half-open and full of pikelet, looked as if she had leaned across and bitten his nose. He was that astonished. Serve him right.

'What about Digger?' she demanded.

He drew back and looked at her. 'Who's Digger?' he asked.

That did it. She gave him a shove then with the heel of her hand against his shoulder, and for all the heftiness of him he very nearly went over backwards out of his chair.

'All right,' he said. He got up, very flushed and foolish looking.

He didn't know how to deal with her. If it was a man he would have flattened him.

'F' Christ's sake!' he said under his breath. He got into his uniform jacket and tugged it down hard, making himself stiff and formal. He was on his dignity now. He strode out.

'I buggered it up,' she told herself miserably. 'It was me best chance and I buggered it up.'

She never saw that driver again, as she had never seen the little boy either. The next time Vic came he drove himself.

When she was very little and Digger just a baby she had been set sometimes to look after him. 'You watch Digger now,' her mother had told her, 'there's a good girl. I'm depending on you.' She had believed always that the time might come when she would have to do it again.

Digger thought he was protecting her, and he was too, she was dependent on him. But he was too trusting, Digger. He knew a lot, he knew heaps, he could *do* things. But he didn't know about the world, and she did. She knew how cruel it was. It didn't matter what you knew or where you'd been – Digger had been overseas even, to the war even, she'd never been anywhere. To Brisbane. That wasn't anywhere. But she did know what the world was. It could come at you, all the evil and cruelty of it, in a single blow: a big hand wet as a mackerel coming slam at the side of your head, knocking you sideways, and in just a fraction of a second you'd got all there was to know of how wicked it could be. Sister Francis of the Wash, that was. All six foot of her, looming up in a cloud of steam just as you were hoiking a stickful of sheets out of the copper, and knocking you sideways without a word. Wuthering Heights, that was. Or to give it its proper name, All Hallows Convent, The Valley, Brisbane, Queensland, Australia, The World. *Hell*.

Some girls, all lined up in buff-coloured uniforms and pale stockings, got a good education there, or so they said. They paid for it. Others, who had fallen like her and had nowhere else to go, worked in the laundry. Except she hadn't fallen at all – or not till Sister Francis got going. All she had done, once or twice, was lay down.

While she was still carrying her baby she scrubbed floors, and after she'd had it and they took it away without letting her see it even, to see if it had all its right parts, she worked in the wash. Bloody terrified she was most of the time of that Sister Francis, but even more of having to leave.

'Please, please, Sister,' she'd jabber, ducking under the fat palms, 'it wasn' me. Honest, Sister, I swear t' God!' But they kept coming down just the same, all suds, over your left ear or across your face, with all the weight of a six-foot Irish virgin behind them, her temper got up by the fact that you had fallen, and been picked up again, and were *still* no good. The weight of the whole Catholic Church as well – and she wasn't even a Mick!

She had run away, oh, heaps of times, heaps! On trams. But that didn't get you anywhere.

'Sorry, girlie, this is the terminus.'

A feller in a blue uniform and a little round white cap told her that, a conductor bloke with a leather pouch at his waist and a punch for clipping tickets.

It was Dutton Park that time. She got off the tram, which went on sitting at the end of the line, and climbed up to a bandstand all painted but peeling. From there you could see the whole city, not too far away: the three bridges, the river switching back and forth, even Wuthering Heights with its steep black roofs on a cliff above the water.

The tram, all silver, went on sitting on the line and you could see right through it except for the driver and the conductor bloke who put their feet up on the seat and smoked.

At last the conductor got down. He stood for a moment looking up at her, then swung the pole, and the tram moved off.

It began to get dark. A couple of sailors came, Yanks, with girls, and she got scared.

She ended up walking all the way back. Hours it took. In the blackout, with men and women barging about the pavements and searchlights swinging overhead and crossing, catching stars.

Another time it was a different terminus: New Farm Park. She sat on a bench this time among the rosebushes and a feller come up and started talking to her very fast and with a lot of spit, but kind really. He put his arm round her. He was a bit smelly. Grog. Then he put his wet mouth to her ear, which wasn't as bad as Sister Francis's fist, and whispered something dirty; then shoved his hand up her skirt. It was no good her saying anything. But when some people come past she got up quickly and followed them, but turned after a minute to look back.

He was still sitting on the bench. He looked at her like he was ready to cry – he was that disappointed – and she thought, 'Well, I might as well let him have what he wants, poor bugger, why not?' He looked that hopeless. Wanting something and seeing you take it away.

She walked back, sat beside him, and they spent a while sleeping in tram-sheds and that. It wasn't too bad. But when he got on the grog he bashed her about, just like Sister Francis, and called her a dummy, so she went back.

It wasn't the fear of being alone out there that took her back each time. It was all the hands, even in a crowd of strangers, that kept reaching out to grab or squeeze or pinch or turn themselves into fists and go smash at you. Some of those hands, she knew, might be gentle, but you couldn't take the risk. Even if they started off gentle, you never knew when they were going to switch. So she went back.

She could have tried a different tram (there were lots), to some other terminus. But she'd already seen two and two was sufficient. She didn't reckon Ashgrove or Enoggera would have been any better. Or Kalinga or The Grange. So she stuck, and then one day Digger appeared and said, 'I've talked to the boss here, the Mother, and you c'n come back home,' and that was it. Digger too had been shut up somewhere and had got out – she didn't know where.

So that was all she had actually *seen*.

But it was so astounding that it stopped her breath even now just to think of it. The terror of what was possible out there, the cruelty of some people, and how helpless you were once they got stuck into you. You don't need all that much *experience*. Two seconds flat and she'd got to the end of her own power to bear it, that was the point. There's nothing more.

The difference between her and Digger was that Digger had *not*. He'd never come up against whatever it was, out there, that could utterly flatten him.

'That sister of yours is a hard nut to crack,' Vic had said once in the early days, when he still had some hope of winning her over.

'Yairs, well – she's got a mind of her own,' Digger told him. 'I wouldn' worry about Jenny.'

But he did.

Today, as she bashed the crockery about – 'There, that's yours, mister!' – she kept fixing her eye on him. She had something on her mind.

They sipped their tea and she was still looking. At last, in her abrupt way, she came out with it.

'Hey,' she said, cutting right across something Digger was saying, 'what've you done with that little kiddie?'

When they failed to catch on she got furious and shouted.

'The one you *come* with!'

It was Digger who saw what she meant.

'Jenny love,' he told her, trying to pass it off, 'that was ages ago, you know that. That was Greg.' He shot a glance at Vic. 'He's grown up. Ages ago.'

That little feller with the sticky fingers that she'd given a lolly to? She couldn't believe it. How could he? She felt a real dill. Ages, Digger said.

It was true she hadn't seen him, or even thought of him, for a bit. But ages! And in just that little while he'd grown up into someone. 'Who?' she wondered, and was about to ask but thought better of it.

But she felt sad. Something in the news put a real damper on her. Something she had been looking forward to she knew now she would never have.

She glanced up. And that Vic had the oddest look on his face, like there was suddenly nothing to him. Like something, some*one*, some Sister Francis, had loomed up out of nowhere and king-hit him. She saw right through him to that feller in the long overcoat who had come looking for Digger the first time, nothing to him, thin, pale as potatoes, and she found herself thinking, in spite of herself, 'You poor bugger! Now what's gone wrong with *you*?'

Part Two

1

The basin was enamel, white, chipped black at the rim. In the year his mother died Vic brought it to her three and sometimes four times a day. When he was at school or out playing one of their neighbours did it.

He held it close and in the early days had had to turn away not to be sick himself. But there was no escaping the smell of it or the sounds she made as the last strength was torn from her. 'I'm sorry, love, I'm sorry,' she would murmur over and over.

When he had cleaned up some of the mess he would carry the basin out and empty it in a place in the yard that was all rusty cans, chop-bones and bleached pippies and crab-shells, then kick sand over it, turning his head away in disgust and taking quick gulps of air that had a taste of coal-dust in it.

The yard backed on to barren dunes. The rise behind was always on the move. There was a time, not so long ago, when he had had a rabbit cage out here, but it was gone now, yards back under the dune. There had even, further back, been a couple of trees. He remembered climbing them. He wondered sometimes how long it would be till their whole house was covered. He would lie at night hearing the wind and the individual grains rolling. The great white slope of a wave would rise up and break in his sleep, come trickling first through the cracks in the walls, then press hard against the windows till they fell with a crash and sand came pouring over their table and chairs and the rafters caved in and the whole hill went over them. He would be fighting to get above it.

The shack they lived in was just one room knocked up out of timber, old packing cases mostly, and patched with fibro and corrugated iron – anything his father had been able to scavenge.

There was a dunny behind, and for privacy a curtain his mother had sewn out of bags.

Their neighbours down here were all squatters like them, families that in one way or another had got into trouble and been evicted. It was four years since they had lived in a proper house, in a street with fences between the yards and a number on the gate. Number 6, Marlin Street.

He swilled the basin with water from their tank, once, twice, then went in and sponged her brow with a damp cloth; then poured water so she could clean her mouth.

'You're a good kid, Vic,' she would whisper as he settled her pillow. It was grey and stiff with dirt. 'You're all a mother could wish for.'

He did all he could for her. Sitting beside her on a butter-box, he read the books that one of their neighbours, Mrs Webb, got from the library behind Williams' store. At nine he was an excellent reader. He hardly ever stumbled over the words.

When he slipped away to play cricket with the other kids in the hour before dark, he would pause a moment and bury his nose in the sleeve of his jumper.

That smell – ingrained dirt, coal-dust, salt from the sea, mutton-fat, sour milk – he loathed it! Stripped to the waist in their outhouse, with a cake of Sunlight soap and a scrubbing-brush, he would punish his flesh till it was raw, but the smell persisted. It was a condition, like a disease, and went so deep you couldn't get at it; or like character, or family features. It was *their* smell, *them*. Whatever the ads said, it was beyond the power of Sunlight.

The other kids at school held their noses when he appeared. Pooh! they went, even the ones he was mates with. He flashed out but his spirit squirmed. He loved his mother and hated to feel ashamed of her. His father was another matter. There was nothing anyone could do about *him*.

All this he bore in silence, he was proud; and they were all outcasts, more or less, the kids like him who lived along the railway and down the dunes.

He wasn't by nature morose. The brightness of his blue eyes and their steady gaze, his quickness and sturdiness of limb, belonged to a disposition that was meant to be sunny. He should have moved easily in the world. But circumstances had taught him to hold back. Indirectness, an intense secretiveness about all that mattered most, had become second nature to him, the first surviving in an assurance, which belonged to his physical side, that the world must some day lay itself at his feet, though he was pretty certain now he would have to force it to.

As for the ready smile and liveliness of manner that came so easily to him, they could leave you vulnerable, he had discovered, unless used as a mask. They disarmed people. That was their use.

He ought to have been without hope. But his body was hopeful and he trusted it. Everything he did he looked forward to with an eager impatience. As a little lad he would come rushing in from play and suddenly stop dead on the doorstep, wondering, now he had arrived, why he had been in such a hurry to get back; as if he had expected the house to have changed while he was away. His mother saw the look on his face and it went right through her.

When he examined the world he was in he could only assume that an error had been made in the true workings of things. He was harmed by this. It would make life hard for him. But he intended to rectify the situation any way he could and would have no mercy on whatever it was that had sought to rob him of his due.

Standing still out there in the fading light and knowing that the moment he went in his eyes would lose their capacity to follow the flight of a ball or catch a disturbance in the grass, he would try to keep contact with the animal part of him, trusting to *that*, and would feel his whole body come to the edge of something – something he could have too, if he could only grasp what it was.

Here, at the smoky edge of darkness, even stones lost their sharp edge and their heaviness a moment and seemed ready for flight. He felt his body leave the earth. That was the animal in him, which was sure-footed and had perfect timing. It took off in a long leap and he held his breath.

The land breeze had fallen, just on the turn. Everything was suspended, hanging for one last moment between daytime and night, between its day life and that other darker life of the night hours. His body too was suspended.

But after a moment of almost miraculous lightness in which he felt he had actually done it, and worked the change, he came back to earth. The weight of his body, light as it was, reclaimed him. It was too heavy to shake off.

The sea breeze quickened and in kitchens all down the shore they would be feeling its coolness now. His eyes had adjusted. The lights were hard window-squares.

'Maybe,' he thought grimly, 'there *is* no other life to be broken through to. It's all continuous, and you just keep getting thicker and

73

thicker and heavier and heavier as it builds up in you, and that's *it*.'

He thought this but could not believe it. That sort of fatality was not in his nature. He would sigh and go home disappointed, but not hopeless, never entirely without hope.

Mornings, out early to fetch the milk, he would see the local men gathering at bus stops on their way to the mine. Other fellows from villages down the coast would be on bikes and would call to them as they passed. Happy enough they seemed, with their little lunch-boxes. They were the lucky ones who still had work. The rest, unshaven, in pyjamas some of them, would be pottering about behind fences, digging a bit, keeping busy. Later, still unshaven but dressed now in collarless shirts and braces, they would be hanging about in groups outside the pub, quiet enough till they got going. Horses were what they were passionate about, or greyhound races or football teams.

At the weekends you could see them, in the same groups, walking to matches with their hands in their pockets. Younger blokes in flash suits, their girls in stockings and high heels, would be stepping along beside them, occasionally calling across to a fellow they knew, or the girl would call to a neighbour she recognised. They would have a fifth share in a lottery in their pocket, these youngsters, maybe a frenchie just on the off-chance.

'Doin' all right, are yer?'

That question from an older man, with just a touch of envy in it, would satisfy in most of them the need for recognition.

'Can't complain,' was the conventional, understated response.

A raw, scrubbed look, hair cut short around the ears and palmed down with California Poppy, a suit. Kids like Vic, still barefoot, in an old knitted jumper with a hole at the elbow from leaning on a desk, were supposed to be impressed by that and to catch in it a hint of what they too might step into, if they did what they were told, stayed on the right side of the law, and the Depression ended.

Vic considered this and didn't think much of it. He would make his own life, not just pick up what was passed on to him. He would. He knew it.

His father was a miner, or had been till an old war wound asserted itself – 'came good', as the cynics put it. He had a pension and spent his

74

days now, winter and summer, down at the jetty where the coal-loaders put in and there was always a little crowd of men lounging about or casting a line for whiting. There or in one of the town's three pubs.

He was a well-set-up dark fellow with the same blue eyes Vic had (Vic resented this, whatever value they might have in the way of foxing people), and a natural slovenliness in all he did that affronted the boy. It was to assure himself of the impossibility of there being any link between them that Vic tormented his spirit into hardness and punished his skin with the scrubbing brush.

Easy-going – that was the word for him. They had both been easy-going, Dan and Till Curran, in the days when he was still in work and she was a big woman who liked a beer or two and a hand of poker. They had friends all over. Vic was little then, but he remembered Marlin Street and the rowdy nights.

His father now was a byword in the town. A drunk and a scrounger, he was always dancing about on the edge of whatever crowd there was at the Pacific or the Prince of Wales, and there was a point in his booze-sodden day – Vic had been witness to it more than once, and could not, young as he was, wipe out the horror of it – when he would, with a show of clownish good humour, easy-going as ever, do whatever was demanded of him so long as there was a beer at the end of it: run messages for people, tell tales, swallow insults – always with a silly smile on his face and a fawning eagerness to make himself agreeable.

He had no shame, and it amused some of the smart-alecs of the town, a good many of whom had no shame themselves, to see how far he would go. With a mixture of low pleasure and fascinated disgust, a touch of fear too at what they might have in common with him, they would taunt him with insults, amazed that he should just stand there smiling, blinking, and make no effort to defend himself.

He would do anything, Dan Curran, if he was far gone enough. Lick up your spit and thank you for it, laughing. Then swallow his schooner at a gulp.

There were others, decent men who had worked in the pit with him or been in the same class at school, who felt humiliated themselves to see a man with so little regard for himself.

'That's all right, Danno,' one of them would say stiffly, 'have this one on me.' A couple of coins on the linoleum would save him then from his own weakness. But after a minute or two he would have an empty glass in front of him and start making up again to his tormentors, since they were more reliable in the long run than the occasional benefactor.

When he got home he would be in a shouting mood. Then suddenly he would break down and weep.

Every stage of this daily drama disgusted Vic and confirmed him in the view that this vicious crybaby who claimed to be his father had nothing to do with him.

The shame of it was that in the early days, when things had not yet come to their worst, when his father was just newly out of work and had time, since he was home all day, to take Vic fishing and tell him stories of the war, they had been mates, and Vic had been inveigled on more than one occasion into going round to the back door of the pub, just on closing time, to fetch a couple of bottles. Jimmy, the Pacific's barman, would slip them to him and he would get back fast to hear the end of whatever it was his father had been telling. It was a secret between them – Jimmy, his father and himself. The bottles came in loose straw jackets and they went out and burned them quickly in a corner of the yard so that his mother wouldn't find them, a real blaze. The empty bottles they sent sailing into the dunes.

But Jim Hardy the publican got to hear of it and told his wife, and when she told Vic's mother, she cried and was angry with him. Didn't he know, couldn't he see what was happening?

He did see then. His mother and father, who had always been so lively together, began to have brawls, and in no time at all, or so it seemed, were forever clawing at one another.

'You're a bloody wowser,' he complained when she refused to drink with him. 'I din' expect that. I din' expect you t' turn into a bloody wowser. If there's one thing I can't stand it's a bloody whingein' woman an' a wowser!'

He would come home belligerent now, ready, on a point of honour, to take offence at everything.

'You shoudn' be sewin' for bloody Sam Goddard's bloody wife,' he bellowed. '*That* bitch! Here, gimmee that,' and he would wrench the bit of work, whatever it was, a skirt to be let down or a new blouse, right out of her hands. If she resisted he would hit her.

Now, when his father tried to get around him, Vic used his elbows to push him off.

'You git away from me,' he would hiss, quite prepared to fight if he had to. 'I won't do yer scroungin' for yer.'

He would go out in the dark and sit on the woodpile and look at the axe swung down hard into the block. There would be a breeze from the sea, cooling the sweat on his upper lip, and he would sit there letting it cleanse him.

But when he went back in his mother would say: 'You oughtn'ta speak to 'im like that, Vic. Don't think you're doin' it for me.' She would have a cut on her lip or a puffy eye, and still she said it.

He hated that. The way she found excuses and put up with things. He was a fighter. He wanted her to be.

'Vic, love,' she told him, 'you don't understand these things. Don't be too hard on me.'

Later, when they thought he was asleep, he would hear them in the double bed. She would be saying his father's name over and over, gasping it, and with her cut lip kissing and petting him.

He loved her, but her weakness enraged him. When his father flung about with his fists and they were all in a savage moil, shouting and using their shoulders and elbows, he would have given his last breath for her, and was in a frenzy of such rage and blind impotence that he thought he might die of it; of being caught up with them – between them at one moment, at the next outside and beating with his fists to get in, and of shame at being so big for his age and so helpless to do anything.

In the closeness of such moments, when they were all three struggling and shouting, they were like creatures trying to give birth to something, some monster, that's what he thought, and he saw at last what it was: a murder, that's what it was. One day soon, as soon as he was strong enough to keep hold of the axe, he would kill this man.

Then his mother took sick. In just weeks she fell away from being a big soft woman to skin and bone. He brought her the basin, and watched her, one hand clutching her side, drag herself from chair to table to doorknob, then across the sandy yard to their dunny. His father was nowhere in sight. Never home now. He had stayed sober for a day or so, right at the start, but now he was drunk from morning to night, though he stayed quiet enough. There was no more shouting. He slunk home after midnight and went to bed in his boots.

Too young to see beyond the immediate horrors, it did not occur to Vic that his father was a man in panic: that what subdued him, drove him deeper into himself, but also kept him away, was an animal terror of what was happening here, the wasting of the big body he had clung to, so that he barely knew it any more, her pain that was like a wild thing in the bed between them, all teeth and claws. He never came near her, that's all Vic saw. When he did, he couldn't wait to get away again.

His mother knew what he was thinking. 'You're wrong about yer father, Vic,' she told him, but her voice was no more than a whisper. She was too weak to elaborate.

She died at last. Vic was ten. His father wept and tried to cuddle him. 'There's just the two of us now, Vic,' he said. But Vic was not deceived and offered no sympathy. When his father held on he pulled away.

His own sorrow was overwhelming. He dealt with it. But what feelings he had left over were for himself. He had none for this drunken bully who whined and snivelled and laid claim to him but did nothing but bring them shame.

'You're a hard man, Vic,' the father said bitterly. 'I wouldn' wanna be in a world where you was God. God help me if I was. There's no softness in yer. Not like yer mother.'

He was trying to get around him again. Vic shut his ears.

So long as his mother was there to see it, for her sake, and to set himself at a distance from his father's slovenliness, since *he* would do nothing, Vic had tried to keep things in order, wiping the oil-cloth after they ate, rinsing the galvanised iron tub they washed up in, sweeping the floors.

It was hard enough. No matter how often you used the broom there was always a grist of sand under your feet. It settled on the skirting boards and along the windowsills, got between the sheets and scratched when you climbed in. There were always a few grains of it in a teacup when you took it down from its hook.

He had been concerned, in those last weeks, when his mother lay all day in a coma, with her mouth open, that he might come home and find her choked with it, and had nightmares of having to use his fingers to scoop sand out of her throat.

Once she was gone he did nothing. To spite his father he let the dirt accumulate as a witness to all he was responsible for. Food lay about the table, a mess of bread-crusts, open jam tins, knives smeared with fat. Flies gathered and big cockroaches swarmed and scuttled. The beds were unmade, their sheets growing filthier from one week to the next. Milk soured in the jug. Dirty socks and shirts piled up. The whole place stank of fish and sour milk and sweat, and when the windows grew thick with coal dust and salt they stayed that way. He wouldn't lift a finger. He too stank, he knew that, worse than ever, and was itchy.

He loathed filth of every kind, but he let it accumulate, and lived with it out of spite, to torment himself and as a witness against his father.

The one thing he kept clean was the edge of the axe. He would stand stripped before the bit of broken mirror in the outhouse wall and make a muscle with his arm, the right one. A hundred times, in fantasy, he went through with it. Without these acts of assertion he might never have been able to tolerate it, the muck they lived in, and the look on his father's face when he sat in his singlet on the bed with one dirty foot across his knee, sore-headed and sorry for himself.

'Givvus a hand, son. Git yer dad 'is boots, eh? There's a good lad.'

'Fetchem yerself,' the boy would tell him, pulling on his shirt for school and jerking in the belt of his hand-me-down trousers.

'Yer a callous bugger,' the father whined, while Vic stood at the window chewing a bit of crust and taking a good swig of tea, and the whine was enough to close the boy's ears if he had been inclined to respond. 'You don't give a bloke a chance, do you?'

The roof of the house had no lining. You could look up at night and see, under the corrugated iron peak of it, the bare rafters with mice skipping along them. It was, Vic had thought when he was younger, like living inside a huge tree, all branches. An owl lived in this tree, and sometimes, in his childhood sleep, it flew right into his head, and quietly, very quietly for all its heaviness, flopped about there among the rafters woo-hoo-ing and blinking its yellow eyes. He would feel its warm droppings come down. He would wake sometimes with his arms flailing to keep the big bird off.

He had not had that dream for ages. Now the big bird reappeared. It flew about, its wings beat, warm droppings fell. But when he woke in his dream and looked, the owl had a mouse in its beak. The droppings were blood. He woke with warm blood in his mouth and was too choked to cry out.

*

A night came when his father brought a woman home, a big girl of seventeen called Josie.

Vic had seen her round often enough, with three or four littlies, her brothers and sisters in tow, and had heard stories about her from the older boys. *She roots.*

At breakfast, which she had ready by the time he got up, she looked at Vic without hostility but without attempting to win him over either, as if she already owned the place and he came with it. She had, it seems, laid her hand on everything she needed, the right teapot, the only one with a decent spout, and had solved their curious way with labels – tea in the cannister marked sago, sugar in the one marked rice. She had chopped her own wood, too, and laid a proper table. She was the sort who got on with things and knew how to make do.

Vic resented the ease with which she had discovered the oddnesses of their male housekeeping. He was embarrassed – as usual he had woken up with a horn – at having to dress in front of her, though she paid no heed. When he came in at lunchtime she was still there and was cleaning the house. He was furious, but realised, when he saw the windowpanes clear again and the floorboards scrubbed, how important it was to him, this orderliness and the smell of suds.

His father did not change and Josie did not demand it. She took things as they came. Vic could hear them at night, and the fury of it tormented him. He was nearly twelve.

She was soft with him, but expected nothing in return. She was a person, it seemed, who had no expectations of any sort, and this touched him but he held back. He was wary of her. He resented the way she took over things his mother had treasured and changed their use.

She kept the house clean, did their washing and sang a bit as she shifted the clothes-props and hung it out. In the afternoons when he came in she would be reading a magazine, *Photoplay* or *Pix*, with her bare feet up on a chair, and was glad to have someone to talk to at last. Putting the magazine aside she would ask him about school, and despite himself he was drawn into talking things over with her.

'No,' she admitted, 'I never was much good at parsing. Algebra I am – that was my long suit.'

Occasionally she read things out to him: 'Myrna Loy and William Powell,' she read, 'are close friends, both on and off the set. Since appearing together in *The Thin Man* . . .'

Sometimes they played Ludo, which was the only game she seemed to know.

When boys at school, or outside the pictures, taunted him, he found himself standing up for her. This was just what they wanted. 'Gettin' a root now, are ya Curran?' the older boys jeered. He reddened and went for them.

He continued to exercise at the woodpile. She thought he was doing it for her, a boyish gallantry, and his fantasies became more complicated: she kept getting in the way of what had been a simple act of violence. What it was now he could not quite determine. The fantasy was its own satisfaction. He did not want to give it up.

In the end it was taken out of his hands. One night his father, who had lately become combative, got into a brawl. A man came to the door to call Josie, and she and Vic went running. For once, it seems, he had stood up for himself, refused some piece of self-abasement no worse than others he had complied with (but who can tell how he saw it?), struck out with an empty glass, and the other fellow, one of his persistent tormentors, infuriated that he should be challenged, and by a fellow for whom everyone had contempt, struck the top off a bottle and took his guard.

No one could say what happened then. The man's account was that Dan Curran had thrown himself at the jagged edge and cut his throat. When Josie burst in, with Vic behind, though rough hands tried to hold him back, he was dying. There was a six-inch gash in his throat and blood all over.

Vic was astonished. The blood in his own throat thundered. He looked at his hands.

The men were standing back in a ring, their boots making a cordon round the head with the long open wound across its throat, the cheeks and brows grey as mutton-fat, and the sawdust floor like a butcher's shop all pooled with blood.

People were kind to him. They took him aside and gave him a nip of something that burned and brought tears to his eyes, but it was this unexpected kindness, not grief, that made him weep.

Josie was inconsolable. They sat at the table together under the branching rafters and he looked up for the owl. He had shown no grief.

'You're a real shit, Vic – you know that?' she told him fiercely.

She was white-faced and looked childlike in her big-girl clothes. They had the house to themselves.

'Don't you worry, mister high-and-mighty virtuous – you'll find out, one day.' She saw the look on his face and laughed. 'What's that?' she asked, though he had not spoken. 'Well, there's a *lot* you don't know.' She leaned close and for a moment he thought from the scornful look of her that she might hit him. If she did, he would not defend himself.

He was shaking. Her face was very close now. Two inches closer and he could have kissed her.

They sat like that for a full minute, then she burst into tears and he put his arms round her till she cried herself out.

Later, when she had crawled into bed, he went out to the woodpile and sat. The axe was where he had put it, with a good swing, when he had chopped the wood for her at teatime. In the block.

His father's blood. It had stunned him, that, the thickness of it, the liveliness. He had had a vision of his own blood rushing with a thump to his heart, swirling through him, pushing out into the roots of his hair, swelling the veins in his wrists.

He felt obscurely, and not for the first time, some limit to his imagination, his grasp on the complexity of things, that sent a wave of depression over him. You could be so wrong! His mother had warned him of that. He felt himself butting against something, some wall that would not yield. He might never discover now what was on the other side of it, though he knew there was a wall and that his failure to penetrate it was important. Without thinking, he smelled his hand.

Sweat. His sweat, with the grime in it of things he had touched. He rubbed hard at his shorts. Guilt moved in him but he did not know what it was for since he had done nothing.

Maybe (and a shadow cast itself across his heart) it was for something that was still to come.

And the anger he had hoped to relieve himself of? To throw off forever with one swing of the axe? It would have no relief now, ever. He would be left with it.

He rubbed his hands again on the rough of his shorts. So his father had got the better of him after all.

He sat in the dark of the woodpile with the wall of the house behind him and the moonlit slope of the dunes in front and saw the great wall of it shift and begin to move. It rolled towards him. He did not move. It covered the pile of rubbish in the corner where he had so often emptied the basin, covered the smell of it and the old rags and papers there, and the burned ash of the straw jackets off beer-bottles, and the rusty tins and fishbones, then the woodpile till only the axe-handle poked out above it; then it covered that too and rolled on to push against the windows of the shack and break in and cover the chairs and table and the stiff grey sheets on the beds, and climbed into the teacups high on their hooks, till the whole room was filled to the ceiling and the rafters and roof were covered and there was no sign any more of them or of the life they had lived except in his head.

2

His life changed abruptly, and in ways so like his own secret wishing that he wondered later if he hadn't, by some power he only half guessed at, brought it about, and that *that* was the guilt.

His father, though he had nothing to leave, had made a will. Vic was the sole beneficiary. But more important, he had named an executor, a Captain Warrender of Strathfield, Sydney. For three years during the war Dan Curran had been Captain Warrender's batman, and the officer had agreed, in the event of Curran's death, to act as guardian to any children he might leave. He appeared now, nearly twenty years later, to make good his word.

He was a large shy man in a three-piece suit. He patted Vic on the shoulder, then shook his hand, and Vic saw immediately that of the two of them it was Mr Warrender who was the more ill at ease.

He had come up from Sydney by train. The dirty little town, scattered at the edge of the sea, all unpainted timber and rusty iron, the sandy yards full of rubbish, the coal dust which that day was blowing all about in a stiff south-easterly making the sea air sharp with smuts – all this was unfamiliar to him. So was the barefoot boy with his raw haircut. At home he had only girls.

But for all his shyness he had eyes that looked right at you, not unkindly but with perfect frankness about what they were up to that showed you frankly, as well, what they saw.

Vic, who had put on a clean shirt and wet-combed his hair, stared straight back. He knew his best qualities and was confident they would show. He trusted this man to see them.

Mr Warrender looked for a long time, then patted Vic's shoulder again and nodded.

Vic did not relax, not quite yet, but he saw that Mr Warrender did, and that was a good sign.

What he had grasped by instinct was that Mr Warrender was innocent and had better remain so, whatever glimpses he might have got into the truth of things from the squalor of their shack. He could have no idea how much Vic really knew, and Vic saw that he would need to be careful about this, hide it, bury it deep inside him and be a kid again. He would learn about life (or pretend to) all over again, on Mr Warrender's terms. He could see, just from looking at him, that this was what he would expect.

When Mr Warrender explained that he was taking him to Sydney, Vic said nothing. He let him go on.

Mrs Warrender and the girls (there were two of them) had been told about him and were looking forward to his arrival, to having another man in the house. Vic still said nothing, but smiled to himself as Mr Warrender, in order to set him at his ease – which wasn't necessary really, he *was* at ease, it was Mr Warrender who was nervous – made this acknowledgement of their shared masculinity.

He would have a room of his own of course and would go to high school. Only first, perhaps, they ought to go into town and get him some shoes.

Out of a fear of upsetting him, or out of embarrassment at the whole business of 'grief', Mr Warrender said nothing at all about his father, and Vic wondered at this. He wondered, too, what Mr Warrender had been looking for when at first he stood there studying him. Not what he had found – he was confident of that – but what, knowing only his father, he had expected.

Sitting beside him on the train, impressed by the smell of damp wool he gave off, which was oddly comforting, and watching the landscape fly through his own ghostly face in the glass, in a new pair of shorts, a sweater and boots that they had bought a size too large, Vic felt his body draw into itself, compact and sturdy, as solid on the velvet seat as the man's, and got hold at last of the consequences of the thing. 'I'll never see this place again,' he told himself as stretches of flat beach flew behind. It was a promise. There was only one thing he regretted, his mother's grave.

He stayed quiet and would continue to be until he knew where he stood. He saw that Mr Warrender, who was observant, was impressed by this, and by the pride he showed in not feeling he had to be saying 'thank you' all the time, though he was very polite. He squared his shoulders and, when Mr Warrender spoke to him, looked up very frank and steady, so that what Mr Warrender saw was a reflection of his own lack of guile. He was grateful for this chance to show himself in the best possible light, and to be looked at as if frankness and steadiness could be taken for granted in him. He felt a wave of affection for this shy man.

'You'd better call me Pa, Vic,' Mr Warrender said, 'if that's all right. It's what the girls call me.'

Vic relaxed and smiled. By now he had done some observing of his own.

When Mr Warrender smoked he held the cigarette between thumb and finger like a pencil, and sucked, like a kid taking his first puff, which was odd in so bulky a figure. But he did it voluptuously. Vic thought that very strange, and after a time he decided that Mr Warrender, for all his air of solid assurance, *was* strange. That lack of ease he had felt in him hadn't had to do only with the uncomfortable nature of the occasion. It was part of the man. He wasn't intimidating at all, Vic decided, not at all. I needn't have worried.

It occurred to him then that his father must have found Mr Warrender easy to fool, and this brought him up sharp. All the more reason, he decided, why I should be open and honest with him.

They were coming in to Sydney now, and as street after street flashed by, little backyards with chook-houses and rows of vegetables, and off in the distance smoke pouring up out of giant chimney stacks, he felt some wider vision open in him as well, an apprehension of just how large the world was that he was being carried towards, and the opportunity it offered of scope and space.

Strathfield, when they came to it, was an older suburb not too far from the centre, with avenues of big detached houses that had once been fashionable and were now in a state of elegant disrepair. Along the railway line there were some meaner streets, workmen's houses in terraces that were quite scabbed and shabby, the alleys behind them piled with filth. Still, it was Sydney at last, the big smoke, and Vic had never seen anything like it.

Mrs Warrender, Ma, accepted him with open arms.

The girls, Lucille and Ellie, were sceptical at first, he saw that; but he knew just how to deal with them.

There was also an old lady, an aunt of Mrs Warrender's, who wasn't in her right mind and thought he was someone else.

*

Mrs Warrender showed him his room and they stood for a moment, the two of them, not knowing what to say to one another. Mrs Warrender was plainly embarrassed.

'Well, Vic,' she said at last, 'I'll leave you to get used to things.' She thought he might want to be alone with his grief. 'The bathroom, when you want it,' (maybe it's only that, she thought, she wasn't used to boys) 'is first down the hall.'

She stood at the door, looking at him as he stood with his boots on the carpet in the middle of the room, and his look said, Don't go, I don't need to be alone. But she fiddled with her hands a little, then went.

He sat on the edge of the bed, which was rather high, and looked at his boots. They were heavy. His shoulders slumped and he heard himself sigh. A wave passed over him. Not grief, but desolation, a feeling of utter loneliness that surprised him after the confidence he had felt downstairs. Maybe it was the largeness and whiteness of the room, which he was afraid he would betray himself by dirtying with the grime off his hands; its emptiness, too, since he hardly thought of himself as occupying it – it was so big.

He looked at the case he had brought. It was a little cardboard one with a leather strap. His mother, in the days when she had taken in sewing, had kept buttons and snips of ribbon in it, and off-cuts she could use for patches. What it contained now were the new shirts Mr Warrender had fitted him out with, underpants, even socks. He had brought nothing out of his old life but what was all the heavier for being invisible, and he would have left that too if he could, or shoved it down the windy lav in the train; only there was no way you could get your hands on it. It came along in the roots of his hair, in the mark his fingers left on everything he touched.

Another boy, with his sour miseries and anger deep hidden, had come along with him, and would push his feet each morning into the new shoes, leave dirt marks round the collar of his shirts, soil the bed, these clean sheets, with the sweat of his dreams.

He felt the despair of that boy flow into his heart and sicken him. Getting up quickly, he went to the long mirror of the lowboy, and in an attempt to drive him off stood very straight and square, as he believed Mr Warrender had seen him, in his new clothes.

He turned sideways, and as far as he could, rolling his eyes, looked at himself from that angle too. Then he put his face close to the glass, breathed, and his features vanished in fog.

After a moment, when they came back again, he went to the door along the hall and found the bathroom. It had green tiles. Unbuttoning his shorts, he lifted the seat of the lavatory, pissed, and when he was finished stood for a time and played with his dick till it was stiff. Then he pulled the chain and watched the bowl flush.

In a china shell above the basin was a fresh little cake of soap, very smooth and white. He smelled it, then carefully washed his hands. The smell was allspice.

He looked at his nails, took a little brush, and scrubbed them. They didn't come clean, not quite, but with soap like this they would eventually, he was sure of it.

When he dried his hands the soap smell was still on them. It was still on them when he came downstairs. He checked, in a new rush of confidence, just before he went into the room where Mr Warrender, Pa, was waiting to show him about.

The Warrenders' was a big old-fashioned house, dilapidated in parts and modern in others, with a cast-iron verandah in front, another wooden verandah at the back that had been closed in with pink and green glass to make a sleep-out, and on either side a squat, steep-roofed tower. It stood in a garden of firs and bunyah-pines, and to the left, with no fence between, was a factory, a square brick building with bars on the windows and a paved yard behind that was flagged and full of carboys and barrels. The barrels were brought in on trucks with 'Needham's' painted on the side in a flourish of gilt. When Vic and Mr Warrender came up, one of these trucks was parked at the loading bay. Two men in leather aprons were rolling a barrel down a plank.

'Hullo, Alf,' Mr Warrender said to the older of them. 'How's it going?'

Alf set his boot against the side of the barrel to steady it and said: 'She's right, Mr Warrender. Got a good load on today.' He drew the back of his hand across his nose, which was running, and looked at Vic.

'This is Vic,' Mr Warrender said. 'Vic, this is Alf Lees – and Felix.'

Felix was a dark youth with muscles and a smirk. He said nothing. He stood with his hands under his leather apron and flapped. Vic thought at first that this was some sort of insult. He reddened and looked about to see if Mr Warrender had noticed. But Felix was rolling his eyes up, bored, his big hands under the apron, which flapped and flapped.

'Vic's come to stay with us,' Mr Warrender explained, as if these men needed to know, and Alf, with his boot against the side of the barrel, nodded.

'I thought I'd show him round.'

There was a long pause.

'We won't get in the way.'

Mr Warrender's shyness suddenly overcame him, and Alf, his boot against the barrel, steadying it, also looked uncomfortable.

Vic saw for the first time now another of Mr Warrender's oddnesses. He had difficulty in bringing things to a conclusion. He started off well enough but didn't know how to go on. He stood looking down at the pavement, lifting his huge bulk up and down, very rhythmically, on the toes of his shoes. After a moment, to Vic's surprise, he began to hum.

'Well,' Alf said abruptly, 'no rest for the wicked. C'mon, Felix. Don't just stand there,' and, ignoring Mr Warrender, he took his foot away and allowed the barrel to move on to the bottom of the plank.

Mr Warrender, relieved of his difficulty, said genially, 'So long, boys.'

Vic, glancing back, saw that Felix, under his flop of black hair, was smirking after them. Alf made a gesture to him to get on.

The moment you went through into the dark, high-raftered gloom of the factory itself you were aware of activity; not visible activity, there was very little of that, but a brewing and bubbling that made the air tremble and produced a perceptible heat. It was like crossing the line into a new climate. The atmosphere was thicker. You began immediately to sweat.

A great vat was the source of all this. Mr Warrender led Vic up to it, and for a moment he stood regarding the thing with a kind of awe that struck Vic as surprising; the continuous low hum of it seemed to put a spell on him. He bent his head to the metal surface as if he were listening for a message there that would provide the clue to something that had long puzzled him. Only the message, it seemed, was in a language he had failed to learn.

The bulk of the thing under the high rafters, and Mr Warrender's respectful silence, made Vic think of an altar. It was, little as he knew about churches, the only thing that would explain the sense Mr Warrender gave of being in the presence of something that was both grand and invisible.

Two men wearing white coats appeared round the side of the vat, and one of them, after a brief nod, went back again. The other, looking none too pleased, Vic thought, came on.

'What is it?' Vic was asking. 'What are they making?'

The man in the white coat had come right up to them now, and Mr Warrender made a little gesture in his direction, as if the right to answer, perhaps, were his. But when the man said nothing, he was forced to go on.

'Soap, Vic. It's soap. In this vat here we've got fats – tallow mostly – that's what Alf and Felix were bringing in – and caustic soda. That's right, isn't it, Hicks?'

'That's right,' the man in the white coat said.

'This is Vic,' Mr Warrender told him. 'Vic, this is Mr Hicks. He's our manager. Then,' he went on, 'when it's all been boiled by the steam that's going in there – you can feel the steam, eh? – the soap separates out from the glycerines,' (he sounded like a boy repeating a lesson) 'and when we've boiled it again, only with brine this time, we get soap.

'Well,' he said, after a pause, 'that's a very superficial version of what happens, eh Hicks?'

Vic could see that Mr Hicks, in his white coat and round gold-rimmed glasses, thought it was very superficial, and that Mr Warrender had not explained it very well, but Vic's sympathy was with Mr Warrender.

Mr Hicks moved round now and stood between them and the vat, as if he had to protect the thing, and what was mysteriously happening there, from the sort of superficial interest that might actually prevent it from taking place. Vic felt the hostility he projected. Impatience, too. No doubt he wanted to get back to his own part in the process. Mr Warrender might be the owner, but they were on *his* ground.

Vic, who had a strong sense of these things, of territory, saw that and found himself feeling protective of Mr Warrender and a little injured on his behalf. He seemed out of place here, yet the factory was his.

'Further along,' he was saying, 'we have what we call pitching and settling.' Vic looked for the curl of Hicks's lip. 'One day, Mr Hicks will take you through the whole thing – eh Hicks? – and you can see it all from whoa to go.'

He was running out of steam. In a moment they would come again to one of his awkward silences. But this wasn't quite the end.

'All these processes,' he said, and you could see that it was the first thing so far that really interested him, 'are called "the changes".' He reddened a little as he said this. The word, for him, was charged. 'Pretty poetic, eh, for just soap?'

Mr Hicks was scowling, he couldn't hide it. He was affronted. Maybe he felt something proprietorial about this word, and did not care, since it had a precise scientific meaning, to have Mr Warrender use it in his own way; or maybe he objected to his even telling it at all. Mr Warrender, he guessed, from Hicks's point of view, was not being respectful enough, or his respectfulness was of the wrong kind. The look was dismissive.

'Well, thank you, Hicks, for letting us into your sanctum. Mr Hicks is pretty strict about visitors, Vic. We're privileged.'

Mr Warrender was talking of Hicks the way you talk about a child, humouring him, but in a way that Hicks, you could see, did not care for. He shook hands with Vic, nodded briefly to Mr Warrender, and stepped back behind the vat. Mr Warrender visibly relaxed.

'Times are a bit rough, you know,' he explained to Vic as they turned and went out under the lintel into the blinding sunlight of the yard. 'The big companies have got us by the short hairs, if you'll pardon the expression, we're all men here. The makers, you know,' and his voice took on the fruity tones of an ad on the wireless, 'of Lux toilet soap. We're out of our depth.' But even this he said as if he were repeating a lesson. 'So, young feller,' he said, 'what do you think?'

'I liked it.'

'Good,' said Mr Warrender, 'so do I. But I didn't grow up with it, you know. That was Mrs Warrender. Her father. And liking, old fellow, isn't quite good enough.'

He paused, looked at Vic, and, after considering a moment, decided not to go on.

'Now,' he said, 'we'd better go and take a look at the girls. Otherwise they'll feel neglected. You'll like the girls.'

Some of the girls, it turned out, were over sixty. They were packers and they worked in an overwhelming scent of that allspice Vic had been so delighted by upstairs. Mr Warrender was very gallant with them, and they made a fuss of him and of Vic too.

'So,' Mr Warrender said, 'now you've seen the whole show. We'll just slip round to the kitchen and see if Meggsie can find us a nice cup of tea.'

3

He grew fond of the Warrenders, especially of Mr Warrender, Pa. He was delighted at last to give his softer instincts scope. He had wanted, always, to be the perfect son, and this was easy because the Warrenders were so nearly what he might have conceived of as the perfect parents. He put the past behind him, rediscovered a kind of innocence, and let his spirit loose, slipping back into his heavier nature only when he had shut a door behind him. He could look grim then, and Mrs Warrender, if she had seen it, would have been stricken. A nervous woman, always on the lookout for what was about to go wrong, she might have had to ask herself what they had done to the boy to make him so miserable.

The Warrenders were a source of endless astonishment to him. He had known a life till now that was too harsh to allow for playfulness. The poker games his parents had gone in for, all cigarette smoke and beer, had been rough affairs.

A spirit of boisterous exuberance prevailed in the Warrender house. The games they preferred were childish ones, played at night with all the lights off and a lot of noise. Even Ma, rushing about in her stockinged feet and with her hair flying, would give herself up to easy recklessness, shrieking louder than either of the girls. The girls were wild enough – they were encouraged to be – but Ma outdid them.

Aunt James, who was too old for what she called 'high-jinks', would sit in the dark of the dining room and laugh under her breath, while Ellie or Lucille or Ma tiptoed in and hid behind her chair, and lights flashed on and off in the hallway, and there were rushes, stumblings, evasions that took no heed at all of chairs or vases, then shrieks of childish laughter as the seeker shouted: 'I've got Pa' – or Lucille or Ellie or Vic.

These night games were not the only ones they indulged in, and Vic, who was prudish, found he was often tested, and not at all in the ways he had expected. He had thought he might be too rough for them, so he was surprised when Pa, with no sign of embarrassment, talked about farting, and the girls took it up and elaborated, and even Ma had a laughing fit.

There was a carelessness about the Warrenders, an indifference to what he had imagined was good behaviour and propriety, that would always be foreign to him. They had a passion, all of them, for practical jokes, physical ones, the rougher the better; even Aunt James was not spared. It was a test of character here to take these raw dealings with equanimity and a show of sporting humour. He was delighted when he was at last included and became the butt of one, but never got used to being caught out and mocked. He thought too, after a time, that there was something false in it. What they pretended was that they were all very thick-skinned and impervious to hurts; whereas in fact, as he soon discovered, they were always protecting one another from truths that really wounded, and this rough-and-tumble was a way of disguising it.

Lucille, for instance. He realised after a little that all these eccentricities and raw jokes her parents went in for were a mortification to her. She hated them. She was very proud, and he had thought her hostility to him had to do with that. But he saw at last that what she really had against him was the extent to which they had exposed themselves to him. She was afraid he might take it upon himself to judge Ma and Pa and despise them. She did herself sometimes and was ashamed of it, but her pride would not allow him to.

In the beginning he was flattered by this, but saw that he would have to sacrifice his vanity if he was to make her see he could be trusted. And he could be, too. His loyalty to Pa and Ma was beyond question. It had to be, and especially this matter of loyalty to Pa. The whole household was based on it. Pa's moods, his whims, had at every moment to be respected and allowed for. Ma saw to this, and the girls and Aunt James, even Meggsie, for all her grumbling, complied. Mr Warrender tyrannised over his house of women. They spoiled him and made a great show of it; but the spoiling was a substitute for something he wanted more and which they thought he might never get. The fuss they made was to conceal from him that he had no real authority. But Pa was too intelligent to be deceived. If the household was shaky, and it was at times, it was because of this.

He was an odd fellow, Pa. For all his generosity of flesh he was not expansive. People who thought that all large men should be jolly and lovers of life were disappointed in him. He was not jolly at all, and the roughness of the games he liked to play, the practical jokes, far from expressing a crude vitality, belonged to a version of himself that he reached out for but could not catch. He was often despondent, and sometimes downright gloomy. On nights when he did not happen to be in the mood for noise he would sit with his eyes closed, his brow lowered, while Ma or one of the girls rubbed his shoulders to soothe the ache he felt in being all locked up in himself.

He was a man who had spent a day in heavy traffic with the world, which had buffeted and exhausted him. He needed to be restored now with the ministering of soft hands. The fact that all this had been *mental* traffic made no difference. The results were the same.

He had spent his day getting under everyone's feet, as Meggsie put it, poking about the house looking for things that he or other people had mislaid, making angry phonecalls to lawyers in town, to the council or the newspapers, enervating himself with trivialities to the point where he was quite incapable of settling to any work.

What this work might be, if he did settle, remained unclear. Sometimes it was the regimental history he was writing, in which, Vic supposed, his father might figure – he would be interested in that. More often it was 'something literary'. He had an office and a desk, all leather, that had belonged to Mrs Warrender's father; but he had no sooner got himself in there than he was out again, calling for a pencil-sharpener or his tobacco pouch or the paper, or the volume of Gibbon he had been reading that morning in the lav, or his glasses or his old boots.

On the day each month, 'our dreadful Fridays', Ma called them, when he had to appear at the Needham's board meeting, he would be exhausted, utterly drained, a mere shadow of himself. He would sit through these meetings in a state of maddened irritability, listening to gloomy reports from auditors that he could make nothing of, and angry ones from travellers that he kept rewriting in his head, illiterate accounts, full of irrelevant details or diversions, of encounters with the managers of department stores and chemist shops and beauty parlours, and all the while, under the eye of the chairman, he would be filling the margins of the page with doodles, little half-imaginary animal figures or scornful caricatures.

He would laugh at these meetings the day after, finding in them a source for extravagant mimickry, but the occasions themselves were painful to him. He knew he was of no use there, a straw man, invited only to make up the numbers and have a member of the family on show. He was ashamed of the frivolous manner he assumed but could find no other. He felt humiliated.

Vic was surprised, and sometimes in a painful way, by the differences between this baffled household figure and the one he had sat beside in the train, in whom he had found so much manly steadiness, and warmth and ease. But he continued to honour without qualification the understanding that had been struck between them. What he would remember always was that on that occasion of their first being alone together, and at leisure to observe, Pa, out of an innate generosity, had seen only his best qualities, and accorded him, even if he was just a kid, the full measure of his possibilities. It was for Vic a matter of feeling. The affection it evoked in him, and the loyalty, endured.

Of course he had been presenting himself in the best possible light. It was an opportunity and he had taken it. If Pa had been deceived in some ways, what he had seen was also the truth; it was what Vic, in his deepest nature, aspired to be.

Perhaps Pa too had recognised an opportunity to show the better side of himself. What he had shown, as Vic soon discovered, was the mere externals of his nature, but Vic understood that and would not allow it to make a difference.

He did not reason these things out. He could, with Pa, move back into a state of feeling where those first moments on the train extended themselves and covered all the years to come. The understanding between them, once achieved, was undiminished.

And there was a further dimension to all this. Pa's difficulties offered him an opportunity, or so Vic felt, to step in and show that the qualities that had been accorded him were actual and could be put to use. One day he would do for them what a son might do, and that perhaps was just what had all along been intended.

It was under this aspect of a larger and as yet undeclared purpose that he considered Aunt James's refusal to see him as a stranger. She had simply assumed, from the first day, that he was a member of the family, but, in the weird view she took of these things, a secret one. The fact that she had got the details wrong was neither here nor there.

'I kept all your letters,' she told him in a whisper the first time they were alone. 'I knew you'd be back. They told me you were dead, Stevie, but I knew *that* couldn't be true. And it isn't, is it, sweetie?' She laughed and poked him in the ribs, as if it were a good joke between them that he was not a ghost. 'Well, I would have thought your own sister might have known you.'

Stevie was Mrs Warrender's brother. Years back, at a time when Ma and Pa's marriage was being settled, he had got into some sort of trouble, been despatched to New Zealand, and died there by taking his own life.

Vic felt uncomfortable. It was crazy, and spooky too. She was herself a kind of spook. When they played their games he would keep away from the dining room where Aunt James was sitting, her eyes, her ears too, made sharper by the dark. 'Ah, Stevie,' she would whisper as he tried to tiptoe past the door, 'is that you? You come and hide by me. I won't let *him* get you.'

It did not trouble him in the daylight. He could treat it as a joke. But here in the dark, seeing her grey hair lit up in points where the light from the garden touched it, and hearing the passion in her voice, which was so low and croaky, he would feel a coldness on the back of his neck, and stop still sometimes, unable to move.

For all Mr Warrender's generosity to her, Aunt James was still loyal to the scapegrace Stevie, and for more than twenty years had looked forward to his return. Mr Warrender knew this. No doubt it upset him. But he accepted it as another of Aunt James's disconcerting eccentricities.

So when she saw in Vic's appearance among them the return of the prodigal, the banished brother-in-law, she was making mischief. She was enlisting him in an alliance against Pa.

Vic decided (they were all so open about it) that he could take this side of the thing lightly, presenting himself as a victim, as Mr Warrender himself was, of the old girl's crazy fits. But it worried him a little and made him more determined than ever to do nothing, whatever turn things might take, that could be construed as disloyalty to Pa.

He was helped in this by Aunt James's inconsistency. There were occasions when her mind skipped sixty years rather than twenty and he became her own brother Bob, a spoiled and sickly child who had been killed in a riding accident when he was just the age that Vic was now. In this guise she would poke her tongue out and, snatching the bread off his plate, shout, 'Let him go without, the little bugger!' being pretty well certain that no one else could see him; or she would lean out and pinch him hard, daring him to cry out and show her up.

He did not know how to react. He felt a fool just sitting there and letting an old lady pinch him. He could hardly pinch her back. But the girls, who had put up with Aunt James's tricks for as long as they could remember, were delighted, they thought it hilarious. Even Pa was amused, but did give him a look as if to say, 'Well, you see how it is, old man. It's the same with me. But what can we *do*?'

But he saw now why the girls asked their friends to the house only when Ma could guarantee that Aunt James would be out of the way, and why they had been so uneasy at first even with him.

Ellie wasn't – or not for long. But Ellie was just a little girl, rather wild and tomboyish, glad to have someone new to play with and a boy in the house. Lucille he had to win.

He did it by not trying to, by letting her discover for herself how solid, how utterly loyal he was.

They were the same age, and she too was glad at last to have a boy in the house, though for other reasons than Ellie's. At thirteen she was quite grown-up, or thought she was, and very aware of the power she had over people, only a little scared as yet of the consequences of it.

She did not set out to make a worshipper of him, but he became one. The little game he had been led into, of getting around the difficulties of her character, of impressing and pleasing her, became a habit, then a pleasure and a misery. Before long he was, he told himself, in love with Lucille, and in his usual way began to include her in the visions he gave himself up to of what his life would be.

She accepted this at first. She was just the age for it, for talking dreamily of ever afters and for being in love. But she grew up faster than Vic did; he could not keep up with her. He found himself, more often than he would have wanted, turning to Ellie for the rough-and-tumble games that the boyish part of him still hungered for, and he was hurt when Lucille drew her mouth down and mocked at him.

By the time she was fifteen Lucille Warrender had become a young woman, very demanding and wilful and with a tribe of followers. He did not despair when she began to go about with older boys. He knew he had a year or two yet in which to grow up. But he agonised, and wore such a long face that Ma, who saw all this and was increasingly fond of him, was at a loss. For all his stolidity he was easily hurt. And he had a romantic streak. Other people might miss it, but Ma didn't. She didn't know how to help him.

The fact was that she was scared of Lucille, who seemed to her too grown-up altogether. She thought too highly of herself. For days on end she would be all moods and little female fads and whims that Ma had no time for. Then suddenly there would be floods of tears and she would want to be cuddled and forgiven. She was neither one thing nor the other. She was proud and critical and unthinkingly cruel; not so much by nature as from inexperience. She did not know herself or how to act in a way that would spare either her own feelings or other people's. It was Vic who bore the brunt of it.

'After all, Vic, you're not a stranger, are you, so it doesn't matter.' These were the words Ma used when she came up to his room, as in time she often did, to consult with him. 'I can talk to you, Vic. Goodness knows, I can't talk to the girls or Pa.' She meant she did not want to alarm them with her fears.

She believed, young as he was, that Vic was tough and practical. Practical was one of her favourite words, and a great compliment. He would sit feeling pleased with himself, tough, compact, and yes, practical, while she gave herself up to visions of disaster. That was the word she kept flying to.

She was a worrier, Ma. With a magazine in one hand, *The Bulletin* or the *London Illustrated News*, which she would snatch up as a guarantee that she had something to do, and in the other a cigarette that she mostly forgot to smoke, she would prowl the house like an unhappy ghost, peering into rooms that her mother, in the days when they had five maids, had filled with whatnots and the souvenirs of travel – Venetian glass and little boxes and figurines in porcelain or Parian or bronze, that they could afford to keep dusted then but were impractical now. On Pa's urging, and for reasons of common sense, she had cleared it all out, all the gloomy mahogany and velvet and bric-à-brac, and furnished the place in modern veneer.

The trouble was, she missed the old things. She would put her hand out for a bit of familiar furniture and be shocked that it wasn't there. Or she and Meggsie would spend half a morning going through drawer after drawer looking for some old newspaper cutting she wanted to consult, or a bunch of artificial violets she thought she could use on a hat, or an earring to match one that had turned up again after seven years, and she would realise with a pang that she had left it in one of the sideboard drawers when it went off to Lawson's to be sold.

This was her parents' house, the one she had grown up in. What she had done, she felt, for all her talk of what was sensible, had been an attempt to drive their spirits from the place. She felt ashamed now. She ought never to have done it. And anyway, she had failed.

Standing at the long drawing-room window and looking across to the factory, she would feel her father there in the room behind her. He would be wearing a savage look and waiting, not too patiently (he had been a rough, uneducated fellow), for her to explain herself. What had she done with his splendid enterprise?

She thought of the answer she might give him. 'For heaven's sake, Pop, this is 1936!' (As if this improvement on 1919, when he died, could stand against the other figures she would have had to give him, which these days were always down.) 'I mean, there's a depression on.'

All this was nonsense, of course. 'I ought to have been a boy,' she would tell herself, and she would tell Vic this too. 'Then they would have taught me how to *do* something about it.' But Stevie was the boy, and her father, in a fit of self-righteousness that was to be fatal, had destroyed that possibility by driving him away. So who was to blame? And why did *she* feel guilty?

Wandering about the house in her stockinged feet, elegant but careless, she could be there, as Meggsie complained, before you knew it – unless you smelled the smoke.

'Lord bless the Irish!' Meggsie would exclaim when Mrs Warrender appeared, anxious to have a sit-down at the kitchen table and go over some problem about the girls, 'You scared the daylights outa me!'

Meggsie had girls of her own: two of them unhappily married and settled, the other still getting her glory-box together. She had known Lucille and Ellie since they were babies. She spoiled them, always took their part and could see no problem with either of them.

But Mrs Warrender was in no mind to be convinced. As if by habit, and ignoring Meggsie's clear displeasure, she would go to the dresser, find a sharp little knife and set herself to help Meggsie peel and core apples while she went over the thing.

Meggsie fumed. She had her own way of doing things, and Mrs Warrender's did not suit her. As Ma got more and more excited, a good half of the apple she was working on would disappear as scrap. If it was peas she was shelling she would pop at least one from every shell into her mouth. Finally Meggsie would stand no more of it. Ten years older than Ma, she took the line that Ma was not much more than a girl herself. Taking the knife out of her hand, or pulling the bag of unshelled peas to her own side of the table, she would say: 'Now you listen to me, dear. You should stop stirrin' yourself up like this and just let things go their own way. Let *nature* take its course.'

Mrs Warrender was appalled. She had seen nature take its course. That was precisely what terrified her.

'They're good girls, both. Let me tell you, you don't know how lucky you are. Now *trust* me. Did I ever serve you up a brumm p'tata?'

Mrs Warrender would sit a moment. In fact she did feel easier. Maybe it was the few minutes of working with her hands and actually doing something. More likely it was the light in Meggsie's kitchen, which she had loved since she was just a little thing and would come to make patty cakes in the stove. Or Meggsie herself and the rhythm she imposed on things. It was different from the rhythms of the rest of the house, which were either too hectic or too lax – she should do something about that, but what? Just being in this cool, back part of the house was refreshing and she found herself wishing that Meggsie, who was proprietorial, had not made it so exclusively her own. She would have been happy to work here if Meggsie would have her: peeling potatoes, chopping vegetables, putting her hands into greasy water, acting as a slavey in her own home. But Meggsie, polite but insistent, couldn't wait to get rid of her.

'Now you go and putcher feet up on the verandah, dear, and I'll bring you a nice cuppa tea. I'm busy. I got the pudding ta think of. If I don't, pretty soon, there won't be any.'

Mrs Warrender went, feeling quieter, but dismissed.

'I wish,' she was fond of saying, 'that my father had let me learn typing or something – or serve in a shop even. At least then I would *know* something and people wouldn't talk to me as if I was some sort of dimwit. I mean, we aren't *born* impractical.'

Quite soon after Vic arrived in the house she took to waylaying him in the hallway as he came in from school, and later, when she began to see in his sturdy and sometimes grave figure a kind of equilibrium that came, she thought, from 'experience' (and how in the world, at his age, had he come by *that*?), she would at the oddest hours wander right into his room and, settling herself on the edge of the bed, start in on whatever it was that was fretting her.

Sometimes, abstractedly, as she talked, she would pick his dirty socks up off the floor and begin to roll them, or a shirt or a pair of underpants. Once she held one of his socks up to her nose and smelled it, and did not look at all offended – in fact, rather pleased. Or she would open and close the drawers of his dressing table, moving things about and seeing they were properly folded. She wasn't spying, he knew that, because she wasn't actually looking at things. Just touching them and reassuring herself that one article was cotton, another wool, so many pairs. It helped her order her thoughts and re-established, in a motherly way – socks and shirts and underpants were a mother's business – her intimacy with him.

'Mr Warrender, Pa,' she would tell him, 'is a wonderful man. He's the kindest, most generous – . People don't realise. Look how he is with Aunt James! But like the rest of us he has his limits. He can't do wonders. They keep asking too much of him.'

Vic would sit silent and follow her restless pacing about the room, wondering at this way she had of putting a case for the defence as if she were a lawyer addressing an unseen jury, and Pa always the man in the dock.

He was too young at first, and too unused to being confided in, to do more than take it all in and hold his tongue. But he did wonder who *they* could be. Ma's parents? Aunt James, Meggsie, Mr Hicks? He decided then that Ma was rather queer in the head, or overwrought, hysterical. For a time he took an amused attitude and regarded her, secretly, with a kind of affectionate contempt.

But as he got to know the household better he saw at last that she was the only one here who really thought about things. He did too, and she saw that and was grateful. As he got to be older and more responsible, their little 'confabs', as she called them, became serious discussions about family affairs, that took up the whole business of the factory and its running, loans, interest rates, finances. She knew more than you might expect, Ma, about loans and such things. What she knew she shared with him. They were in a bad way: that was the heart of the matter. That's what she was trying to face up to.

They did not give themselves airs, the Warrenders – they had too much style for that. They would have been ashamed to appear opulent when around them so many others were being crushed. The car they drove, a grey Hup, was the same one they had been careering about in for fifteen years. You still had to crank it. The house was large enough, but a lot of it was in poor repair and half the rooms they never went in to except when they played games. There was only Meggsie to do anything. The girls had been brought up to think of themselves as poverty-stricken, and might have been ragged if Meggsie hadn't taken a hand.

All that was a kind of insurance, a sop to the fates. They were *not* poor, not by most people's standards, but they soon might be. Poverty these days could hit you just like that. Ma had seen it happen to others, and she was scared. What scared her was that she did not know what it was, or how, when it came, she would meet it.

Vic knew and could have told her, but what would she have learned from that? He would have had to bare at last what he was determined to keep hidden, even from her.

Occasionally, when he came in from school, there would be a man in the yard, often, as he grew, a boy not much older than himself, chopping wood for Meggsie's stove. Normally this was his job.

Resting on the axe a moment, his shirt dark at the armpits and sticking to the small of his back, the man would draw a wrist across his brow, which was dripping, and nod under the greasy hat. Some of these fellows were not used to it, you could see that. They were making a mess of the job.

They were men out of work, battlers who came to the back door looking for any employment they could get: chopping wood, cleaning out gutters or drains. Meggsie had authority, or had assumed it, to give them something, usually bread and dripping or a bowl of soup. The work was an acknowledgement that what they got they had earned, a gesture towards masculine pride and the insistence that what they were after was work, not charity. Meggsie knew them like her own. They might have been her sons or brothers. Just the same, she kept an eye on them.

They haunted Vic, these men or half-grown boys who a few months back had been storemen or clerks in shipping offices or drillers in mines. He felt his shoulders slump a little at the sight of them. He felt humbled. When he had taken his school jacket off and rolled his sleeves, he would go out sometimes and have a word with them – nothing much, but he knew the language.

They were embarrassed. He didn't talk like a boss, but he was at home here. So what was he? What did he want? They wished after a while that he would leave them alone to get on with it. He felt the hardening in them of something he had touched and offended, and knew what it was but could not help himself. He found excuses for hanging about the factory yard with his hands in his pockets, kicking stones under the firs.

Worst of all were the times when he came on one of them hunched over the soup Meggsie had given him, apart and feeding.

They scared him, these men. Not physically – there was very little that scared him that way. It was his spirit that shivered and got into a sweat. They were everywhere you went: hanging about with no change in their pockets outside the picture shows, the boldest of them still flash enough to whistle at girls; in lines on the pavement. You would have had to tag on to the end of one of these straggling, endlessly shuffling lines to find out what it was, up ahead, that had drawn them. He didn't really want to know, but felt there was something wrong. He had got off too easily. He was in the wrong dream.

He went out for a time with a girl, not one of Ellie and Lucille's friends, but a girl he had met at a dance. She lived at Granville and worked as a salesgirl in the city. She had two older brothers who were out of work, her father too, and could type a hundred words a minute and take shorthand, but the only job she could get was selling paint in a hardware shop. He was getting nowhere with her but he didn't mind, he liked her so much; she was so lively and certain of her own competence, and so pleased with herself because she had a job. Her whole family depended on her.

But one hot night when he went out to meet her, as he sometimes did, at the tram, she was in tears and would not speak to him, just went rushing past in her neat high heels, sobbing, and when he caught up with her she pushed him off.

She had been sacked. They'd sacked her for coming in three minutes late from lunch. It had been so hot that she and another girl had stopped off a minute in the park, sitting on the edge of a fountain to bathe their feet and let the spray blow over them. Three minutes! In a mood of over-confidence set off by their moment at the fountain, which was still bubbling away in her, she had stood up for herself and the manager had sacked them, both of them – and the other girl hadn't said a word! She was inconsolable. She just looked at him. Didn't he see what it meant? Was he too stupid even to see that?

What angered her was the vanity of his assumption that he could soothe an outrage in her that he had not even understood.

She had lost the one little bit of ground she stood on that gave her a choice. It was that, and the shame of what she had let them do to her, that had beaten the spark out of her.

They were in a world in which forces were at work that took no account of ordinary lives, and as things everywhere got tougher he saw that Ma's fears, which he had thought exaggerated at first, were real. All around them people were being swept into the gutter and could not save themselves.

Friends of the Warrenders, a family that had seemed quite safe and prosperous, were revealed overnight to have been living on nothing but show. The father, a solicitor, went to prison. The mother, and the boy and girl, moved to Melbourne.

Things were closing in. It was for Ma's sake now, as well as Pa's, that he set to work, but in a practical way, to save them. Pa was too high-strung and sensitive to be a businessman. 'Well,' Vic told himself, 'I'm not sensitive, I can't afford to be. Business will do fine for me. I'm not so particular.'

He had thought at first that he ought to be; that his readiness to muck in and dirty his hands with money-making was an indication that even his finest instincts might be coarse. But when he got to see things more clearly he began to ask himself what the value was of so much fineness if all it did was spoil you for action – and it was in action that he meant to prove himself.

He took a second look at his coarseness. What it amounted to was a wish to get on in the world, and a view, a hard-headed one, of what you might have to be to do it.

For one thing you had to see things the way they were. No good giving people credit for virtues they did not have. Most people were selfish. They had low motives rather than noble ones. You had to start from *that*. You ought to act nobly yourself (he always would), but you couldn't expect others to.

He could live with that, he wasn't squeamish. The times had revealed pretty clearly what sort of world they were in. Lack of fastidiousness might be an advantage when things got rough.

He kept faith with the glimpse Pa had given him that first day of 'the changes'; he had been moved by all that, and if it was a term he had any use for he too might have called them poetic. He was not without idealism, or imagination either. But this did not prevent him from seeing these processes, in their real physical form, as what they were:

natural occurrences accountable to strict chemical laws, and also, if need be, to the balance of costs.

He had been fascinated by the vat from the moment he saw it sitting there so cool and mysterious, the great rounded girth of it with its rows of darker rivets, the pipes climbing away at all angles, the activity it set up in the air around you, which throbbed with an added heat. Twenty-four hours a day it sat there, quietly humming to itself, and it wasn't just soap it manufactured, the pure white cakes that moved up and down on conveyor belts, went out at last to be wrapped and packed by the girls in the work room, and from there, in trucks, to the department stores and chemist shops and beauty salons where it was handled by sales ladies, and came back at last in the form of the ready cash that Pa jingled in his pockets and doled out on Saturday mornings as pocket money, and which Ma used to run the house. No, it made something else as well, and they lived on that, too. It was a dynamo pouring out energy that when it crossed the yard was translated into the little actions and reactions that made up their daily lives. (Not literally, of course. He was thinking now in terms that in Pa's mind would have been 'poetic'.)

Standing at his bedroom window he would look across the dark of the yard and be reassured by the faint glow of it there, still humming away. He saw it in his sleep as well. Awesome and huge it looked, but comfortably familiar. The energy from it fired his dreams.

In the afternoons after school he would slip across to the factory to 'bother' Mr Hicks. But the manager, once he saw the seriousness of him, and that his interest was not just boyish curiosity in the nuts and bolts of things, was happy to show him all he knew. The boy was bright, that's what he saw. And he had imagination, too. He saw things large.

'That's a good question,' he told Vic once, chewing on his moustache. 'If we knew the answer to that one, young feller, we'd be on the way to millions.'

'Would we? Really?'

Hicks paused a moment. Vic, he saw, had taken him literally. The word millions meant something definite to him.

'Well, millions is an exaggeration,' he said. 'Let's say: to setting ourselves pretty firmly on our feet.'

But that wasn't enough for Vic. It might do for a start. But millions!

He put this bit of information, which was still a question, at the back of his mind. He'd work on it.

What Hicks had failed to see was that millions, even if you took it literally, wasn't simply, as Vic saw it, cash. It was an evocation of scale rather than an accountable sum. In an action of that size, Vic thought, coarseness would blur into insignificance.

He still smarted over the presence of this negative quality in himself, but was determined not to deny it; to find instead a means of using it in an action that would be fine. At least his *motives* were fine. He would be doing it for *them*; anything that might accrue to himself would be sheer profit. He would be repaying his debt a thousandfold. Wasn't that noble enough? In millions! Even Meggsie might be impressed.

He had an irritant, Vic, a grain of scepticism about his own nature that would not let him rest. He could never quite prevent himself from looking, on each occasion, for the little giveaway flicker in another's eye that would warn him he had failed to get away with it; that for all his swagger, he had been sniffed out. It gave him a dark pleasure, that, which he could not account for. It was always the one person in any company who had not been taken in, who had not succumbed to the tricks he used to win people, that he was drawn to.

He went on trying to, of course. That was only natural. But with half of him he wanted them to resist.

What he was after was a truth that could not be mocked.

He had seen at once, when Mr Warrender first took him round to the kitchen to be introduced, that Meggsie was the one here that he would have to be on guard against.

'Vic is it, eh?' she had said, looking once and weighing him up. 'Well, you just watch them boots, young feller, on my floor. I jest mopped it.'

These were her first words to him. He looked at the floor. It was lino in big black and white squares like a draughts board.

'Oh, Vic's all right,' Pa assured her, but lost confidence under her glare.

He knew what she really meant because they spoke the same language.

'Never seen a floor like that, have you, son?' That's what she meant. 'Floor and boots both, I dare say. Well, the floor's mine, I'm the boss here. As for the boots, don't you get too big for 'em, that's all. You may fool some people but you won't fool me.'

It wasn't hostile, but it was a warning. The look of amusement on her face suggested that she would be watching with interest but he could expect no quarter. She had her girls to think of. She didn't care for boys.

He went easy with her. No good trying to get around Meggsie. She'd see through that right off. She knew the world he had come out of and she knew, because she had scrubbed them, the grime he got on the cuffs and collars of his shirts and the state of his sheets. A kind of game developed between them. It wasn't the sort of game the Warrenders would have understood. It was a joking game, watchful on her part and contentious, but not without affection. 'I know you, young feller, I've known lots a' fellers like you. Believe me, I can read you like a book.'

So far as Meggsie was concerned, he would always be on probation. That was the nub of the thing.

Apart from Mr Warrender, to whom she was fiercely loyal, there was only one man Meggsie had any time for. This was the actor Sessue Hayakawa. Vic knew him because he had been one of his mother's favourites too.

'He's a dream,' Meggsie would tell Vic and the girls when they came bustling into the kitchen to scrape bowls.

'I thought he was a Jap,' Vic would say cheekily.

'Well, 'e's a gentleman. Which is more than can be said fer you, young feller, with them *hands*.' She meant his nails weren't clean, but he was ashamed of his big hands and hid them. 'Yer not in the race.'

'The Jap race,' he said under his breath (this was for the girls), and giggled. But the girls were not amused. A year back they would have been, but only Ellie laughed now, out of loyalty, and he felt oafish.

'He's *suaaave*,' Meggsie told them, and Vic had a vision of the sleek, cruel, broodingly attentive lover she must dream of, who stood at the furthest possible distance from what she had known in the flesh. From 'fellers', as she would have put it, 'round here'.

'Well,' he thought, 'yes, but she's never had to change *his* sheets.'

'What does Meggsie think of her dreamboat now?' he wrote home after the Japs hit Pearl Harbor, still smarting, long after, from the snub he had felt and the disadvantage she had put him at in front of Lucille. But it would be four years before he got his answer.

Part Three

1

The early days at Changi were all idleness and neglect. The Japs, caught out by the suddenness of the collapse and the falling into their hands of so many thousands, had no idea as yet what to do with them. Left to their own devices, they did nothing. Even Doug, after his first picnic vision of it, fell quiet and was depressed.

To Digger it was terrible. The daily hanging about in irregular groups, the looseness, the disorder: sudden outbreaks of rebellious anger, then periods when the whole place seemed ghostly and they were struck, all of them, with the sleeping sickness.

The time they were in, like the unenclosed space of the camp, was limitless. Without boundaries it had no meaning. Young fellows who only weeks before had been full of fight and spirit, setting up races with one another, or boxing, or riding out on bicycles to the Happy World to have their fortunes told and play rough and find girls, shuffled about now like old men in a hospital yard, sucking fags, swapping rumours, feeding petty grievances. They neglected everything: let a grain of rice fall for the flies to swarm over; at the latrines were too lazy to cover their shit. Their insides went liquid. Everything they ate turned to slime.

This was despondency in its physical form, so childish and shameful that grown men wept at it. 'I hate this,' Digger told himself. 'It's worse than anything.' It was the sun scrambling their brains. It was lack of activity. It was the shame and desperation they felt at being sold out by the higher-ups. It was the failure of the officers to impose order. It was their native slackness and refusal to accept authority – those were the theories.

But slowly, as the days went by, a kind of order began to emerge. It was rudimentary enough, a simpler version of the old one, but it grew in such fits and starts and bits and pieces that you could make nothing of it.

Makeshift shelters began to appear, flimsy affairs knocked up from whatever the men could scrounge. Cook-houses were established.

Three times a day food was doled out, rice and a few vegetables with maybe a lump of fish in it, and you spent a good hour sometimes hanging about in lines. A few of the officers, who still had faith in the civilising power of education and saw in the enforced idleness and boredom of the lower ranks an opportunity that might never recur, set up a school. They had textbooks, and a blackboard and chalk. They called themselves a university and gave lectures on all sorts of things. Digger went along once and heard a talk on Ancient Rome – the monetary reforms of the emperor Diocletian. Another time it was the Soviet Union, but that occasion ended in a ding-dong battle over Stalin's pact with Hitler, and the anger on both sides was murderous.

Mac tried to talk Digger into doing French. They sweated over a lesson or two, but learning a language would take years, even Mac saw that, and they had no idea what they would be doing next week.

'You'd be better off learnin' bloody Japanese,' Doug told them. 'On'y I don't s'pose they're bloody offerin' that. Bad for morale.'

Standing in line one day, waiting for his issue of rice, Digger found himself addressed by a fellow he had never seen before. He was muttering. All Digger had done was turn his head a little to see who it was.

'They're all bloody thieves in this camp,' the boy told him passionately. 'I lost a fucken good fountain-pen. Some bastard swiped it straight outa me pack!'

Another fellow, half behind the other, half beside, gave a scornful laugh. 'You could'a done worse,' he said. He turned to Digger. 'He don't even know how to write.'

'Yair? Well what's that gotta do with it?' the first boy shouted. 'Eh? Eh?' and he began to jab the heel of his hand into the other's shoulder. 'I traded that pen fer a fucken good pair a' socks. A man oughten'a steal from 'is mates.'

Faced with this fiercely honourable proposition the other fellow shrugged and turned away.

'Me name's Harris,' the boy told Digger, 'Wally' – as if he had seen that Digger was the one man in all this throng who might remember it for the rest of his life. He waited for Digger to respond but Digger drew away. He had nothing to do with these men. He had been late lining up, that's all. He had his own mob. But the boy would not be put off.

'I oughten'a be here by rights,' he confided. 'I'm on'y sixteen. I lied to 'em. Me mum didn' mind.'

Standing with his dixie and spoon in hand and the hat far back on his curls, his expression was a mixture of cocky satisfaction at his own cleverness and dismay at where it had got him. He was trying to interest Digger. He was one of those fellows that no one notices and he was eager now to pick up with someone, anyone, having grasped by instinct that you could only survive here if you had mates.

'I could'a done a good swap for that pen,' he said, 'it was a real goodun. Listen,' he said, dropping his voice so that the other fellow could not hear, 'waddaya reckon I oughta do? I don't feel so good. I got the shits all the time, I'm crook. What can I do?'

But Digger was at the head of the line now. He took his rice and moved away. He saw the boy turn and look after him, but there were dozens of fellows like that, who once the ranks were open were helplessly adrift.

'I don't eat it,' another man told him, another stranger, when he was once more in the line. 'I don't eat the shit.' Digger wondered then why he was lining up for it. He was a big, heavy-shouldered fellow, blond, red-faced, pustular.

'If they keep feedin' us this muck, and we keep eatin' it, our eyes'll go slanty. Dja know that? This professor tol' me. It's what the bastards want! T' make fucken coolies of us. They hate white men.'

Digger frowned. Was he crazy? He was dancing about behind Digger with his dixie all washed and ready in his hand. Half crazy with hunger, he looked.

'On'y I don't eat it, see? They can't make yer, can they? They won't get me! I'd rather bloody starve! All it does anyway is give yer the shits.'

But a moment later Digger saw him, big-eyed and wild-looking, shovelling the stuff into his mouth. Their eyes met and Digger looked quickly away.

More than ever now he clung to Mac and Doug. Only in those who were close to you was there any continuation of cleanness and sanity. But now they had Vic as well and were an uneasy foursome, un-balanced, as they never had been when they were three. Forever looking about to see what you might be thinking of him, Vic was all little burrs and catches, always uneasy with himself yet at the same time cocky, and anxious at every opportunity to put himself forward or to get the better of you. Digger couldn't stand him.

'Oh, Vic's all right,' Doug would say. 'Take no notice of 'im.' But the foursome began to split into unequal twos.

Digger missed Doug. He missed his lightness and good humour. He was civil enough to Vic but resented his butting in. He and Mac thought alike on this. They thought alike on lots of things.

He was an odd bloke, Mac. When he was in the mood for it he could talk the leg off an iron pot. Not like Doug, who loved an audience and to joke and pull people in, but in a quieter, more reflective way.

He was full of stories, odd anecdotes and theories he had picked up from meetings or lectures he had attended or fellows he had heard on Sundays in the Domain; or from books, or from conversations he had had up at the Cross.

For a time he had had a flat there and known all sorts of people: radicals, poets, fellows who wrote for the *Herald* and *Smith's Weekly*. It was an education. 'Sydney wouldn't be Sydney without the Cross,' he told Digger. 'That's where you oughta head for when you get outa this. The Cross. No place like it.'

It seemed to Digger he had seen nothing really, for all the places he had been. Not after what you heard from other men. Mac's tales of life round the city and on the trams, the different depots, and the runs he went on out to Bondi, Bronte, Clovelly, Watson's Bay, the best pubs and pie shops, and Sargents, where his sister-in-law worked, which made the best cakes – all this brought Sydney to life for Digger and fed his hunger for a world of ideas and talk and action that he thought he would never get enough of, not if he lived till he was a hundred and three. He took in every detail, and each one was sharper for his having to picture it in his own head.

The walk up the long gully at Cooper Park, for instance. Could any place be greener on a nice Sunday afternoon? Mac and Iris and the boys would go for picnics there, and after an hour or so, when their meal had gone down, Mac would coach the younger boy, Jack, in the high jump.

'I dare say he'll be out of the juniors,' Mac would say a bit regretfully, 'by the time we get back. Grows like a beanpole, that kid. No stopping 'im. He'll be five three or four by now, I reckon. You should see 'im take off – the spring he's got!' Digger could see it: the boy's legs scissoring as he went over the bar, Iris seated on the grass with a chequered cloth spread out in front of her, and the scraps from their tea, with maybe a bottle of pickles. In time, out of Mac's bits and pieces of description, and stories and instances, the whole household came into view.

The house itself, in Bon Accord Avenue, Digger could see as if he had lived his whole life there.

Mac slept on the side verandah in a room he had closed in himself with the help of a mate, another trammie. It was floor to ceiling books and there were more books in stacks under the wire frame of the bed and along both sides of the hall. Mac had not read these books, or not all of them; they were for his retirement. But the majority of them he had at least dipped into. How could you resist? On the way home, last thing Friday nights, when he had just picked up a new lot, he would take a good long look and be content then to have the rest of it stored up and waiting for him.

Technical manuals on everything from book-binding to telegraphy, novels, journals, books of travel, psychology, history – that's what he liked. He'd been reading since he was a kid, like Digger – anything he could lay his hands on: Shakespeare, Shaw, Dickens, Jack London, Victor Hugo. They swapped favourite characters, told over incidents, laughing, and Digger, a bit shyly at first, recited out of his head from *Hamlet* or *Henry the Fifth*. They were Mac's favourites.

'Amazing, that is,' Mac would say. 'Ruddy amazing. Honest, Digger, you oughta be in a sideshow. What I wouldn' do with *your* gift!'

'What?' Digger wondered.

It had become clear to him, even before any of *this* happened, that his 'gift', as Mac called it, even if it turned out to be the one thing that was special to him, was not to be the source of any fame or fortune. It would never be useful in that way. It had some other significance, or so he thought, that was related to the image his mother had put into his head, that room where all the things were gathered that made up your life. He was a collector, as she was. He hung on to things. But his room was of another kind, and so were the things he stored there.

Mac had been married – still was, in fact. Two years it lasted. The girl left him; not for another bloke, as it happened, but to live her own life and run a nursery in the Blue Mountains.

'She got fed up with me,' Mac told him, and put on a humorous look; but Mac's humour, Digger knew by now, was a way of protecting himself, and you too sometimes, from the pain of things. 'I never understood what she wanted, really. I reckoned I did, like most blokes,

on'y I never had a clue really. She had a bad time, poor girl. Me too.'
When his brother died in a shipping accident in the Islands he had
moved in with his sister-in-law, who was glad of the extra money and
to have a man's help with the boys. Mac got letters from her and had a
pile, five in all, that he read over almost every night.

'If anything happens to me, Digger,' he said once. 'I'd like you to
have 'em.'

It was a solemn offer, and Digger, who felt the weight of it, was
moved. 'OK,' he said.

He had had only one letter himself, from his mother, an angry one.
His father had got himself wounded in Crete.

But more important to Digger in the end than Mac's yarns, and the
passionate and sometimes pedantic flights that put him pretty firmly,
as Doug said, in 'the ratbag brigade', were the times when they just sat
cleaning their gear or doing a bit of mending; saying nothing much,
just quietly enjoying the company.

Self-possession. That was the quality in Mac that drew Digger. It
was rare, and seemed, the more he thought about it, to be the one true
ground of manliness. It was a quality he had never attained himself,
and he wondered sometimes if he ever would. He had ants in his pants.
That's what his mother would have told him. Everything grabbed his
attention and led him away from himself. He was always in a turmoil,
never steady or still. The world was too full of interest. He got lost in it.

One of the things Mac introduced him to was music. It stood, for
Mac, in some sort of middle position between talk and silence, with
similarities, if you could imagine such a contradiction, to both, and it
was this, Digger thought, that explained the link he felt between music
and Mac's particular brand of self-possession. If you understood the
one, perhaps you would get a clear sight of the other.

He encouraged Mac to talk about the pieces he liked. Mac, who was
a born teacher, was only too pleased to introduce him to bits of opera
and things by Chopin and Fritz Kreisler.

'*Nessun dorma*', 'none shall sleep'; that was a good one. They heard
that one night during their first week in Malaya, in the early days
before the Japs landed. Digger was amazed. It was in the open, under
the stars, and almost a thousand of them had been sprawled there on
the grass. But there was a lot of music to be heard at Changi, too.
Fellows who had carried their records with them would bring their
favourites along, and dozens of men, hundreds sometimes, would

come in out of the dark to listen. Digger would sit back a little and take his cue from Mac.

Mac's characteristic expression was a long-faced, half-woeful, half-comic look that went with his being, as Doug said, a 'black-stump philosopher'.

'The big trouble with you, mate,' Doug would tell him, 'is that you know too much fer yer own good. All it does is make ya mournful. Now, I ask you, what's the use a' *that*?'

'I'm not mournful,' Mac would insist.

'A' course you are. You're about the mournfullest bloke I ever laid eyes on. Honest, Mac, you oughta take a dekko at yerself. I tell ya, mate, you look as if the world ended last Mondee and you just got news of it.'

These sallies were pure affection. They took in a side of Mac that in Doug's opinion was excessive. He needed to be jollied out of it. It was his ratbag side, the side of all those failed, unforgotten utopias that blokes like Mac, dyed-in-the-wool idealists, would give their lives for – and other people's lives as well if they could get them, all in the name of some future that most fellers didn't want and couldn't use and weren't fit for, and couldn't be *made* fit for either, unless you wrenched them this way and that till there was nothing left that was human in them.

Mac defended himself, lost his temper, became just the sort of angelic storm-trooper Doug accused him of being, then laughed and put on his self-deprecating, comic-suffering look, but refused to admit defeat.

Doug's rough cynicism beat him every time, but somehow, when it was over, he was not beaten. He was self-possessed, Mac, but he was also passionate, and contradictory too. Only when he was leaning forward into the music and utterly absorbed by it were the different sides of him resolved. What you saw then – what Digger saw – was the absolute purity of him.

'I'll never be like that,' Digger thought. 'Not in a million years.'

Then Mac would catch him looking and wink, and what you saw then was the odd humour of the man.

When the chance came to move out of the camp and do some real work they leapt at it. The work was coolies' work, hard labour at the docks, but they wanted the exercise. There was nothing dishonourable in it, if you didn't see it that way. Besides, there would be good pickings among the piled-up stores in the godowns. Best of all, they would be on their own again, away from the sickness of spirit and irregular violence and filth of the camp. Nearly three hundred strong, they were to set up quarters in the abandoned booths and tea-gardens of the Great World, an amusement park where in the early days they had gone to drink Chinese beer, dance with taxi-dancers and have their pictures taken. From there they would march, each morning, in parties to the docks.

'This is all right, eh?' Digger said when he saw it. A fairground. It was like coming home.

They spent the first night cleaning the place up a bit and fixing showers. There was plenty of running water. Then, all washed and spruced up, they went for a walk through the alleys and lanes between the stalls. A real maze, it was, of lathe and crumbling plaster, with sketchy paintings, half-faded, of horses and misty-looking mountains and clouds, and avenues of bulls with bulging eyes and miniature pagodas. It seemed unreal with no crowd to fill it, none of the noise and sweat and cooking smells from food stalls or the smell of charcoal from smoky stoves.

They wandered in groups and kept meeting other groups at the end of alleys. Very odd they looked too, in their boots and baggy shorts and nothing else. Like kids, Digger thought, who'd got locked in after the store keepers had shut up shop and the taxi-dancers, the actors in the Chinese theatre and the sellers of potency pills and balms had all gone home.

They greeted one another shyly and had to make themselves small to get past in the narrow lanes, their skylarking self-conscious in so quiet a place. There was a moon. Everything looked blue. The walls were mostly blue anyway, 'celestial' blue. The reflections from them gave men's faces, from a distance, a luminous, rather ghostly look. It was weird though not scary.

It was an interlude of pure play, but they were so subdued by the emptiness of the place, its peeling vistas and derelict squares, that it became dreamlike. At last they went whispering through the alleys like quiet drunks, still full of high spirits but afraid to wake someone.

Ourselves, Digger thought, as their boots echoed on the gravel and laughter came through the walls.

2

They had been working all morning, a small party inside a larger, mixed contingent of Australians, British and Dutch, in one of the biggest godowns on the docks. It was an immense place like a cathedral, a hundred and fifty yards long and sixty wide, all slatted walls where the light that beat in was dazzling, and, high up in the gloom under the rafters, sunshafts swarming with dust.

The dust was from the chaff bags they were lumping, or that others had lumped before them. They were choking with it. Their eyes were raw, their hair thick with it, they were powdered to the navel with a layer of fine dust that streaked where the sweat ran and where it got into their shorts, and went sodden round their balls, painfully itched and rubbed. It was a kind of madness they moved in. Half-naked, and barefoot mostly, they stumbled through a storm in which they were shadows bent low and tottering under the hundredweight sacks.

The guards too suffered. They had swathed their mouths and nostrils in knotted scarves, but the dust got in under the collars of their uniforms, clogged their lashes, and hung on their brows with an eerie whiteness. They wore heavy boots and leggings, the sign that they were masters here, but sweated for it.

Generations of coolies, Chinese for the most part, but Tamils too, had worked to unload ships and stock these godowns with bales of rubber, wool and cotton; sacks of flour, salt, sugar, rice; and cartons of corned meat, condensed milk, apricot halves and pineapple chunks in cans. A new sort of coolie, they were clearing it now to be shipped as spoils of war to the new masters of this corner of the earth.

Vic humped his sack with the rest. It was an animal's work though a man could do it, and the dust was a torment, but none of that worried him. Neither did the weight, the two hundred pounds laid on his neck, which he had to trot a hundred yards with. He could do it. He was strong enough. And there was something in him that these things could not touch. He was lit up with the assurance of his own invulnerability. Had been all morning. There was no reason for it.

He knew the danger of such moods. They had dogged him all his life. In the drunkenness of his own power and youth he would lose track of things, grow reckless, and out of sheer physical exuberance say something sooner or later that he did not mean to say, or blindly strike out. That was the danger. He knew this. He was watching himself.

What hurt him, and in the most sensitive part of himself, was that somewhere not so very far away, fiery battles must be taking place, fought by fellows no older than himself, and no more daring either – part of a war that would be talked of for all the rest of his life, and which he would have no share in; no campaign ribbons, no medals, no stories to tell except this shameful one. He would live through this stretch of history and be denied even the smallest role in it.

He was sufficiently certain of his own courage to believe that in the ordinary circumstances of the soldier's life he would, given the chance, have acquitted himself in a quite superlative way. He had spent his youth studying to be noble. But the world he was in now was a mystery to him. You do not prepare yourself for shame.

The guards were edgy. All this dust and the heat of the place maddened them. They too were young. They resented having to stand guard over coolies. To restore their own sense of honour they would suddenly strike out, and there was no way of knowing when the blow was coming or where from. Out of the storm of dust, that's all, whack! and you took it.

But for all that, he could not convince himself that the conditions he was under held force. All morning his spirit was light and he swaggered. In brute fact his back was bent and he was tottering like the others in a dense haze, choking, streaming with sweat, feeling every ounce of the two-hundred-pound sack on his neck, but his spirit was coltish. Nothing could touch him.

After a time a rage of frustrated power began to build in him. If there was a girl here his energy might have been taken up in some other way; but there wasn't. Each time he straightened he felt a surge of exultation and the bitterness of having to rein it in. This was one of his moments – every nerve in his body told him that – and he would miss it for no other reason than that the timing was wrong. That's what hurt him. The moment, and with it the event – whatever it was – that belonged to it, would be lost and would not recur. The unfairness of it maddened him.

He could never be sure what happened next. As he passed, the most bad-tempered of the guards, a smart young corporal, out of boredom it might have been, or the idle spite of those who have been given power for a moment but no scope to use it, or more likely because, in his own youthfulness, he had caught from the mere look of him the state of rebellious excitement Vic was in – this guard, idly, almost indifferently, leaned out and jabbed at him very lightly with a cane. There was no contact. But Vic, with the load still on his back, stopped, turned, and his spirit acted in spite of him.

Even when he saw it happen he was not dismayed. Some part of him was, and he went cold at the enormity of it; but in the other part, in a kind of triumph, he was exultant. Time stopped dead while he hovered with the two-hundred-pound sack on his back and he and the guard faced one another across a distance of perhaps two feet. He was aware of the hair on his scalp as a dense forest, of his body soaring up from where his feet touched the earth. The moment released itself from the flow of things, expanded and was absolute. He spat in the guard's face.

He ought to have been a dead man then. That was the logic of the thing. But as the guard hurled himself forward, Mac, who was next in line, stumbled against him, was knocked off balance, and his sack went. There was a soft explosion and they were immediately, all three, swallowed up in a storm of white.

In a moment Japs had rushed in from all directions, and when the others in the party swung round to see what it was, they were using their rifle-butts, their bayonets too, all screaming and out of control.

Vic, his own sack still heavy on his neck, stood at the centre of an absolute fury in which boots and heads and rifle-butts and steel went everywhere. The bayonet blows were synchronised grunts and screams. He too had his mouth open screaming, but it was Mac they were going for.

For Digger it was a moment that for as long as he lived would remain apart and absolute, its real seconds swelling till he felt as if his body had been suspended over a gap where the sun was stopped and chronology had ceased to operate. Duration was measured now only by the mind's capacity to grasp all that was taking place in it.

He had turned at the first hint of trouble (Vic, that would be, it had to be), slewing on one foot. Heard shouts. Saw the rush of guards, and then, in a storm of dust, saw that someone had gone down. He was thirty feet away and still had the sack on his shoulders. He could see nothing clearly.

Madness was loose, that's all he knew. From a time, just seconds back, when they were in a world, however harsh their lot in it, that was familiar and human, they were hurled into a place where anything could be done and was done, in animal fury and darkness, in blood, din and a thick-throated roaring before words. They were all in it, all shouting.

It would pass. It had to. But until it did, for what seemed an age, they were outside all order and rule, in a place of primal savagery.

Digger had risen on one foot. He did not come to earth. That's how he saw it. He hung there as from hooks in his shoulder blades, weighed down by the blood that was being pumped into his hands and the big-veined muscles in his neck; by the weight of the sack he was carrying too. But his limbs, no longer attached or subject to gravity, were flinging about in a passion like nothing he had ever known, that took him right out of himself, over horizons he had never conceived of.

It was a kind of dance, in which he shouted ecstatic syllables that passed right through him, lungs, mouth, consciousness, as if he were no more than the dumb agency of the rhythm he was pounding out in the dust of the godown, beyond smashed bones and the gushing of blood. The cries that came heaving out of him belonged to a tongue he did not recognise, and for all his gift (he who knew whole plays by heart), when his foot came back to earth at last, and the seconds linked, he could not recall a single one of them. They were in a language that his mind, once the moment was gone, no longer had the shape to receive.

His foot came down; he took the full weight of the sack again, and found himself gasping for breath. Like a man who had run miles bearing a message he was too breathless now to deliver – and anyway, it had gone clean out of his head.

Still in a panic, shouting and slapping now even at one another in their recriminations over what had occurred, the guards forced them into a mass, drove them with canes, battens, a wall of rifles, till they were huddled in a close heap on the floor of the godown, hands locked behind their heads, heads hard down between their kneecaps.

They kept their eyes lowered, not daring to look up. To show the guards something as alive and jelly-like as an eyeball might be to set them off again. They were still shouting and shoving at one another, entirely out of control.

Digger forced his head down, his fingers so tightly knuckled that he felt he might never get them unstuck. His heart hammered. He was rigid but quaking. The guards were all round them, kicking up dust, dancing about in a rage at one another, uttering gutturals and shrill howls.

On one side incomprehensible crazy activity. On the other this heart-pounding, frozen immobility in which they sat squeezed into a single mass just where they had fallen.

Digger had Vic's mouth at his ear. He could smell the foulness – terror was it? – of his breath. The sweat was pouring off him, off all of them. What he had thought at first must be Vic's arm twisted and caught between them was another man's altogether. It hardly mattered.

He saw very clearly then what they were at this moment: meat, very nearly meat. One flash second this side of it.

'There is a line,' he thought. 'On one side of it you're what we are, all nerve and sweat. On the other, you're meat.'

All herded together and with the breath knocked out of them, they were right on the line. Things could go either way with them. Only when the Japs stopped yelling at one another, and rushing about in a panic, and began to move again at a human pace, and they were allowed to unlock themselves from one another and lift their heads, would they be back again on the right side of things.

For Mac it was too late. He had already been pitched across, and was lying over there somewhere – even Digger did not dare shift his head to see where it might be, but it was unnervingly close. Back in the half-dark of the godown, in a scrabble of wet dust; but further than that too, in a dimension, close as they all were to it, that was already beyond reach.

Vic too sat hunched and painfully twisted, in a silence he thought must be a kind of deafness – one of the guards must have deafened him – since all round he could see them shouting. There was an invisible membrane between him and the world. Inside it he was choking for breath.

They were jam-packed together in a heap, no space between them, hard bone against bone; but he felt himself entirely cut off; at an immense distance from the shouting, the panic, the hot presence of the others as they pressed against him. It was as if space now had developed the capacity to expand that just a moment back had belonged to time. He tried to make the laws of time and space operative again in his body, to get himself back into the world the others were in. If there was a price to pay for that he would pay it. He had no illusions about what they must think of him.

Everything that came to his senses had a ghostly quality, yet he had never been so aware of his own physical presence, the sensitivity of his lips which when he ran his dry tongue over them were all puffed with blood, the lightness of his belly, the terrible flexibility of his wrists.

Whenever, in flashes, his mind worked, all that had happened came back to him, and he was flooded with shame. But always it was his body that had the final word, and his body thought differently. It lived for itself and did not care.

'How could I let it happen?' he asked himself, 'how could I?' When the moment for action came and he should have moved into the gap he had opened, he had hung back and done nothing. He had stood there, too slow to move, too astonished that the moment he had been waiting for had actually come. Or this body he was lumbered with, always slower than the spirit, or cannier, or more cowardly, had acted in its own interests, and while it hovered there – it could only have been a second or two – the world had moved on, pushing him away to one side. The blades had come down and missed him. His body saved itself, *and* him, but shamefully, leaving him with a lifetime to face of the life it had bought for him. And the most shameful thing of all was that he could live with it. He was breathing hard. All his blood was pumping. He was full of the smell of himself.

His body was driving it home to him. You won't die, son. Not of this.

The guards, themselves shocked to silence now at what had been done, began to get them to their feet, urging them gently, like children. No one among them, guard or prisoner, was ready yet to meet another man's eye.

Vic too got to his feet. No one looked at him, and he felt a little rush of defiance come over him, like a child who has been unjustly accused. He began to find arguments in his own defence. He hadn't asked Mac to step in between him and whatever fatality he had provoked. 'I didn't ask him to!'

They formed a line again and went quietly to their work, and when they came back through the godown with their load Mac's body was no longer there.

They moved quietly, scarcely daring to breathe. As if sound, any sound at all, might set something off again. When one man jostled a chain and a length of it fell and rattled, they jumped like frogs, all of them, as if even the clank of iron against iron could send out ripples and break a head.

When he got his meal Vic did not know how to act, whether or not he could sit with them. He was still tense and close to tears, but determined now to tough it out. He took his dixie and sat a little way away from where Digger and another fellow, Ernie Webber, were already eating.

But when Doug came in he saw immediately how things were and came without fuss and sat at Vic's side, but did not look at him.

Digger did. He looked up, noted what had happened, then looked away and went on chewing.

Seeing it, Vic put his head down, animal-like, and plunged his spoon into the mush. He ate. He was ravenous — that was the body again. He was ashamed but he couldn't get enough of the sticky mess he was shoving into his mouth. He could have eaten pounds of the stuff, and still it wouldn't have satisfied the craving he felt. He ate fast, with his head down like an animal, and the tears that welled up in him were tears of rage.

Slowly in the days that followed his life came back and began once again to be ordinary and his own.

His wound was still raw in him, and when his mind moved back to that fraction of a second before Mac went down, his blood quickened, he stepped forward, and his youthful spirit did what it had to do to save his honour. He died happy.

The awakening from this dream sent a wave of new shame over him. He would flush to the roots of his hair and look about quickly to see if any of the others had seen it.

He went out on the usual work parties and in the same group; taking the weight of the sack on his bent back and trotting with it to the place where it could be dumped, welcoming the opportunity it offered to lose himself in the exhaustion that extinguished thought. The young guard was there each day and acted as if nothing had happened. They ate their meal in a group just as before, shared what they scavenged, and Vic got his share. When he scavenged something he offered it round and even Digger took it. The lump in his throat began to melt.

'I am nineteen,' he told himself. He did not offer this as an excuse. His youth, if anything, was an affliction. It made things hard for him. What he meant was, 'Nineteen is all I've got.' It seemed, as the sum of what he had experienced, a large thing. But what he was thinking of was the future. 'All this,' he thought, 'can be made good in time, if I get it. All I need now is time.' Putting his head down in an animal way and getting on with it was the first step.

It wasn't simply a matter of outliving his shame and the blood on his hands; but of proving to them, whoever *they* might be, that this life of his that had got itself saved, by whatever means, had been worth saving.

Meanwhile he dealt with the others as they dealt with him. He was prepared for the hostility Digger showed him.

They had never been close, but there was in Digger's avoidance of him now a harder quality, a kind of contempt. What it said was: for me you are not there, you're dead; you died back there where you ought to have done, instead of *him*. And in his old way, while deeply resenting this, he also, in another part of his nature, accepted it. Digger became the one among them whose good opinion he most cared for – because he knew Digger would not give it.

He deliberately put out of his mind the Warrenders and his old life, feeling that in betraying himself he had betrayed them, too. It hurt him to look at what he had done through their eyes, even more through Lucille's. He set himself to live in the present. That is where he would remake his life. But once, in a dream, his father came to him. It was something he had dreaded. He shrank into himself.

He was drunk, of course, and there was a smirk on his face. 'Well,' he said, 'fancy meetin' you here. Fancy you an' me bein' in the same boat, eh?' He was delighted that Vic had been brought so low. 'We're the same kind after all.'

'No we're not,' Vic told him. '*You* might think we are.'

'Oh? Why don't we ask yer mates?'

He laughed at that, a dribbling laugh, and Vic thought again of all those hours he had sat out in the dark of the woodpile in a trance of blood.

'So how does it feel, eh? Still think yer better'n the rest 'v us? I s'pose you'll be askin' now fer a second chance.' He paused, and Vic quaked. 'Well, good luck t' ya! – But did you ever give me one?'

It haunted him, that, but he put it out of his mind with all the other things he had decided to turn his back on. He had his life to save.

3

Digger too was in turmoil. It shook him that he could feel so much hostility, and to one of their own blokes too, not even a Jap. The thoughts that came to him, the wish to see Vic pay or for the events in the godown to take a different turn and for *him* to be the one, scared Digger. He wouldn't have believed he was capable of that sort of vindictiveness. But the loss he had suffered was too raw in him to be amenable to reason. There were things, he decided, that you couldn't be reasonable about – and oughtn't to be, either. But then he thought: 'Where was I when Mac needed me? What did *I* do?'

He and Mac had crossed for the last time at the loading point. Mac had been next in line behind Vic, and as he took the load on his neck and tottered past he had caught the look Mac flashed him, just the tail of it, through the sweat and his lank hair which was streaming.

It was nothing special. One of those little gestures of easy, affectionate contact that keep you going, that's all: that make the ground firmer, that's all. But in that moment they had been just twenty, maybe thirty seconds away from it. Would he have seen something if he had been more alert? That's what stumped him. Mac was just thirty seconds from death. They had been looking straight into one another's eyes.

Fifty feet further on, trotting now with his neck bowed under the weight of the sack, he had heard a ruckus and turned awkwardly on one foot to see what it was.

It was Vic. He had known that immediately. Who else would it be? A sack had burst, and figures were struggling in a storm of white, one of them, from the bulky shape of him, a guard.

Could he have glimpsed Mac's face then, in the confusion of the moment, through the cloud of floury dust? He thought he had; the image of it was so clear in his head.

A face wiped of all expression is what he saw. Or maybe that was just the flour Mac had been showered with in the exploding storm. But what Digger *thought* he saw was the look that might come over a man who is on the brink of extinction, and knows it, and has already let the knowledge of it possess and change him. An impersonal look of neither panic nor despair; which was the certainty of his own death passing physically from head to foot through him, a kind of pallor, and changing him as it went.

It was Mac's sad-faced mournful look, as Doug would have put it, which they had seen him wear on a thousand occasions, only raised now to the highest pitch, so that everything that was personal in it was gone, and yet it was utterly his own look that you would have known anywhere.

Had he really seen that, or was it what his mind had pictured to fill some need of its own? He could never be certain now. But as time went on the image stayed clear, if anything, grew sharper. So in the end it was what he might never have seen at all that meant most to him.

He also had the pile of letters Mac had left him. When, months later, they were organised into forces and sent to Thailand, the letters went with him.

4

They were at a place called Hintock River Camp, one of dozens of such work-camps that stretched for three hundred miles between the Malay and the Burmese borders. The map of it was not clear to them, because their knowledge of these countries was limited to the patch of jungle that shut them in, and because the line they were on was as yet an imaginary one.

It ran in a provisional fashion from Bangkok to Rangoon, and their job, under the direction of a Japanese engineer and several thousand Japanese and Korean guards, was to make it real: to bring it into existence by laying it down, in the form of rails and sleepers, through mountain passes, across rivers, and even, when the line met them, through walls of rock. Eventually all the bits of it would link up. Till then, they were concerned only with their own section, with bamboo, rock, rain and the rivers of mud it created, the individual temperament of their guards, the hours of work the Japs demanded of them (which kept increasing), the length of rail the authorities decided should be laid each day or the length of tunnel completed, and their own dwindling strength. The limits of their world were the twenty or so attap huts that made each encampment – one of which was set apart as a hospital, or rather, a place for the dying – and the site, off in the jungle, where their daily torment took place.

They had come up here from the railhead at the Malayan border in a series of night marches, since it was too hot to move by day, and had passed many such camps, some better than the one they were in, one or two of them a lot worse. These camps either had native names like Nakam Patam, Kanburi, Nan Tok, or they had been given the sort of name you might have used for a creek or a camping spot at home: Rin Tin Tin Camp, Whalemeat Camp. One, however, was called Cholera Camp.

The work was killing. So was the heat. So, once they started, were the rains.

Back where they came from they had belonged, even the slowest country boy among them, to a world of machines. Learning to drive was the second goal of manhood – the first for some. Fooling about under trucks and cars, tinkering with motorbikes and boat engines, rigging up crystal sets – all this had become second nature to them, a form of dream-work in which they recognised (or their hands did) an extension of their own brains. It had created between them and the machines they cared for a kind of communion that was different from the one they shared with cattle and horses, but not significantly so. For most of them machines were as essential to the world they moved in as rocks or trees. Tractors, combine harvesters, steamrollers, cranes – even the tamest pen-pusher among them had dawdled at a street corner to look over the wire in front of a building site to see the big steamhammers at work driving piles. It had changed their vision of themselves. Once you have learned certain skills, and taken them into yourself, you are a new species. There's no way back.

Well, that was the theory.

Only they found themselves now in a place, and with a job in hand, that made nothing of all that. It might never have been. They had fallen out of that world. Muscle and bone, that was all they had to work with now. An eight-pound hammer, a length of steel, and whatever innovative technology they could come up with on the spot for breaking stone.

Some of these men had been storemen and book-keepers. Others were shearers, lawyers' clerks, wine-tasters, bootmakers, plumbers' mates, or had travelled in kitchenware or ladies' lingerie. They had had spelling drummed into them, the thirteen-times table, avoirdupois and troy weight. 'You'll need this one day, son. That's why I'm caning you,' a lady teacher had told more than one of them, when, after getting up at four-thirty to milk a herd, they had dozed off at their desk. They were all labourers now. Someone else would do the calculations. So much for Mental! The number of inches a pair of drillers, working closely together with hammer and steel, could drive through sheer rock in ten or twelve hours a day. The amount of rubble, so many cubic feet, that could be loaded, lifted and borne by a man who had once weighed thirteen stone, now weighed eight and was two days out of a bout of malaria. All this to be balanced precisely against the smallest amount of rice a man could work on before he was no longer worth feeding and could be scrapped.

The work was killing. So was the heat. So, once they started, were the rains. But they also suffered from amoebic dysentery, malaria, including the cardiac variety, typhoid, beriberi, pellagra and cholera.

The doctors among them diagnosed these diseases, but that didn't help because they had none of the medicines they needed to cure them, and it didn't help a man to know that the disease he was dying of was pellagra, any more than it helped to know that the place he was dying *in* was called Sonkurai. The name, however exotic, in no way matched the extraordinary world his body had now entered, or the things it got up to, as if what *it* had discovered up here was a freedom to go crazy in any way it pleased.

Only one thing set them apart from the other coolies who for centuries had done this sort of work for one empire and then the next. They knew what it was they were constructing because it belonged to the world they came from: the future.

It was as if someone, in a visionary moment, had seen a machine out of the distant time to come, a steam engine, and had set out with only the most primitive tools and a hundred thousand slaves to build the line it would need to move on if it were to appear. If you could only get the line down, then the machine would follow – that was the logic. It was true, too. In this case it would happen.

So, if they could only finish the line and link up all the sectional bits of it, they would have made a way back out of here to where they had come from: the future. When the engine came steaming round the bend, its heavy wheels perfectly fitted to the track, the sleepers taking its weight, its funnels pouring out soot, they would know that time too had been linked up and was one again, and that the world they had been at home with was real, not an unattainable dream.

5

The fevers came on every ten days.

The first time he was hit Digger looked up out of his delirium and saw Vic was there; squatting on his heels like a child and with a quick, animal look in his eyes. He was spooning rice up from a dixie, shovelling it fast into his wet mouth. Between his feet was a second dixie. Empty. When he saw Digger was watching he stopped feeding a moment and just sat, his eyes very wide in the broad face. Then, without looking away, he began to feed again, only faster.

'That's my rice he's eating,' Digger thought. 'The bastard is eating *my rice*.' But his stomach revolted at the thought of it. 'Well, let him!'

When he woke again, Vic, a little crease between his brows, was sponging him with a smelly rag. He wore a look of childish concern, and Digger thought: 'That's just like him. Steals the food out'v a man's mouth, an' the next minute he's trying to make up to him by playin' nurse. Typical!' But the dampness was so good, so cooling, and the hands so gentle, that Digger closed his eyes again and drifted.

What puzzled him was the utter candour of Vic's look when he had caught him like that with the second dixie. He didn't try to cover up. He wasn't ashamed. There was something in that look Digger did not want to let go of. Some truth he needed to hold on to. He worried at it.

It was so different from the look he wore when he was offering you some bit of a thing as a gift. He would look sly then, calculating; but when he was stealing the food out of your mouth you saw right through into the man. It was an innocence of a purely animal kind, that took what it needed and made no apology, acting on *that*, not on principle.

Digger saw there was something to be learned from it: a hard-headed wisdom that would save Vic, and might, when the time came, save him as well.

The time came almost as soon as Digger was on his feet again and could go out to work. The fever took Vic now, and it was Digger's turn to eat the second dixie, hold Vic when he raved, and use the cloth.

There was an affinity between them that was almost comical. When the one went down with it the other was well, time and about, ten days at a stretch. Vic accepted it as a fact of nature, a utilitarian arrangement that was good for both of them. Digger resisted at first – he had something against this cove that was fundamental – but when the fever struck him he had no option.

Their natures, though wildly out of order in other ways, were matched in this. They were made for one another. Digger was struck by the irony of it, but they were in a place now where ironies were commonplace.

Under the influence of this arrangement – the close physical unit they formed, the right on occasion to eat the other man's rice, the unpleasant and sometimes revolting duties they had to perform for one another, and which Vic especially carried out with a plain practical tenderness and concern you would not have suspected in him – under the influence of all this, there grew up between them a relationship that was so full of intimate and no longer shameful revelations that they lost all sense of difference.

It wasn't a friendship exactly – you choose your friends. This was different; more or less, who could say? There was no name for it.

The old bitterness died hard in Digger. Vic knew that and accepted it. It seemed to Digger at times that Vic sought him out just because of it. But that was *his* business.

There were days when they couldn't stand the sight of one another. That was inevitable up here. They were always on edge. The petty irritations and suspicions they were subject to in their intense preoccupations with themselves made them spiteful and they would lash out in vicious argument. Digger was sickened by the hatefulness he was capable of. And not just to Vic either, but to poor old Doug as well. He would crawl away, humiliated and ashamed.

But there was something cleansing in it too. What came out in these senseless flayings of one another was the contempt they had for themselves and the filth they lived in; the degradation they accepted at the hands of the guards: and what was especially shameful to men who had thought the spirit of generosity was inviolable in them, the peevish grudging they felt for every grain of rice that went into another man's mouth. It was a relief at last to get rid of the poison in you.

'It's amazing,' Digger thought after a time. 'I never meant to be, but I'm closer to this cove than to anyone, ever. Even Slinger. Even Doug.'

Then another thought would hit him: even Mac. Mac wouldn't be as practical as this bloke is.

He hated himself for letting that thought through. It would just be there, a thought like that, because he was at his lowest. His resentment of Vic would be strong then, fed by guilt. He would draw off in revulsion from him, which was really a revulsion from himself, and was surprised each time at the way Vic bore it and put up with him.

It went back to that animal-innocent, candidly guilty look he had seen on his face when he was finishing off the second dixie. It was a look that risked judgement, even invited it, then revealed, through its utter transparency, that there was none to be made.

6

In his fever bouts, Digger found himself passing in and out of his lives.

There were, to begin with, the conversations with his mother. They took place outside time as clocks or calendars measure it, neither before nor after.

He would be floating. He had a mouth and ears. He had his sex. But they were far off; further anyway than his fists, if he unclenched them, could have reached. She was talking to him in their old way, without words.

Digger? she was saying, Digger? You come on now. I will *not* let you die on me. You hear me, boy? You get breathing now, get feeding. I've given you this, Digger, and I'm determined you're goin' t' have it. You know how I am if I set my heart on a thing. There are stars, Digger, there are gerberas, I planted 'em. There's a whole lot more as well that I haven't got time to go into. So you just buck up now and come on.

You see this? This is earth, boy, dirt. You'll eat a whole peck of that before you're through, before you die, I mean, an' you haven' had more than a few grains of it yet, you've got a whole lot more eating to do. So you just start to get it down, you hear me, Digger?

This is your mother talking. Oh, you know me, boy, don't pretend you don't. Don't pretend you're not awake, I won't let you off *that* easy, you don't fool me. I've got a whole lot more to say, Digger, and I won't let you go deaf on me. I can be a terror, you know that. You're always running out on me, or trying to – you an' your father both! But believe me, Digger, I'm coming after you, there's no running away from fate. You know that. I've got enough ghosts on my hands already, without you trying to be another one. I won't have it, hear? Now you get breathing, boy, you *breathe*! You come back into the real world and give up this dreaming. Here, take this.

She passed him something. It was a thread and he saw now that she was unravelling the sleeve of an old grey jumper he had worn holes in. Beginning at the shoulder, he watched the stitches hop back over invisible needles as the rows ran backwards from shoulder to cuff and the sleeve passed through an invisible wall into non-existence. He had to wind faster and faster to keep the wool running over his fist.

It was another version of her talk, this, and he couldn't resist it. The thread ran between them, dark and fast, till the whole jumper, which he had worn through four winters and slept in, and which had his smell on it – sleeves, front, back – was gone, and there were nine balls of clean knitting-wool in her lap.

He began to fear almost more than the physical racking this having to face up to her each time the fever took him.

She never let up. He would thrash about, drowning in sweat, but she wouldn't let him off the hook.

He made himself an eel, eels are slippery. He reduced himself to just a mouth and eyes – no ears, no sex, no fingers; but she got furious, hauled him out and thumped him into shape.

He tried going on all fours. Digger, she yelled, are you out there, you little grub? That's Ralphie's. Now you come in.

He stayed out. There were stars, there were gerberas. It was thundering and Ralphie was tonguing his neck, he could feel the thickness of Ralphie's tongue rasping.

He knew he was out of his body. Well, good, he thought, that's *one* way! It was the lightness of his head and his sex that told him that.

He got down in the dirt. He was swallowing it, getting down his peck. When he found Ralphie's water-tin, the water he lapped up was the water of life – cool, sweet, slaking this thirst he had been tormented by, which was not the thirst of his body but of what his body had left when it shook him off.

He lapped and lapped – Ralphie didn't mind, didn't begrudge him the water he got from the dried-up bowl; or the bone either, which was alive with maggots. He got his teeth into it, defying the flies. It filled the hunger in him, fed some earlier body than the one he had abandoned, and did him good. Some animal part of him, which he loved as he had loved Ralphie, and which *was* Ralphie, wolfed it down, maggots and all, took the strength from it and was enlightened. He felt the strength gather in him; and lightly, on all fours, began to run light-footed over the earth. Under the moon, past bushes that lay low before him so that he could leap over them, across plains that burned but did not blister. He ran and ran and had breath for it, and came in the early morning down the track to Keen's Crossing.

He woke feeling refreshed and fed. His dreaming body had fed his thin, racked frame, slaked its thirst, licked him into life again.

'I'll live,' he thought, 'this time. I'll live.'

7

Coming in from the line they would be so exhausted sometimes that a man might nod off with his bowl in his hand before he had taken a single mouthful.

'That horse is done for,' he would shout, right out of his sleep. 'Better shoot the poor brute.' Or: 'Don't you move, Marge. I'll get it.'

The others would stare in wonder at his having got so quickly away, and would be reluctant to call him back.

That was one of the things the body could do.

Once they were sitting over their bit of a meal when Ernie Webber, one of the fellows who had been with them since the Great World, made one of his 'remarks'.

He was a likeable fellow, Ern, but very poorly educated, a windbag, inclined, with great assurance and whether you asked for it or not, to give you the benefit of his thoughts. 'I was perusing the papers once,' he would say – it was one of his typical openings – and go on then with some rigmarole of a thing, half-heard and largely misunderstood, that was so plain foolish it was hard to keep a straight face sometimes. Newcomers took it for a subtle brand of humour and might offend Ern by laughing outright. What he said on this occasion was no more foolish than usual. 'I knew there was gunna be trouble,' he said. 'I said we're gunna have trouble with this feller Musso. Soon as I seen he was linkin' up with them niggers, them Abbysiniums.'

'Them who?' This was Clem Carwardine, a fellow who generally said very little. His tone now was so scathing that they sat up shocked. Ernie was a joke and his ignorance under protection. He sat blinking now.

'My God,' Clem said with a savagery he had never shown them before, 'I thought a chook was about the most brainless object in the universe, but compared with some of you blokes a chook is Einstein.'

'That your last word on relativity, is it Clem?' Doug put in. He was trying to turn the thing into a joke, but Clem's look was murderous.

'A half-witted six-year-old knows more than you,' he told Ern. 'You brainless article!'

Ern was too confused to be indignant. He couldn't believe that Clem Carwardine, who was such a nice bloke, could turn on him, and so savagely. Older than the rest of them, and very well spoken, he had never acted superior. He was looking at them now with such utter contempt and fury that they felt embarrassed for him; but there was a kind of puzzlement in his look too, as if he was as surprised as they were at what had just come out of his mouth. The puzzlement increased, then, without another word, he jerked his head back, shot his feet out and keeled over backwards.

He was dead. Cardiac malaria. Just like that. It seemed wicked to Digger, who liked the man, that his last moments should be so uncharacteristic, and that it was this they would remember of him. Ernie was especially upset. He kept harking back to it as if there was something in the event that he had failed to grasp and for which he was to blame.

The body could do that too.

They had never given them much thought, these rough and ready bodies of theirs. You got that drummed into you early: not to look at it, not to touch. A half-dozen schooners got down fast before closing time, and if it was too fast you puked. A run at football on Saturday arvo. A bit of love-making, easy exercise. Nothing fancy or too passionate. Nothing out of the ordinary. If you got a scratch you dobbed a drop of Solyptol on it if you were particular and waited for the scab to form. Warts maybe, whitlows. Chilblains in winter if it was cold enough. Measles, mumps, chickenpox. That was about the limit of it. The body went its own way. It was serviceable. You could forget it was there.

Up here the body ruled. You watched it night and day, you got obsessed with it as you saw the flesh fall away and the ribs and the big knuckle-joints come through.

They wouldn't have believed, if anyone had told them, how fast it could go, the meat they carried, all that their grandfathers and great-grandfathers had shoved into their mouths to build the big frames they had brought up here and the muscle to stock them with. They needn't have bothered, those black pudding and porridge eaters, those kids tucking into the dripping, spreading it thick and wiping a crust round the bowl. It could fall away overnight under the right circumstances, till you looked like someone who had never, in all of time going back and back, known more than the few mouthfuls of pap they were getting now, that were as thin as slime and went right through you, and when you squatted, ran down as slime.

They had had no idea that the equality they claimed and thought they had already achieved would be like this. For each man the same scoopful of thin gruel morning and night.

The big blokes were the first to go, and took hardest the indignity their bodies heaped upon them of needing more than their fair share and of being the weaker for it. They went quickly, some of them. It was pathetic. They hadn't known (and might have expected, in the normal way of things, never to have brought home to them), how much of what they were was dependent only on the meat.

It was all you had, all they had left you. You kept feeding it and it kept falling away. Up here only the tools you carried, the picks and shovels, had the power to keep their true weight in the world. Just getting a fist around them, feeling the solidity of wood and steel, was a guarantee of something, as in straggling lines you picked your way towards the beginning of a path, stepping gingerly, always on the lookout, however hardened your feet had got, for a hidden stump or thorn, since the merest scratch could cost you a leg if the flesh broke and an ulcer formed. An ulcer could cover half a man's leg, eating it away till there was more bone to be seen than flesh. The doctors would use a hot spoon then to jelly it out. If you were lucky you kept the leg. If you were less lucky you lost it. Being unlucky meant it lost you.

You got to be an expert at last on the tricks it could play, this body that was so crude and filthy a thing but was also precious and had to be handled now with so much delicacy. You watched for the smallest change in it, fixing your attention on every square inch of yourself, even the skin under your balls, and what normal man among them had ever done *that*? It had an imagination of its own, and fellows who had none at all, or not of that sort, looked on astonished at the horrors it could produce, stared in amazement as the first brown patch appeared, then spread, and they began to go black.

Digger remembered a joke that Slinger had made. 'Maybe yer a blackfeller, Digger, on the *inside*.'

He saw fellows now turn inside out. He saw the skin of a man's face grow thick as elephant hide. He saw thin boys blow up till they were the size of the fat lady, though no one would have paid to look at them – there was no market for it, not up here. They got so big at last that they couldn't move, even to turn on their pallets. Two of their mates would have to roll them; but gently, like a two-hundred-pound drum full of some dangerous fluid. Their balls would be the size of footballs, their dick eight inches round; but no one laughed, it wasn't a joke. Only the skull with its familiar features stayed normal; but they were pin-headed now and the eyes in the tiny head were lost in terror at the dimension of what was happening all round them – ankles thick as tree-trunks, feet like balloons, but *heavy*, weights they couldn't even think to lift.

'If they keep on feedin' us this rice our eyes'll go slanty.'

Digger had laughed at the man who told him that – or might have done if he hadn't seen the fury in the fellow's eyes. He had felt superior to that sort of dirt ignorance.

But what was happening now made slanty eyes the mildest of changes. Their bodies had gone berserk and were dragging them back to a time before they had organised themselves into human form and come in from chaos.

There were occasions now when he thought Mac might have drawn the best bet after all. He was scared of these thoughts, which came without his will. They were dangerous. If you gave in to the least bit of despair the body would be onto it; it was on the watch for that sort of thing every minute, and you had to watch *it*. They watched one another. He would catch Doug's eye on him, or Vic's, or one of the others, and think, God, what is it? What can he see? Has it started?

When it did start, in Doug's case, they pretended not to notice, not to see, either, the terror he was in, because he had discovered it even sooner of course, felt the little worry of it growing, beginning to swell.

They rolled him like a drum when the time came and carried him out on work-parties to make up the numbers as the Nips demanded. It was, all the time, a question of numbers. The Nips were fanatical about it.

'Watch it, fellers,' he joked as they lay him beside the track, 'I spill easy.'

He lay there all day, patient and uncomplaining, every now and then shouting across to them just to keep himself in the swing of things and one of their number – the living. Then at nightfall they carried him back.

It was the jokes, Digger thought later, that kept Doug going. That little bit of health in him, a stubborn refusal to give in to the sheer weight of things, a belief in lightness. He emerged again out of the huge bulk of himself in the old form, rangy, tough, and more certain than ever now that he could survive whatever they put up to him.

Vic too felt he had passed through the monstrous stage and emerged in something like his old form; but in his case it was mental. The work was what saved him, or so he felt. Even the weight of a basket full of rubble cutting into the rawness of your shoulder could be a reminder that the body was still with you, still in the same line of gravity as stones.

If you accepted that, you could begin to live. If you couldn't, you were done.

There was a way in which absolute deprivation confirmed him in a thing he had known from the start. Basically, when you get right down to it, we've got nothing.

He thought, and there was bitter humour in it, of the times Aunt James had snatched the bread off his plate and shouted 'Let him do without!' There had been so much malice in the old girl. Or maybe in her crazy way she had seen through into the future and was warning him.

He thought of those fellows under the tree outside Meggsie's kitchen, wolfing soup from a bowl, and how he had felt then that he was on the wrong side of things, that he had got out of some shame and humiliation that had been meant for him too. Well, he had it now. Did that balance things?

'I'm at rock bottom,' he told himself. 'I can face that. I didn't get into the world on the promise of three meals a day and a silver spoon to bite on. There was no promise at all – not for my lot. If I have to live like this, right through to the finish, on nothing but will, I can do it. I know what *real* is. I'm not like Digger. I don't need dreams.'

There were times when Digger's way of seeing things maddened him. 'This time next month,' Digger would tell them – or next year, or by Christmas – 'we'll be outa this. The line'll be joined up an' they'll take us back.'

There were plenty of fellows who thought like that. They were dreamers. Always on about the future.

He denied himself that luxury as he denied himself the luxury of the past. There was only one place where you existed with any certainty. That was here. The only *line* was the one that went downward, straight down through you into the earth. He clung to that with a dumb tenacity.

He reckoned this way because he was of a reasoning nature, taking pleasure in the hardness, the harshness of it, stripping himself of all illusion.

But in relying only on the body, he reckoned without its power, which he had already seen in other circumstances, to go its own way and think for itself. One day, in one of those moments when he had fallen out of space into mere time, when his mind lapsed in him and the moment he was in lay open to the flow of things, he raised his head and saw just ahead of him, coming from the opposite direction but in the same line, so that they must inevitably collide if one or the other did not leap aside, a figure he recognised, or thought he did – a big-shouldered, white-haired fellow for whom he felt a flicker of inexplicable warmth and interest. The feeling surprised him; and it was because he was diverted by it that he failed at first to see who it was.

It was himself: far off in a moment that was years ahead and which he was, it seemed, inevitably making for. He had no sooner realised this than the figure was on him and he felt his body open and let it through.

He did not look back. It was forbidden, he knew that. If he looked back they would both be lost.

Still in a state of astonishment, he kept his eyes dead ahead, and when the next breath came, he took it. But a little of the warmth and affection he had felt still glowed in him.

'Well,' he told himself, 'if that's how it's to be I've got no option, have I, but to stick it out?'

8

Digger's most precious possessions, since he had only the one short note of his own, were the letters he had inherited from Mac. Folded small, he had carried them from camp to camp and got them safe through all searches.

He knew them by heart, of course. No trouble about that when he knew so many plays off and had in his head the names and numbers of the whole unit. The letters were just a few hundred words. But the words themselves were only part of it.

Reading took time. That was the important thing. Constant folding and refolding had split the pages, and in the continuous damp up here the ink had run and was hard to read. Each time he took them out, especially if his hands were shaking and wet, he ran the risk of damaging them. But he liked the look of the unfolded pages, their weight – very light they were – on his palm. Even the stains were important. So was the colour of the ink, which differed from letter to letter, even from page to page of the same letter, so that you could see, or guess, where Iris had put the pen down in mid-sentence to go off and do something. So what you were reading was not just words.

He would close his eyes and imagine her being called to the door. The baker's lad, that would be, with a basket on his arm and the warm loaves covered with a cloth. (He would tear the corner off a loaf while they weren't looking and pop it warm into his mouth. Lovely, it was.) Or one of the boys would be calling. Ewen looking for his football socks – weren't they dry yet? – or Jack nagging for a coconut ice-block. Digger let his mind rove. He knew enough from what Mac had told him at one time or another to find his way about the house. It was one of the ways, just one, of getting back.

He did not gorge himself. He read one letter only and took his time. But there were days when he *needed* to gorge himself, and then he would read all five at once, then over again.

It was a strange business. Since the letters already existed in his head before he even started on them, it had to be a process, almost simultaneous but not quite, of letting each word fall out of his mind just before he came to it, so that he could discover it anew.

Playing music must be like that. Even if you had played a piece a thousand times over, and your fingers knew it on their own, you would have to clear your head of all knowledge of the next note so that your fingers, when they found it, could surprise themselves.

'I've planted sweet-peas,' she wrote on St Patrick's Day.

That was over two years ago. The sweet-peas would have sprouted, climbed the trellis, come out, filling the yard with their sweet smell, then died again; but he could still smell them where they had gone back into the earth, and still see them as well in the colours she named, pink, mauve, white. He could see the whole wall of them, pale green, with leaves that were scratchy to the fingertips, like the legs of a praying mantis, and the light shining through; the trellis repeating itself in shadow on the sun-blasted weatherboard; the poles tall as a row of men, but sweet-smelling, opening their buds that were set flaglike at a stiff right-angle to the stalk, white, mauve, pink.

Cut, in a tight little bunch, they would sit in a glass in the front room. He saw the room empty, with the curtains drawn against the sun, which could be strong, even in winter, and the glass with its two kinds of light, one air, one water, and the pale stalks and paler blossoms on a table in the centre of it. He would stand in the hallway and breathe the smell of sweet-peas and it revived him.

When the sun went down and the room grew dark, the glass was still there, the water still central and a source of light. He would lower himself into its coolness, its clearness, at the centre of the dark, quiet room. In the rooms on the other side of the hallway opposite, the breath of sleepers: in one room Iris, in the other the boys, Ewen and Jack, still safe in their boyish dreams, and out the back in a third room, the closed-in sleep-out, Mac's records and his piles of books.

Back and back he went to that house he had never been in. He let Mac show it to him again, room by room. They were shining, both; all cleaned up, their hair combed wet, their feet washed.

There was a wooden rack over the sink with plates in it, thick white ones. They leaned there, drying, and had been washed a thousand times with a block of Sunlight soap in a little wire cage-like contraption, and rinsed, lifted out of the water and left. Beautiful, they were. He could have sat at the table and just looked at them forever, over and over. Because it happened that way, over and over.

Regularly, three times a day, the plates were taken down, set on the cloth, used and washed again. That was the beauty of it. Order, repetition.

But how boring! The same thing, day in day out, over and over! For him that was just the beauty of it. The cloth shaken out in the yard and the sparrows flying down. Light on the lovely glazed and crazed smoothness of the plates in the rack. The calendar on the wall turned to the right month, and the days, black or red, coming up in their numbers, workdays, weekends, the next page already there, and the next and the next all the way to Christmas.

In the dark, while the house slept, he waited quietly in the kitchen, his spirit touched by the light off those plates, in his hands the dryness of a bit of stale bread. There was a whole bowl of it, set out for the morning, to feed the chooks. His spirit broke off a bit and swallowed it – the chooks won't mind, he thought, though he could hear them shifting their claws on their perches in the dark.

Once, standing there, he heard a movement behind him and Iris came in in her nightgown. She didn't see him, of course. She walked right past him to the sink, took a glass, filled it with water from the tap, and drank, very slowly, gazing out into the dark yard.

He watched her as if the ordinary act was miraculous.

It *was* miraculous. It slaked his thirst.

9

Memory was a gift, when they really set themselves to it.

Lists. You started one and it could be extended forever, back and back, and gone over endlessly, and what you called up became a magic formula for keeping yourself in the world or for wiping yourself, temporarily, out of it.

For some it was a numbers game. What they went back to was the number-plates of the various cars they had owned or had driven at times for the firms they worked for. These numbers were *it*. Got into the right order, like the combination of a safe, they were a key that would unlock the universe. Only you had to get the order right, and it wasn't all that easy since the right order had nothing to do with the one in which these numbers had first come into your life. The right order was the *right order*, the one that would *work*. If you got it at last the engine would kick over, and powered by the six or eight cylinders of all those Buicks and Chevvies and de Sotos and Fords, it would take you out.

For others it was railway stations. The stations for instance out from Redfern on the Western Line. They went through them slowly, in morning heat sometimes but at others in the chill of smoky winter, on their way to work. The line ran high above the street. Below you could see barefoot men walking greyhounds alongside parks, kids on their way to school with little satchels on their backs, leggy girls, the older ones in checked gingham. Then, after a bit, you took the same journey back. Only at dusk this time and with the names in the reverse order. Factory sirens would be howling over the flat swamplands. You would have a slick of grease on your thumb. The faces along the platform blurring, and the train moving too fast now for you to catch the headlines on the news-boards as you plunged into sleep.

For others again it was the names of all the girls they had done it with. Even if you only got a finger in, it counted. The Muriels and Glorias and Pearls and Isobels going right back to when you were in sixth grade and first could.

The names first, then details. Where each one was: behind the baths, or on a bench under a school somewhere, or in the back of a parked truck. And when: in the Christmas holidays or on a Queen's Birthday long weekend, getting hold of the weather if you could, what she had on – the shoes, if any, the bra and panties, the colour and pattern of her frock, and the sweat-smell, or the soap-smell of what it had been washed in. Or the feel of leather (smooth or with seams) where it stuck to your bare arse in the back of the Vaux, or the splintery floor under the canvas seats at the Elite, and the taste of vanilla malted or popcorn in her mouth, or Wrigley's Spearmint, or the fried fat of chips. Ah, chips! Now that would be something.

On the menu at Maher's Boarding House for Men, the same menu each week over the seven nights, beef stew, shepherd's pie, etcetera. The gravies – lovely! And the picture over the sideboard, a Pears' print of a little girl about two in a sun-bonnet, standing in the nuddy in a galvanised iron tub . . .

Or the words of all the songs in the *Boomerang Songbook* for March 1941: 'I was watching a man paint a fence'. Or the rhymes their sisters and other little girls skipped to in the evenings after school, on the hot concrete under the sleep-out, while they were doing their history homework (Oliver Cromwell and the Civil War), or setting the wing of a balsawood plane with a dob of glue on a matchstick, and might stop a minute to have a quick pull on the bed –

> Over the garden wall
> I let the baby fall
> Me mother come out and give me a clout
> That almost turned me inside out –

cleaning up quickly afterwards with a stiff hanky, the smell of it and of the glue.

Others the no-hoper horses they put good money on, that never came in, and all the winners of the Melbourne Cup back to 1870, Archer.

Others the cows in a dairy herd: Myrtle, Clover, the Gypsy Princess, Angel, Sugarpie, Queenie, Minnie the Moocher.

What Digger remembered, and after a certain time in an official capacity, was the name and number of every man in the unit; including those who had been killed or gone missing and been replaced, then the replacements; and where each man was sent after the surrender; to Sandakan in Borneo, to Blakang Mali Island, the greatest bashing and punching show in Malaya, so they said, or who drew paradise and stayed on in Changi, or who went to Thailand, and in which force and to which camp. Official. All stored that information, safely, permanently, in the last place the Nips would think of looking.

He was so unremarkable, Digger, looked so like all the rest of them, barefoot, filthy, in a lap-lap, all bones, that no one could have guessed what he carried along with the pick over his shoulder or the basket with its weight of rubble and stones.

Once committed to memory these names would be there forever. The whole unit could be called up and paraded in his head, the dead right there with the living, all clean and in good shape again, whether they had drawn a short straw or a long and wherever they were.

Digger remembered *them*, and their names and numbers. And they, each one, remembered whatever it was they needed to keep them halfway in the world or halfway out of it: number-plate numbers, girls, songs, stations, all the flavours of milkshakes and malteds they served at the Mermaid Café, all the shops up and down Elizabeth or Queen or George or Swanston Street, both sides, the names of horses or dairy herds. Put it all together and something, secretly, was being kept alive. What an army marches on when it is no longer marching.

But there were others, Vic was one, who had no time for memories, even sweet ones. What they clung to were the things they could touch, the few bits and pieces they had managed to hang on to, some of it from back before Changi, the rest picked up along the road, at this stopping place or that, and were keeping for the day when it might come in useful: Singer sewing-machine needles, nails, screws, bits of rope or twine, keys, batteries, cards out of a broken pack, folds of newspapers – objects that elsewhere would have been trash, hardly worth stopping for, but were precious relics up here, and useful too, since you could trade them one for another and have something new in hand.

Vic had started off with quite a hoard. Small things mostly, that all went into a single pocket of his shorts, where he could turn them over; not idly, but letting his mind go with them. His fingertips knew every one.

But over the months he had traded some for a fag-end or a bit of something he needed urgently and didn't have; or for things, once or twice, that had taken his fancy in a childish way though there was no point to them. Other things, infuriatingly, had gone lost. Stolen maybe – he had his suspicions; about some things and some men. Or they had fallen through a hole in his shorts that he had found too late. In the end he had only one thing left: two and a half yards of white cotton thread tied in a loop. He had that in the left-hand pocket of his shorts, quite safe, and was keeping it, come what may.

He could have traded it a dozen times and had refused. A length of thread like that would come in handy sooner or later, it was bound to. He'd need it to keep his shorts together, or for some other reason, and if he didn't have it then, where would he be? Besides, he liked the feel of it. Hours he spent just rubbing his thumb and forefinger over it. He got teased for that: 'Watcha doin', Vic? Playin' pocket billiards?' Finally he hung on to it just for itself, whether it was useful or not. Because it was the last thing he possessed.

It had been white at first. Now it was a brownish colour. What worried him was that it might go astray. He kept checking every five minutes or so to see that it was still there. He took precautions. If he lost it he would be done for.

10

'Coolies,' the man behind him whispered, and Digger had time to take a quick look. Just a glance, because one of the Koreans was close, who would knock you down as soon as look at you.

They were working at night now, a real *speedo*. Bamboo fires were blazing all down the lines. They reddened the walls of the cutting and threw weird shadows. Other, more substantial shadows stopped, shovelled, staggered under basketloads of rubble in a din of bellowing and raucous shouts and blows as the guards ranged up and down. There was a haze of dust that the fires turned to hanging flame. Their bodies in it were alight with sweat, but high up, where it thinned out in the dark, the air was bruise-coloured, a sick yellow, then black.

Through the sweat in his eyes, and the hanging dust, Digger saw them on the track: Indians, Tamils probably, half-naked in lap-laps (like us, he thought) and carrying little bundles of next to nothing, a water bottle, sometimes a stove or lamp. For nearly an hour they passed, and every two or three minutes, stretching upright and keeping an eye out for the guard, he dragged his wrists across the sweat of his brow and got a quick look.

Here and there among them were families, women with babies on their hip, but they were men mostly, and mostly young men, though a few of them were old.

He had seen them working along the railroads up country and in road gangs in the towns, camping just off the pavement in orange tents or stretched out on a bedroll in the dirt. Now they were here. They had changed masters, that's all. Another empire to build.

He thought of the look on that fellow's face who had told him once, 'They wanna make coolies of us': the savage indignation of it, at the violation of all that was natural in the world, their unquestionable superiority as white men; but there was also the age-old fear in it of falling back and becoming serfs again.

Whatever indignities that fellow's people might have suffered — mine too, Digger thought — at the hands of bosses or schoolteachers or bank managers or ladies, all those who had the power to humiliate or deny, there was always this last shred of dignity to chew on: I'm not a coolie, I can choose. Whatever you could be deprived of, by bad luck or injustice or the rough contrariety of things, there was this one last thing that could not be taken. That's what they had believed. Only they knew differently now. It could be taken just like that. Easy.

That fellow would be here somewhere, in one of the other camps up or down the line; if he hadn't been clubbed or kicked to death by one of the Koreans, or fallen on one of the murderous night marches that had brought them here from the rail-head at the Thai border, or succumbed to beriberi or dysentery, or to cerebral malaria, or died of blood poisoning or gangrene from an ulcer; or, like so many of the youngest among them, simply from exhaustion and despair. Wearing a lap-lap and filthy shorts, barefoot, covered in sores, he would be stooping to take the basket on his back, pouring with sweat and chewing on the bitterness of it.

'This,' Digger said to no one in particular, to the part of himself that stood apart a little and observed from a distance still, 'is what happened to us in the world. Maybe it wasn't meant to. It was meant for those others, those coolies. It happened to them too, and now it's happened to us. So what do you make of that?'

It was part of an argument he had been having, for weeks now, with Doug; except that it seldom got put into more than a few words. They were too exhausted to argue. But the words went on arguing in their heads, and some of it got across; they got the drift of it. It was an argument, really, that Mac ought to have been making. He would have done it better. Digger was doing it for him, the best he could.

There were fellows now who had begun to take a religious view – that was understandable, Digger could see that – and one of them, astonishingly, after he came through the beriberi, was Doug.

They could hardly believe it at first. They thought he was putting it on and making a mock. But he was dead serious. In the horror of what was happening to them, some teaching had come back to him out of his hellfire youth. Some grim Presbyterian view that had been opened up in his head in the days before he asserted himself and said 'Stuff it' and refused to go to church – half-heard on hot Sunday mornings while he was gazing out a window, his mind a slingshot loosing itself after a sparrow, or his own dick, hard as iron, working its way up a girl's thigh – struck him now, ten years later, as an incontrovertible truth. 'Look about you, lad, and mock if you can. Isn't this what they were trying to make you see? Isn't it?'

'Isn't it *what*?' Digger wanted to know. 'Hell? Is that what you think it is?'

He thought of his father and those Sundays when they had been out on the line. Hell was just a name people had for the worst thing they could think of, the worst thing that could ever happen to them. Well, it happens, that's all. Nobody deserves what they get. You better believe that, son, because every other sort of belief is madness. We don't *deserve* this. Nobody does. We haven't done anything *that* bad, even the worst of us, even you, Douggy, you old bastard! But it's what we've got. Thailand is just a place. Some people spend their whole lives here. It's normal. These coolies, for instance. For them it's normal, it's all they'll ever have — not for any *sin* they've committed. It rains a lot, that's all. The jungle's as thick as a wall. Things rot. Flies breed maggots in everything. Us too, if we get a bit of a nick. We weren't meant to be here, but we are. Eight hours a day and time off for smokos — that's one sort of justice, a pretty rough one; but it's not for everyone, and it's not for us now either, maybe ever again. Oh, it's unfair all right. But who ever said it would be fair? And who can you complain to, anyhow?

'I'm not complaining,' Doug said.

'But you should be,' Digger told him fiercely. He hated to see Doug, of all people, so meek.

Doug just looked at him, half-smiling, and it was true, Digger had hanged himself on his own argument.

But he stuck to it just the same. He had to.

It was so hard to keep your head in all this. It was a kind of madness, but there was a thread of sanity in it, there had to be; in all the twists and turns, a clear straight line into life. He was determined to hang on to it. Sometimes he could.

Later, half-asleep, he sat in the stink of himself and spooned up gruel. He had something fresh to brood over. Coming back from the embankment he had stepped on a thorn. It would fester, blow up and ulcerate. Bound to. That was enough to worry anyone.

Down on the track a new lot were passing, you could hear their feet scuffing the leaves; and a new rumour was being passed among them. 'Cholera. They're Tamils. They'll be carrying cholera!' That whisper on the track.

'As if we didn't have enough on our plate already,' Digger thought bitterly, using a phrase that had lost all meaning up here.

But what really worried him, right now, was his foot. Each time he got up in the dark and trotted to the borehole (four or five times it was, in less than an hour) he could hear them, still passing. Thousands, it must be.

Cholera wasn't just bad, it was the worst. They had seen a bit of it in one of the camps on the way up and had been eager to get out and away. As if they didn't have –

But immediately his foot touched the ground his mind went *there*, to the immediate sore place where the thorn had gone in, and worried and worried.

It was a new eye, this opening in his flesh, and had its own point of view. Darkness was what it was obsessed with. It loved the dark. When he lay down and tried to sleep again he saw nothing but what *it* saw: the road it would take, dragging the rest of him (what was left of him) into bruise-blackness, till his whole body began to drink darkness from the hungry mouth that had opened there – mouth or eye, whichever way you saw it, both hungry for something other than the flesh, but also for the flesh.

The trouble is, he thought, they never tell you anything that's of any real use. Even the books. Even the great ones. You have to learn it for yourself, just as it comes.

Well, he was learning all right; so were they all. Some of it their bellies were teaching them; like how little a man can live on and still drag himself from one day to the next. The history of empires, that lesson was, and what it costs to build them. Top grades he had been getting. Now it was his foot that was beginning to instruct him. God knows what lesson that would be.

It was swelling with the illuminating darkness of an ultimate *wisdom*. First principles. The original chemistry of things. Flashing it throb after throb to the furthest galaxies at the limits of his system. 'This is how it starts,' he thought, 'this is genesis. This is the truth now, spreading fast, beginning as just a pinprick and eating its way through flesh to the very bone. Nothing abstract about this. You can see it if you want, you can scoop it out with a hot spoon. That's real enough surely for any man.'

11

To top it all they gave them the glass-rod test and Digger was discovered, along with about eighty others, to be a cholera carrier. Sent to the isolation ward across the yard, he discovered a little deeper hell inside the larger one. It had been there all the time but he had known nothing of it. New cases were brought in each day, and in the morning, two or three of them, sometimes more, would be dead. Fellows who only hours before had been able to whisper at least, with a fleshy tongue and lips, would be mummies, their skin as dry and yellow on their bones as if they had been laid out like that for centuries. Dried-up twigs, their fingers were. Their feet were wood. You could only tell one man from another by the tag he wore.

A little away from the camp, in a jungle clearing, they had their burning-place. Each day there were new dead to be cremated, and because he was in reasonable shape, except for his ulcer, Digger did it. The wood had to be chopped the day before. The bodies were carried on rice sacks on bamboo poles.

Entering the place Digger felt a sleepiness come over him. It began the moment you stepped off the common path that the work parties used and took this one that led sharply away from it and then a hundred yards or more, in impenetrable gloom, into the forest. Only the dead came this way, except for those who carried them. To enter here you too had to become one of the dead, at least in spirit – the place demanded it. A sleepiness came over you, a torpor of the mind, though your limbs worked well enough.

You were in the antechamber here of the next world – that's what the perpetual blue-grey gloom and the external dampness of the place told you; and the stillness, the suspension of all activity, including the fall of the ever-falling bamboo leaves.

You were at the furthest point now from where you had come from, wherever it was, and could bring no human qualities with you. The place did not recognise them, had never known them from the beginning of time. It was a primeval place of a vegetable dampness where nothing human had yet been conceived.

The air was blueish and so cold that your breath went always before you, as if spirit here had more substance than flesh.

The leaves kept up a slow drizzle, and long streamers of mist floated through just at head level. More breath.

The slowness of the blood that overcame you belonged to lizard life, reptile life. To stand upright and take on the sensations of men might be fatal here; no space had been prepared for it. You preserved yourself by letting a reptile sleepiness come over you and your spirit sink down towards the earth.

There were no ceremonies. The words would have blown back damp against your mouth.

All the more terrifying then that the dead, who after twenty-four hours were no more than the driest sticks, should suddenly, when the teak logs under them roared into flame, sigh and sit upright, start bolt upright in the midst of the flames. This recovery, and the heat that came from it, was too much. You found your limbs and hobbled away as fast as breath would take you. You fled.

12

'Listen mate,' Vic whispered. What was he doing here? 'I heard about something. One of the other blokes tried it and it worked on him. Can you hear me Digger? I'm gunna get you up. Sorry about this.'

The place was full of voices. In the attap roof where rain dripped continuously small lives were on the move, lizards, mice, scorpions, cockroaches – occasionally one of them fell and you would hear a man cry out in alarm and claw at himself to drive it off.

The other hospital inmates, if they could drag themselves to their feet, were never still – that's how it seemed to Digger. They were forever trotting off to the boreholes, five or six times a night some of them, or restlessly wandering up and down between the bunks, in violent conversation with themselves.

Bugs rattled in the folds of his rags, he could hear them. They clattered against one another in the joints of the rack. Sighs, groans, a burst of shouting out of some man's nightmare.

Get up? He would never get up, that's what they had told him. Not on two legs anyway; one maybe. He had begun a light-headed descent towards a place of light, and had decided to go with it. He was letting his body have its own way now. That was the best thing.

'Digger? C'mon. I'm going to get you up, right? It'll hurt, I know. I'm sorry. But it's our only shot. You don't want t' lose ya leg, do you?'

It was Vic's voice but the tone was his mother's. He wondered what Vic had been tuning into that allowed him to get it off so perfectly, but was not surprised. The walls between things had been breaking down for a while now.

'Digger?'

He was being hauled up, away from the light. When his eyes opened it was dark. The hospital hut was all shadows of men moving against the light outside.

'What are you *doing*?' he complained, feeling Vic's arm hooked under his own and hauling him up. He was light enough, but was surprised just the same that Vic could manage it. 'I can't *walk*.'

Vic ignored this. He had him up and hanging. Digger could hear Vic panting and could smell his breath. He began to drag him out under the overlap of the attap roof into starlight. Other men, ghostlike, were wandering about out here but took no notice of them.

'Where are we goin'?' he asked when they had crossed the open space in front of the huts and entered a thicket.

Vic was grunting. He did not reply. 'This is the hard bit now,' he said at last, after they had come some way into the thickening forest. 'Hang on, eh Dig? Digger? Dig?'

They were at the edge of a muddy bank that sloped steeply to a glint of water where blackness swirled. Digger looked out across the wide expanse of it. The river.

'Listen,' Vic was telling him. 'I'm gunna put you down on your backside, right? You gotta slide. It'll hurt, Dig, I know that. I'm sorry. But it's the only way. You ready now?'

He had no power to resist. He felt himself settled with his legs over the edge of the bank, then he was sliding. His bones wrenched. They would break, they must; he was waiting to hear what he had heard often enough in the hospital hut, the unspeakable sound of a legbone snapping, crack! where some bloke turned in the dark. But there was only a shock of pain that he blacked out on, and he was in thick mud. It was oozing all round him. It was in his mouth and eyes, stinking. But he did not have enough weight for it to take him down. No pack, no boots, and there was no meat on him. So in his own case gravity did not function. He floated on top of it, floundering, and the mud was grey-black river-slime with roots in it.

'Digger? Are you OK, Dig?'

That was that Vic again. 'For Christ's sake,' Digger thought, 'doesn' 'e know any other name? Why doesn' 'e torment some other bastard?'

'All right,' Vic said, 'all right, we can rest a bit, no hurry, Dig. You have a rest.'

Vic lay with his face in the mud. It stank, he thought, like an old slate-rag at school. He was sweating. 'No, there's no hurry,' he thought.

He was light-headed. That was the pain. But more than that it was the revulsion he felt that part of him stank worse even than this river-slime, and had the stink of a dead body. He was carrying the beginnings of a dead body along with his live one.

There was no hurry, but he couldn't wait just the same. Another moment of this death touch on him and he'd go crazy now that the cure was so near. But Digger couldn't move again. Not just yet.

'I can wait,' he told himself. 'There's no hurry. The fishes'll wait. If I can just get my ear out of the mud' (he lifted his head) 'I'll be able to hear them.' The tiddlers, he meant, in their shoals at the edge of the river; swishing their tails, waving their gills to breathe, and smelling them: flesh. He reached out and touched the edge of the water. Very gently it tripped over his fingers. It was going somewhere. It would clean them, even if it was itself thick with mud.

'Digger?'

He pulled himself up, put his face close to Digger, who was all mud, and, as if he could by sheer willpower breathe life into him, said, 'Listen, mate, I'm gunna get you up again, right? Digger? Dig?'

Digger rolled his head a little. There were stars, big ones, very close, and so bright that it hurt. They were heavy, he knew that. Tons and tons of gas and luminous minerals burning, rolling, travelling fast but managing to stay up. The weight of them, that light balancing act, was an encouragement.

'Right? *Now*,' the voice said, 'this is it. Right, mate? I'm gunna get you *up*. Upsadaisy! Right?'

Vic was astonished. Digger was just skin and bone but the weight of him was enormous. It must be the mud he was coated in. No, he thought, it's something else. It's the weight of death, heavy as lead in him. So heavy maybe I can't do it. He struggled and the sweat began to stream faster on him.

'That's *good*, that was good, Digger. We're there now. We've made it.' He stood still, supporting Digger who also supported him. He could hear the mad activity there on the surface of the water, where the stars touched it and you could see them beginning to swarm.

'Don't worry, fishies,' he said, in a voice he recognised as his own from when he was maybe three years old, 'we're coming. Only a little while now.'

'Now,' the voice said, and half-supporting, half-dragging him where he hung under the stars (what was supporting *them*?), led him forward.

It was a river. Digger saw the gleaming surface of it, coal-black and churning. 'What *is* this?' he thought. 'What does he think he's doing? This won't help.' The word that had come into his head – it was a word he had never used as far as he could recall – was baptism. But all Vic did was lead him a little way in: one pace, another. He felt the warmth of it rising to just below his knees. It was alive. He could feel the life of it.

'What is it?' he asked, childlike. 'What's happening?'

'It's the fishes,' Vic said. 'Don't worry, they won't hurt.'

'What?'

'Shh, don't scare 'em, you'll scare 'em. They're only tiddlers. They won't hurt.'

Vic too was in a kind of wonder at it. The idea of it had sickened him at first, just the idea: of being fed off by greedy mouths. But in fact it was soothing. The stars high up, so still; and underwater there, in what seemed like silence but wouldn't be, close up, the jaws fighting for their share of the feast. And all you felt from up here, from this distance, was a pleasant *contact*. The touch of their savagery was soft.

'It tickles,' Digger said foolishly.

'Yair, they're just tiddlers,' Vic told him, and he was laughing now. It was so weird, and he had such a sense of the good they were doing him. 'It'll be over in a minute.'

It would be over when they drew blood.

Digger understood at last, but thought it must be a dream. He could hear the fish in a bright wave swarming at the edge of the bank where they stood offering themselves.

There was a smell these last days that had got right into his head. He knew what it was. It was the news of his own corruption, the smell, still as yet a little way off, of his own death. It had sickened him. Now, slowly, he felt the smell recede. All the stink and ooze of it was being taken back into the world, away from him, into the mouths of the living and turned back into life there. He felt the bump bump of gristle as the small fry darted in and their snouts bounced off bone. They were feeding off him, savagely, greedily tearing at the flesh, and what they were giving him back was cleanness.

When he came back into himself and looked about he was standing knee deep in oily water, stars overhead, so close he could hear them grinding, and he could hear the tiny jaws of the fishes grinding too, as starlight touched their backs and they swarmed and fought and churned the blackness to a frenzy round his shins.

'Did any of that happen?' he asked Vic later, when they lay exhausted in the dark.

'Yes, it happened, an' it'll save us. I told you it would. It *works*.'

13

Digger, in the methodical way that was habitual to him, kept track of each day that passed. He could tell you, if you were bothered to know such a thing, what day of the week it was, in which month; how long it was now till Christmas (how many weeks and days), how long since they had left Changi, how many days and nights they had taken on the road up, how many they had been at work on the line. It mattered to Digger that this bit of order should be maintained in his life. In a place where so much had been taken from them, perhaps permanently, this business of time-keeping, which was after all something the Japs had no control over (it was between you and the sun) represented a last area of freedom to him, a last reminder too of what had been essential to the way they had lived back home.

It was no small thing, this capacity to place yourself accurately in time, this bit of science it had taken so many centuries to get right. It was worth holding on to, gave a form to what otherwise might run right through your hands.

So in his monkish way, which Doug teased him over, Digger could be relied on, when any question of times or dates came up, to deliver an answer on the spot.

The surrender? That had been Sunday, 15 February 1942. Not long after, third week in April, they left Changi for the Great World – Mac had died on 7 June. (This was a date in Digger's personal calendar. He did not mention it; but three times now he had kept the anniversary.) In October, the 4th to be exact, they had gone back to Changi, and on 22 April the next year, 1943, had begun the long journey into Thailand: five days and nights on the train, crowded into cattle wagons, then a series of night-marches through jungle camps where cholera was raging, twenty nights in all. From then till the day they started back down the line and crossed the border again into Malaya was a hundred and eighty-nine days. Eighteen months it was since then. Just on.

Other things, big and small, had been happening in the world. Most

163

of it they knew nothing of. The dates Digger recorded, the periods – Changi, the Great World, Thailand, Changi again – that was *their* war. It was three years and six months since they had become prisoners.

He knew well enough how little these measurements told. The days were not equal. Nor were the hours. Nor were the minutes, even.

That minute and a half in the godown, for instance, in which Mac had been killed – there was no way of fitting that into a system that needed sixty minutes to an hour and twenty-four hours to a single revolution of the earth. Some of those days they had worked up there, *speedo*, as the body recorded them, had been centuries, strung out in an agony for which there were no terms of measurement at all. He knew all that.

Their history took place in its own time. But it had to be fitted to the time the rest of the world was moving through or you wouldn't know where you were, outside your own sack of nerves. The two times didn't fit. They never would. Digger knew that as well as the next man. But you kept both just the same and made what you could of it.

So it was three and a half years, just on, as the calendar showed it. August 1945.

14

All the signs now were that it was coming to an end, might even be over already, days, even weeks ago, so that in *fact* (in one version of it) they might already be free. If that was true their watches would be showing the wrong time. They had no certain news, but *something* had happened. You could feel it.

For the past six months they had been at work on a series of tunnels the Japs were digging across the strait in Johore Baahru, a protection for their troops in case of invasion. Vic was with Digger, and Doug had been there too till he got caught in a cave-in and lost an arm. The work was dangerous. They tunnelled into the side of a hill with just picks and shovels, shoring the walls as they went; but the earth was waterlogged after the rains and there were many accidents, the air in the tunnels was foul, and the heat so fierce that they could work for only minutes before they were gasping for breath. If one tunnel collapsed they started in on another just yards away. Now there was this rumour that it was all over anyhow.

Some fellows said no, it couldn't be. It wouldn't end. If it did the Japs had orders to kill the lot of them. They knew too much of what had gone on. They would be herded into the tunnels and machine-gunned or walled up there. That sort of talk, Digger argued, was madness. They couldn't have got this far, come through so much, those hundred and eighty-nine days for instance, to be gunned down like dogs.

He was used to the wild speculations that spread among them. For years now they had been living on them. Like the great sea battle they had got so excited about just after they arrived in Thailand, which had raged for days and days with terrible casualties and would certainly now bring an armistice. Off the north coast of Western Australia, that was supposed to have been, near Broome; the whole Jap navy done for. Only it must have taken place nowhere at all, or in some bloke's head, because nothing more was heard of it.

Sydney was wiped out by incendiary bombs. The Japs were at Coff's Harbour, and Menzies, pig-iron Bob, had flown to Manila to sue for peace. That was another bit of news. What had come of that?

The Japs had set up a puppet government at Townsville. Artie Fadden was at the head of it. Artie Fadden!

The Russians had moved into Manchuria. The Yanks had invaded Japan from mainland China and were in the suburbs of Tokyo. It was a matter of days now – two weeks at the most.

This phantom war, whose triumphs and defeats they clung to because their lives depended on it, would in some ways remain more vivid to them than the real one, when at last they learned of it; or they would go on confusing the two, uncertain which was which.

It was an odd thing to have lived and died a little in a history that had never actually occurred; to have survived, as some of them had, on the bit of hope they had been given by the fall of Yokohama at Christmas 1943, or succumbed, as others did, in the gloom that descended when a few weeks later Churchill died and New Zealand surrendered, both on the same day.

Occasionally, by accident, some fact out of a quite different set of occurrences would get through to them and they would be utterly bamboozled. What were the Japs doing in New Guinea if the Americans were already swarming over the home islands?

They lived off rumour, and rumour, often enough, sprang out of some man's sleep. So what could you believe?

This latest thing, for instance, that it was already over. Best to take it with a grain of salt – that was Digger's view. Let it get your hopes up, if that's what you needed, but don't put money on it.

Still, it affected them as everything did, and in different ways.

Some men who had hung on till now, bad cases of malnutrition or beriberi, just gave up and died. It was good news as often as not that finished a man.

Others seemed dazed. The prospect of going home again scared them. They couldn't imagine how they could ever settle to it. How they could just walk around the streets and pretend to be normal, look women in the eye again after what they had done and seen, ride on trams, sit at a table with a white cloth, and control their hands and just slowly eat. It was the little things that scared them. The big things you could hide in. It was little ones that gave a man away.

Vic was one who thought like this. The more the rumours spread and the closer it got, the more fiercely he rejected the possibility.

'They're fooling themselves,' he told Digger. 'They're mugs.' He was vehement about it. The optimism of some people infuriated him.

'We've heard all this before. It won't *end*. Not like this, it won't. It can't end.'

The truth was he didn't want it to, that's what Digger thought. He's a difficult cuss. You never knew which way he was going to jump – he didn't himself half the time.

They began to draw apart now that they no longer needed one another. Digger shrugged his shoulders. 'Well, if that's what he wants.'

Vic kept away from Doug too, and from all their former mates; turned sulky, drew into himself.

'He's a bastard. I knew that all along,' Digger told himself, but was hurt just the same. He owed a lot to this fellow. His life, maybe. Certainly a leg. These were things that Digger could not easily forget. There were times, up there, when they might have known all there was to know about one another, things you'd never find out about a man, never have to, in the ordinary run of things. It meant something, that. But back here, at the edge of normality, these were matters that could not be alluded to.

'He's ashamed of all that,' Digger thought. 'It's something he doesn't want to know about.'

What surprised him was that Vic seemed closer to breaking down now than in any of their worst moments in Thailand.

It was time that troubled Vic. The opening up of a line into the future would take him back now into the life he left four years ago.

So long as he had been able to hold a view of things in which time was just moments, then days, each one destroying itself in the next; so long, that is, as it was a process without sequence, he could face himself and hang on. Living was vertical. You stood up new in each moment of it, and if you were strong, and luck was with you, you got from one moment to the next. It was all moments and leaps. But now he had to take on again the notion of a self that was continuous, that belonged to the past and was to have a life again in the future. That's what scared him – the need to carry forward into the ordinariness that was coming a view of time, and of your whole life in it, that he had had to suppress in himself simply to stay alive.

He was twenty-two, just turned. Years, he would have, if the vision that had come to him, back there, was a true one, and his body told him it was.

He had done better than some others. Digger had lost all his teeth.

He was gummy. Doug had lost an arm. He himself *looked* whole but felt that he had lost everything.

He had had no word from the Warrenders for more than two years. They had written often in the early days, Pa had anyway, and there was always an added word or two from the girls or Ma, but they had had no mail at all in Thailand, and he had got nothing in the hand-outs since they got to Malaya.

In his years with the Warrenders he had never spoken of the life he had known before he came to them, of his parents and all that world up the coast. He had buried that, kept it to himself.

Of course Pa had got a glimpse of it. But then Pa, amazingly, had known his father, though he couldn't imagine *what* he had known. Pa, understanding by instinct how he might feel about it, and in accordance with his own manly principles, had never alluded to it. So he had kept all that to himself, hoarding it up in the most secret part of him as a thing he would not speak of or let anyone see.

He would not speak of this either, once it was over; since it was pretty certain now that it soon would be. He would push it deep down into himself, face it on his own, and deny, if asked, that he had ever been here: 'No, mate – not *me*.'

That's how it would be for him, and how it had to be. Strange? Is that strange? It's the way I *am*.

Maybe he wouldn't go back at all, that's what he had begun to think. He was too changed. He didn't want them to see (*them* least of all) what had been done to him, and he knew only too well what that was because he could see it in others. It would kill him if he had to see himself through *their* eyes. Lucille's for instance.

He had (he couldn't help it) a kind of contempt for what he had become that was the last resort of his wounded pride. The mere sight of other men sickened him. Their necks all vein and gristle, the tottering walk they had, like old blokes you saw going home just on closing time with a bottle of cheap plonk in a brown-paper bag; the silly, hopeful chatter they went in for, the rumours, the schemes – chicken farms were what they were all for running when they got back; most of all the smell they carried, which wasn't just sweat or shit or green vomit but of what four years of slavery had done to them, sickness of the spirit. It marked you forever, that. There was no way you could get rid of it.

But as the time got closer and the rumours wilder and maybe nearer the mark, old needs and desires began to reappear for no other reason than that they might be capable again of fulfilment; he was racked. And with them, quite unsought, came visions, so real at times that his whole body would be filled with such sensual warmth and yearning, raw need, happiness, and sudden choking emptiness, that he thought he might pass out. Was that what it was to be like?

The visions appeared of their own accord, and in no particular sequence: a stockinged foot, a hairpin, the unbuttoned strap of a suspender. They were the ingredients of spells, his body practising its own form of witchcraft, or they were the symptoms of madness – that's what he thought. But their power was overwhelming. His blood raced and burned, he hardly dared close his eyes. And they came as well when his eyes were open. His mind, or his body, was an infinite storehouse of such vision, of acts and objects he had pushed down into the dark and which were reappearing now to claim connection. Was this madness or some deep healing process? Either way it was a torment to him.

One image especially kept coming back and back, a kind of waking dream. It was of the house at Strathfield, the hallway just inside the front door, with its high white ceiling and pavement of blue, white and brown terracotta tiles.

A radiance as of the westering sun filled it – but that, his reason told him, was impossible: the house faced south. Still, there it was and there he was.

As the light settled out and his heart, which appeared to be the real source of it, slowed at last to normal pace, and since it had been free-floating, came to rest again under his ribs, he saw that Lucille was there, just turning on the second step.

Something had caught her attention. She was looking towards him with a little line of puzzlement between her brows, as if she knew someone was there but was too dazzled by the unaccustomed light to see who it was. He knew he could not call out to her. But his heart was beating so loud he thought she might hear that.

After a moment, still puzzled, she turned and went on up and he was left standing, but quietly now and full of contentment, as if some sort of assurance had been given him.

None had, of course, and with the part of him that was rational and clear-headed he knew it, so what was he doing?

Still, the image, or the dream, or whatever it was, stayed warm in him and kept coming back.

15

Vic, freshly washed and combed, in clean shirt, clean shorts and a new pair of boots, a bit light-headed just with the knowledge that he could go anywhere he pleased, down this alley or that, was out walking in the freed city. They were all out somewhere, rushing here and there like kids in a fairground, not knowing what to try first.

He had come out alone and was in a part of the town he did not know, along a foul canal. He didn't know anywhere in Singapore, not really. He had never had a chance to.

It was a low place, all peeling walls, coal smoke from kerosene tins, and footpaths filthy with squashed fruit and dog-turds and cinders and bloody-looking spit. He had wandered down here looking for he didn't know what. Nothing. Anything. It wasn't any place he had intended to be.

Bicycles passed in droves, all honking. Children sat half-naked on the ground. Salesmen, squatting, had laid out on upturned butter-boxes, or low tables covered with a cloth, the few things, whatever it was, that they had to sell. Suddenly he stopped dead and stood stupidly staring.

What had caught his eye was a pyramid of six cotton-reels on a tray, one of them a sickly green, another royal blue, the rest white, but all dusty and soiled looking. The only other thing on the tray was a packet of needles.

The old woman squatting beside them glanced up under heavy pads of flesh, happy to have attracted his attention. She was preparing to call out to him. But the look he was wearing, or the threatening bulk of him, must have warned her of something. Her hand moved out to cover the single reel at the apex of the pyramid she had made. To save it. She sat staring up at him.

He was in a rage, a kind of madness, and close to tears.

In the left-hand pocket of his new shorts was the length of thread he had kept. His fingers went to it. He hadn't thrown it away – you never know. Its value to him, anyway, was absolute. And here now, in this dirty bit of a place, this old crone of a Chinese woman had six reels of it on her mean little tray, six whole reels – and beyond that, on shelves somewhere in a storehouse, there would be cartons-full. They were common as dirt. He had a vision suddenly of how small it was, all that had happened to him.

The old woman's hand, which was yellow and wrinkled like a duck's foot, kept hold of the reel, expecting this crazy boy to use his boot now and kick the whole tray aside. They were like that, these blond ones. But instead he let out a cry of rage, flung something out of his pocket and ran off.

She watched him go, her hand still protecting her wares. Then she leaned forward over the edge of her tray a little to see what it was. A bit of dirty thread. Nothing.

Minutes later he was back. With his eye crazily upon her, he stooped, snatched up the bit of cotton as if she might be intending to rob him of it, and was gone.

Part Four

1

On hot nights late in Darlinghurst Road Digger found what he had always been in search of, a crowded place with the atmosphere of a fairground, but one that did not have to be knocked down and set up again night after night. It was simply there, another part of town.

It was a rowdy place, the Cross. It could be violent, sordid too at times, but it had put a spell on Digger just as Mac had told him it would.

Girls, some of them toothless and close to sixty, worked out of mean little rooms up staircases smelling of bacon-fat or sharp with disinfectant. The pubs were blood-buckets.

You would see a couple of fellows come hurtling through the door and in seconds a full-scale brawl would be going on, right there on the pavement, with passers-by ducking aside to get away from it or standing off on the sidelines to watch.

Often it was seamen; but mostly it was young blokes, louts, who had come in on motorbikes to roar about and see what was doing, keen to get a reputation and discover how tough they were.

They wore second-hand air-force jackets, duck-tailed Cornel Wilde haircuts and wanted blood.

They would roam about putting their shoulders into the crowd, waiting to be challenged, with a Friday night ferocity in them that had the pent-up frustration of a week's work behind it, and would only be content at last when the man they were bludgeoning was in the gutter and they heard his ribs crack – 'Ah, that's it, that's the sound' – or when they had gone down themselves and were sitting with their head in their hands, hearing a whole lot of new sounds in there that might be permanent and with their palms wet with blood.

Occasionally it was a woman you saw, still clutching her handbag but with her mouth bloody, one arm like a broken wing, and the man who had done it shouting right into her face, spitting out obscenities but weeping too sometimes, justifying himself. This was peacetime again.

And in between these savage episodes the delivery boys would be out and old people, or women dragging a suitcase in one hand and a reluctant child in the other, would be going about their daily affairs. Well-dressed ladies walked pug dogs. Kids sucking sherbet sticks dawdled back and forth to school. Old fellows slept it off on benches or stood with their sleeve up to the elbow in bins.

There were coffee shops, continental, with mock-cream cakes in the window, and other, darker ones downstairs where it was rumoured that satanic cults were being practised. The paintings on the walls, which were pretty bold, gave you a hint of what they might be: a woman with her legs round a shaggy male figure with horns above his ears, another in which a girl was coupling with a gigantic cat.

Then there were the milk-bars, all fan-shaped mirrors and chrome, spaghetti places where men in business suits lined up for lunch, and barber shops, some with a dozen chairs; always with two or three fellows lathered up for shaving while the barber, razor in hand, harangued them while others, further down the room, would be snipping and chatting or showing a customer the back of his head in a glass, and in the doorway one of the idle assistants hung on a broom.

Barber shops, billiard saloons, dark corners in pubs – this was where the SP bookies followed their trade, using runners and a 'nit' to watch for the cops. But everyone up here had something to sell: petrol, stuff without coupons that had fallen off the back of a truck, nylons, second-hand cars, pre-war of course, and girls.

Towards five, with paperboys shouting the headlines and running out barefoot to cars, working men, still in their singlets, would be strolling home with the *Mirror* under their arm, taking it easy and eating a Have-a-Heart or a Grannie Smith apple; going back to a room in a boarding-house, or up three flights to where a girl was cooking sausages in a two-roomed maisonette, the only place they could get in the housing shortage.

This was the rush hour, the hour before closing. Sailors would be up in mobs from the ships you could see moored at Woolloomooloo, and along with them came fellows, newly demobbed, wearing suits you could pick a mile off (Digger had one) that they had been given to start them off in Civvy Street, but still with their old army haircut, and with the half-expectant, half-lost look of men who were waiting for life to declare a direction to them, now that they were free to go wherever they pleased.

Digger kept away from these fellows. They depressed him. He knew their story. It was his own. They were men who for one reason or another had never gone home – or had done so and come straight back again, one or two of them on the first day. They hung about feeling sorry for themselves and keeping close to one another, looking on at a show they were not part of, not yet, and wondering if they ever would be.

Digger felt that too, on occasions. He hadn't been home either, but not because he was scared of what he might find there. He was putting it off, that's all; enjoying himself, getting back into the stride of things. There was such a sense abroad of streets being swept for a new day, of ties off, sleeves rolled up, girls walking with a new bounce to their heels and their handbags swinging, full of what the world might offer them now and what they could do with it. 'Me too,' Digger thought. 'The war is over and we won!' – Except that it wasn't quite like that.

'We didn't win our war because it wasn't a war we went to. It was something else. It's victories that are all the go now. This is a victory parade. No one wants to know about *us*.'

There were men who were bitter about that, and not just on their own behalf. Digger shared the feeling but would not give in to it.

He wrote to his mother nearly every week and she sent back sharp replies. His father was in Japan now, a hero of the army of occupation. Jenny had run away, she didn't know where. Yes, he assured her, he *would* come back, she knew that. But from week to week he put it off, still dizzied by all that was going on here, all he saw and was trusted with. Once he went back he would be caught. For a little time longer he wanted to be off the hook.

People trusted him. He didn't know why.

A man he hardly knew, though they might have spoken a couple of times, would thrust an envelope into his hand. 'Here, mate, keep this for me, willya? Don't worry, I'll find you. Next week or the week after. Somewhere. Just keep it under ya pillow, eh?'

Digger would sock the thing away behind the mirror of the little room he had at the Pomeroy and forget about it. A week later the man would come up to him in a pub, fool about for a bit, then say casually: 'How's the bank vault? – That envelope I give you, I s'pose you still got it.' With the envelope safe in an inside jacket pocket he would slip Digger a twenty. 'Thanks, mate. I'll do the same f' you some time.'

What had he been part of? He didn't ask. That's why he was trusted.

Someone who had heard that he knew how to look after himself and was handy with his fists put him on to one of the clubs. He got a job as a bouncer at thirty quid a week, working from seven till five in the morning at a place where sly grog was served, and in a room at the back, poker and blackjack were played. He helped clean up afterwards, went out and got himself a cup of tea at an all-nighter, then, in the early-morning coolness, walked home.

He loved the Cross at that hour. Greeks would be setting up fruit stalls, apples and oranges in glossy pyramids. Men in shorts would be unloading fresh flowers, setting them out in buckets on the pavement and sprinkling them from a can against the coming heat. He would buy a paper and scan the morning news.

'Haven' you got any better place to go than this, feller? You don't want to hang around here.'

The man who offered him this advice was a cop, a thick-set fellow with close-cropped straight black hair and freckles. Mid-thirties, a bit flash, with a good overcoat, a soft grey hat, and eyes Digger had taken a liking to. They were very steady and blue. He could offer the advice because he did it lightly. It was a joke between them. His name was Frank McGowan.

Digger had seen him about often enough and they'd got talking. He didn't mind having a drink with him, though he knew he was breaking a code.

'I seen you drinkin' with that dingo McGowan,' one of his acquaintances observed. 'I s'pose you know what 'e is.' There was a little beat of silence. 'Yair, well, 'e's a cunt. An' 'e's crooked as shit, you ast anyone! SP – they're all in on it, you ast anyone!'

Digger listened but did not reply. It was all such tales up here. The Cross was a village, full of intricate alliances and drawn lines. A thing had barely happened, they'd hardly picked the body up off the pavement, before it was in the mouth of every barber's boy and saloon-bar lounger. McGowan was in the Vice Squad. That was enough. It embarrassed Digger sometimes that McGowan should take an interest in him, but he did not believe it was a ploy. He was no use to McGowan.

'So,' McGowan would say each time they ran into one another, 'you're still here. Go an' get lost, why don't you?'

But once, in a darker mood, when they were sitting quietly together, he said: 'I don' understand you, Digger, a feller like you. What are you doin', hangin' about with this sorta rubbish?'

Digger looked up, a shadow of doubt in his eyes. His experience in the camps had given him an ear for the various forms of self-hatred that men go in for, and he thought now that some of the venom in McGowan's voice was directed at himself.

McGowan saw the look. 'Yair, well,' he said, and made a brusque movement with his thumb across the tip of his nose. There was a grossness in it that was deliberate. He had given himself away and was drawing back again. Digger too withdrew.

It was the word he had used, rubbish, that Digger wanted to go back to. What came back to him at times, and too clearly, was that break in the forest and the fires he had tended there. It had given him such an awareness of just what it is that life throws up, and when it has no more use for it, throws off again. Not just ashes and bones, but the immense pile of debris that any one life might make if you were to gather up and look at the whole of it: all that it had worn out, used up, mislaid, pawned, forgotten, and carried out each morning to be tipped into a bin. Think of it. Then think of it multiplied by millions.

What he would have wanted, given the power, was to take it all back again, down to the last razor blade and button off a baby's bootee, and see it restored. Impossible, of course.

He wanted nothing to be forgotten and cast into the flames. Not a soul. Not a pin.

He said none of this to McGowan, but wished later he had done and taken the risk.

'I'm like one of those old blokes you see poking about the bins,' he would have had to say, making a joke of it. But he was serious.

'Not a soul,' he would have said. 'Not a pin.'

2

One Saturday around three o'clock he did something he had been meaning to do for weeks. He got himself ready and took a tram out to Bondi Junction to find Mac's sister-in-law, Iris. He carried with him the letters Mac had given him. It was all he had to pass on to her.

He recognised the house easily enough from the description Mac had given him, but the woman who opened the door was not at all what he expected.

He had seen her often enough. He had stood behind the door in the kitchen and seen her come in, turn on the tap, pour herself a glass of water, and then, with wonderful slowness, drink it, all the time looking out through the window in a dreamy way at the stars.

That woman had worn her hair in a style he remembered from before the war. She was very sober and tall. This one, with the light of the hallway behind her, was shorter, heavier too, and she stepped out of a moment of hilarity that had to do with something that was still going on in the depths of the house. There was a radio playing. He heard thumps from back there and saw the flash of a blue shirt – one of the boys that would be – between the hallway and the back stairs.

'I'm sorry about this,' she said in the midst of her laughter. 'Come on in.'

He stepped into the narrow hallway. He was cleaned up, his hair combed, his feet washed – that was normal now. But he wore a tie as well, feeling the constriction of it, and had the letters, in a clean envelope, in his right-hand breast pocket.

'Here,' she said, 'let me take your hat.'

'Oh – good,' he said. He had been just standing there, staring about.

He had thought he would know the place, and he did in some ways; Mac's sleep-out would be the bottom of the hall to the right. But the whole house was lighter than he had imagined, more airy. More cheerful, too. Mac had described only the things his own plain taste would have put here; the rest he had left out. A lot of what Digger saw now was fanciful: a tall Chinese vase with umbrellas on it, and a little

Alpine house with a man and woman in peasant costume, who came out, the one or the other, according to whether it was fine or would rain.

She settled him in the front room, then went out to turn the wireless down, put a kettle on, and at the same time to shout something through a window into the yard. Digger had a chance to look about.

Above the upright piano, which was covered with a green velvet cloth, was a certificate showing that Elizabeth Iris Ruddick had her letters from the Trinity College of Music in 1921 – the year, as it happened, of his birth. There was a metronome, a bust of Beethoven, a bronze rose bowl with a wirework lid. Another object that took his eye was an ornamental tray in mother-of-pearl. On it was a young fellow in olden-days dress, a satin coat and breeches, who sat with two shepherdesses in a moonlit ruin. In a corner, on a little lacquered stand, was a basket of a kind he had seen before only in the foyers of picture theatres, where it would have been filled with gladiolus spears. This one had half a dozen dolls in it, their spangled skirts fixed to bentwood crooks.

Nothing in her letters suggested any of this. She had subdued her liveliness there, limiting herself maybe to the way Mac saw her. Anyway, it had given him the wrong idea, and when she came back now, bringing in tea and a slice of Napoleon, he observed her with different eyes. She apologised for the Napoleon. It came from a shop.

'Oh,' he said, 'Sargents.'

She was surprised at that, and at his knowing already that she worked there, and he restrained himself from telling her greedily how much more he knew: the sweet-peas, the tomato jam she made that he and Mac had so often talked about and smacked their lips over, the forty-nine piece dinner set Mac had given her and Don as a wedding present, and how upset she had been when she broke the lid of a soup tureen the first time she washed it up. These facts seemed trivial now. He had made too much of them.

Several times, as they drank their tea, he caught her eye on him, a frankly puzzled look, and it was a while before he saw the reason for it. She had no idea really who he was. Mac, he saw, had never mentioned him, or if he had she had forgotten it.

She asked questions of him: where he came from – he gave her a quick sketch of Keen's Crossing – what he was doing in Sydney, where he lived. She came from Queensland herself. Had he been up there? He told her about the boxing. He had never found it so easy to talk about himself.

Once the preliminaries were over they barely mentioned Mac. She simply took it for granted that what he had come for, now that he was here, had to do with her.

The idea alarmed him at first. It took him a little time to get used to it. But once he did he had to admit that it was true, and had been right from the start. How quickly she had seen it! That was a woman for you. She was over forty, he guessed, working backwards from the date on the certificate, but hadn't lost the assurance of her own attractiveness.

She called the boys up to get a piece of Napoleon. They came in barefoot and in their house clothes, shorts and ragged shirts, and were awkward at first but found their tongues at last under her meaningful looks. He knew them already, of course. Ewen, the eldest was. He would be sixteen. The younger boy, Jack, was the high-jumper. They were making something down in the yard and were keen to get back to it. They shifted from foot to foot, and after a decent interval she relented and let them go.

So they came at last to the letters.

He had expected them to provide the climax of his visit and had prepared a speech. But so much had already happened that they seemed like an afterthought now, and when he said what he had to say it was in such a confused, emotional way that it sounded false.

'Goodness,' she said, when he told her what the envelope contained. She looked at it a moment, turned it over in her hands, then lay it, unopened, on the piano stool; and there it sat, very white and clean, for the rest of his visit.

He had expected her to open it and see how soiled the letters were, and from that how many times they had been unfolded and read. When she did not he was disappointed. She would do that later, he guessed, in private, after he left. Or would she? Once they got talking again she seemed simply to have forgotten they were there.

'I make too much of things,' he told himself. He knew how fond she was of Mac because he knew the letters. 'There's a lighter way of handling all this.' It would go, he thought, with the rowdy good humour the house had been filled with – till he stepped in and put a damper on it.

'Thanks for coming,' she said when he was on the doorstep again. 'Really. I appreciate it.'

He swallowed hard. He wanted to say something to her. 'Listen,' he wanted to say, 'You don't know this – how could you? – but I watched you drink a glass of water once and it was amazing. It wasn't you, I see that now. It was a you I made up. But it was amazing just the same. An ordinary glass of water, can you imagine it?'

What he actually said, and he was staggered later by his own temerity, was: 'Would it be all right if I called again?'

If she was surprised she gave no indication of it. 'Of course,' she said. 'Any time. Only not on weekdays. You know, because of the shop. This time Saturday is good.'

'Oh, I saw you coming,' she laughed. 'Saw you a mile off.'

They were lying together on the narrow bed in his room, high up on the third floor of the Pomeroy.

'What d'you mean?' he asked, turning his head so that she wouldn't see his smile. He loved it when she presented him to himself. It was like seeing someone else. He had had no opportunity before this to indulge himself.

'You had messages written all over you,' she told him. 'In nine languages.'

'Did I?'

All this delighted him.

But after a moment he said solemnly: 'It was Mac that I was coming about, that first time.'

She might have questioned this. She did not think so. And the second? But Digger was sensitive on the point. He did not want it to appear that he had used Mac, or the letters, to come to her. He was too scrupulous, she wouldn't have minded; but it was his own integrity he was concerned with. When she saw that, she let him have things his way, and clung to what she knew.

He had gone out the second time on foot. It wasn't much more than a mile and he wanted to take things slowly, no need to rush.

He was going now on his own account. The other business, Mac's, had been settled on the first occasion; so far as it ever would be. He felt light-hearted, youthful. It didn't worry him that he didn't know the right forms for this sort of thing. She would understand that and make allowances. She had an infinite understanding (that's the impression he had taken away) of all sorts of things; things he had no notion of.

He was very conscious of the fact that at twenty-five he was entirely without experience in some matters. Courtship and that – the sort of gallantry that some fellows can manage by instinct, he had none of. But he had a great tenderness in him. Surely if he let that speak it would be enough.

Still, he had armed himself, just in case, with a bunch of flowers, purple and red anemones wrapped in pale tissue. The old girl he bought them from, who looked after six or seven buckets in a laneway, and sat reading the Bible all day on a folding stool, had recommended them as the freshest at this time of the week, and seeing how nervous he was had taken trouble with the wrapping. The flower heads with their strong colours and black furry centres, as if fat bumblebees were at them, just peeped out over the sky-blue tissue, and there was a bit of ribbon, a darker blue.

He felt awkward carrying flowers. He held them downward at arm's length where they were not so noticeable; he wasn't one of those blokes in light suits and polished shoes you saw ringing the doorbell of apartment houses, stepping about impatiently in front of the bronze door and checking how they looked, their parting, their ties, in its diamond panes. Still, he didn't care if he looked foolish. Who was looking, anyway?

He had felt such a warmth of life in her. He was chilled to the bone sometimes, for all the strong sunlight here.

She was dressmaking when he arrived. She came to the door in her stockinged feet, in a frock of some shining material, green, with the pins still in it; and when he followed her into the front room a neighbour, a young newly-married woman, was there. They were drinking beer. Snips of the material like big pointed leaves were in pools all over the floor, and the neighbour, who was a blonde, had a mouthful of pins. She said hullo through them and giggled.

Apologising for the mess, she put the flowers for a moment on the piano stool, just as she had the letters, and promising him a beer in just a moment if he would be patient till they got round the last bit of hem, climbed on to a chair. He saw then that the hem was not quite fixed.

The blonde girl, whose name was Amy, got down on her knees with the pins in her mouth and went on with it, glancing up every now and then to take a look at him. He guessed from this that she already knew about him. So Iris had mentioned him! Her quick little glances were glances of appraisal; she was a second opinion. He laughed at this and did not feel intimidated. Quite the opposite, in fact. He was enjoying himself.

Iris turned in a slow circle above them – Amy kneeling, he in one of the genoa velvet chairs – shifting her stockinged feet very daintily, an inch at a time, with her arms at her side and her head lowered a little to follow the progress of the work.

It was a quiet business and took a bit of time; the quietness imposed by the fact that one of the two parties (he thought of himself as a mere spectator) could not speak because of the pins.

To Digger it was a lovely moment, he had known nothing like it. He was happy just sitting. But the hem was done at last, found satisfactory, and she got down, told him how patient he had been, took the flowers to put them in water, got him a beer, brought the flowers back in a glass vase, and they sat and chatted.

She was a lively girl, Amy. She kept them laughing with tales about her three sisters-in-law, who were called Faith, Hope and Charity – could you believe it? – so that they hardly spoke to one another. Just sat sipping the cold beer and looking. Once or twice Iris turned away in profile and he saw that the hairs on her neck, where she had pinned it up so that Amy could fix the collar of the new frock, were darker, damp with sweat.

'Do you dance, Digger?' Amy asked him in her uninhibited way. 'Ben and I go every Friday night. Do you like Perry Como? Have you seen *The Sign of the Cross*?'

As she fired off her questions, and he answered them, Iris gave him half-amused, apologetic looks that assured him that she was not responsible for this inquisition, and he believed it; she was quite capable of putting her own questions. But she didn't cut Amy short either.

The only thing that worried him was that he might be too old-fashioned for them, for *her*; too out of it. He was embarrassed still by the number of things people took for granted here that he had not yet caught up with. Amy was full of them. He didn't want to be shown up. He bluffed, made a mental note of these puzzles, and wondered who he could go to later and ask.

When the boys arrived they came in a storm, shouting and dumping their boots in the hall. Ewen's team had won, six-three. That was a cause for celebration. With a quick little look that dared her to protest, he took a good swig of his mother's beer. His eyes were on Digger, summing him up, Digger was aware of that, but gave no indication of what they saw.

Jack, the younger boy, was already off out the back and was soon calling.

'I've got to fly,' Amy said, gathering up her things. 'Here,' she told Ewen, 'leave your mother's beer and finish mine. It's only a few drops,' she told Iris. 'I'll get murdered if Ben's tea's not on time.'

She took one last look at the frock, which was hanging now from the picture-rail, to satisfy herself of her own workmanship, took a look at Digger too, actually *winked* at him, and went.

He went himself a minute later; he had to be at the club by six. So that was all there was to it. But it was agreed that he should pick her up after work on Monday and they would do a show.

Lying quietly at his side she got him to tell her stories, and what he had to tell – his mother and father, Jenny, everything about Keen's Crossing – seemed stranger than it had been in the living of it. Why was that? Because he was seeing it through *her* eyes.

One thing he told her shocked him. He hadn't thought about it for nearly twenty years. If his memory were not so good he would have said he had forgotten it. It was the cruellest thing he had ever done.

Once, when she was about eight years old, Jenny had gone up to the highway above the house and somehow or other got herself to the other side. This was forbidden, and she knew it. Why had she done it this time? Anyway, once she was across her courage entirely failed her and she dared not cross back.

It started to get dark and, lost out there, she began to whimper and call. He heard her, crept up under cover of the bushes, and sat there, well hidden on the other side, and watched to see what she would do. She would come up to the edge of the road on her stumpy legs, screw up her courage to cross, then sit down again and weep; then come to the road again and walk up and down the edge of it as if just minutes ago it had ceased to be dirt and gravel and become a deep-flowing stream. He watched for a long time, appalled, but fascinated too by her helplessness. Finally she sank down in the growing dark and in a hopeless way sobbed his name. Over and over, 'Digger, Digger' – it gave him the creeps. At last, pretending he had just arrived, he stepped out into the middle of the road, stood a moment, then went quickly and took her hand.

He was a long time silent after he told this.

'Where is she now?' Iris asked.

'That's just it,' he said, and realised why it was that the occasion had now come back to him. 'She's run off somewhere. My mother thinks Brisbane. She's terrified – mum, I mean. She's scared we'll all do it, go off one after another. Dad did. Now Jenny.'

'What about you?'

'Oh, I haven't gone off. She knows that. I'm different.'

He told her stories of his mother, too, and was surprised to see from her reaction that he had made his mother fearsome, whereas what he had meant her to see was what a fierce grip on life she had – how she had given that to him too at times up there, when it was her presence, her demands on him, that had got him through. She sounded hard, but she wasn't, not by nature. It was circumstances that had made her hard.

'We think the same way,' he explained, partly to himself. 'On'y she doesn' see that. Because the things I've got to hold on to aren't the same as hers. Some of them are. But most of 'em aren't. She can't see it.'

He described the things his mother held on to and told Iris of the room she believed she would sit in one day surrounded by all her worldly possessions; only by then they would be *otherworldly*. Still real and touchable, useable too, but as she too would be then, past all possibility of loss.

'Just ordinary things,' he explained, in case the picture wasn't clear to her. 'She's not grasping, it's not that. She does want the things for what they are now, but what she really wants them for is what they will be then. What they will show about her. Her life.'

Iris looked at him rather hard. 'And what about you?' she asked. She was only indirectly interested in what he had to say of his mother. 'What are the things you need to hold on to?'

He told her a few of them. At last he told her how the two officers had come and asked him to keep a list of the names – the names and what happened in each case, insofar as it was known, to the men: a record, a kind of history. That was one thing.

Billy, James, Leslie, May, Pearl – that was another.

Then he told her, as well as he could, what he hadn't told McGowan, and actually said the words: 'Not a soul. Not a pin.'

The flames he was thinking of were the ones that had leapt up round the teak logs in the clearing at Hintock Pass, which was just one fire of the many into which all the cast-offs, all the refuse and broken-down and worn-out rubbish of the world, goes when its newness has worn off, and those who have scrabbled to get and keep it no longer care whether it goes up in flames or down the sewer, or simply gets stamped back into the earth.

You couldn't save it from destruction. And you couldn't make it whole again. Not in fact. But in your head you could.

She listened. She touched his cheek, and lay the tips of her fingers to the place, just above the line of his hair, where a vein beat, feeling its steady throb.

He also told her at last how Mac had died. She listened without looking at him, holding his head against her so that his breath, while he spoke, was on her flesh. After a time she asked quietly: 'Was he buried?'

'What?'

The question surprised him.

'No,' he said at last. 'We never saw him again, the body or that. The Japs would've buried 'im.'

'The word they sent,' she told him, 'was that he was missing. That's all we ever heard.'

'No,' Digger said. 'I saw what happened to him.'

She was silent a while, then sat up a little and told him a story of her own.

'Listen,' she said. 'When I was little, ten or eleven, maybe, we lived up near Gympie in Queensland. My dad had a farm. There were four of us, four girls, I was the second eldest, and my mother's mother, our grannie, lived with us. She was very difficult. She and my mother never really got on. She had asthma and was too weak to get about. She'd sit all day out on the front verandah, and what I remember best is the rug she had. I'd never seen the sea then, but it was sea-colours, all blues and greens and purples in waves. She'd crocheted it herself, so they must have been her favourites.

'They used to tell me I was like her. I mean, I was supposed to be difficult too. My mother would say: "You're just like your grandma," but in fact I didn't like her very much, and if my sisters said it, you know, copying her, I'd pull their hair. Can you see me doing that?

'Anyway, there was a flood. They came out to warn us. Our place

188

was out of town, so we had time to save things. I remember they put a whole lot of furniture, beds and chairs, a sideboard, our sofa with a birdcage on it, on the grass in front of the house waiting for a wagon to take it. I remember how strange it looked. But the river came down quicker than they expected, and in the end there was a real panic. We had to get away in the night, and all the chairs and the sofa and that were swept away. I saw the water take them, it was amazing.

'The thing is, grannie wouldn't go. Or there was a quarrel or something at the last minute and she wouldn't get into the boat. I don't remember exactly, and later the story my mother told was different somehow. When we went back there was no sign of her. But for some reason I kept expecting her to turn up. I'd hear her wheezing in the middle of the night and get up and go to the verandah rails and expect to see her there.

'My mother got furious with me. I was just, you know, at the most difficult, growing-up stage, and we didn't get on either and she was upset by it. Maybe I was being difficult on purpose, I don't know. But I wouldn't accept that she was really dead.

'All our other relations were buried right on the property. We used to go off and play funerals there and pick flowers and put them on the graves. You could read the stones. Being buried was what dead was, and we had never buried grandma. We'd never even seen the body. You can't bury people in water, and water comes back, those floods did. You'd see the light of them off in the trees. I used to go out in the moonlight and look at the light there in the paddocks, under the trees, and the strangeness of it, to me, had somehow to do with my grandmother.'

That was the story. She did not add to it, and he saw after a while that it was her husband she was speaking of, though she did not name him.

What they were doing with the things they told was revealing to one another, in the only way they could, all that was closest to them, but tracing as well the limits of their freedom.

The one or two nights a week that she came to his room were when they had been out to a show and the boys could be left with something cold. Digger could always get someone to cover for him. She never stayed late, nor did she ever invite him to stay at Bondi Junction; and even later, when things were on a settled basis and he came up from Keen's Crossing and stayed overnight, they preserved the fiction of being no more than friends. She made up a bed for him on the sleep-out and came to him there.

It was the boys she was thinking of. 'I'm a middle-aged woman,' she told Digger lightly. 'Forty-three,' and she shook her head in a girlish way, as if in her real self she didn't believe it. 'Oh, you mightn't think of that, but *they* do. I'm supposed to be past all this. That's how young people think.'

The boys wouldn't have worried, even at the beginning, and certainly not later; or so Digger thought. She was observing her own code.

He would lie, still in his singlet, and watch her undress, liking best the moment when, in just her petticoat at last, she would tilt her head first to one side, then to the other, and take off her earrings; then her rings; the pearl-and-diamond engagement ring first, then the wedding band, placing them carefully on the marble top of the wash-stand. This was the real sign of her nakedness. That she kept on her petticoat and he his singlet had nothing to do with it.

Later, when she got up, he would lie and watch her do the whole thing in reverse.

Only when she came to the earrings, then the engagement and wedding ring, was she no longer naked for him.

3

In the afternoon he liked to sit quietly for an hour or so in the bar of the Waratah. Towards five it got crowded, and by half-past fellows would be ordering in half-dozens and lining the glasses up along the sill. He'd slip off then, get a bite to eat and stroll round in a leisurely way to the club.

One afternoon he was holed up in a corner, just enjoying the soft light and the scent of coolness, when he glanced up for no particular reason and Vic was there. He was on a stool at the other end of the bar and had been watching him; goodness knows for how long.

Digger felt a jolt of panic. It was uncanny the capacity this cove had for unsettling him. The once or twice they had run into one another there had been a kind of constraint that had grown at moments to open hostility.

Vic eased himself off the seat, and when he came up it was with a look of surprise and feigned indifference that made Digger furious. Why could he never be open with you? This was no accidental meeting. He had been hearing all week about this bloke who was asking around for him.

'So, what've you been up to?' Digger asked when they were settled over a beer.

Vic looked at him, and there was a little play of light in his eyes. He was preparing some cock-and-bull story, some lie maybe, that he wouldn't even expect you to believe. He would just throw it out in contempt, and defy you to take offence at the effrontery of it. 'Blast 'im,' Digger thought. But when he spoke it sounded like the truth.

'Been out west,' he said. 'Moree.'

'Oh? You don't come from out there, do ya?'

Digger was holding himself in, keeping calm and at a distance. It struck him how little he knew of the bread-and-butter things of Vic's existence. What he did know he wanted to keep away from. It was too intimate for here. He felt a weakness in his gut. He was inwardly trembling. At the mere sight of Vic a shadow of fever had flickered over him and his body was responding to it now with shivers.

'Nah,' Vic said. 'Thought I'd go out an' take a look at what we were supposed to be fighting for.'

Digger looked up enquiringly.

'We might as well 'ave let the bastards have it,' he said, 'if you want my opinion.' He laughed, tipped his head back, opened his throat and poured down the rest of his beer.

'He's been on the booze,' Digger thought. 'Or he's off-colour somehow. Crook.' He felt the pull on him to say something now, as if, for all Vic's offhandedness, what was really being appealed to was an arrangement between them that was still in operation, because there was no way it could not be. Digger was shaken. He had thought, back here, that he might be finished with all that, that this place was to be all beginnings. But once bitten there was no shying away. The medicos had told them that.

'What about you?' Vic was asking. 'How they treatin' ya?'

'Oh, good,' Digger said, and swallowed. 'Pretty good.'

He could barely speak. Suddenly he had seen what it was in Vic that touched him, and it was something he did not want to touch.

They had been prisoners of the Japs up there; anyway, *he* had been; so were Ern and Doug and the rest. It was one of those things that just happened to you, if you were unlucky enough to be in the wrong place. But that wasn't how Vic saw it. The Japs for him were only part of it, so it hadn't ended for him. It was still going on. 'What's more,' Digger thought, 'he wants to drag me into it.' He had even kept the look of a prisoner. And deliberately too, or so Digger thought.

It was a sickness he did not want to get too close to. Maybe you could pick it up just by seeing it in someone, someone you were too close to; or just by realising it could exist.

'Thought I'd try the big smoke again,' Vic was telling him. 'Give it another shot.'

He looked up. There was only one thing Digger could say. 'Got a place?' he asked, and looked quickly away.

'Yair,' Vic said after a moment, and Digger could feel the tension break between them. 'Yair, I'm all right that way. Thanks, mate.'

They sat for a time in silence, Digger all emotion, Vic calmer now. They talked. Digger's mind began to wander. He kept falling through holes in the conversation that were no bigger than single words sometimes, but the distance he fell was hundreds of miles. He began to sweat. All that brutalisation up there had left a weakness in him, a part of his mind that was open on one side to absolute darkness, and the stench that came from that direction was so powerful at times that he gagged on it, not daring to turn his head, even in the clearest sunshine, for fear of having to face again the tattered columns of them, big-boned, filthy, with their muddy eyes and outsized hands and feet.

They went out into the street together, stopped at a pie stall and sat down side by side in the gutter to down a pie.

Digger barely tasted his. Vic offered to finish it. When they parted on the footpath outside the club he was still shaking, and he knew for certain now. It was the malaria. A return bout.

It hit him harder than he expected. He was carried back, not just months, but three or four thousand miles, to a place of jungle heat and wetness that had nothing to do with geography – he knew about geography – but was a condition his body had surrendered to once and could never now be free of. With the physical symptoms came all the troop of events and visions and ghosts he had thought he might be rid of back here. He had thought *she* might rid him of them, but no power on earth could do that.

He was one again among others and could barely make himself out among them, they were all so tattered and thin. They closed in on him, stifling his breath, and when he tried shifting in the ranks to get a glimpse of her, of her sunlit figure through the press, they were too many; thin as they were, mere bones some of them, as if they had just hauled themselves upright out of the mud, they stood between him and even the smallest chink of sunlight, holding their hands up like begging bowls with nothing in them, and each one in a whisper saying the syllables of their own name over and over, as if only in that way could it be kept in mind, in their own mind or anyone's. Anyone's.

Digger tried, against the great hissing sound they made, to speak his own name, but his mouth was dry and he had no breath. He tried to think it, but his head now was filled with *their* names, and he had given his word, officially, and was afraid in his weakened state that he might forget one of them, let it slip. How could he ever face the man, knowing he had let go of him so that he was no longer present and accounted for?

But his own name was safe enough. It was buried somewhere. He would dig it up again later.

He had to survive. If he didn't, how could they, since so many of them were now just names anyway, with no existence save as syllables in someone else's head? In *his* head.

His mind went back to that swarm of tiddlers in the river. He felt the touch of the stream, then the tiddlers striking and striking in fury as they tore at his flesh; but with a touch, though it was all selfishness and savagery on one side, that on the other was the gentlest healing. It could also be like that.

His eyes clapped open. The voices now were roaring up from the street. There must be a huge mob down there, all shouting their names and holding their faces up like empty bowls.

A face tilted towards him. Hands brought a coolness to his brow. *She* was here. No, it was a man's hands. Vic's. The whispering rose in a great shuddering wave and he was swept under again, and he battled with it, half-drowning in scald.

He blinked, opened his eyes again, this time on silence, then lapsed a moment, rolling back months into wet heat; then blinked himself back again into the room.

'So. You've decided to come back to the living.'

It was Frank McGowan. He was looking up over a newspaper, with glasses halfway down his nose. He lay the paper aside and took them off.

'How you feeling?'

'I'm all right,' Digger said weakly. 'What are you doing here?'

'Playing nurse. Any complaints?'

'Was that you?' Digger asked.

'Yair. You want to try an' eat something?'

He got up off the cane-bottomed chair and busied himself for a bit at the gas ring with a little saucepan and a tin of soup. He was in shirt-sleeves and braces.

He brought a bowl and spoon and sat on the edge of the bed, preparing to feed Digger with the spoon, but Digger put his hand up. He put the spoon back in the bowl.

'How long have you been here?'

'Not too long. You've been sick for three days.'

He opened his mouth and let McGowan feed him warm pea soup.

'I suppose I've been saying things,' he said after a moment.

'Not much. Here, you should try and get a bit more of this down you.'

'How did you know?' Digger asked. 'That I was crook. The room and that.'

'Oh, I'm a cop, remember?' He met Digger's eyes with his own and there was a flash of humour in them.

'I should be at work – it must be nearly six.'

McGowan took the bowl away. 'It is,' he said. 'Six in the *morning*. Anyway,' he added, 'you're out of a job.' He was fussing about at the gas ring. He turned and faced Digger.

'The club was raided,' he explained. 'Wednesday night. Stroke a' luck, really – f'you. Being crook when it occurred.' He seemed pleased with himself.

Digger frowned. He didn't need anyone to take charge of his life.

'Nah, that was just good luck,' McGowan said, as if he had seen what Digger was thinking. 'Or maybe you'd prefer to have been taken in.'

'I'd be safe enough,' Digger said sharply. 'I've got friends in the force.'

McGowan looked at him and laughed. But Digger was failing. In just seconds he was delirious again. But he saw what McGowan was now. He was an agent for his mother. How on earth had she recruited him?

4

When Digger was in the third grade at primary school, and the teacher allowed them for the first time to take home books, he had for several months been obsessed with atlases and maps of every sort. Kneeling up at the kitchen table to get closer to the lamp, he would screw his eyes up so that he could read even the smallest print, and making himself small, since whole towns in this dimension were no larger than fly-spots, would try to get hold of what it was here that he was dealing with, the immensity of the world he had been born into, but also the relation between the names of things, which were magic to him, and what they stood for, towns, countries, islands, lakes, mountains.

Countries, for instance, the shape of them.

Each one was its own shape entirely, cut out of the whole, out of earth and water, and resembling nothing in nature but itself. The shape was random, determined only by the way a bit of coastline ran or the course of a river, or by the language people spoke, or by battles that had been fought whole centuries ago; but once you were familiar with it you couldn't imagine how it could be otherwise – Spain or Italy or Australia – any more than you could imagine a different shape for the things that nature had evolved or that men had designed to fit a use. A moth, for instance, a sleeve. And the names also fitted. 'Moth' was perfect for the furry thickness and powdery wings of the creature, as 'sleeve' was for what you slipped your arm through. But 'Italy'? 'Australia'? Yet once it was in your head the name perfectly evoked the shape of the country and contained it; the fit was perfect.

Patagonia, the *Pamir Plateau*, the *Great Bear Lake*. You let these names fall into your head and, by some process of magic, real places came into existence, small enough to find a place there with other names and places, as they also fitted on to a page of the atlas, but existing as well in a latitude on the globe that you could actually travel to, where they were immensities of water and rock and sky.

The world was so huge you could barely make your mind stretch to conceive of it. It would take days and nights, months even, for your body to cover in real space what you could spread your fingers across on a page; this is what Magellan and Vasco da Gama and Abel Tasman had had to prove. Yet whole stretches of it could be contained as well in just two or three syllables. You spoke them – it did not have to be out loud – and there they were: *Lake Balaton*, *Valparaiso*, *Zanzibar*, the *Bay of Whales*. And among these magic formulations, and no less real because it was familiar and he knew precisely what it represented, *Keen's Crossing*.

It wasn't in any atlas. You could hardly expect it to be. How could you get yourself small enough even to contemplate it, when a city of millions like Sydney was just a dot? But it was there all right, even if they hadn't put it in. He was sitting there. At a table, with the atlas open in front of him under a lamp.

He would fall into a dream. Letting his mind expand till it was as diffused and free-floating as a galaxy off at the limits of space, he would rove about, searching till he had located the world, a pin-point of light, far off and spinning. He would home in on it then, till he could see the exact point on its surface, in New South Wales, where *he* was: Keen's Crossing. He would find Broken Bay first, the mouth of the river; then, moving high up over it in the dark, follow the twists and turns of it till he saw the wharf, the store, the lighted window, his head like another globe bent low over the atlas, and could slip back into it.

His mind would be dazzled, like a moth that had been drawn in out of the dark and was at the centre now, dazed but excitedly fluttering. Around him, in pitch darkness, the Scotch firs soaring sixty feet towards the stars, the pepper tree, the clothes-lines touched with moonlight, the beginnings of an immensity of scrub.

How much of all this was contained by the name he could not determine. There was no visible border. Not enough, clearly, to make a showing in the atlas, but quite a lot if you thought of all the dust you had to wade through to get from the ferry to where the highway crested the ridge; or considered the millions of ants that were scurrying about over the dried-up leaves and twigs of it.

He did see a map at last on which Keen's Crossing was marked. A fellow at the ferry showed it to him, a government surveyor, unfolding the big sheet across the bonnet of his car while they rode across. A dotted line showed the river-crossing, and there was a dot, a red one, to mark the store. Beside it, in italics, *Keen's Crossing*.

So there it was: his own name, Keen, making an appearance in the great world. On a map, along with all those other magic formulations, *Marcaibo, Surabaya, Arkangel.*

There was a tie, a deep one, between the name as he bore it and as the place did; they were linked. And not just by his being there. He could leave it – he would too, one day, he was bound to – but the link would remain. The name contained him, from the soles of his feet to his thatch of roughly scissored hair, wherever he might go, whatever might happen to him, as it contained as well this one particular bit of the globe, the Crossing, the store, all the individual grains of dust and twigs and dead leaves that made up the acres of the place, along with the many varieties of ants and insects and spiders, and the birds that flew in and out of it; all covered. There was a mystery in this that he might spend the whole of his life pondering, beginning at the kitchen table here; except that it was just one of the mysteries, and he knew already that there were others, equally important, that he would have to explore. Still, this one was enough to keep him going for the moment, and he saw, regretfully, that he might have to forgo all those other places, Mont St Michel and Trincomalee, however attractive they might be, if he was to get hold of this one, which he was linked to because he was born here, and because his name was on it, or *its* name on him.

What had Keen's Crossing been, he wondered, before his grandfather stopped here and claimed the crossing and built the store? Did it have any name at all? And, without one, how had anyone known what it was or that it was here at all?

It *had* been here, and pretty much as it was now, if you put back the trees that had been cut down to build the store and the ferry-landing and to make way for the road, and if you took away the clothesline, the three Scotch firs and the rosebushes and gerbera his mother had planted: the same high ridge of sandstone with its forest of flesh-coloured angophoras.

Nameless it would have been; untouched in all time by the heel maybe of even a single black. But here all right. And not even in the dark. You couldn't say that, just because *people* had no knowledge of it.

The same hard sunshine would have beat down on it, the same storms and slow winter rains. The same currawongs and magpies would have been here, blue finches, earthworms, tree snakes, frogs. But it was not Keen's Crossing. It wouldn't have known that there *were* any Keens, to drive their horses across the river and cut down the first tree and make a camp. It hadn't been waiting.

But then the two things met: his grandfather's axe and the hard trunk of one of its trees, and the first letter of a syllable cut into it. Keen meant sharp. The axe's edge was Keen. So the place got a name and he and it had found a connection that was unique in all the world. The shared name proved it.

Years later, in some of their worst times in Thailand, this connection would sustain Digger and help keep him sane, keep him attached to the earth; to the brief stretch of it that was continuous with his name and, through that, with his image of himself. He could be there at will. He had only to dive into himself and look about.

Time after time, in his own shape, or taking on the secret shape of some four-footed creature that could move freely past the guards, he would start running, and, with the air streaming behind him, leap bushes, rivers, over seas at last, and come down through the moonlit trees to where the store stood back from the edge of the river, with the great sandstone ridge behind it, and on the other bank a forested bluff rising sheer to the stars.

He was there now, sweating a little after his run; having come down again from where his fever had dragged him. He stood in the trees at the edge of the clearing and watched while his mother hung out the wash.

She wasn't expecting him, except that he was always on her mind; so she *was*, too. When he stepped out between the trunks he would not alarm her.

In a moment he would do it. But just for a bit he stood panting, letting the big drops of sweat roll off him, and watched her lift up and peg one wing, then another, of a sheet.

Part Five

1

Vic, with the drowse of afternoon sleep still on him, stood in his undershorts, one bare foot on the other, his elbow against the dusty wall. The telephone receiver was loose in his hand. He stood with his head dropped, shaking it hopelessly from side to side. Round the old-fashioned speaking-horn fixed to the wall were scribbles in indelible pencil, numbers, names (some of them horses), an irregular heart doodled in a waiting moment, which was bleeding purple at the tip. Down the hallway a race was being called.

It was a men's boarding house in Surry Hills. He had been summoned to the phone just before tea.

Sprawled on his back in the airless heat, legs spread, mind empty, his body as flat as paper – one of a string of such fellows cut out of a single folded sheet – he had been tempted to call out 'Not in,' but had staggered up, still half in a dream, scratched his head and applied the receiver to his ear. It was Ma. Every Friday night she rang and they had the same three-minute exchange.

She wanted him to come home, of course; but after the first time she had never again tried to persuade or bully him. But she rang each Friday at the same hour, and though he was often tempted not to, he took the call. She was clever, Ma, and had infinite patience. Eventually he would give all this up and come back. She knew that and so did he. In the meantime, as lightly as possible, she hung on.

Sunday dinner – that was the open invitation, a surprise for Pa; no pressure, but the invitation was always there. One Sunday, yes, he promised, but he continued to put her off.

Back in the room he lay on the bed, not thinking, and stared up at the stamped-tin ceiling with its design of circles within squares, and inside the circles, fleurs-de-lis.

In these last years, when the population of the city had very nearly doubled, the big front room of the place, with its long sash-windows and fifteen-foot ceilings, had been partitioned with three-ply to make smaller rooms, he had no idea how many, each with its bare bulb hanging, its wardrobe, washbasin and cot. The long gap between the top of the partition and the ceiling meant there was no privacy here. All night you heard other men coughing, hawking, turning the pages of the Zane Greys they were reading, shifting on the rusty wires and groaning in their sleep. You participated, whether you cared to or not, in their dreams.

He was earning good money now and could easily have had a room of his own. But he couldn't sleep in a room of his own. He wouldn't have admitted it, even to Digger, but he couldn't get through the night. The one time he had taken a room in a hotel and tried it, he had woken in a cold sweat, filled with a panic he could not contain. He had had to go out and sit with the tramps at an all-night pie stall.

The proximities of this place, the indifference, the low-keyed despair of the other men, who were mostly older, were what he wanted; they suited him. So did his job.

For six months he had been out west, moving on from one township to the next and picking up any work he could get; as a greenkeeper in one place, a fencer in another. Out past Bathurst to Orange, then to Moree, Walgett and across the Queensland border. He had done that to lose himself for a while, but in the end had worked his way back. He was employed by the council now as a ganger on the roads, spreading gravel in front of a steamroller, all day in the heat and reek of tar. It was fierce work in the December sun. His hands were calloused and black. There were burn-spots where the hot tar spat. Some nights his arms felt as if they had been torn out of their sockets. But it was what he wanted.

He was home, he accepted that. It was a fact. But some stubbornness in him, a sense of outrage that he would not relinquish, still kept him captive, not to a place but to a condition. He did not *want* to be free of it. To be so would be to accept at last that what had been done to him could be ended and put behind him, and he could never accept that.

He was back, and could have whatever he wanted now, a room of his own, a girl, what Ma called a normal life. But he chose not to. The right to choose, even if the choice was against his own interest, was important to him. By living as he did now he made what had happened to him 'up there' – the deprivations and shame he had suffered, the misuse he had been subject to – that much less of a violation. 'You see, I might have chosen it anyway. Like I'm doing now.'

But he also chose, out of pride, not to let the Warrenders see him like this; however fond they were of him and whatever allowances they might be willing to make. He did not want allowances made. When he saw them again it had to be in his old self as he was before he went away. Those were the conditions he set.

In his last days in the camp, among other letters from Pa and Ma and Ellie, had been one from Lucille. It was written in a style that had immediately enraged him, which pretended to make light of the facts it had to tell and was entirely false. She was married, that's what she had to tell. To a Yank. And had a child.

He accepted these facts. He had a high regard for facts. What he did not accept was their finality. Like the things that had happened to him, they were a result of the extraordinary conditions of war, and were to that extent accidental. He chose himself not to be a victim of accident, in this case or any other. He would in time reverse these facts, but only when he was strong enough to take hold of things with something like his old power. Till then, he would have to wait.

The other men in the house were mostly winos. He met them in the dark hallway or on the steps outside, tottering home with a bottle of port in a brown-paper bag, or stopped halfway up the stairs and lolling. 'G'day, son,' was all they ever said. But one or two of them were old fellows, respectable enough, who had nowhere else to go. No woman any longer, maybe a son or daughter somewhere who had no room for them; or they had never had a family at all. They read the papers, took an interest in the races, exchanged cheap mystery books. To these men all this was normal. They did not look at him and wonder what he was doing here. They assumed he was as they were — only a few years earlier on the road.

He kept away from people he knew, or tried to; but occasionally, in a panic, would need the comfort of a familiar voice. He would go out shakily and ring someone. Douggy mostly, since Douggy was settled; more rarely, but he had done it once or twice, the Warrenders, hoping that he might catch Lucille. It was enough on most occasions just to dial the numbers and hear the phone ring. He could go back to sleep then. Or he would wait for the answering voice and stand listening a moment, too ashamed to speak.

But there were times as well when only one person would do, and that was Digger.

He hung off as long as he could. He hated this dependence and didn't understand it. But sooner or later he would give up fighting and seek Digger out. Once it was up the Cross. The next time he had to hitch-hike all the way up to the Hawkesbury, to Keen's Crossing.

Facing Digger took him right back. He would be shaking so badly at times he thought it must be the malaria coming back; it was *physical*. But it wasn't malaria, and after a little he would be calmer, then a great calmness would settle and spread in him; his spirit would go sleepy with it and it would last for days sometimes, like a laying on of hands.

He did not know why this was. He was moved, and grateful, and wished he had some way of showing it, but Digger needed nothing from him, barely knew, he thought, what had taken place. Digger was patient with him but also held him off. He felt hurt. He was touched at times by a spirit of generosity and affection for the world that broke something in him which needed, he knew, to be broken. He would blunder about empty-handed then, looking to some as if he were drunk, to others crazy, with the light-headed, swollen-hearted sense of being a bearer of gifts that would appear and declare themselves, *must* do, as soon as he found someone who would accept them from him.

2

'Well, he's coming,' Ma said, turning aside from her accounts. 'He's promised this time. But I'm not telling Pa till he's actually here. He'd be too disappointed. Oh,' she added, 'and I think it would be better if we didn't say anything, any of us – you know, about where he's been.'

Ellie did no more than glance up briefly from her book. It was Lucille who said sharply: 'For heaven's sake, why not?'

She was feeding creamed pears to little Alexander. The child, peeved at the interruption, at anything that came between him and the big warmth that shone so continuously upon him, shifted his gaze to his grandmother and his lip dropped. His mother was turned away from him. The spoon was in mid-air, inches from his mouth.

Mrs Warrender did not immediately reply. She understood Lucille's position. It was difficult to be a married woman and a mother, and to have a husband who was thousands of miles off and no household or home of your own. She knew too that where Vic was concerned Lucille was proprietorial. She had no right to be, but all that did was make her touchier.

'Well,' Ma said at last, 'I know Vic and he won't want to talk about it. If he brings it up himself it's a different matter. But he won't, I know he won't.'

Lucille glowered. In these last months she had grown increasingly impatient with Ma, and now that she was about to break free, increasingly critical, scornful even, of the way they lived, the evasions and half-truths they were driven to in being so sensitive always of one another's hurts. She wanted a life now that was robust, and open and honest, even if it hurt, and such a thing was impossible here. She was tired of being a married woman and still a child in her parents' house.

All the months she was pregnant she had felt wonderfully separate and self-contained. She had eaten what she liked, slept till midday, spent her afternoons stretched out in the sun; with none of her usual restlessness, and none of the vexations either that went with her 'difficult' nature. And there was no selfishness in it, because she was no longer thinking only of herself.

Separate, but at the same time connected and in the line of something: real *forces*, by which she meant forces that were outside her will.

Time, for instance.

The clock that had begun ticking in her, which was perfectly synchronised to the sun, was real time, not just clock time, and it synchronised her as well. It could not be stopped or slowed or quickened. She submitted herself to it and felt no violation; in fact the opposite, a kind of release.

Gravity, too.

One afternoon, in the dreamy state she fell into under the blazing sun, she had had a vision of herself as a cloud, so light and transparent that she might have dissolved or risen up and floated. But inside the cloud, far off in a spotlight at the very centre of it, a little figure was performing, not for an audience, not at all, but for himself. In a state of perfect self-absorption he was turning somersaults, and she could see him quite clearly, though in fact he was such a long way off. He wasn't weightless, but he appeared to know enough of the secrets of gravity to play the most astonishing tricks with it. She kept her eye on him; she wanted to learn the secrets of all this – of lightness, but also her own true weight in the world.

For months, with her eyes screwed up against the sun, her feet propped on the arms of a squatter's chair and a jug of Meggsie's lemon drink at her elbow, she had watched him perform. He was very small and far off at first, but the far-offness had to do with time, not space. He grew as he got closer; till he was so close she no longer had to squint to make him out.

Never for a moment in all this did she feel anxious for him, or for herself either. She would not float away and he would not fall. They were held, both of them.

And she did not have to feel impatient either. He was moving in his own time and would not be hurried. *He* was the clock. Somewhere up ahead, at a point they had not yet arrived at, he was already sitting up in his high-chair and banging with a spoon. All she had to do was wait the days out till they were there.

'Well,' she said now, 'I know Vic, too.' She urged the child to open up for a last mouthful. 'You're doing just what he wants. All this carrying on! It's to make us see what a sensitive soul he is and how careful we ought to be with him, that's all. And to make himself the centre of things.'

Ellie looked up again. It was the note of vehemence in Lucille's voice, not the words themselves, that shocked her.

'That's got nothing to do with it,' Ma said, and she too was angry now. 'Honestly, Lucille, there are times when I don't think I know you at all.'

Lucille flushed. It was humiliating to her to come under her mother's criticism and be rebuked. She took up her things, set Alexander on her hip, and stalked from the room.

'Why are you so down on Vic?' Ellie asked later, when they were alone together in Lucille's room, the child on the bed between them. Lucille was sitting up cross-legged threading a needle.

'Am I?' she said.

'Yes, you are. And you haven't even *seen* him. You upset Ma, too. You know how fond she is of him. What's the matter with you?'

Lucille went on with her needle. After a moment she lowered her work and said fiercely: 'He thinks he's the only one in the world that anything's *happened* to. I know Vic. I don't have to *see* him.'

Ellie drew back. She knew these stormy, half-tearful, half-defiant moods in her sister. They were close, and had been even closer in these last months since Lucille was alone.

The three years between them made a difference.

Ellie had been too young to go out with Americans – Pa wouldn't allow it; but she had hung about when they appeared (just as in the movies) with an orchid in a square cellophane box, or chocolates, or nylons, had sized them up in her quick down-to-earth way, and afterwards, when she and Lucille, still in her dancing dress, were rolling about on one of their beds, whispering, laughing, comparing, criticising, could catch just the drawl with which this one said, 'We sure do, ma'am,' or the self-satisfied sprawl or little military stamp and snap of others, or the boiled look of this one, or the muscle-bound, collar-jerking shyness of another, a certain Virgil Farson Jr of Greenwood, Mississippi, who had not been Lucille's favourite at the start, not by any means, then was. In the Virge business she had known at every point what Lucille was up to. To the extent that Ma actually blamed her for not telling and had not spoken to her for a week.

When Vic went away Ellie was fifteen. They were friends and she was fiercely loyal to him. She had taken it for granted that in the end Lucille would choose *him* – there was such a tie between them – and that their other little affairs and flirtations were no more than a kind of teasing play to conceal the inevitability of it.

'No,' Lucille told her gravely, 'that was just kid's stuff. Don't you know the difference?' She was so sure of herself that Ellie wondered what she had missed.

Still, when she got pregnant there was the sense all round, but especially on Ma's part, that a mistake had been made.

Lucille did not think so. She broke the news to Ellie as a sworn secret, and with so much awed excitement and triumph (Ellie had never seen her at once so elated and sober and overwrought) that Ellie had felt a little thump in her own belly at the immensity, the serious adultness of it.

Lucille, she told herself, was right. She was still a schoolgirl and had no grasp of things. Even in the midst of the war, when so much that was terrible had occurred, she had simply gone on in the old way, believing that life, their life, was a story that could end only one way, according to the rules of the films she went to and the romances she read. Lucille had broken through all that, and for all their closeness she had not seen it.

For the two weeks that she had Lucille's secret to keep she had looked on her sister as a being transformed, suddenly endowed with urgency and purpose.

The germ of light that with each passing second was swelling and rounding in her had drawn Lucille into the line of life; and it had been put there, amazingly, in such a precise and effective way, though also no doubt in his usual barging manner and with no clear intent, by Virgil Farson, a big slow boy of less than twenty. At that moment three thousand miles away in the Islands he was lounging about an Air Force base reading his Felix the Cat comics, quite ignorant yet of what he had done.

These facts astonished Ellie. She had gone about the house in a dazed state, aware suddenly of how fragile and important things could be and feeling her bond with Lucille immeasurably deepened. Lucille had crossed a border. Ellie felt that she too had come to the edge of it and was shining now and swelling in sympathy.

It was an exaggeration, of course. She had been stirred by her own possibilities, that's all, had felt the pull in her own nature of the change in Lucille's. She soon came back to earth.

But the little life she had been so aware of then as a mere floating presence, a new, nameless one that had turned towards them and was starting for a point maybe sixty or seventy years away was no longer nameless. It was this odd little Alexander; who filled the house with his squalls and hungers, his smells too, and was at this moment lying on the bed between them, singing to himself, kicking up his heels, and when she put her face down into his naked belly, uttering squeals of ecstasy.

'Do you think he'll be so different, then?' she asked, lifting her head. She was asking on her own account, rather wary now of what it might be that she had not understood.

Lucille was more upset than she would admit. She made a mouth and turned away. It was too difficult. She couldn't put it into words.

He would be, of course he would. He must be. Weren't they all? So much had happened in these last years. But Vic, she knew, had a way of closing himself off from mere happenings. It was a strength; it was also, from another point of view, a weakness. The more he was touched by a thing the more he did it.

He would be changed, sure enough, perhaps horribly, and the possibility of that, however small her own part in it, was painful to her. But he would pretend not to be, and at the same time would want you to see through it and pity him.

So when Sunday came round and he did appear as promised – she heard the bell, then the clamour they were making in the hall, even Meggsie and Aunt James – she did not go down immediately. She took a little extra time, not on herself, she spent no time at all on herself, but on the child. When she came to the door of the front room they were all gathered around him, Ma, Pa, Meggsie, Aunt James (Ellie was still out at her tennis match), in a close family group. He was the lost son come home; they were making a royal fuss of him. She felt shut out. Had she always, secretly, been resentful of his place among them? Was Ellie? But when he turned, and she saw the quick, clenched look of him, she felt ashamed. She went up quickly, holding the child and relying on his warmth and weight to steady her, and kissed him on the cheek. She was shocked. He was no thinner than in the old days but he had a flayed look that went straight to her heart.

The others, Ma, Pa, Aunt James, were watching. She told herself that she had to be careful now of her own emotions. The moment was critical.

His hair, which was brutally short, shaved right up above his ears, gave him the look of a convict. Was that deliberate? She was moved by this but warned herself that she could not trust him. They stood very close, with the child between them, who was crowing and working his fingers in the air.

'How old is he?' Vic asked.

He was staring at the child in a perplexed way, as if he had not expected him to be quite real or had underestimated how much innocent energy and egotism he would possess. The child was laughing and looking from one to another of them with no doubt at all that he was the most important person here.

'Hello, cobber,' Vic said when the child reached out and made a grab for his shirt.

'Alexander,' she told him.

'So you see,' she wanted to add, 'we're no longer the youngest ones – not any more.' She thought this might reconcile him a little, make him see things, as she did, in the longer view.

He put his hands out then and took Alexander from her. She felt the weight go, saw how rough and scarred his hands were, and was surprised by his gentleness, but did not lower her guard. The child had knocked him off balance, that's all. He would be looking now for a way of restoring himself. The child was on his arm and Vic was hefting him up and down as if assessing his weight.

It made her want to laugh, that. He could not enter into rivalry with a fourteen-month-old child. It was too undignified and the odds were too much on the child's side. He was looking for a way round. 'What funny creatures we are,' she thought, and relaxed a little. 'So transparent.'

'He's heavy,' Vic said, and all the time the others were quiet and watching.

'Oh, he's heavy all right,' she thought. '*I* could have told you that.'

She did laugh then. She was filled with such a wave of joy at the weight he added to the world, which she felt even when she herself was not holding him, and in the rush of it felt an affection for *him* too, for his hands that were so scabbed and swollen and for the sureness with which they held the child.

'Listen,' she wanted to say, 'can't we make this easy? There's been a war. Extraordinary things have happened. A boy came all the way from Mississippi to sleep with me; drafted into it by the War Office in Washington. He was nineteen. He had never left home. Now he's gone again, and it may be months before I can go to him, and Alexander is here, and the whole world is different. But it's all right. We're all fine – we're *alive*, aren't we? You can see just by looking at him how easy these things can be.'

He was very quick. She saw from his eyes that he had caught her moment of weakness towards him. He passed the child back, and when he put his hands in his pockets there was a little smile at the corner of his mouth, though he tried to conceal it. He had felt his strength again and was preparing to be difficult. There was a lightness in him and a little buzz, she could hear it, coming off the surface of his skin. She drew away.

She could say none of the things that just a moment ago had come to her lips.

He had felt like a ghost coming back here.

When he got off the train he had walked up and down the platform for a time consulting the timetables, the adverts, and deciphering the graffiti in the glassed-in waiting room; giving a good imitation of a man who had another train to catch.

What he was doing was hanging on to his last moments in limbo.

On a railway platform you can wait without question. You walk up and down with your hands in your pockets; stop to light a cigarette or unwrap a new stick of gum, and that's the limit of it; no obligation to justify yourself, or to greet others or even acknowledge their presence. You stand lifting yourself up and down on your toes and whistling. You stroll to the end of the platform and look down the quarter mile of lumped gravel that serves as a shunting-line. You turn and stroll back. Only when you have passed the boy in the cap and waistcoat who idles at the gate, given up your ticket, gone down the stairs to where taxis are waiting, have you arrived. 'I could stay here all day,' he thought when he had read the timetables twice, and the Bible message, and the ads for Vincent's A P C Powders and Bushell's tea, 'or I could catch the next train back.' But suddenly, without thought, he walked to the end of the platform, took the stairs, and before he knew it was in the street.

It was a good walk to the house, but he knew every step. Only four years ago he had been a schoolboy here.

He stopped once to peer through the fence of a canning factory where he had gone with other kids to collect metal scrap.

Just beyond it was the ghost house, a verandahed ruin set far back behind beds of cannas and rusty-looking palms. It had been inhabited then by a batty old girl who wheeled a pram with a Pomeranian in it about the streets. The house was empty now and boarded up.

At the corner of Crane Street there was a place where eight or nine years ago, when he was thirteen, he had used his house key to scratch his initials, V.C.C., into the wet cement. They were still there under the prints of a dog's paws.

But there was a quickening in him as well, the re-emergence of a sense of himself that had been there from the moment he first told Ma that he would come.

The familiarity of the walk itself began to work on him, as his body, which had a memory of its own, slipped back into the easy knowledge of how many steps it was from the station to their front door. When he got there, he found himself, out of habit, feeling in his pocket for the key.

Two surprising things occurred when the front door was at last thrown open. Meggsie hugged him and burst into tears, and Aunt James, for the first time, recognised him as himself. 'It's Vic,' she called, just behind Meggsie in the hall.

'My God,' he thought, and felt a bubble of laughter rise in him. 'If *she* knows me I really must be a ghost!'

There were other changes. Pa announced them, a little too quickly, Vic thought, before he could discover them for himself, adopting a humorous tone that gave no indication of what he might really feel.

'I'm retired,' he told Vic. 'Put out to pasture, I reckon. Though officially it's so I can get on with my book.' Ma was making little sounds of disavowal, keeping up the game Pa made of it. 'Meet the new manager.'

'It's true,' she said, rather shy about it. 'I took over three years ago. Now there's a surprise for you!'

'Got rid of *me* first thing she could,' Pa said. 'Sacked for incompetence. For loafing on the job.'

'Rubbish!' she said. 'He couldn't put up with having a woman for a boss, that was the real trouble. Thought it was beneath his dignity.'

'Oh?' said Pa. 'I thought you were always the boss. I thought I was used to it.'

'Anyway,' said Ma, 'we're on top again, that's the main thing.'

'All these years,' Pa said, 'we had this secret weapon an' didn't even know it. We let Ma loose and the buggers fled.'

Behind all this raillery, Vic felt, there were tensions that only humour, their old rough-gentle humour, could deal with.

But it had changed Ma utterly, this move to the centre of their lives. All that had previously been lax in her had come to attention. The vagueness and languor that had seemed constitutional in her, the restless anxiety, had belonged only, it now appeared, to the conditions she had imposed upon herself – against nature, as it were; first to make way for her brother Stevie, then for Pa. When wartime changed the rules, she had simply stepped in and done what she had all along been intended to do; temporarily at first, while Pa was down with dengue fever, then, with scarcely a protest on his part, for good.

War economies had put a premium on local products. Ma, seeing the opportunity it offered, had acted and made a killing.

It astonished Pa that this woman he had lived with for twenty-five years, and known for more like forty, should suddenly reveal herself as a 'buccaneer'. She was a Needham, and her father's daughter, that's what it was. Pa, who had found the old man intimidating, a bit of a ruffian in fact, was amused, but awed too, by the extent to which he reappeared now in female form. He teased Ma and made a joke of it – that was his style – but was disturbed.

Ma too found it easier to present what had happened as a freak of the times. She was pragmatic, Ma. It was one of the qualities she had had no opportunity to reveal till now, but once liberated, she gave it rein, like the rather salty humour that went with it. The agent of her liberation had been, of all things, the Japanese Imperial Army, though that, like so much else that had happened, was by the way. She had not been part of their Co-prosperity Plan.

It was too humorous a view, this, too odd, far-fetched even, to be admitted. She kept it to herself. People, she had discovered, were not very sympathetic to unusual views, however humorous they might be, or to those who expressed them.

Vic had caught the new note in her voice on the telephone. It was partly, he felt now, what had drawn him to come. There was a confederacy between them. It did not have to be evoked. All that had been settled years back in their uneasy consultations, when she had felt his commitment to her and had seen already, as he had not, that they might one day make a team.

She led him off now to see what she had been doing *out there* – in the factory, she meant – and without words, and taking the old relationship between them quite for granted, put it to him: we're partners, eh?

There was no coquettishness in it. She did not play up to the male in him by pretending to be weak or in need. It was an offer between equals. On both sides an opportunity that was too good to miss.

They were standing, dwarfed as you always were here, under the great cross-beamed ceiling of the factory, a place that bore an eerie resemblance, Vic thought, to a godown – but the shadow this threw across his spirit he immediately drove off.

You came in out of strong sunlight into coolness. But it was a coolness of a particular kind, a climate all of its own, and at the touch of it he felt something restored in him. It was like that first waking up into the real temperature of your body after days of fever, the crossing over a line between zones. He felt a goosepimpling all over the surface of him, and what came back, and with an immediacy he was quite unprepared for, was the last occasion he had come here, the eve of his departure.

A self-conscious, self-important eighteen-year-old, he had stood here to take temporary leave of his life, knowing nothing of what lay ahead. Now, five years later, with the knowledge of all that, which was still bitter in him, taken fully into account, he found he could look on his former self with none of the angry disappointment he had been consumed by in the months since he got back. He could face that humourless schoolboy, standing there so full of himself and making so many promises to the world, with detachment and a wary tolerance. There was no shame – or anyway, none so deep that it demanded the penalty of death – in having been eighteen, and so ignorant of what the world could do to you.

It was the place itself that brought this home to him, and he remembered something he had heard when he went down to Keen's Crossing but had dismissed till now as one of Digger's mystifications.

'It's all right for *you*,' he had thought, looking about the clearing and observing how completely Digger fitted in to it; so much so that he had found it difficult to imagine him in any other place – had he really been up *there*? But now he too felt it. Some impression of his presence had remained here and was waiting to be filled. He could, with no difficulty at all, step into it now as if he had never left.

3

At last Ellie arrived, dropped off by a noisy group in a red convertible. She stopped in the doorway a moment to apologise for being late. 'No, don't look at me,' she told Vic when he tried to go to her, 'I'm a mess,' and she ran off to change. When she came down again it was in a cotton dress with little ties at the shoulder and no stockings. 'Ah,' Pa said, 'here's our girl.'

When he left she had been at school; they were mates and had told one another everything. She threw her arms around him now as if nothing had changed between them.

He glanced across to see if Lucille was watching, but she was absorbed with the child, refusing, a little too deliberately he thought, to acknowledge him.

Ellie had a job. She had been drafted at first into a munitions factory, but was working now in a motor pool, driving a six-ton truck and doing all her own maintenance. She showed him her hands. She loved zooming about all over the city, and the long trips up to Lithgow or down the coast to Wollongong. You could tell this from the way she talked about it, and the others, who must have heard her tales a dozen times, seemed delighted to hear them again.

She got up now, still talking, and fetched a bowl of unshelled peanuts that Meggsie had set out. Taking one she cracked it in half, popped one nut into her mouth, then cracked the other half and, just as she would have done in the old days, passed it to him, all the time going on with the story she was telling.

It was as if he had never been away. She had never had for him any of the intimidating glamour of Lucille, so they could fall back now, almost without thinking, or so it seemed, into little unselfconscious habits, like this one with the peanuts.

The story ended, he laughed and she looked up and said, 'Eat your peanut.' He had been sitting with it in his hand.

Food had an almost mystical importance to him; any food, even a crust of bread. He hoarded things, even the most useless scraps and leftovers, but knew how odd it was and hid it.

He looked now at the peanut he was holding. Very slowly, he put it in his mouth and began to chew.

All through Meggsie's long Sunday dinner he did not look once at Lucille. In the front room afterwards he lounged, hands in pockets, in the window and watched her at play with the child.

There were just the three of them in the room. Ellie was on the phone in the hall. He could hear her laughing. The others had gone upstairs to rest. Lucille did not like being alone with him, he knew that, but was unwilling to make an issue of it.

It was a typical summer afternoon in Sydney, muggy, the sky heavy with a threat of storms. He had longed, up there, for the peculiar drowsiness of these long Sunday afternoons, with the luxury they offered of infinite time before afternoon tea, to trail across the golf links and down through the sticky paspalum to Hen and Chicken Bay, then supper, and afterwards, in the dark, their Sunday games. Now here it was.

Lucille had a pile of building-blocks. She would build them up in a pyramid, and the child, with a laugh, would punch out with his little fist and send them down. The same game over and over.

They had not spoken, but her eyes, even as she occupied herself with the child, kept touching him. He could feel it. He smiled to himself and began, very lightly, to whistle.

Lucille was disturbed. They had got through dinner well enough, but she saw that he had accepted nothing. She could feel the little pressure he was exerting on her to make a scene. She could not allow that.

It wasn't true that she had no feeling for what he had been through. But he was too full of his own experience to give any weight to hers, that's what she saw, and it angered her. He really did believe that only he had been touched. It was a way of telling himself that, unless he wanted it, nothing need be changed between them. That's what she was up against. But she didn't want a scene.

He went on whistling, very low and tunelessly. He was keeping his eyes peeled. She was pretending to be absorbed with the child, but that was a bluff; the real game, and she knew it, was with him. 'So,' he told himself, 'I've won *that* round.'

But the advantage was a weak one. She was weaving around herself and the child a circle of magical containment, and kept looking up now to see if he saw this and understood what it meant.

She was a mother. That is, she had become a woman – guaranteed. But there was no guarantee that what he had been through had made him a man. It was a way of putting herself out of reach. By treating him as if he were still a boy – the same one who had gone away.

He was hurt by the unfairness of this. It seemed to him he had earned the right to be treated as a man, but could not demand it. So he was caught all ways.

In this game they were now engaged in he was, for all his swagger, inexperienced. He knew that. But what else could he be? He had lost five years. The unfairness of it choked him, but he kept whistling.

She saw the truculence in him. She knew what it was, too. He was telling himself how hard life had been on him, urging them both towards a scene. She sighed. Then suddenly she saw their situation from outside all this, in the long view, and what she had to tell him was very clear. It's silly, all this. Our being so cross with one another. Don't you see, your unhappiness doesn't depend on me. But neither does your happiness. Don't you see?

She got to her feet and stood with her hands at her side looking at him.

He stopped whistling, his hands still in his pockets. He could not tell for a moment what she was up to, but did see that something had changed in her. The child felt it too. He was sitting on the floor with his face lifted, puzzled by her having got up so suddenly and removed her attention from him.

She came closer. His mouth was a little open. Quickly she bent forward and kissed the corner of it. It was what he had exerted all his powers to make her do; but now, when her lips touched his, his willing had nothing to do with it. He could claim no triumph and he felt none. She had deprived him of it by acting entirely unexpectedly and of her own free will; in a tender way, but one that dismissed the possibility of all passion between them.

She touched his cheek very gently with her hand, then calmly turned away to where the child had his hands up to be taken.

'That's the boy, Alex,' she said lightly, and lifted him, and took him off for his nap.

Vic looked about. He felt let down. Something critical had occurred but his understanding had not caught up with it. He pushed his hands deeper into his pockets and began to whistle again, but his heart failed him and after a bit he dropped it. He stepped from the window and went out to the hall.

There was no one in sight. Treating him as one of the family again, they had simply gone off without ceremony.

He walked up and down on the coloured tiles, feeling the assurance he had built up lapse and drain from him.

He sat down in one of the low-backed cherry-wood chairs that were ranged along the wall. They were ornamental. No one ever sat in them.

He got up quickly and went through the house to the kitchen to see if Meggsie was about. The big tiled room was immaculate, as always, but empty, everything washed up and cleared away.

He came back to the hallway, looked about a little, then went upstairs and tried the door to his room.

It was just as he remembered it. Nothing had changed. It gave him an odd little start, the thought that it had been here, clean, cool, ready, all the time he was *up there*, always in such filth and with nowhere to lay his head. A feeling of anger and self-pity came over him. He rested his brow against the closed door and clenched his fists.

When his passion had passed he turned back into the room and opened a drawer of the dressing table and saw socks there, underpants, too, all neatly folded.

He stood and looked at himself for a time in the mirror, then lay down full-length on the bed.

He did not sleep, but saw himself standing, as he had just a moment ago, at the open door, and the room he was looking into was empty again.

After a supper of cold meat and salad and his favourite pears and junket, Ma insisted on a game of hide and seek. She was apologetic about it – it was to keep Aunt James happy, who loved to sit in the dark and hear them scampering about; but it was really, Vic guessed, for him. It was a hectic affair. They were playing at play, and to make up for their lack of commitment, banged about more than they usually did.

Upstairs, under a net, little Alexander was sleeping, and Lucille, fearful he might be disturbed by the row they were making, kept one ear tuned for his cry. She was barefoot, her hair damp with sweat. Vic too was only half in the game.

At first Pa was It and he found Ma; then Ma found Vic. While the others trooped off to hide he stood with his face to the wall like a dunce in school and counted to a hundred before he was free to go off in his socks and look for them. Once or twice earlier, while they were rushing about seeking places to hide, he had collided with Lucille, but he was shy of her now. He set off to check the pozzies where one or other of them was sure to be squeezed in holding their breath. He knew all the hiding places.

He had let these rooms and their clutter of familiar objects go out of his life. But now, moving through them in the dark, his foot remembered every loose plank, he could judge without fault the precise distance from table-edge to sideboard. He never once bumped into anything. Whatever he felt for was there.

He covered the hallway, all the rooms down one side of it, including the dining room where Aunt James sat laughing, then crossed to the other. A southerly had come up. Each door he opened set the curtains blowing, and from beyond the windows he heard trees in motion. The moon was up, but all this side of the house was dark.

Hidden behind a curtain in what they called the piano room, Ellie saw the door open a crack and a figure appear. 'Damn,' she thought.

There was a time, years back, when she would have been breathless at this point with the wish to fool whoever it was that there was no one here. All she thought now was that if she was found *she* would be It and they would have to begin all over again.

The crack of half-light widened. It was Vic. She could see the shape of him poised there at the threshold, his body so alert that you could feel the energy of it like a new kind of heat in the room. She drew back against the wall. He wasn't so much looking as setting himself like an animal to catch a scent. His body was hard-edged, separate, intent.

She had seen this quality in him, or thought she had, from the very first day Pa introduced him, and he had stepped out, very sturdy and solemn, to shake hands; looking, with his hair chopped off short as it was again now, and his ears sticking out, very tough and little-mannish, but watchful too, as if for all his squareness and solidity he could be hurt. He had been hard-edged even then, aware of the precise point where *he* left off and a world began that might not be entirely well-disposed towards him, and which for that reason he had always to be on his guard against.

He was standing just inside the door, compact, firm, tense with the effort of feeling about for some other presence in the room, his eyes in the darkness taking up the light there was, oily-bright.

'Like a cat,' she thought.

Caught like this, with her heart beating fast, she too felt like some creature, a rabbit perhaps, but was determined not to be mesmerised.

Then something happened. He gave up playing, that's what it was; and having decided there was no one there, simply stood, his body eased, in the belief that he was alone and unobserved.

He stood where the light fell. There wasn't much, but Ellie was accustomed now to the dark. He was looking straight to where she was but did not see her. The curtain rose and fell like a veil, brushing her face. And something in the way the breeze moved and the leaves of the trees clattered gave her the feeling that they were not inside, not any more, but out in the dark somewhere on an unlighted road, and she had come upon him by accident, sleepwalking there. She was looking past his known face to one she had never seen. It was the one he wore when he was too deep in himself to be aware any longer of what he might have to conceal; the face he showed no one, and which even he had not seen.

She heard him sigh. He was very close. Then, thrusting his hands deep into his pockets, he turned on one heel so that he was in profile. He might have been deliberately showing himself to her: first full-face, now this. She was tense, but the little touch of panic she had felt at the beginning was gone. She had given herself up entirely to looking.

She must have made a sound of some kind, just a breath. He turned his head sharply and his face was covered again. He leaned towards her in the dark.

'Who is it?' he said, his voice very low. 'Ellie? Is that you?'

His brow was creased but he was not perturbed, or did not seem to be, that she had seen him. He put his hand out. She froze.

This was the game now. There were rules and they were in operation again. The tips of his fingers came close to her face. He did not touch her but she felt that he had. Her skin tingled.

There was a smile on his mouth. What light there was, which was really no more than a transparency of darkness, was full on him. But what she was seeing still, behind the smile and the clear roundness of his pupils, was the look she had seen earlier, an afterglow as when a bright light has imprinted itself on your eyeball and remains for long seconds after you have looked away.

'Ellie?'

There was a note of amusement in his voice.

In just a moment now, as the game required, he would grasp her wrist, give a shout, 'I've found Ellie,' and bring the others into the room; but he did not want that, not yet.

He brought his fingertips to her cheek, through the light gauze of the curtain, and she flinched. 'Don't,' he said. 'Don't be scared.'

They stood for a moment longer, neither in the game nor quite out of it, very still, with the breeze moving and the curtain lifting and falling with her breath. She had seen him, he knew that, and for some reason it did not bother him. If anything he felt relieved, as if a weight had been taken from him. Only one other person had ever seen him like that, and that was different. It was a man. It put you at risk, of course, but Digger had not let him down.

He took Ellie's wrist, very gently at first, and they stood a little longer without moving. Then he tightened his grip and called.

Part Six

1

Digger's first days back at the Crossing were spent clearing an infestation of blackberry canes that had invaded the open area between the store and the river and overgrown all that remained now of the ferry, the old wheelhouse and its machinery and the planked approaches to the wharf. Stripped to the waist in the November heat and armed with a machete, he waded into the massed entanglement of it. He used a gloved hand to push aside the barbed shoots, hacking at trunks as thick in places as his own wrist and grubbing out strand after strand of fibrous roots.

It was a single dense growth, its root-system as extensive and as deeply intricate below ground as above. Somewhere at the heart of it was the tap-root, but he never found it. Over and over again he thought he had; he put the machete in and dug out a fleshy tuber. But further in there was always another, tougher stock. At the end of the day his arms, chest and back were criss-crossed with scratches, and despite the gloves he wore his hands were torn, but the work was a pleasure to him. It was a way of getting down to the ground of things. In his sleep that first night he went on with the work, moving with almost no effort now and scarcely feeling the sting of the thorny shoots as they whipped out and clung to him. He saw the bones of small animals that had got trapped in the undergrowth, bandicoots, bush rats, a feral cat; turned up objects he had thought never to see again, that shone out of the over-arching growth with an unnatural luminescence, as if they had managed somehow to preserve the last ray of sunlight they had been touched by, or the last moonlight, before a new shoot launched itself, knitted into the thicket and shut them in.

There was a sun-bonnet of his mother's that had once been blue and was sodden and stained now to a colour he could not name. He tossed it on to the pile he was making, along with a smashed storm-lantern, the crumbling head of a spade, some bald tennis balls, and from deep under, where so little light got in that the undergrowth was hollow, the battered pudding basin that had been Ralphie's water-tin. He saw it glowing like a full moon in the half-darkness, reached in, pulled it out, and sent it clattering on to the heap.

His mother came out to bring him cups of scalding tea or jugfuls of iced water, and would stand there while he drank.

She took no interest in the progress of the work. She would have preferred him to begin on the roof, which leaked in places, or to put in new slumps for her lines, and he would get around to these too, in time; but it was the blackberries that had priority. So when she stood waiting for him to finish drinking it wasn't the work that held her, it was him: the fact that she had him here. Gulping down cold water, he watched her over the rim of the glass, hungrily taking him in.

At the end of the day, casting his gloves aside, he set fire to what he had hacked and torn out and dragged to the bank. The thorny strands crackled and burned fast. The place began to resemble the Keen's Crossing he had left, though there was much that could not be restored. The Crossing now was a dead end. The highway had moved a mile downriver and there was a bridge, a three-spanner, high above the stream.

It surprised him, given this and the war and all, that his mother had been able to hang on so long, but she would, of course, if anyone could. He was struck again by her tenacity, that strength in her that he too had drawn on 'up there' and used to pull him through, and was conscious once again of how alike they were, and how different.

At the table, still shirtless in the heat but with the grime and ash washed off him and peroxide on his cuts, he listened in a numbed way to her talk, which was ceaseless as she went over the list of her grievances: the same bitter anecdotes and illustrations of the hardships she had put up with and his father's many deficiencies. Her war with him had intensified. He was a more powerful presence to her now that he was gone than he had ever been when he was sitting out on a stump somewhere in the dark, sulking and cursing, or when he was traipsing mud from his boots over her floors.

What she could not forgive was his refusal to knuckle down to the hard truth of things: which for her meant marriage, home, family, all she had spent her spirit over the years in amassing and preserving, and which she had expected they would share.

'He's a conquering hero now,' she told Digger. 'Lording it over the Japanese. I *ask* you!'

Digger felt sorry for her. There was no end to the injustice she felt, and since no story she told in illustration could contain the whole of it, no story was ever finished. It opened out at one point or another into a new one, approached some new and deeper injury, and that one led on to the next. The worst of it was, he wasn't even here to face her. He had escaped even that. Digger learned to listen and not to hear.

She told him as well what she knew of Jenny. It wasn't much. She was in Brisbane somewhere.

At the end of the week, when the yard was cleared and he had dealt with the roof, Digger made his own enquiries, took the train to Brisbane and brought her back.

So there they were, all three, united again. Back, Digger thought, despite the seven years and all that had happened, in a life that was barely different in its essentials from the one he had left.

His mother still weighed out and packed orders each Friday night in the room behind the store, and a boy called Cliff Poster came on his bike at eight on Saturday morning and went back and forth, as he had, making deliveries.

She still had her garden, and a war now with the cats. She set Jenny to watch out for them if she couldn't do it herself. A bucket of water was kept ready under the clothes-line to slosh at them.

She still did the washing out in the yard, using a tin tub and a scrubbing-board, and ironed in the kitchen late at night.

She and Jenny shared one room now, and Digger slept in his old bed on the other side of the wall. They could talk right through it if they wanted.

He was surprised, lying on the narrow cot and looking past the windowsill at the same moonlit view, to recall how light-headed and restless he had been in the old days; waiting, fully awake and counting the seconds till the rest of them were asleep, then easing himself off his cot so that the springs didn't squeak, pulling on his pants, and tiptoeing out, his boots in one hand, his shirt in the other, to finish dressing in the dark.

The difference now, he thought, lay in the load of ballast he had taken on; none of which might be measurable in *real* terms. He could still have made the grade as a featherweight, and none of what he was carrying would have registered on his mother's scales, out there in the shop. But it made a difference just the same.

He worked as an odd-job man, and, since it was all word of mouth up here, soon had a reputation as the man to get: 'Get Digger. He'll fix it.'

He had a way with generators, old fridges, every kind of engine, and since the day his father first put a hammer and nail into his hand, and gave him a slab of four-by-two to practise on, had been a dab hand at all sorts of carpentry.

Building restrictions were still on in the early days, so it was repair work mostly, and it remained so, even when the bans were lifted and they moved into a boom. People who wanted new homes got a contractor from Gosford, or brought their pet architect and builder up from Sydney. He worked with other men's blunders, patching and restoring; or with what the weather ruined – they got too much rain up here, too much sunlight too: replacing floorboards, closing in verandahs, hanging doors. He took over the tools his father had left – however careless he may have been in other respects, he was a scrupulous workman and they were in excellent nick. He was happiest when he was straddling the line of a roof with the whole river-country laid out below him; in summer expansive and glittering, on early mornings in winter trailing a line of heaped cloud between its forested bluffs, while up where he was, crouched on the side of a fibro roof and hammering, the sun on his shoulders would be making him sweat.

On Thursdays he went up to town and spent the night at Bondi Junction. He did it without fail, not missing a single Thursday in twenty-six years.

He would walk round to pick Iris up at the cake shop and they would stroll home together, have tea with the boys and maybe go to a show. But more often than not they just sat like a long-married couple and listened to the wireless, while Iris mended socks or did a jigsaw puzzle, and Digger took a toaster to pieces and put it together again. Around eight, Ben and Amy Fielding came in and they would have a game of five hundred or a bit of a sing-song while Iris played.

He began to read his way through Mac's library. There were, he estimated, about seven hundred volumes. Mac had intended them for his retirement, and it pleased Digger that, even if he made not a single addition of his own, there was reading enough on the stacked shelves, and in the unsorted books that were piled under the bed, on top of the wardrobe and round the walls of the little closed-in porch beyond, to keep him going for the rest of his life.

He didn't push himself, there was no need. He read steadily through biographies, travel books, books of history; the collected writings of Wilhelm Stekel, and Adler and Freud; the whole of Havelock Ellis; the novels of H. G. Wells and Arnold Bennett and Conrad and Theodore Dreiser, including the book the Human Torso had given him, novels by Balzac and Stendhal and Tolstoy and Dostoevsky, wondering, as he went, how often he was travelling a path Mac had already been on, and, when he came on something that challenged or shocked him, what Mac might have made of it.

Occasionally, in turning a page, he came on a slip of paper that Mac had put there to mark where he had left off reading – or was it so that *he* could come upon it, five, ten, fifteen years after his death?

Once it was a list of birds.

What was that doing, Digger wondered, in the scene towards the end of *War and Peace* where young Petya Rostov, with his fondness for sweet things and his ten pounds of seedless raisins, does ask after all, in spite of his embarrassment before the older men, about the little French drummer boy, and has him brought muddy-footed into the tent.

Mac's presence, as Digger turned the page and interrupted his reading, imposed itself on the scene. So that for ever after, recalling it, he would think of Mac as having actually been there along with Denisov and Dolghow, and the actual birds, unlikely antipodean angels – the white throated honey-eater, a flock of fire-tails, a Regent bower bird among others – would also be there, flashing about the courtyard where young Petya hangs down from the saddle and Denisov grips the railings of the fence and howls his grief.

At other times it was tram tickets, and Digger would look at the numbers to see if they were in any way significant.

Once, with a dirty mark along the crease where Mac had used a thumb blackened with ink off the tickets he had been pulling, it was an official letter from the tramways office, in reply to a complaint he had made.

These relics moved Digger, and reminded him, if he was ever tempted to forget, of the continuity between Mac's life and his own, which had not been broken after all in the godown that morning. He would look at one of these scraps of soiled paper, taken out of a back pocket or from Mac's wallet when he was called to collect a fare on some late-night run out to Clovelly, and feel the other man's presence as a physical thing, a heat in him that was different from his own, something added. Till it faded in him, the pages he read had a sharper meaning. It was a private thing. Not secret, but he found no reason to speak of it.

He and Iris seldom spoke of Mac. He connected them only lightly. Their life together was made up of things they had discovered in one another, separately and in their own way. Digger never again saw the letters he had brought her, and he did not ask about them. What they had once stood for in his life had been replaced, and filled a hundred times over, by the woman herself, who was quite different, as he now saw her, from the one who had written them. He was not, in that sense, devoted to the past.

He kept the different parts of his life separate from one another, though there was no separation in him; no conflict either.

He told his mother nothing of Bondi Junction, but she knew of course. He was astonished all over again by the extent to which she could get into his head still, and was aware, in a way that disturbed him sometimes, of what he was thinking.

Each Thursday morning she laid out clean clothes for him, shirt, socks, underpants. She did it to show him that however secretive he might have become – and he had been such an open little fellow – he could hide nothing from her.

She would have preferred him to have some local girl, and kept trying to set him up with one. She wanted him married. She wanted grandchildren. But she knew too well his capacity for loyalty, for sticking at things, to challenge him. The laying out of his clothes each Thursday became a ritual, and when she died, Jenny did it, without knowing quite what the ritual meant, except that it was one.

2

'I understand,' Ern Webber said, 'that you an' Douggy got an invite to the weddin'.' There was a good deal of scorn in his voice.

'That's right,' Digger told him.

'I thought you might of been best man,' Ern said. It was what passed, in his mind, as a stroke of wit. 'Considerin'.' When Digger failed to take this up he went back to his own grievance. 'Well, he was never all that shook on me. An' I know why, too. 'Cause I seen through 'im, that's why, 'e never fooled me. Not after that Mac business. I notice 'e never turns up to reunions.'

'No,' Digger said, 'an' neither do I. So what does that prove?'

This sort of talk was painful to him. It raised too many ghosts, put a finger on wounds that were still raw in him. But it was no good saying any of this to Ern. He was a tactless fellow with fixed and emphatic views, and besides, was bitter now at the snub he had received.

'Oh, Vic's all right,' Digger found himself saying to cut off further argument.

In fact Digger had not been entirely happy at the wedding, which was a very grand affair, but he did not intend to tell Ernie this.

Vic had never spoken to him of the Warrenders, not once. He was unprepared for the house at Strathfield, with its turrets and the big hallway laid with blue, white and brown terracotta tiles and lit with a fanlight, and on either side of the door coloured panels of glass. A good deal of renovation had been done for the occasion. All the stonework of the façade had been repainted and the ironwork of the upstairs verandah given a lick of paint. The vision it presented to Digger was of an opulence he had no reference for, outside of books.

He went quiet and felt awkward in his old suit. He had taken it for granted that Vic's people would be like his own, or Mac's or Doug's. That was the impression he had given. Now this! 'All that time,' he thought, 'he was making mugs of us.' He felt himself flush with indignation, though there was shame in it too.

He tried to hide it. He had told Iris a good deal about Vic and of the tie between them. He did not want her to see now how shaken up he was. When Douggy raised his eyebrows and cast a look around the room where they were to leave their things that said, 'Well now, what do you make of this?' he played dumb, and only Douggy's extreme good nature prevented him from taking offence.

A marquee had been set up on the lawn behind the house. It was of a transparent blue stuff, very light and airy, and all round the edges of it alcoves had been created as at a proper ball, each one hung with loops of cornflowers and pink roses and with a medallion above on which the couple's initials, V and E, were very prettily entwined. Iris, who had been at a good many marriages, had never seen anything like it.

There were waiters in Eton jackets with burgundy cummerbunds, stacks of champagne in dry ice, whisky, beer, soft drinks for the children. Waxed planking had been laid to make a dance floor, and there was a three-piece band to play foxtrots, quicksteps, slow waltzes, gypsy taps. They shared their alcove with Doug and his new wife Janet and some younger friends of the bride.

Meanwhile Vic, sometimes with Ellie at his side, sometimes alone, was moving through all this as if he had never known anything else. Not the least sign now, Digger thought, of the close-cropped, half-crazy character who had come to him at the Crossing. When was that – two months ago? No sign in fact of anything Digger had known of him, or of any of the things they had been through. The ease with which he wore his wedding suit, which sat very smooth and square across his shoulders, the big carnation in his lapel, the freshness and youth he suggested as he clapped older men on the back and called them Gus or Jack or Horrie, and made himself agreeable to their wives – all this appeared to make nothing of what he had been, what they had *both* been, just a year ago. It denied that as if it had never been.

Digger felt injured, and not just on his own part, but strangely enough on Vic's part too, the Vic he had once been close to. And on Douggy's and Mac's. He didn't know where to look.

The Warrenders, you could see, doted on him, no doubt of that, and he plumped himself up with it; you could see that too. He glowed. And the assurance of it gave him the power to submit others, the whole world maybe, to his charm.

'What does it mean?' Digger asked himself miserably. 'Is he so shallow? Or is it just that he knows as well how to hide himself among this lot as he did with us?' Either way he didn't want to have anything to do with it. He felt empty and hurt, but sorry too, and if it wasn't for Iris, who had been looking forward to all this, would have gone straight back to the station.

She felt the tightness in him. 'What is it, love?' she whispered. 'Aren't you enjoying yourself?'

She was. The Warrenders were generous people, there was no mistaking that, and some of the warmth of the occasion, and some aspects of the ceremony too, she took as extending to her and Digger: the vows, which she was always moved by, the confetti, the three-tiered wedding cake with its little columned tabernacle on top, and under it a bride and groom, which would be cut up and passed around in slices soon, and eaten, just a mouthful each, by the guests, or sent off in flat tins stamped with wedding-bells to other parts of the country or overseas. When Mr Warrender got to his feet, and instead of making a speech recited a poem he had written, she took Digger's hand, feeling that the words, in a way she had not expected, spoke for her own emotions, which were so full that only poetry perhaps – and she knew nothing about poetry – might contain them.

Some people, she saw, thought it rather queer that what this big man, who looked like an alderman or a Rotarian, should have embarked on was a poem.

The occasion till now had been a mixture of formality and a suppressed but growing rowdiness. Some of the male guests, skylarking about in their restraining collars, and restrained as well, but only with glances, by their wives, had been making rough jokes, hinting broadly at the cruder side of things. The groom had taken this in good part, as he was bound to do, and unmarried girls, caught in a position where they could not help but overhear (which in a good many cases they were meant to), let it appear that they had not caught on; or they drew their mouths down in a disapproving but half-amused and indulgent manner and turned away. Even one or two of the formal speeches had taken advantage of what is allowable and struck a ribald note. So when Mr Warrender started, a group of the noisier fellows took it as a spoof. Only after a good many hard looks were they shamed into silence. They put on expressions of honest bemusement and let themselves be stilled. But others, Iris saw, were, as she was, moved.

As for Mr Warrender, he gave no indication that there was anything out of the way in what he was doing. He spoke as if poetry was his normal manner of address, and after a moment or two it was accepted as such.

He wasn't solemn. There was often a little kick to what he had to say that was quite humorous, and this surprised Iris; she didn't understand it. She had to get Digger, later, who had a gift in that direction, to repeat some of Mr Warrender's lines (he could too, word for word) before she got hold of what she had been so moved by:

> 'Eternal.' On our lips the extravagant promise
> That spirit makes. The animal in us knows
> The truth, but lowers its dumb head and permits itself for this
> One day to be garlanded and led
> Beyond never-death into ever after, being
> In love with what is always out of reach:
> The all, the ever-immortal and undying
> Word beyond word that breathes through mortal speech.

That was one bit of it.

When Digger spoke these lines they lacked some of the ordinariness Mr Warrender had given them. Even under the circumstances of the tent and its decorations, which were unusual enough, and the guests all subdued and with their hands held back a moment from the clatter of knives and forks, and from glasses even, gravely or politely listening, there had been something very natural and straightforward about it; as if, at the moment of his getting up and looking around at them all, the words the occasion demanded had simply come to him of their own accord. It all seemed so fitting to Iris, and so easy too, because the words Mr Warrender came up with might have been her own, even if some of them were a puzzle to her.

But when Digger repeated the lines, they seemed fixed and formal. He might have been reading them off a printed page. And now that it was long past, it was not simply the one occasion they referred to but all such occasions, and this too, Iris thought, she had understood, if only vaguely, at the moment itself. As if there were more of them present, many more, than the guest-list would have shown:

> Noon here in this garden, and the daystar
> Shakes out instant fire to call up earth, water, air,
> Grass, flowers, limbs and the still invisible presences

That hold their breath and stand in awe about us.
We are all of us guests at a unique, once only
Occasion – *this* one, *this*, the precarious gift
Alive in our hands again, the mixed blessing
Offered and accepted . . .

'The mixed blessing'. That was one of the things that had puzzled her. It had seemed out of place, suggesting as it did a kind of doubt rather than the easy conviction that is usual to such occasions. But she had come, in time, to see that it said several things at once – that was just the point of it, and she saw then what it was in Mr Warrender that had struck her. He did not take things for granted or just as they appeared. What he said was: 'Yes – but,' in this way allowing for what really was, as well as what you might want life to be.

Vic had sat very attentive through it all, with a single deep crease between his brows, either because he thought he might have at some point to defend Mr Warrender against the rowdy element or because what his father-in-law was saying was important to him and he too was struggling to get hold of it.

Ellie on the other hand was following the poem with her lips, as if she already knew it, word for word.

Later, going over the events of the day, the spring heat that had set their skin prickling and given everything such a fresh glow, then the coolness as shadows began to fall, the music, Mr Warrender's poem, even the magpies sitting humped and patient, waiting for the crowd to thin out so that they could dive after soaked crumbs – going over all this, they came to feel that the occasion had been a special one for them too, and that it was Mr Warrender who had given expression to the various moods of it, and his words, as Digger repeated them, through which they could best recover what they had felt.

But there had been something embarrassing as well. Later in the day Digger had gone up to Mr Warrender to say a few words, and to see if he could find in the man himself some indication of where it came from, the poem, but also his boldness in being able to get up in public like that and deliver it.

Nothing came of the meeting. Mr Warrender was all noise at first, all bluffness and easy affability. Digger was embarrassed. Then Mr Warrender was too and stood ignoring Digger altogether, lifting himself up and down on the toes of his shoes, observing the ground and humming. Digger had had the greatest difficulty in getting away.

Except for a moment outside the church, when he and Iris and Doug and Janet had gone up together to shake his hand, Digger had not spoken to Vic, and Vic, he thought, had gone out of his way afterwards to avoid them. After what he had seen, Digger was not surprised by this, but he did find it uncomfortable. Why had he bothered to invite them? To show himself off? Was that all it was?

Towards the end of the day, while Iris was taking the opportunity offered by bathrooms and such to look over the house, Digger, still chewing on the grievance he felt, went to moon about for a bit under some firs. It was over against a high brick wall where there had till recently, he guessed, been a chicken run; maybe they had got rid of it for the wedding. There were still some feathers about, clinging to the fir branches and caught in the needles underfoot, and resting in a corner were the planks that had made up the perches, all split along the grains, encrusted with droppings and beginning to be overgrown with moss. It was quite secluded in here. He walked up and down and was too deep in himself to see that someone had come up beside him and had been standing, he could not guess for how long, just a few feet away.

'Hullo, Digger,' he said lightly. 'What are you up to?'

He spoke as if there was no constraint between them – not on his part. He had seen nothing, Digger realised, of what *he* was feeling. His mood was entirely calm, joyful even – well, why shouldn't he be? – and Digger felt abashed, as if he was the one who was at fault.

'They looking after you?' he enquired. 'Had a piece of wedding cake?'

He had a piece himself and was holding it, half-eaten, in his palm.

'Enough to drink?'

It pleased him, you could see, to have this opportunity to play host. He did it in a very grave way, but with a kind of shyness too, in case you thought he was being smug, that communicated itself immediately to Digger and made him feel again that he had done him an injustice and was in the wrong. He mumbled something, but could not come up with the light reply that might have made things easy between them.

Vic stood, swaying a little, and looked over his shoulder at the crowd. He had an empty glass in one hand and in the other the remains of his piece of cake. They stood a moment. Then, with a gesture Digger had seen him make a thousand times, but under very different circumstances, he tilted his head back, cupped his palm, and, very careful not to lose any, let the crumbs and mixed fruit roll back into his mouth.

It was utterly characteristic. That, his concern not to let a single crumb get lost, and the way too, when he tilted his head back, that his whole throat was bared, gave so much away to anyone who could feel it that Digger found himself choked. All the resentment he had felt went right out of him.

Vic meanwhile was examining his tie and the front of his suit for crumbs. He picked one off and put it on his tongue; then looked up, half-shy, as if he had been caught at something, and they were back immediately in an intimacy that was so strong, and appealed to something so deep in both of them, that they had to draw back from it.

'What a weird bloke he is,' Digger thought. 'Honestly, I'll never get the hang of him.' One moment he was all smooth impenetrability, and the next he opened up and gave himself away – but only, Digger thought, when he was afraid he might have lost you. How did he manage it? Was it calculated, or were they as guileless as he made them seem, these moments when he put himself entirely in your hands? Digger was inclined to protect himself against his own weakness. 'A man'd be a fool,' he told himself, 'to make anything of this. He'll drop me eventually. He's bound to.' It was so clear to him, from what he had seen, that Vic's was a life he could have no part in. In the normal course of things they would never have met, and they were back now in the normal course of things. Still, something was restored between them, and for the moment he was relieved.

When, soon after, Vic was captured by a woman who wanted her husband to meet him, Digger excused himself. He wanted to think things over. He went off through an open arch into a factory yard. It was mostly in shadow, but the archway, where the sun broke through, cast a skew, truncated reflection of itself across the flags. He dragged a packing case out of a heap of rubbish, set it down in the sun, and rolled himself a smoke.

It was here that Ellie, coming to the archway in search of Vic, found him sitting with his head lowered, his tie loose, his new shoes set far apart on the flags. She knew who he was. Seated on his packing-case in the sun he looked ordinary enough, but there was something too that appealed to her.

239

He glanced up, startled. He had an odd, thin-faced, rather wooden look, and very deep-set eyes.

'Sorry,' she said. 'I didn't mean to make you jump.' He was getting awkwardly to his feet. 'You're Digger, aren't you?'

'Well,' she added, and laughed, lifting her arms which were sheeted in a shimmering white material, 'you can see who I am,' and any embarrassment there might have been between them immediately vanished. Digger dropped his fag and ground it out. It was a way, for a moment, of not having to look at her.

'I'd have known anyway,' he found himself saying, and blushed because he couldn't think, once it was out, why he had said it or what it meant.

She smiled. 'Well,' she said, 'I'm glad we've met at last. I was wondering what you'd be like.'

'Me?'

'Vic's talked a lot about you – well, not a lot, but – well, you know.'

They were standing just inside the arch. Behind Digger lay the empty yard. Looking at her the sun was in his eyes so that he squinted a little, but he could feel the edge of the archway's shadow on his shoulder, creeping in.

Outside on the lawn the party was beginning to break up. Many of the guests were already gone. Those who remained were scattered in groups, the men all fired up with the last of the day's arguments, sport, politics, business; some of the women now with their high heels kicked off, easing their stockinged feet in the grass. The band still played, but the floor was occupied now entirely by children, little boys in long pants and long-sleeved shirts and ties, some of them bow ties, and girls in party frocks with ribbons. They were pushing one another about on the waxed boards like perfect little adults while one or two real adults looked on. One of them, Digger saw, was Ellie's father, Mr Warrender. He looked rather tipsy, and Digger saw him, over Ellie's shoulder, step on to the dance floor in a top-heavy, deliberate way, as if he feared he might not make it, and begin to weave about among the couples, who looked sideways at him, embarrassed by his dancing alone like that, and steered away from him towards the corners of the floor.

Ellie, seeing Digger's intent look, turned her head, wondering what it was that had caught his eye; but what she saw was not her father making slow circles with his arms raised among the dancing children, but Vic. He was standing just off to the side in a group of older men, all with their heads together. He had turned away from whatever it was they were discussing. With his hands in his pockets, he was watching Digger and her.

He glanced down when her eye caught him and pretended to laugh at something that was being said. But a moment later, when she looked that way again, he was again watching. This time Digger saw it too. And immediately Vic detached himself from the group, one or two of whom turned and looked after him, and came over the lawn towards them.

Ellie looked at Digger, made a face, and smiled.

'Well,' her look said, 'that's that. This is the only moment we'll have. But that's all right, isn't it?'

Digger found that he too was grinning.

'He's scared. You know – that we might get on too well together. I mean, of what we might find out – you know, about *him*, not about one another – if he leaves us alone too long. He's like that.'

'I know,' Digger agreed.

'He can't help it.'

'He's a difficult cuss.'

'Oh, you don't have to tell *me*.'

These were the thoughts that flew between them.

He wondered what it was exactly that Vic had told her; not about him but about the rest of it. Not a lot, he thought. There would be things she would never know. She would wake nights and find him sitting on the edge of the bed (Digger knew these occasions himself) with the sweat pouring off him; stuck in the real heat of a place he had been dreaming about, except that it was never just a dream and there was no way back from it.

'You've found Digger,' he said brightly, coming up and taking her arm. 'That's good.'

He stood looking from one to the other of them, aware of the warmth between them. They were quite easy, gave no sign that anything they had been saying had had to be cut off short by his arrival. But the smiles they wore were conspiratorial, and Digger reddened and looked down. Vic knew him too well to miss it. But Ellie was not intimidated.

'I was just asking Digger to come and see me sometime,' she said, contradicting what Digger thought had been agreed between them. 'You will, won't you, Digger?'

He glanced at Vic. He too was smiling, quite amiably you might have thought, but he said nothing, and he did not want it; Digger saw that quite plainly. Why had she suggested it?

'I should find Iris,' he said quickly. 'She'll be wondering what's happened to me.'

3

A blustery day, late August. High up, flat-bottomed clouds were in flight, sailing fast around the world, but the air was clear and up here on the hill above the Crossing she could see in all directions at last, north, south, eastwards towards the river's mouth and the ocean. The whole landscape was laid out for her.

Downriver, in a dozen little bays and inlets, boats were stuck like bits of paper, white on blue, unmoving at this distance. Upstream the bridge, its traffic silenced by the sound the wind was making, the wrenching of branches, fistfuls of leaves rattling at the ends of twigs and the gulls' crying.

To one side below was the store in its elbow of low land, high and dry and isolated: the ridge of its tin roof, the four posts of her washing-lines, old barrels and kero tins with her bits of shrubs in them, Digger's workbench under the pepper tree. Jenny was there, mooning about in a cotton frock chasing birds.

'She doesn't know yet,' she thought. 'She hasn't realised I'm out of the house.' The panic there would be when she went into their room and found the empty bed! The moaning and flapping! She was sorry about that.

On the high bank opposite, on one of the roofs of the weekenders that dotted the hillside over there and flashed among the trees, Digger would be working, a hammer in his belt, a stub of pencil behind his ear.

She knew it all; where everything was. Only up here was new to her.

And why had she left it thirty-three years to come up here and see it?

Because she didn't want to see things too clearly, that's why.

And why had she done it now?

Because she did.

She had left it till the very last, not to disappoint herself. She could face it now. She was past disappointment.

Far off, forty miles it would be as the crow flies, in a soft haze in which houses, whole streets of them, and trees and harbour water were smudged to the same pastel blue, as if it was a lake not a city, and just the highest towers were visible above the surface of it, was Sydney.

That wasn't what she had come to see. She hadn't even known it would be visible. In her mind it was further off than that. Halfway to England, practically. Thirty-three years off. She had knuckled under and hung on here – somebody had to; kept things together, turned her back on the rest of the world, taken on its name, Keen, and would now be buried under it.

But suddenly, just this afternoon, she couldn't bear to be in the house any longer, in the stuffy little back bedroom, on a day when the wind was up. Everything, every stick of furniture, every inch of the curtains she had ordered and sewn and hung in their three rooms, every teaspoon, and the wedding picture of her husband's parents on the sideboard, and the bags of sugar, rice, salt, and the scales in the back room on which for thirty-three years she had weighed them out in pound and half-pound packets – all that, and her kitchen chairs and saucepans, and the bucket and mop behind the door, and Jenny flopping on the counter, and all the ghosts of the others, squeezed into a corner by the stove and sucking a rusk or pushing ashes into their mouths, Leslie and James and May and Billy – all that and more, weighed on her heart and crushed her. She could have set a match to the lot of it in this high wind and watched it blaze up in a roar of smuts.

So what sort of woman, at last, did that make her?

The very kind she had set out *not* to be.

Tearing off her bedclothes she had rushed out barefoot to the kitchen, snatched up a box of matches and struck one and threw it down, then another, and looking wildly about her said, 'This is the sort of woman I am.'

But the box fell from her hand, the matches spilled. Without looking back she had broken out of the house and, plunging off into the scrub with no thought in her head, only the wind and the high clouds flying, begun to climb.

Once she was actually climbing she was all excitement and haste, as if she had wanted to do this every day of her life and was to see at last what she had for years been held back from. She pushed past ledges of rock where she had to use both hands to haul herself up, and the big, flesh-coloured angophoras with their fat-rolls like naked angels, till she was high enough to get a grip on the dimension of things. She wasn't a coward. No one could have called her that. She could face anything.

When she reached the summit, she looked about, took it all in, then, hunched on an outcrop among scratchy, waist-high grass, and with her arms hugging her breast, chewed on the bitterness of things.

Now that it was about to occur, the thing she had dreamed of, the descent of peace and the gathering around her of all the objects of her life, she did not want it, any of it. She did not want her life – the fifty-four years, so many days and days and the disappointments and defeats and little silent triumphs – to be made visible at last and piled up around her so that she had to say: 'So this is what it comes to.'

That's what she had wanted to get away from, and had, in her head, already burned the evidence of. Not to have, forever, to sit at the centre of it.

Gibbons. That was the name she had been born to.

'My God,' she thought, looking about at the spiky heads of the blockboys, 'where is she? Where's Marge Gibbons? And Bert. Marge and Bert.' It disturbed her that she could no longer actually see them: two hopeless little kids she had let wander off and get lost. They had been so real in the world, and still were, in her mind somewhere, if she could only get back to them past all the things she had accumulated that shut them out.

She began to pluck at the wool of her bedjacket. Little bits of pink fluff blew about in the air and joined the light little seeds and balls of pollen that were streaming and tumbling. The wind could not tell the one from the other of them.

Keen. She had taken that name, and the result was she would be buried under it.

And him? Billy? He was off chasing another war, and had found one too, in Korea this time. He would go on till he found the one that would do for him. She had known for years now that he would not come back.

She plucked at the bedjacket, pecking at it with the hard tips of her fingers. The pink stuff rose up and sailed. But suddenly there was a barging about in the bushes close by, then a wailing, and she was found, which was just how it had been the first time. The big blubbery girl found her and kept clutching and clutching and would not let her be.

*

245

'She won't come in,' Jenny told Digger. 'She says she never wants to. Ever again.'

She was wheeling about in the yard under the clothes-line and wringing her hands. Their mother, wrapped in an eiderdown, was in an old cane chair that had been chucked out as rubbish, her back to the house and shivering.

Digger put his tool-box down. 'Don't worry,' he said, but his calm was pretence. 'You go in an' make us a cuppa tea. I'll talk to 'er.'

He did, but she remained woodenly silent, as if she could no longer hear.

Jenny brought tea. She took a cup, but just sat with it while he drank, and Jenny, who was terrified, kept well away on the kitchen step.

But she would not go back into the house, and though he talked and tried to tempt her with things she had once cared about, she did not hear or would not listen. When it got dark he brought more blankets, wrapped her, put on another sweater himself, and they continued to sit as night deepened and the stars came out, and Jenny, behind a lighted window in the house, looked on.

Jenny brought him something to eat. It wasn't much. She was too upset to make anything proper. Digger sat on an upturned can and ate potatoes with a fork, with bread and a bit of gravy, and their mother continued to sit with her back to the house. It was ashes in her head. The house, the store and all its contents. She had put a match to them, whether or not the flame had taken. Digger could do nothing with her.

He had faced this sort of thing before but had not expected to see it again in his lifetime, and not here. She was willing herself out of the world, and she would do it too.

It was a strange thing, to have the house there, all lighted, and her sitting in the dust in front of it in a broken chair, with the scrub and all its night sounds around them.

Towards dawn he dozed off and she did at last begin to speak to him. The things she told him were terrible. He had not known she was in such despair. Bert, she called him. 'No,' he wanted to say, 'that's not my name. I'm Digger. Remember?' but he was afraid of interrupting her.

But he was wrong, or she did not remember or did not want to. 'Bert,' she called, and he woke, and the conversation they had been having went deep down into him and was gone.

*

'Digger,' Jenny said. 'Would you mind if I ast you something?'

She had come out to where, in an old pair of shorts and with his shirt off, he was at his workbench in the yard. There was a smell of freshly sawn timber.

'Fire away,' he said without looking up. He had thrown himself into work as a way, for a time, of not thinking. He needed a little time always to recover himself, and had settled now for the pleasure of putting a saw into soft wood, the smell of it, very sweet and spicy, and the warmth of the sun on his back.

'What's gunna happen,' she got out at last, painfully twisting her brow, 'to Mumma's *things*?'

'Her clothes, you mean?' He went on working, taking a pencil from behind his ear.

'No. Her *things*. They're *her* things.'

He looked at her now.

'The furniture an' that,' she said hopelessly. 'Saucepans. You know.'

'Nothing's going t' happen to them,' he said gently. 'What did you think? They're yours now. Ours.'

'Are they? Did she leave 'em?'

What had she expected, he wondered. He had no idea, even after so long, how her mind worked. Perhaps she too had taken their mother's vision literally, the one she had herself in the end turned her back on, and expected all the furnishings of the house, right down to the serviette rings and the tea-strainer, to be *taken up* in some way. Maybe literally. If not that, then in essence. Was that it? So that they were no longer, as they had been till now, quite solid and useable.

Or perhaps she thought their mother's spirit had appropriated them and made them dangerous to touch.

The chair she had sat in all night still stood in an awkward place under the lines, but neither of them had thought to move it. It was broken, its canes cracked and bleached by the weather; so much more like a natural thing than a piece of abandoned furniture that after a time, as it sank lower on one leg, they would barely notice it.

'Yes,' he said very quietly, 'she left them to you. They're yours now. You just do whatever you want with 'em.'

'Oh,' she said. 'All right.'

She stood a moment, looking serious, then went off, and he heard her shifting things about in the kitchen, clearing the shelves and rinsing things, instituting little changes that she might have been wanting to make for years – who could know the order her mind followed? – and wouldn't have dared make while their mother was alive.

4

Digger was to discover that he had been wrong on two counts that day of the wedding. Against the odds he did see Ellie again, though not for more than six years, and then only by accident, and Vic did not, as he had put it, 'drop him'. Two or three times a year, sometimes more often, he turned up unannounced at the Crossing and they would pass an hour together. He would sit out under the pepper tree and watch Digger at work at the bench he had there, getting up to steady the other end of a four-by-two Digger was sawing; or Digger would haul out a spare rod and they would go off and fish.

It wasn't always easy. There were times when he was in one of those moods where everything was an irritation to him. He had come for no other reason, Digger thought, than to pick over some old resentment or injury and provoke you into wounding him. Sometimes he succeeded, and Digger would be irritated himself when he saw Vic's satisfaction at having got him to strike out, the odd little smile he wore as he turned his head away. But on other occasions, though Vic went on and on, he would resist. Suddenly, without warning, Vic would be all appeasement, and minutes after in such excellent spirits that Digger could scarcely credit the change in him. It was as if in Digger's refusal to be on bad terms with him he had found the capacity to be on good terms once again with himself.

But there were many occasions when he came only because he had picked up something, some new gadget, that he thought Digger would be interested in and ought to see, or because the mood was on him to do a bit of quiet fishing, or simply because two or three months had gone by and they hadn't seen one another. They never discussed whatever business it was he was involved in. It was only when Doug mentioned it that Digger began to get an idea of what a figure he was cutting out there.

'Ol' Vic's doin' well, isn't 'e?'

'Is 'e?' Digger said. 'What d'ya mean?'

Douggy laughed. 'Don't you read the papers? Needham's —

that's him. He's practically a millionaire. Makin' money hand over
fist.'

There was no irony in Douggy's tone. He was, as he had always
been, sceptical of what he called the bosses, but he took Vic's rise in the
world as reflecting on him as well, on all of them: he did not begrudge
it. But who would have guessed it, eh? Who would have thought they
would have a mate who was on the way – how old was he? twenty-
eight, twenty-nine? – to being a millionaire? Not that he and Vic were
all that close any more. But it was a wonder just the same.

'Doesn' 'e talk to you about it?' he asked Digger.

'No. Why should 'e? I don't know anything about business.'

'Well, 'e was never slow to blow 'is own trumpet – not in the ol'
days. What's happened to 'im?'

'Nothing,' Digger said. 'I dunno.'

'So what *do* you talk about?' Doug asked after a moment, and his
look was humorous.

'Nothing much,' Digger told him. It was the truth. He had to think.
'Cars an' that,' he added at last.

'Oh? So what sort of car does 'e drive?'

'Humber Hawk. Before that a Pontiac.'

Douggy looked impressed. 'Didn' you think from that,' he asked,
'that 'e might be doin' well?'

Digger didn't know what to say. He had seen at the wedding the sort
of people Vic came from and the life they led, and had been too
absorbed with the vehicles themselves, with raising the bonnet and
looking in at the workings of them, to ask himself how much they
might represent in the way of 'getting on'.

Vic liked to show them off, but there was nothing show-offish or
proprietorial in it. They could have been kids who had come upon the
Pontiac or the Riley, the Austin Healey or the Ford Customline,
parked in a street somewhere, less concerned with who owned it than
with the full panoply of its metal power and the wonderful elegance
and achievement of the thing; though it struck Digger as amazing at
times (he shivered and went ghostly under his clothes) that they should
be here to lay their hands on the sun-warmed gloss, and to feel, when
they put their foot down, the full power of these models of 1949, 1952,
1954.

'I believe you're doin' pretty well for yourself,' he said at last, one
day when their easiness allowed it. 'So Doug tells me.'

'I'm holding my end up,' he admitted.

Digger was planing a set of planks, three or four of which stood upright against the trunk of the pepper tree. Pale shavings, almost transparent and showing the honey-coloured grain, curled off the blade as he swept his arm through, fell, turned over, and rolled away in the breeze. Vic sat on an upturned kerosene tin.

'I didn' realise,' Digger said.

'Oh – ' Vic passed it off lightly, 'I've had a bit of luck, that's all.'

It was true: things fell into his hand and multiplied. But that wasn't the whole of it. He was smart, he worked hard, never stopped in fact, he was famous for it; he had an eye for the way things were moving and would be on the spot and ready to go before other men, more experienced men too, had seen there was a chance; and he was ruthless – he let nothing and no one get in his path. But he also had luck. It worried him.

Luck, he believed, was a thing you couldn't rely on. It had let him down once, and badly. It could let him down again. It was his opinion that a man who depended on luck was little more than a lounger in the world and had in no way proved himself. What he believed in was character. His achievements, such as they were, all plain and visible, had to be balanced against what was *not* visible because it was within, but which must exist because *they* did, and could therefore be taken on trust.

Sitting out in the dry wind, under the pepper tree, on the upturned tin, what he was worth was not millions but just what Digger might see and reflect back to him, with no need of explanation or proof.

He looked up very frankly to where Digger had stopped still with the plane in his hand, looking at him, and there it was.

It was a moment Digger would remember; when he saw clearly, and for the first time, what Vic wanted of him. He was to be one of the witnesses to his life. Not to his achievements, anyone could see those, which is why he hadn't bothered to draw Digger's attention to them; but to those qualities in him that would tip the balance on the other, the invisible side.

It had taken Digger so long to grasp this because the idea that a man might need *witnesses* to his life was so foreign to him. But once he had seen it, though the role did not please him, he stuck. It was one more of the responsibilities that had been laid upon him. He would not have chosen it, any more than he would have chosen some of the others, but it was there. Chance, life, fate – whatever it was – chose for you, connecting and binding you into the pattern of other people's lives, and making that at last the pattern of your own.

It was Jenny who did the resisting, and this had its comic side. None of Vic's appearances over the years, or the little presents he brought, ever reconciled her to him.

One night they were watching TV when she suddenly turned and asked in astonishment:

'Is that who I *think* it is?'

'Yes,' Digger told her. 'Vic.'

'So what's *he* done?'

Her quick rule of thumb was that anyone who got on to TV, if he wasn't a pop star or a newsreader, must be a crook.

'Nothing. Made a bit of money, that's all, by taking someone over – You know, buying 'em up. There's some trouble with the unions.'

She screwed her eyes up and concentrated. That didn't tell her anything. That wasn't what it was about.

The interviewer was a girl, and after being very nice to her, or pretending to be, calling her by her name, Jane, but showing too that he didn't take any of what she was asking seriously, he suddenly went cold, then lost his temper. Jenny chuckled. This was what it was about.

'*She* doesn't think much of him,' she declared.

'Good on yer, girlie!' she shouted. '*She* thinks he's a crook. Is 'e?'

'No,' Digger told her. He was amused. 'And that girl doesn't think so either.'

'Why's she after 'im then?'

'It's 'er job. She's doing 'er job, that's all. Being aggressive.'

'Mr Smarty Pants!' Jenny shouted, 'Mr Smarty Smarty Pants!'

5

Vic, still in his shirt-sleeves, pushed back the breakfast plates, shifted the pepper and salt shakers and the toast-rack to a new position, poured himself more tea, lit a cigarette, and leaned back in his chair. He had a habit, when he was about to propose a new idea, of clearing a space before him. You could, Ma knew, judge how large or risky the idea was by the extent of cloth he laid bare.

Their consultations together often took place over the remains of breakfast. With Pa already installed in his office and Ellie off delivering the boy to kindergarten, they had a good half-hour to themselves. The domestic setting, the fragments of the meal ('There is something very reassuring,' Ma thought, 'about burnt toast'), gave an unemphatic quality to their talk; the solid grip on things suggested by teacup handles and spoons grounded what might otherwise have seemed fantastic in the ordinary and commonplace.

It astonished Vic, when he recalled the anxieties she had been racked by, that Ma could be so changed. She had never failed him, not once. If he drew back sometimes, and even he had his moments of doubt, though he did his best not to show them, she saw it and would be there to urge him on.

Her mind was sharper than his. He came up with a scheme, presented it to her, and let her knock it down if she could. If *she* couldn't find the crack in a thing it was foolproof.

He relied on her. They were a team. Arguing a deal out with her was like arguing with his other self, the sceptical one he might not otherwise have made contact with, or not so immediately. He accepted criticisms from her that, if a man had made them, he would have felt bound to reject. They knew one another too well for that, and cared too much, both of them, for what they were doing, to be soft with one another.

He was lingering this morning, deliberately holding back. There was a vagueness in him – not quite weakness, it was never that – which she would have in a moment to acknowledge and deal with. She knew him very well by now. But there was also this new space he had opened up. 'First things first,' she thought.

'So,' she said briskly, 'this is it, eh?'

'Yes,' he said. 'Ten-thirty.'

He saw how she was looking at him. He pushed his plate back another inch.

'I find all this a bit difficult,' he said. 'I mean, he can't be *that* innocent. I thought he'd be tougher, a bloke like that.'

'He *is* tough,' Ma told him. 'Don't be fooled by all that soft talk. He's tough in the old way, like my father. You fellows are a different breed.'

She saw the little flicker across his brow. She had not meant it as a criticism.

'He doesn't seem to realise that he'll no longer have control. What does 'e think we are? A charitable institution?'

He was speaking of Jack Creely, an old school friend of Pa's who had an engineering firm with government contracts. Needham's were taking him over.

'He's so full of himself! He thinks he's been clever, pulling the wool over our eyes.' His pride was touched.

What disturbed him, she knew, was the talk it would generate. He had made a good many enemies these last years. People thought he was getting too big for his boots; he was too sure of himself, too successful. They would be only too eager now to use Jack Creely as further evidence against him.

'Look,' she said, 'we're in for forty-six thousand, aren't we? That doesn't look like charity to me. Jack knows the score.'

The sharpness with which she heard herself say this gave her a start. She too had come a long way in these last years.

As for the forty-six thousand, just saying it straight out like that took her breath away. As if it was nothing!

She thought of her father, and saw him raise his eyebrows, half-shocked, but half-admiring too, at the summary way she had dealt with Jack Creely. But what would really have shocked him, as it did her too a little, was the forty-six thousand. Her father's rule had been a strict one. You stayed within limits, you kept out of debt. 'This feller's a lunatic,' her father would have told her, half-admiring of that too, but with a strong suggestion that she ought to look out for herself. 'Can't you see that?' She heard it so clearly in the room that she was surprised Vic didn't jerk his head up, in that aggressive way he had, and answer him.

He had been a buccaneer, her father, but of shallow waters. They were in open waters now.

For more than three years the factory had been abandoned and boarded up. The brickwork was crumbling and weeds had sprouted, not just between the flags of the yard but on the stone windowsills, and even, in places, from the roof. The little boy, Greg, was scared to go there. She had seen him more than once standing in the archway, peering into the yard and daring himself to go on.

The house and the factory, when her father built them, had been a single unit, two halves when she was growing up of a single world. The girls who worked in the packing room were part of the family. They might step across to the kitchen to get a cup of sugar if they were short at morning teatime, and if one of them took sick she would be brought over to lie in one of the rooms off the verandah. As a little girl Ma had often put aside her dolls or her jigsaw, or left off practising with her roller-skates on the long side verandah, to go across and have a chat with her favourites among the packers, Alice Green or Mrs Danby, or to watch a van being unloaded in the yard. Or she would perch on a stool in her father's office and cut out floral patterns from the Needham's labels and advertising placards and paste them into a ledger.

All this had brought the world of manufacturing and business into their daily lives, so that for her there had been no gap between them, the two worlds were interpenetrable. It was this view of things that she meant to re-establish by making the breakfast table the scene of her consultations with Vic, and all the more because what they were engaged with was no longer something you could stroll across to the other side of the garden and *see*.

Margarine. That had been their first move. Astonishing how easily, given a little capital, you could shift from one commodity to another. Soap, margarine – it was all the same, it seemed, though her father mightn't have thought so. He had brought his knowhow about soap-making from the Old Country, and from the Lake District, where he grew up, the recipes for the perfumes he used. It was all very personal to him, and to all of them. The soaps had been named after English flowers, lilac, violet, musk-rose, and the finest and most expensive of them after her mother, Mary Louise. At

Christmas, special packets were made up as presents to clients and friends.

But there was no call these days for things that were hand-made. Hicks had seen the point of the move straight off, and was delighted to be let loose on a new product, with new premises and a real staff, including a dozen trained technicians.

The amount they had had to borrow was terrifying. Hadn't she just got them out of the red? But Vic saw things in a different way.

'Listen,' he told her, 'things have changed. There's nothing to be gained by playing safe and staying out of debt. A millionaire isn't a man who's *got* a million. He's a man who *owes* a million, and if he owes ten million, all the better. That's how we've got to think. If it worries you, Ma, just you leave it to me.'

'My God,' she'd thought. But once she took the idea in she found she could live quite easily with it. That was *him*. He was all energy and unbounded confidence. What's more, the system worked.

His other idea was what he called *spread*. It had nothing to do with margarine – quite the opposite, in fact. Instead of limiting themselves to one commodity, one sort of venture, they took up, in an opportunistic way, whatever offered, using one company to raise credit for another, or they simply let things sit and appreciate.

So he took them into real estate, buying up corner sites all over the suburbs, odd rows of shops, that could be sold off to the petrol companies for service stations. They got into the building trade, financing new-style units, and quite soon owned a demolition company as well. For no other reason than that it was going cheap, he acquired a factory for bicycle parts, but seeing the possibilities in it, switched to specialist parts for the motor industry. Get a hold on just one of those parts, a reputation for being reliable – no strikes, no hold-ups – a good transport side, make yourself indispensable to an assembly-line somewhere, and you were made. Lately he had developed an interest in mining – sand mining up the Queensland coast, bauxite mining in Cape York Peninsula – and had his eye now on several oil-search enterprises, one of them in New Guinea, another in north-west Western Australia. Sooner or later, somewhere on the continent, they would strike oil. The thing was to get in on the ground floor. All this was *spread*.

It seemed a long step to her, from a place on the other side of the yard to sites they had a stake in that were three thousand miles away. But this was precisely what *he* was excited by, the sense of far-flung spaces to be opened up: a map on the wall, and the geography of the whole continent to move in, and not just what was above ground either, but what was below ground as well; and beyond mere *geographical* space, all those decades to come when these provisional ventures and far-sighted risks and hunches would pay off.

He was astonishing. She kept waiting for the moment to come when her father's voice might prevail and she could no longer go with him; but he leapt, and each time she took a good breath and went with him.

Looking now at the area he had opened up among their breakfast things she did not feel anxious. Part of what sustained her, but forced her too, was the need he had to take her with him. What came back to her then was the times she had paced his room, all anxiety, and he had sat so stolidly on his bed – how old was he? thirteen? fourteen? – and she had relied on him. What she had seen in him then was increased now a hundredfold.

She had never told him, but many years before, when she was not long married herself, she had seen his father. She had had no idea then that they would one day be connected.

A good-looking Irish fellow, a coalminer, who ought to have been rough, and was no doubt, but knew how to act soft if it suited him. All that, she had thought, must go over well with the girls, and he tried it out a little with her – having seen that it might be best, if he was to get what he wanted from Pa, to make an impression on her. He knew Pa pretty well, she guessed. That is, he knew how to get round him.

He had been very much then what Vic was now; the same age too, just thirty. Twelve years later, when Vic turned up, the image of the man had come back to her and she saw what he might grow up to be.

It was a type that appealed to her. She could admit that now. The father had seen it and given her the eye, but in a humorous way that said, 'Don't worry, I'm no danger. You'll never see me again. I've got what I wanted here.'

What she had been struck by was the quickness with which he had summed them up. He had been looking them over to see if they would do. The cheek! She could have laughed outright now when she recalled it. 'You'll do, I reckon,' the look said. The effrontery of it!

But he had known better than she had (*something* had known) what was good for them. For all of them.

Vic consulted his watch. Quickly now he outlined the thing to her. He had needed first to clear the air of that other business, Jack Creely. He wanted to start off with everything clear between them. So here it was.

He had, for quite a while, been buying up shares in a margarine company owned by one of their rivals. He wanted to make a bid now for the whole show. Of course they would have to sell one or two things. He laid them out for her. It didn't look like much: an egg cup with a rabbit on it and the scooped egg turned upside down to fool someone that it was whole, two slices of dry toast, a honey pot in the shape of a hive, with a chipped bee on the lid.

Loans? Yes, a few thousand. But interest rates were down and would go down further, according to his bank manager. Three hundred thousand, tops. Very little risk. Well, a little, you had to expect that, but not enough to spoil their sleep. It wouldn't spoil his sleep, anyway.

That's how he talked.

They went over it. The questions she asked were good ones, and he had the answers. In another moment he was on his feet, touching a napkin to his mouth with one hand and with the other reaching for his jacket.

She sat a moment after he was gone, then put each of the pieces he had moved, the honey pot, the egg cup, the two bits of toast, back where they had been, and turned the egg over in the cup to show its ravaged side. Then she put them all back again as they had been when he left.

In her own odd fashion she was getting used to the thing, coming to terms; as when, years back, she used to pick his socks up off the floor and sniff, then roll them in pairs. It was a form of thinking, all her own, but in their daily sessions it had become his way too; or perhaps it always had been, which is why they understood one another.

An egg cup was just an egg cup, of course; but pick it up, move it, and you could get hold of that other more abstract thing it stood in for, which was not so easily graspable. You made it visible, got your hands on it in its momentary occurrence as egg cup, and a shift took place in your head. Once that happened you were dealing with the two things at once.

The men he worked with, who were all very clever, ambitious

fellows impressed by his energy and utterly loyal to him (though this did not mean that he trusted them with all he was thinking), assumed that his consultations with Ma were a charade, an act put on to reassure the old girl that she still had a hand in things. They would have smiled indulgently at all this business with egg cups and bits of toast. But they were wrong. Something in the presence of those domestic objects, something in Ma too, was necessary to the release in him not of the insights themselves but of his power to believe in them, and in his power to make them real.

He had two ways of working. The public one, the one he showed and wanted people to see, was all hard edges, assured to the point of arrogance. His reputation was based on it, and if people assumed it was all there was, so much the better. It left his other nature unseen. He was not ashamed of it, but it would have worried him to reveal too clearly what he himself did not fully understand.

This side of him was all dreamy vagueness, a lassitude in which he lost contact with the real world and where the sort of activity of which he was supposed to be a master seemed inconceivable to him. Yet it was in just this state, which if he had perceived it in another he might have despised, that he first got hold of the schemes, mere childish daydreams they were at this point, cloud-doodles, that he would knot out later and present to his more active self as proposals, then hard plans.

He trusted this faculty in himself because it had so often proved itself; but he thought of it as a form of childishness, and everything that had to do with the child in him he feared.

These moods in him belonged to the early morning, and would be on him when he woke. A continuation, he sometimes thought, of his sleep, they grew out of what he had been dreaming, though the dream itself eluded him.

Careful not to wake Ellie, he would pad across the room and go downstairs barefoot in his pyjamas, feeling oddly soft and vulnerable. The day's heat would be coming. As he wandered through the darkened house things took on a new shape, even the most familiar of them. They seemed released of their weight. Or maybe that too was part of his mood. He would sit quietly in a swing on the verandah, and as the trees on the lawn grew out of darkness his thoughts ordered themselves, became clear to him, and birds sang through them, the familiar sounds of this bird or that, very sane and comforting. This was how his thinking got done.

But sometimes, after only a minute or two, he would go through the house to Meggsie's kitchen.

Meggsie, already up and dressed, would be sitting with her plump arms on the table, her hands round a heavy cup. Wordless at this hour, she would swing round to the stove where the teapot sat, haul it across and pour him a steaming cup, the pot so heavy, even in both her hands, that she could barely heft it. He would sit then, his shoulders hunched a little, his hair a mess, and drink.

They were close. As if to make up for all the years when out of loyalty to her girls she had held out on him, she spoiled him these days as she had once spoiled Ellie and Lucille.

She still teased him. He liked the abrasive form her affection took, and would have felt cheated if she had gone soft on him. But the teasing now was no more than the old form of a game through which they could, without embarrassment, explore their affection for one another.

It was a different world out here.

The cups, for instance. They were so thick you could barely get your mouth round them. The handles too.

If it was winter the kitchen would be fuggy warm, the windows still dark. They would sit and watch them turn blue, and after a little she would get up and bring him a bowl of porridge and watch him eat.

In summer she would already have propped the screen door open with a flat-iron, and magpies would be flopping about the dewy lawn. Little points of light on tips of grassblades would be catching the sun a moment before it quenched and dried them up.

They barely spoke. If they did it was in monosyllables and half-finished sentences that to anyone else would have made no sense.

They might have been a quite different pair: she the mother who had just roused him, heavy-headed and unwilling, for the early shift at a factory or in the pit; he a big, loose-shouldered, barefoot fellow, rather lazy and fond of drink, fond of the girls too, but still tied, with only a show of rebellion, to her apron strings.

Often it was Greg who would come out at last to look for him. He would hang there in the doorway, his hair a bird's nest, his stance very like his father's, whom he imitated in everything. He was a timid little fellow, and Meggsie scared him. He wouldn't come in.

'Mummy says,' he would say, 'where are you?'

6

It surprised Vic, as the years went by, that, leaping right over what had been the grimmest period of his life, he so often found himself back in the year before his mother died and the time afterwards when he had lived with his father. He would go itchy under his clothes – the well-cut suit, the shirt Meggsie had starched – and would find himself standing high up on the dunes under a sky that was just on the turn between day and night, waiting for his body to release him into the future and send him hurtling out of himself into a new life. A kind of despair would come over him. The future he yearned for would not appear – and yet here he was right in the midst of it, assured and powerful beyond anything he could have dreamed.

He would stand and watch the wall of sand-grains shift, his mouth agape but unable to cry out as in a vast wave it rose and covered him.

He did not drink, or very little. He saw too clearly the connection between it and a violence he feared was in his nature, and which drink might let loose. It was his son who showed him this. One day, when Vic was especially angry with him, the child suddenly flinched and drew away, as if he had seen the shadow of Vic's hand before he had raised it.

'What are you doing?' His voice was full of shock, but all the boy heard was anger. 'I'm not going to hit you. You know that. Why are you crying? Nobody's going to hurt you.'

This scene, which Vic found so distressing, took place at just the time that Greg was old enough to be a presence in the house, a new focus of energy and will, subtly changing all their lives by exerting pressures this way and that to make room for itself. He was very spoiled, and when he was challenged gave way to tears. His mother, his grandmother, even Meggsie, made excuses for him, and the more they did it, Vic thought, the more the boy whined and the more resourceful he became at getting his way.

He seemed very much, as he developed, a smaller version of the father, with Vic's stance and squareness of frame, his expressions too – everyone noticed it. But the father's qualities had taken their own direction in him, so that what might have appeared as sturdy self-confidence had in the boy become a defensive petulance.

He was sorry for the child, feeling he knew only too well what he was suffering. He was afraid for him. But the likeness was unnerving. It showed up in a naked, even shameless way – though only perhaps because the boy was too young as yet to have learned how to disguise it – all that he, Vic, had taken such pains to conceal.

When Greg was still quite young, not yet seven, he developed the habit of lying. His lies were stupid ones that were bound to be exposed, which was, perhaps, just what he intended. They were lies whose only purpose was to win attention. But what was the point of *that*, Vic demanded, when all it showed was that he was a liar? In low voices, in bed, he and Ellie argued over it.

'Don't be silly,' she told him. 'You're making too much of it. Children grow out of things.'

He tried to talk to the boy man to man. He hated untruth. He found him playing with his Meccano set and made him stand still and listen, but his attention kept wandering and Vic grew angry and did not know how to go on. He was infuriated to see a little smile at the corner of the boy's mouth, as if he was not fearful at all, despite his seeming so timid, and was getting just what he wanted out of him.

By twelve he had found a kind of strength, but it was covert and indirect. On the one occasion when Vic did at last raise his fist the boy's look was of such contempt and triumph, still with that flicker of a smile at the corner of his mouth, and Vic saw himself so clearly reflected in it, that he was appalled.

He tried to pass the thing off with a recognition of fault on both sides, but the boy knew he had won and was defiant. Vic was powerless.

Everything in himself, in his inheritance too, that he had worked to push down and control, had come to independent existence in the boy and acted against him. That's what he saw, and he saw it the more clearly because Greg was just the age that he had been in his last year with his father.

He looked at the boy, saw his contemptuous smile and the likeness between them, and on the other side saw his father; and there was likeness there, too. This was what Ellie and the others could not know. He felt powerless, and at a time when power was just what came to him so easily, and publicly, elsewhere.

7

On one of his usual Thursdays, a bright winter day when there was a little chill to the air but the whole of George Street, all the way to the harbour, was bathed in clear soft sunlight, Digger was just about to cross at the Market Street lights when a woman spoke to him. He recognised her immediately.

'Hullo,' she said. 'It's Digger, isn't it.'

They stood smiling at one another.

'Oh,' he said, 'it's you.'

He did not feel free to call her by her name; but whether it was the unexpectedness of being caught together like this at the lights, forced by something quite outside themselves to come to a halt, or the softness of the day, or simply the pleasure he always had at being briefly in town, among so many people, Digger felt a wave of light-headedness catch him up – as it had, he recalled, the last time they had spoken, as if whenever they came together they were immediately translated to a special place where his awkwardness left him and he was entirely at ease.

They might have been stepping back here into a relationship that went back ages, in which all the usual difficulties had had their edges worn down through long acquaintance and habit. There was no shyness between them.

'I thought you lived – where is it? –'

'Keen's Crossing.'

'Yes. Don't you?'

'I come up to town sometimes. Every Thursday in fact.'

Their eyes met and he thought she might be wondering, in that case, why he had never taken up her invitation and got in touch. But she knew why.

'I've been buying a few things,' he told her, to explain the packages he was carrying. They were outside a hardware store where he liked to potter about for articles he couldn't pick up so easily at home, the new products they had these days, the magic glues and power tools.

'It's Vic's birthday Saturday,' she told him as the lights changed and they stepped off the kerb. He did not know that. 'I'm shopping. Why don't you come with me, if you're finished.' They were on the other side now. 'We can have morning tea. I won't be long.'

'All right,' he said.

Downstairs at Farmer's Ellie looked at ties, holding one or two of them up to Digger's shirt-front as she talked. They were wide ones, too colourful for him – for Vic too he would have thought, though no doubt she knew better than he did. When at last she had chosen one she bought two Island cotton shirts, then silk socks, then handkerchiefs.

Digger hung back. It was a slow business and might have been boring, but it made the talk between them so easy, and there was for him so much novelty in it, that he stopped being impatient and found he was enjoying himself. By the time it was all done they had caught up on a good many facts that it might have taken them much longer to uncover if they had not been continually on the move, and if the gaps between one question and the next had not been filled, for him, with the distractions of the store itself, the banks of lights in the ceiling, the escalators, so many women, some of them with children, some with a husband in tow, all happily spending, and turning things over on the open counters while they waited for their parcels to be wrapped; all of which he took in – the dummies too, looking so perfect with their real hair and eyelashes and doll-like eyes – while Ellie was engaged with one of the sales ladies or going through the drawers of hand-sewn handkerchiefs. At last they went upstairs into a big room overlooking the street, found a table away from the mothers and children, and ordered tea. They could relax now. A silence fell and they were forced to look at one another; but they could face that because they had already, in their half-hour of movement and talk, got so far with one another.

Ellie looked at him in a candid, clear-eyed way that sought to see, Digger thought, what there might be beyond his shyness; something she had glimpsed, and been looking for too, he thought now, when she held up to his open shirt-collar one of the expensive ties.

She looked at his hands and he saw her register something – that he worked with them? At his eyes again – What did she see there? (He found he did not mind her scrutiny.) It would be nothing of what really mattered to him. So when he looked at her, and saw the way her hair curled in just at shoulder level, the neatness of her brows, the colour on her lips, he took it for granted that what mattered most to her was also invisible, and would remain so unless she found the words to tell him of it.

She surprised him by speaking almost immediately of her father.

'I remember that poem he read,' Digger told her, 'at your wedding. "The precarious gift alive in our hands again, the mixed blessing".' He did not say, though she might have guessed it from the quality of his voice, that the lines meant something special to him.

'But fancy you remembering it,' she said.

'Oh, I know the whole thing off by heart,' he told her. He didn't mean to show off, and blushed in case she suspected him of it.

'The whole poem?'

'It's a trick,' he said, sorry he had ever let on. 'It's nothing.'

She told him of the work she did. Her father had published two books in the past five years, one a book of poems – Digger could find the Wedding Ode there, if he looked – the other a collection of essays. In the small world of writers, reviewers, university lecturers and other people who cared for these things, he had begun to be well known, but it was a very small world of course; most people didn't even know it existed. She did his secretarial work for him. That, together with the house and her little boy, was enough to keep her going. The next time they met she would bring copies of the books, now that she knew he was a reader.

Digger said nothing, but did observe her assumption that this meeting was not to be their last. He would not have made the suggestion himself but was pleased that she had. They talked on after that, with no hurry to get everything said. There would be time for the rest of it next time.

He told her about his mother, who had been gone for nearly a year now, but whose end, all her bravery and defiance gone down to despair, still haunted him. About Jenny too. At last about Iris. She told him about the little boy, Greg. Some time, she promised, when Vic was going to the Crossing, she would send him along.

'Now,' she said, 'I'd better go. Next time, I promise, the books.'

She was proud of what her father had done. He liked that and wondered what Vic made of it.

It was odd that in all the things they had touched on, they had never once referred directly to *him*. Not deliberately – it wasn't deliberate on his part, and he thought it wasn't on hers either, but to preserve an area between them that was for them alone. If they had tried to include Vic, he would have swallowed up the whole of what they had to say to one another, especially in the beginning, when he might have seemed the only thing they had in common.

She had a particular look, he thought, at moments when the natural thing to do might have been to say 'Vic and I' or 'we', or at moments when, though she did not directly speak of him, he was clearly in her mind. There would be a little change in her then, as if something had come to the surface in her that was secret, not to be spoken of, yet was on the very tip of her tongue. It was, he felt, the thing he had been wondering about that was most important to her. When it came up he could feel the heat of it, as in his case it had been there (had she felt it?) when he spoke the lines of her father's poem, but especially just afterwards, when he had owned up to his trick of recall, which always evoked what was deepest in him.

The meeting, when he thought back over it, was a joyful one. They repeated it over the years, sometimes weekly. At other times, depending on what else was happening in their lives, whole months would pass before they could arrange it.

They would go for tram rides to Watson's Bay, and walk round the path under the coral trees from Camp Cove to where the sea crashes against South Head. They took ferry trips across to Cremorne and Mosman, shopped, went to the art gallery or the city library, or sat in the gardens and watched the crowds. Each time her father published a new book she brought him one.

He did not mention these meetings to Vic, though there was nothing secret about them. He thought it was Ellie's right to tell. If she did, Vic gave no indication of it.

Iris teased him, but only mildly, about his 'lady friend'. She liked to pretend she was jealous. Was she? he wondered. Just a little? She had no need to be.

8

It seemed to Ellie, when she gave thought to the matter, that things could not have fallen out otherwise than they had; and this was strange, because when she looked back ten years and saw them all as they were then, she could find no sign of what was coming – none at all.

A good deal of this had to do with Lucille.

Lucille had been gone for seven years. Her marriage to Virge had broken up almost as soon as she joined him. She was married now to an older man with children of his own, a company lawyer in Denver, Colorado, where she too had a business, in real estate.

These changes dismayed Ellie. They had been very close over the Virge business, which had appeared then to be a culmination and had turned out, for all its intensity and the significance they had put upon it, to be no more than an episode on the way to something else. She wrote to Lucille twice a month, and the letters that came back were racy and full of news, but she could no longer connect them to the girl she had grown up with.

As little things they had fought like tigers. Ellie recalled occasions when they had struggled and torn at one another, red-faced and sweaty in their singlets and pants, both tearful with rage, pulling at one another's hair and spitting.

Meggsie's way of handling this had been to close the door and leave them to it. When they came out, still hot and angry but also ashamed, she would say: 'All right now, you little devils. Go an' wash your faces and take off those filthy clothes' (they had been rolling on the floor) 'an' I won't tell yer Ma what you've been up to. Hurry on now. I've made some nice cold lemonade.'

It had been hard for Ellie. Lucille was just that much older. She had already established her rights in the world, and made some things in the house so much her own that Ellie could not take them up without appearing, as she so often was, an imitator.

She was a latecomer in people's hearts too, they had to make way for her. Lucille didn't mean to be imposing, she couldn't help it. People noticed her and only later, Ellie felt, saw that she too was there, trailing along behind and wondering what it might be in her that was anything more than a reflection of her more brilliant sister.

What puzzled her was that none of this appeared to make Lucille happy. Lucille was by nature restless, difficult, discontented. *She* was the easy one.

Then, just about the time that Vic came to live with them, they had discovered how close they were, how even the animosity they felt, the way they jockeyed against one another, was a bond. It was the element Vic added that made them see this.

He was a boy, and they were astonished, angered too, to observe how this simple fact impressed everyone – Pa, Ma, even Meggsie, though she didn't *quite* give in to him.

Ellie had been pleased at first to see Lucille displaced, but soon understood that if Lucille was harmed she was too.

They teased him. That was easy. He was an awkward boy once you got past his cockiness. But he was a novelty, too; that's what they couldn't resist. Quite soon new affinities had begun to form. A secret one at first between Lucille and him, and once again Ellie found herself on the sidelines, a watcher of the little drama that had begun to unfold. Vic was at a loss in this, because although he and Lucille were the same age, he was still just a boy. So Vic and Ellie had ganged up on Lucille. Lucille thought she was so marvellous, so grown-up. Ellie still belonged, as he half did, to the world of animal spirits and fun.

But in all that she had missed something after all, some other, more important strand; some perversity or quirk in Lucille that had made her fly in the face of all that appeared to have been laid up for her, perhaps for the very reason that it was so fixed and had come so easily. She got pregnant, married Virge. None of this, Ellie knew, had had *her* in view, yet her life too had been changed by it.

The point on which it turned was that moment in the half-dark of the piano room, during what was to be the last of their games. Everything had been quite clear to her at that moment, and to Vic too. They saw in a flash all that had led up to it and all that would lead away from it. But Lucille, she thought, had seen it before them.

So the household was hers. Ma, all her energies taken up with business, was quite happy to hand it over. There was no question of their moving into a place of their own. It was as if the house already contained the forms their life would need. She and Vic had their separate life in it but the household went on as it had always done.

It was for this reason, there being so little visible change, that it took her so long to understand what he and Ma were doing.

Their style of life did not change. She and Meggsie settled up the weekly accounts, and they remained pretty much what they had always been. They took the same amount of bread and milk, and these things cost the same whether you are worth thousands or just sixpence. You use the same number of towels, sleep in the same sheets.

Vic talked a good deal at first of the sums they were dealing in. The figures doubled and trebled, you could grasp that. It was worth boasting about. It pointed to a personal agency you could identify, to foresight, boldness, imagination. But when the momentum increased, as if subject to some law of its own that was purely mathematical, the personal side of it disappeared. There was a scale to it now that was beyond the capacity of the mind to grasp. Keep adding noughts, and although the thing is still there, and in fact occupies more and more space, there develops in it a kind of vacuum, as if the noughts, the nothings, had predominance. The mind loses all trace of it.

Ellie was amazed by him. So was Pa. They looked on in wonder at these powers he had, which like the enterprise itself appeared to double, treble, then move in progressions that were inhuman, magical; though this was only because their imagination could not contain him any more than they could the figures.

Where did it come from, she wondered, this energy and animation that she experienced as such a physical thing? He was so full of it that you wondered how so much force could limit itself, when needed, to the merely commonplace business of manoeuvring a knife or getting peas on to a fork, or as she saw it, to the moments they shared when she would watch him pull a clean shirt over his head and walk round the room in his socks and suspenders, or sit, as he sometimes did, very quiet and abstracted with a towel in his hand, his hair still wet from the shower, on the edge of their bed.

It pained her when she went out to hear him spoken of in a cruel and dismissive way by people who did not know him as she did, from within. He had enough success, she saw, to have become a figure who aroused hostility, envy, also fear, and often this was in men, and women too, to whom he was no more than a name. They had never laid eyes on him.

When she met this impersonal version of him, even if it was only in people's eyes across a dinner table or theatre foyer, she went cold. The certainty with which they were prepared to judge! All the more when she found it in print.

But if he thought himself misunderstood, as she knew he did, he bore it stoically, hiding his hurt behind a show of arrogance. He hid things. The more she knew him, the more she saw that, and understood how extraordinary had been that glimpse of him in the dark of the piano room, how completely she had grasped then what it was in him that she would spend the rest of her life grappling with.

He read the papers with a look on his face that even she could not fathom. It was pain. She could tell that, if others couldn't. But he found a kind of satisfaction in it too. There was, just at the corner of his mouth, the play of a smile. Perhaps he felt flattered that they were making so much of him.

To her these assaults were merely painful. How could she not feel them personally when she had given so much of herself to him, and taken into her custody so much that was vulnerable in him?

She spoke to no one of all this, but it was there often enough, unspoken, between her and Pa, who, looking at things from his own distance, and from a very different centre of power, was as struck as she was by the proximity of so much energy. Some of the capacity Pa himself had discovered over these last years, or so she thought, came as an attempt to understand Vic's kind of power and balance it.

Pa too had surprised them. Who could have predicted that his peculiar nervousness, which had kept the whole household on edge and been so aimless and self-consuming, would find a focus at last in what she dealt with daily now, the individual words and lines that sat, when she typed them, so squarely on the page and spoke with so much authority and had such weight in the world?

The one thing that alarmed her, and increasingly as the years went by, was Vic's attitude to the boy. Nothing else caused her such heartbreak or led to so many quarrels between them.

She was by nature optimistic. She believed people were reasonable. Given time, things solved themselves; all you had to do was be patient. But in this case things got worse, not better. By the time Greg was twelve a coldness had developed between Vic and the boy, a kind of contempt on both sides that she did not know how to deal with.

He was a good-natured boy, full of affection and eager to please, perhaps too much so; but he could not please his father, and after a time, out of disappointment, did not want to, or pretended he didn't.

As for Vic, everything the boy did unsettled or irritated him, especially as he grew out of childishness and became a young man.

The more she argued with him, the more unreasonable Vic grew, and at last she gave up. She had begun to fear the things that were said between them. So long as they were unspoken they had no force. Once they got into the world, and could be gone back to and brooded over, they were real.

'Vic,' she told him wearily, 'they're all like this, all these *young* people. He's no different from the rest.' She named Greg's friends, some of whom were the sons and daughters of men Vic knew and thought well of. 'What does it matter how he wears his hair?'

But he clamped his mouth shut and would not answer. He was angry with her, she knew, because she took the boy's part.

'I would have hoped,' he said at last, like a man repeating something he had already prepared, 'that a son of mine would think for himself, not just go along with what others do.'

'Oh,' she said, but gently, 'a son of yours.'

'He's got no character. No character, no interests, no ambitions. What else can I think?'

It was part of the vision he had of the hardness of things, based on his own life and of the qualities you needed not to go under. She could have no idea how afraid he was of every sort of weakness, how panicky he felt, and when he looked at his son, the vulnerable region that opened in him.

Ellie did know this, and it scared her. But she saw something else, too: that things weren't hard any more, they were easy, and he was one of the men who had made them so. Young people had time now to play. That wasn't a crime, was it?

The issues they fought over were small ones, the length of the boy's hair, the clothes he wore: Ellie thought they were small. But it infuriated Vic to see his son, and all these worthless kids he ran around with, dressed in cast-offs. Old waistcoats and shirts without collars that his father might have worn. Grimy old-fashioned suits like the ones they had been given after the war, still with the sweat stains on them (they did not care about that), and all over both lapels the badges of a war they thought they were waging, gaudy passwords and proclamations of revolt. Sweat-stained felt Akubras (except for these clowns only Digger wore a hat these days), greasy ties and evening scarves, all picked up at street markets or at Tempe Tip, or off the racks of the St Vincent de Paul; the fashionable fancy dress of a misery they knew nothing about, and did not care about either, for all their mouthing of slogans and the rag-tag principles of a revolution they would never have to mount.

He thought bitterly of a wet day when he was maybe nine years old and was taken with a gang of other children to a room at the School of Arts. They were the poorest kids of the district, guaranteed so by the headmaster; though you could have seen it for yourself from the reach-me-down clothes they wore, the sweaters that had to be pushed up at the elbows, the trousers drawn in six inches with a bit of string, the little girls' frocks that came down past their knees.

Herded into the dingy hall, they were presented with a row of smiling, sympathetic ladies and a pile of clothes that had been tipped out of bags onto the floor.

Red-faced and ashamed, they were let loose among them like rag pickers. He had snatched up the first thing he saw, eager to do what they wanted, choose something and get away, and had stuffed what he got, without even looking to see how good it was, down the back of a seat on one of the bus shelters along the shore. The rough wool of it still prickled and rubbed his flesh, as if he had worn it next to his skin for years.

Rags, cast-offs, the stink of other people's sweat – all that was horrible to him. It made his flesh itch. Because for him, and for so many others too, it had been necessity. But to these kids it was just play-acting, in uniforms you could change the moment you were bored with them. Poverty to them was just another rag you could put on, if you were rich enough, to make yourself interesting, or different, or to see how it suited you.

Greg lately had taken to going about without shoes; in a suit with a felt hat, and no shoes. He choked on that. He thought of the lines of men he had seen falling in in the drizzle, to whom the lack of a pair of boots up there had meant death. He was not thinking of himself. He did not mean to refer back to his own suffering, though he felt it again, and with a sense of injustice and anger and weak self-pity that sickened him, but of what others had been through.

It would have shamed him to speak of these things. That a man, even a boy, should not know them already, was incomprehensible to him.

When he and Greg argued there was no common ground between them. Ellie felt helpless. What the boy shouted in his own defence was useless, she knew that and felt sorry for him, and Vic set his jaw and would not speak.

9

Meggsie, who was past seventy, sat down in a chair one day at her kitchen table and found she could not get up. Her legs had gone.

She was very shocked, and frightened too, but did not cry out. She thought of doing so, but it seemed so foolish that when her mouth opened she promptly clamped it shut again and sat frowning, feeling a kind of darkness come over her. She had never felt anything like it. She had her moods, but this one came from outside her, like weather, leaving the windows full of clear sunshine but darkening her mind. She felt weak and increasingly helpless and afraid, but could not bring herself to break the habits of a lifetime and shout. When they found her at last it was because of the smell of burning.

All the time she had sat there a custard had been boiling over on the stove, and she had not noticed it. The mess was awful. She kept apologising for it as they lifted her, and for the trouble she was giving them, and it was this more than anything else that upset Pa. She was the sort of woman, Meggsie, who never apologised.

Her daughters were scattered. One lived outside Rockhampton up in Queensland, another out west. The third, Vera-me-youngest as Meggsie called her, and as she had always been known to them, was married to a lawyer on the North Shore. They phoned her now, and two hours later she drove up in a Mazda.

Ma had known her as a girl and had found her very clever and offensive in those days. She was now a good-looking woman in her fifties, very tastefully dressed. Ma, feeling embarrassed at her own shabbiness, still thought of her as Vera-me-youngest, but she introduced herself as Mrs Moreton.

She was cold at first. For several years now she had wanted Meggsie to give up working and come and live with her. Meggsie was torn but had decided she was too well settled to leave the Warrenders. Mrs Moreton believed they had influenced her, and she looked about now for something that would allow her to feel superior.

She found it at last.

The cars in the drive – there were three of them – were what you might have expected. But the house! The furniture, for example. She knew what these people were worth – who didn't? – but there was no decent furniture in the place, not a thing you could look at. No antiques. Shoddy Thirties veneer, old-fashioned and ugly. They had made no improvements. She remembered coming here once a week, when she was sixteen or seventeen, to collect her pocket money and to be given a box of handkerchiefs or a pair of gloves by Mrs Warrender when her birthday came round. In those days she had thought the place unattainably grand. She was angry with herself for having been so naive. Her own house was a dozen times more impressive.

They left her alone with Meggsie and did not hear what was said.

She wanted Meggsie to go to hospital. Meggsie refused. She was happy where she was: they had a night nurse for her. Mrs Moreton was put out. She was grateful for what they were doing but felt snubbed. 'Don't be silly,' Meggsie told her.

She rang daily after that but did not come again till the end.

She was sick for nine weeks. They had the night nurse. Otherwise it was Ma and Ellie who looked after her and put up with her complaints that everything they did was done badly, that the place was going to ruin, that the new girl they had got hold of might be a dab hand at *foreign* cooking but didn't know the first thing about plain food.

In the afternoon while Ellie rested Pa would drop in for an hour or two, to tease her, taste her medicines and tell her jokes. 'Stop it,' she would yell, 'you're killing me.' Vic too liked to sit with her.

He would go out in the early morning in his dressing-gown, send the nurse to make tea, and when she came back, wave her off. Ellie would find her asleep under a reading lamp in the front room.

In these hours he did all the things the nurse might have done. 'Vic,' Ellie told him, 'you don't have to do these things. That's why we've got the nurse.' She meant to spare him something she thought men shied away from, the intimate business that has to do with bodies. 'Don't worry,' he told her, 'I don't mind. It gives us a chance, you know, to talk a bit.'

'Did you know,' he said one day, 'that Meggsie was a twin? Can you imagine it, *two* Meggsies? The other one died of the Spanish flu. She grew up in Chillagoe, did you know that? When it had a population of 7,000. It's a ghost town now.'

He would be half-asleep on these occasions, very tender and talking half to himself. What he was talking about, she knew, was the mystery of other people's lives, how little we know of one another; lying very close to her, just on the edge of sleep, and almost ready, she thought, because of the softness of his mood, to put into words at last the facts and details of his own life, all that part of it that was still secret in him.

One night Meggsie called to him where he sat half-dozing against the wall.

'Vic, love, are you there? I want to give you something – a present.' She sometimes wandered at this hour, but she did not seem to be wandering now. 'Go to the bottom drawer of me dressing table.'

He got up and went to the cedar chest of drawers where her photographs sat in their celluloid frames. One was of the girls when they were little, the other a composite of half a dozen faded snapshots, her husband Len out west somewhere with a lot of other fellows, all standing in a row in hats.

The drawer was stiff. He had to get down on his knees to shift it. It jerked, came open, and in the half-light from the hallway he saw with a little shock that it was full of leaves. Was he dreaming?

'Take one,' she said behind him.

He put his hand into the drawer in a gingerly way, afraid for some reason of snails, and rustled among the dry leaves. But no, it wasn't leaves. It was lottery tickets, hundreds of them, thousands – every fifth share she had bought, regularly on her afternoon off, from Mr McCann the local newsagent, over more than forty years. He felt among them.

But they were leaves. He had taken them for lottery tickets only in the way one's mind works in dreams, though whether it was his dream or hers he could not tell. It was just about the time that ballots were being drawn to send young men up to Vietnam. Greg was eighteen, and he thought it might be Greg's name he was about to draw. Or was it his own? Again? Could they ask you to go again?

'What are you doing?' she demanded. 'Have you got one?'

He took one of the tickets and went to the bed and showed it to her.

'No,' she said, without even looking at it. 'That's not the one.'

He brought her another.

'No.' She was quite short with him, as if he were being deliberately stupid. He felt like a very young child who could not see the answer to some simple problem in arithmetic.

'Meggsie –' he began.

'Go on,' she told him, 'you're wasting time.'

He dipped again.

'Yes, that's it,' she said with a sigh. 'Good boy! You were always a good boy really.' She smiled. 'Now, don't show it to anyone, eh? Don't tell, or you'll lose your luck. Don't even show it to *me*. Put it in your wallet.'

He obeyed. He put the ticket, which had after all never won anything the first time around, in his wallet.

'No,' she said, catching the feeling of despair that had come over him, 'don't worry. It's a good one. I wouldn't give you anything that wasn't lucky, love, you know that. Don't you know that after all this time? Trust me.'

He did not remember it had happened till the next day when he was in the office and in conference. He broke off for a moment to check his wallet, and there was the ticket.

He told Ellie about it, but wondered later if he had made the point clear, since what it had to do with was what he had *felt*; the odd sensation, when he put his hand into the drawer, that he was moving it among dried leaves, going back years, each with its number. Greg's ballot too had been part of it.

With Meggsie's death a prop went from the house. They all felt it and were surprised how her various forms of tyranny, which they had been inclined to laugh over, had determined the way they lived. Impossible to modernise the kitchen – that was Meggsie's province. Part of her power lay in the fact that only she could manage its many inconveniences. Impossible to suggest that nobody these days ate puddings, a different one each night.

But when she was gone and they were free to make all the changes they wanted, they were at a loss where to begin. For the first time Vic talked seriously to Ma of selling the house and the adjoining factory site and moving. He did it, Ma thought, not because it was a necessary move, or one that any of them wanted, but for reasons of his own that for all their closeness she could not ask about.

For a long time now he had felt a kind of emptiness in him that had to do, he thought, with the way he had closed his heart in the last days before his mother's death, had shut out so completely all the pain and loss he felt that afterwards there was nothing to go back to. Now, in grieving for Meggsie he grieved at last for his mother, in the kind of linking over and back (he was thinking of the way his mother hemmed a skirt) that made up the odd, cross-hatched line he was following.

But there was something else as well. For a time, between eighteen and twenty-one, death had been the closest of all realities to him, a daily thing, more common in that place than the sound of a woman's voice, or a bath running, or a clean shirt. He had thought he would never get used to any other condition of life; that those ordinary things – clean shirts, hot baths, a woman's hand – would go on being so miraculous as to be barely graspable, and only the proximity of death quite real.

The whole of his energy at that time had been engaged in pushing it off; in clinging to his own body and dragging the little bit of life in it from one day to the next. It was huge, that, but also simple. Pure, too. The effort was so pure. You knew what the other was because from time to time, when it was necessary, you held a man whose death was near so close against your ribs that his heart was just a paper thinness from your own, and the beating of it was like your own heart flopping and failing.

For years now no death had come close enough to touch him. Now Meggsie's did, and after so long, his mother's death too. (He was not ready yet to think of his father.) Most of all, he began once again to live with his own, but it seemed mysterious to him now because he was surrounded by so much that obscured even the possibility of it, and because when it came to him here it would, given the odds, be of a kind he had not yet faced, a natural one.

10

For more than twenty years Digger's visits to town had followed the same pattern. Thursday was the day, because in the early years it had been Iris's day off. Later, when the cake shop closed and she retired, they stuck to Thursdays out of habit. Digger went up on an early train, spent the night, and came back on the milk train Friday morning.

If it was one of the days when he was to meet Ellie he would not go to Bondi Junction till after lunch. Otherwise, after a bit of shopping on his own, he went immediately. They would take a picnic to Cooper Park, or eat quietly at home, and in the afternoon he would read a bit or do whatever jobs needed doing. Now that the boys were gone there was always some little thing to be set right. In the evening they took in a show, or went round and had tea at Ewen's or Jack's, who were married now with families of their own.

He got on well with the wives. There had never been any embarrassment about his standing among them. The children called Iris Grannie and Digger was 'Grannie's friend'. They called him Digger because their fathers did – he had baulked at 'Uncle'.

They were freer with him than with any uncle. Their mothers had to step in and prevent them, the moment he appeared, from climbing all over him like some sort of natural phenomenon, an especially co-operative tree or rock. He was fond of children. He showed them old-fashioned tricks even their fathers did not know, with balls made of silver paper out of cigarette packets, that if weighted at one end could be made to dance, and how to weave pyjama-cords on cotton reels. He brought them wooden toys he had made and told them stories, serious ones, that left them struck but which for some reason they could not get enough of. Thursdays he was a family man. He spent a lot of his time during the week thinking up tricks to amuse 'the kids'.

The whole tenor of his life on that one day of the week was different, and had been for so long, given the little changes that had taken place in it, that when he found himself at Central Station on a

Monday morning, same hour but a different day of the week, he felt disorientated.

It wasn't simply that his own routine had been broken. The whole feel of the place was different. The Monday morning crowds wore different faces. The streets had a different pace. It felt less like another day of the week than another city.

He had come up for the funeral of the poet, Hugh Warrender. He was doing it out of affection for Ellie, but also out of respect for a man he had spoken to only once, and then in an unsatisfactory way, but whom he felt he had got to know over the years, and grown close to. Iris went with him.

It was an odd gathering. There were groups of older people who Digger guessed would be friends of the family or business acquaintances of Vic's; but there were others whose presence was so unlikely that he thought they must have mistaken the time and come to the wrong ceremony. A lot of the men were in jeans and high-collared Indian shirts, and some wore washed-out combat jackets with Chairman Mao caps. Most of the girls too wore jeans, but some were got up in full-length cotton like Indian women and had children with them in the same outlandish garb. There was a flock of schoolgirls as well, all in gingham and straw hats.

The presence of so many hippies, he thought, was unfortunate. It did not occur to him till later, when he saw how sober and attentive they were, that some of these people might have the same sort of distant but personal relation to Hugh Warrender that he did and had come in the same spirit. He saw them differently then.

It was February, and hot. Outside in the sunken rose garden where they had milled about waiting, the birds were singing, in a regular, repeatable way but at odd intervals just whenever they pleased, breaking in on the organ music. They were a distraction. Very argumentative and bold they sounded, getting on with their noisy lives while people settled and subdued themselves.

The order of things was impressive. Ellie read one of her father's poems, quite a short one that was unfamiliar to Digger though he knew all the books. If it spoke of death, and he was by no means certain of that, it did so in a light-hearted way, closer to the hubbub the birds were creating than to the solemn music. There was an image of night-smelling jasmine – the flower itself out of sight somewhere, its invisible presence in the room, and of a household, also unseen, all busy voices. One word was repeated and Digger was moved by it. The word was 'returns'.

When the poem was over some overtones of it, of its music, lingered in him, and in the others too, he thought. Iris very lightly touched his hand as on that other occasion, and once again what Mr Warrender had to say drew them together.

There was no sadness in it, none at all. Quite the opposite really. It spoke of presence and completeness, of 'returns'. Much later, Digger would think of the poem and be pleased that he and Iris had heard it together. It would comfort him for his loss. But at the moment it was his mother he was thinking of. It struck him with panic, that image of her sitting in a broken chair out in the yard, with behind her the house and its contents, all she had clung to and held against such odds, turned to ashes in her head.

He had spent so many hours in the consideration of it because the law she had lived by was so like his own. What he was left wondering was how, when the time came, he might let go of things without believing, as she had, that he was not only losing them but had never in any real sense had them.

Mr Warrender's grandsons, Greg and an older boy, Alex, who had come across with his mother from America, were to read the lessons; and strangely enough, it was precisely what Digger had been turning over in his head that Greg now spoke of.

It was many years since Digger had seen him. He had been just a lad then, a neat little fellow in a duffle coat and new boots. He was rather gangling now (he had heard something of him from Ellie, from Vic too once or twice), and was so much, Digger thought, what Vic had been when he first knew him that he decided the differences he saw must have to do with his eyesight. He forked his glasses out of his right-hand breast pocket as the boy read, but saw, when he set them on his nose, that the lack of focus he had been aware of was in the boy himself.

He was less compact than Vic had been. But it wasn't that. What he lacked, and it made all the difference, was cockiness. It brought back to Digger, and vividly, considering the years, just what he had felt about Vic in those early days, his intense antipathy – and what had happened to *that*?

'In the day when the keepers of the house shall tremble,' he read, 'and the strong men bow themselves, and the grinders cease because they are too few, and those that look out of the windows be darkened

. . . Also when they shall be afraid of that which is on high, and fears shall be in the way, and the almond tree shall flourish, and the grasshoppers shall be a burden, and desire shall fail: because man goeth to his long home and the mourners go about the streets . . .'

From his place in the front row Vic looked up. The boy did not read confidently. He stumbled in places and seemed unsure of how the words were connected. Vic's face in profile, as Digger saw it, wore a concerned look, either because he was anxious for the boy on this public occasion, as Ellie was too – Digger could see that – or because of something in the words themselves.

Iris had remarked earlier when they arrived how little changed he was. It was more than twenty years since she had seen him. Digger was surprised. When he turned up at the Crossing it was his immediate mood that Digger looked out for – little signs he had learned to recognise that meant their time together would go easily, others which, however much he disguised them, indicated the opposite. Till Iris mentioned it, he had never considered him in the light of change.

'They go fast,' Iris thought, 'when they do go. That sort.' Digger was of the other kind. He was spare and leathery, and under the hat was very nearly bald. She no longer felt any embarrassment when they were out together. He might have been sixty as she was. (Sixty-seven, in fact.)

The other boy, who spoke with an American accent, was *too* confident, Digger thought. He read as at a performance. It jarred.

There was a third speaker, a man from the university who had written on Hugh Warrender and came here, as a good many of the mourners did, as a sharer in his *public* life, though public, as he pointed out, was the wrong word for something which, in the case of each one of them, and in the poet's case too, was so hidden that if one was to be true to the spirit of it, it could be referred to only in terms that were tentative and indirect.

He was speaking of poetry itself, of the hidden part it played in their lives, especially here in Australia, though it was common enough – that was the whole point of it – and of their embarrassment when it had, as now, to be brought into the light. How it spoke up, not always in the plainest terms, since that wasn't always possible, but in precise ones just the same, for what is deeply felt and might otherwise go unrecorded: all those unique and repeatable events, the little sacraments of daily existence, movements of the heart and intimations of the close but inexpressible grandeur and terror of things, that is our *other* history, the one that goes on, in a quiet way, under the noise and chatter of events and is the major part of what happens each day in the life of the planet, and has been from the very beginning. To find words for *that*; to make glow with significance what is usually unseen, and unspoken too – that, when it occurs, is what binds us all, since it speaks immediately out of the centre of each one of us; giving shape to what we too have experienced and did not till then have words for, though as soon as they are spoken we know them as our own.

This speech made an impression on Digger. That 'other history' meant something to him. When they stepped outside into the strong sunlight, which was thick with bees, he saw a few people go up to the young man who had said so much, shake hands and congratulate him; he looked embarrassed but also pleased with himself.

Digger did not make the mistake this time of approaching him. He settled for the words themselves. They had struck a chord in him, and touched, he felt, on the very thing he had been thinking of earlier: what it is that cannot be held on to but nonetheless is not lost.

11

It was the night of Pa's funeral and still hot. Big storm clouds were building over the flat land towards Hen and Chicken Bay and nervous shudders of lightning touched the edges of them. Vic came away from the table feeling displeased with everyone, and with himself too.

Pa's death, which had come without warning, had hit him hard, and Lucille's arrival with Alex, all adding to the adjustments and changes that had to be made in the household, had made these last days painful to him.

The two boys, despite what had happened, insisted on arguing through every meal, but in a way that was inappropriate and put them all on edge.

Greg's arguments, as even Ellie had to admit, were erratic and one-sided. He was idealistic, full of youthful passion and the assurance of being always in the right, but everything he had to say was second-hand, and for all its predictability was so garbled and incoherent as to be very nearly incomprehensible.

The other one, Alex, who was twenty-four and already a graduate of Harvard, was a stiff fellow, equally one-eyed and insistent, but he hid it with an assumption of coolness that outraged Greg and made him more vehement than ever.

Greg had had great hopes of this cousin of his. An American! In his naive and open-hearted way he had been eager to be impressed and to hear at first-hand all that was happening at the centre of things.

He was bitterly disappointed. He hid it at first; Alex was a guest. Then, when he saw that he was being patronised, he adopted an air of open hostility, but in such a hurt and inarticulate and childish way that Vic found it hard to witness. Tonight he gave Ellie a helpless look and got away. He needed to distance himself.

He went first to sit for a time with Ma, who had gone straight up after the funeral to lie down. She too found these mealtimes exasperating.

He sat beside her bed in the darkened room and they talked a little.

What they talked of was an occasion, years back, when Pa had played a practical joke, a particularly silly one, on a dinner guest, a very pompous fellow who was in line to be a judge. Ma began to laugh, then he did, and they both stopped, not in a guilty way, but thinking, if any stranger heard them, how difficult it would be to explain. When he left her and went downstairs he did something he would not have dreamed of doing a week before. He went to Pa's study. Seating himself at the old-fashioned desk, which was carved in Renaissance style, he sat for a time in the dark watching the lightning flicker, then put his hand out and lit a lamp.

The sense of irritation he had felt at the table was still with him. It was associated somehow with the odd shuddery flashes of the lightning. It made him tense and with no hope of release.

It was the hostility between the two young men he focused on, their foolish tearing this way and that of a dead cat, but he was keeping it in the foreground, he knew, because there was something else that disturbed him more, and it was this he needed to think about.

Lucille at forty-six was not at all the girl who had left them more than twenty years ago. He would hardly have known her. She was very brisk and businesslike, and preoccupied, as was only to be expected, with the family she had left back in the States. She took an interest in all there was to catch up on, but what she saw here fell short, he guessed, of some memory she had kept – of the place, of them – and when he looked at things through her eyes he saw it too.

He had thought what he had done – all he had achieved – was so large a thing. Yet what he was chiefly aware of when they sat down to the table together was how *little* had happened, and how little, in the end, was changed. Pa was gone. They were older. There were these two boys now, slugging away at one another. But the only difference, he felt, was that something he had hung on to, a sense of sweet disillusionment that had to do with Lucille and all he had felt for her, was no longer sweet – and not bitter either – but had dulled and was very nearly gone.

He had loved his disillusionment. It gave him such a sense of his own youth. He saw its going now as the beginning, the first approach, of middle age.

And Pa?

How long was it since they had spoken in a way that touched what was most important to them? They were always close. There was no lack of warmth between them. But they had had little to say to one another in these last years that was new. This shocked him, and all the more because suddenly, now that he was gone, it seemed to Vic that everything he knew about Pa was a puzzle to him. From the moment of their first meeting – and before that, too, the days when his father had been Pa's batman and exacted the promise – everything, Pa's playfulness, his glooms, the life he had had in his head, the poems he had written, was a mystery to him. But what really disturbed him was what he had seen at the funeral today: that there were people who had never even met Pa, who knew him better perhaps than he did. He had the panicky sense of having missed the man entirely, but the source of his panic was the ghostly image this gave him of himself.

'What does it mean to *be*,' he thought, 'except *to be known*?'

He had been delighted, as they all were, by Pa's success, but had never got round to the actual books. He saw now that he ought to have done. He had missed something Pa had to say that others had attended to and he had not, something too that Pa might have meant him to hear. He reached out now and drew the four volumes from the shelf. Opening one, the last as it happened, he set himself to go through it from cover to cover. He read for nearly an hour.

It was like a hard lesson at school. He had forgotten what it was to go over and over something and find that it would not go into your head, because there was some resistance in it, or in you, that would not give.

He had come up against this unpleasant fact before, and each time had suppressed it. Looking now at what Pa had got down, he came upon things that were just beyond his apprehension, eluding him at the very moment of his reaching out for them; but they were things, and he knew this too, that were not strange to him. That was the unpleasant part. They did not belong to some other world at all but to the one he was in, and still he could not grasp them.

What he felt in a quite physical way was the spinning of the earth under him at the very moment when he could also say to himself: 'But the room is still.' And then: 'If the world is like this and I have never properly got hold of it, what *have* I got hold of?'

He sat with the book open on the desk but had stopped reading. What the poems, which he had only vaguely understood, had set off in him was going on now of its own accord.

It is a sobering thing, even when you are a father yourself and have some force in the world, to find, in the childish part of yourself that goes on existing despite the years, that there is no hand you can reach out for.

Almost as soon as his parents died Pa had appeared. Since then it was Pa, for all his weakness, who had stood between him and the knowledge that he was alone in the world. For a time, when he was twenty, that knowledge had been forced on him, but it was premature, it did not last. As soon as he got back it lapsed in him, and once again he had moved back under Pa's protection, relegating to him the father's role, and was shielded. Now, for the first time, he felt orphaned.

When Ellie saw a slit of light under the door she had the odd feeling that what she would see, when she opened it, was Pa. So she approached it very quietly, turned the knob, and paused, afraid to startle herself.

He did not see her for a moment. He was seated with a pool of lamplight on the desk before him, his face half-dark. All round the shelves was the flicker of far-off lightning. He did not look up; he was not aware of her. In the moment before he turned, all that she knew of him was confirmed.

12

It was from Ellie that Digger heard of the break with Greg. Vic would not have told him. In the early days he had been eager enough to talk about the boy. He always had news to tell of what a promising little fellow he was, shy, a bit clinging maybe – that was having so many women in the house – but full of questions and his own odd bright little opinions on the world. Vic was young himself in those days. His pride in the boy ran away with him. He would pull himself up, suddenly embarrassed, and laugh it off. But things changed, and after a time he spoke of the boy only with bitterness. In these last years he had barely mentioned him. Digger, hearing of this latest, this last business, did not know what to say. Ellie did not complain but he saw the grief it caused her.

'He does these things to himself. Why? Why *is* that? The very thing he doesn't want to happen he does himself. It's as if he wanted to save himself, you know, from having it done to him. Is that it? You know him, Digger – is that what it is? So he does it himself. "I did it" – that's what he's saying to himself – "it wasn't just done to me." Then he grits his teeth in that terrible way he's got. "Life is *like* this. We have to put up with it. That's what character is for." And he's brought it all on *himself*.'

They were having a cup of tea together in a timbered booth in a quiet little place in an arcade. It was, Digger thought, one of the few occasions when their talk together was openly of Vic, though a lot of what they had to say to one another had him in mind or as a shadow on the sidelines. It was painful, this.

'You know him, Digger – you tell *me*,' she said. She seemed desperate.

'I don't know him,' Digger found himself saying, and he was sorry the moment after. It was true, it was what he felt at the moment, but it seemed like a betrayal. He saw from her look how surprised she was. He was surprised himself.

*

Vic could not have told Digger of the scene with Greg because there was nothing to tell. It was a quarrel like any other.

Vic blamed Greg for the form their quarrels took. All he could do each time was mouth the slogans he had picked up from his friends, no word of it was personal or his own, and all Vic could say in reaction, he felt, was determined by this, and was equally impersonal and beside the point.

They had never found any way of addressing one another in which the truth could be stated or their real feelings shown. So they fell back each time on what they had said before. Greg shouted his contempt for their whole way of life, all the things they stood for, which he rejected utterly and would have nothing to do with. Vic threw all this back at him, and he too shouted, only half believing in what came out. He knew too well the slipperiness of such terms as self-respect and discipline to use them as crudely as he did, but he did use them that way. He talked of the boy's lack of character, his willingness to live off what he claimed to despise, the contempt even his own friends had for his weak-willed parroting of their every opinion and the way he ran after them, in everything he did imitating this or that one of them, with no will or character of his own. The anger in all this was real, but the arguments were the same ones they had been over on other occasions. There was no reason, no apparent reason, why this should be the last.

What Greg had wanted to say was something quite different, but he could not bring himself, out of perversity, out of the sort of pride too that his father did not credit him with, to put it into words. It would only have increased his father's scorn for him, he thought, if he had asked for love.

Vic too had wanted to say something quite different. What he wanted to speak of were the things in his life that when he stopped and looked at them created panic in him.

To have put this into words might have been a relief, but it would have exposed him, and he believed that in his son's eyes he ought not to appear weak.

Then, too, if he put his fear into words he might, in some magical way, give it a place in the world, where it would grow, increase its power and work against him. The desire to keep it inside, where he alone knew what it was and could control it, was enough to keep him silent, even at the risk, as he saw now, of his losing control of the very thing that lay at the heart of his panic—his vulnerability through Greg.

So nothing new was said. They went over the same accusations and counter-accusations they always used and at the end of it nothing had been said. Only this time Greg took him at his word, or decided out of pride to stick to his own. He quit the house.

One Thursday when Iris was in the front room ironing, with the television on 'just for company', there was a ring at the door. It was after nine, too late for neighbours to be calling.

Digger, reading in the sleep-out, looked up with his glasses on his nose. He saw Iris step out into the hallway; then a moment later she was at the entrance to the sleep-out with Vic. Her eyebrows were raised. It was a look he knew well.

Digger too was surprised. He thought there must be some sort of trouble. But Vic had no explanation to offer. He appeared to be in high spirits, he was a little drunk in fact, and had three bottles of Cooper's Ale with him. When Iris took them, and with another little look in Digger's direction went off to fetch glasses, he stepped into the sleep-out as if dropping in on them like this were the most natural thing in the world. Digger found it took a little getting used to.

He had forgotten till now that when Vic first appeared at the Crossing, and Jenny had come up and pointed to him mooching about there under the she-oaks, he had felt the same little sense of intrusion.

It had faded in time. Vic had come to be as much a part of his life at the Crossing as anything else. Only now did the echo of it come back. Why, after all this time, had he taken it upon himself to break in on them?

But if Vic recognised a coolness on Digger's part he gave no sign of it. When Iris, pleading the excuse of her ironing, left them to it, believing there must be something special he had come for, he cast a glance around the sleep-out and said, 'This is nice. All these books yours?'

'No,' Digger said, and folded his glasses, 'not all of 'em.' And then, because he still felt irritated, he said, 'Most of them were Mac's.'

Was it the first time Mac's name had come up between them? Digger could not be certain. Other names came up from time to time. It would have been unusual if they had avoided that one. But they had, of course.

There was a little beat of silence. Outside in the loquat tree Digger could hear a shuffling. Possums. They had possums that sometimes came right into the house and would take a bite out of some piece of fruit in the bowl on the kitchen table, leaving paw marks all over the floor.

Digger was sorry now that he had said anything. He had done it in a moment of spite. He watched Vic take a book from the shelf, open it and look at the flyleaf as if he needed to see the name there: as proof. Or perhaps it was to feel another twist of the knife. But it wasn't Mac's name he would find. Hardly one of these books had Mac's name in it. Other names, yes, and Digger, being Digger, could have reeled off each one of them. *The Nigger of the 'Narcissus'*, for instance, which was the book he happened to be re-reading, had belonged to Janet Dawkins, Year Twelve, at Randwick Girls' High School in 1936. Mac had picked it up at Tyrrell's. He could have gone on to list dozens, even hundreds, more.

What Vic had in his hand was a tooled leather edition of Tennyson. The flyleaf, Digger knew, would read:

To Mr John Darnell
from
B. J. Checkley
10th May, 1889

all in sepia copperplate, and underneath it:

> Kind hearts are more than Coronets
> And simple faith than Norman blood.

He watched Vic read it in a sober way, then close the book and put it back.

He looked around the room, frowning a little. Perhaps he felt the oppressiveness of so many volumes set so close on the shelves, or was wondering how many he would have to open before he came to one (he might find one, an old school algebra maybe) with I. R. McAlister in it.

Outside in the front room, he settled on the arm of a lounge chair, one leg thrown easily across the other, a little subdued at first but quickly recovering his spirits. Iris turned off the television, and offered to put her ironing aside as well, but he insisted he didn't mind, in fact he liked it. So with some embarrassment, since she scarcely knew him, she went on damping down pillowslips, handkerchiefs, an apron, one of Digger's shirts, and the smell of heat and damp filled the room.

She was wary of him, he was out to charm her, and she kept shooting little sideways glances at Digger to see if he had noticed it. But she relaxed at last and began to enjoy herself. He was full of light notes and odd, old-fashioned sayings that surprised her. Nothing she knew of him from Digger had suggested this. Digger himself was surprised. There was no sign now of that moment on the sleep-out, or of any of that side of him; and Digger, who had little to say, went even quieter.

What he was doing, Digger thought, was restoring a kind of order in himself, making up for that little reversal out there, when for a moment his image of himself had been disturbed, by winning her approval.

Digger had never seen him playing up to a woman before. It was new to him, the way he paraded his repertoire of charms; this concentration of energy, of interest in him, that made a woman aware of herself. He was all attention, you could feel it. Digger, who knew him so well, was irritated that Iris should be so easily taken in.

She finished her ironing. He leapt up and helped her fold the board. What he wanted her to do now was play.

Lately she found playing difficult. She had arthritis, all the joints of her fingers were swollen; but she sat down, and it was ages, Digger thought, since he had seen her play so easily or with so much heart.

She played Schubert, a great favourite of Digger's, and once or twice as played she looked aside at him and smiled; but she was playing, he saw, for Vic, and once again he felt a pang of jealousy. Which was foolish, he knew, but he couldn't help it.

Vic sat very silent with his head bowed, and Digger for some reason thought again of Mac, and again of how foolish it was of him to feel hurt, or to feel anything in fact but what the music spoke of – union and peace. Remote, mysterious, yet so full of quiet optimism, it took you right to the heart of things.

'Honestly, Digger,' Iris said later, when she had got out of him what it was that had kept him so quiet. She was half smiling to herself. It did not displease her that he could be jealous. 'All that palaver he goes on with – it doesn't mean anything. Don't you know that? He's a ladies' man. Show him a woman and he can't help flirting with her. Even an old dame like me. There's no harm in it.'

Digger was silent. 'Well, it got my goat,' he said at last, 'him just inviting himself like that. He did it on his own account. I didn't have anything to do with it.'

He waited. He was waiting for some comment from her of what she had felt or seen that would explain it, since he could not; but she lay with her face turned away and did not speak.

Her hair, which had been so rich when he first knew her, was thinning, not quite grey, and he had a particular affection for the freckling of her brow, and the area just below the line of her hair where the skin was almost transparent and the veins showed. He put his fingertips to them, and she turned her head and smiled. It worried her, he knew, that she was no longer beautiful. *She* thought she wasn't.

'He didn't come because he had anything to say, you know. Why do you reckon he *did* come?'

She looked at him. 'Because he was lonely,' she said after a moment. 'He had nowhere to go.' Digger stared. 'Maybe,' she said lightly, 'he fell out with his girlfriend.' She said it carelessly. She saw immediately that she should not have.

'What? What girlfriend?'

'Oh – they say he's on with Susie Stone.'

'Who does?'

'Oh – you know, the newspapers.'

He lay still. He was taking it in.

'Who's Susie Stone?' he said at last. He was amazed by all this, but most of all by her. How did she know these things? It astonished him at times the things that went on in the world that other people took for granted and he knew nothing of. He was surprised, too, how much she accepted now that would once have shocked her. For three years before they got round to marrying, Ewen and his wife Jane had lived together – they even had a little boy. He had been a page at their wedding.

'Susie Stone's a designer,' she told him. 'Sportswear. She's pretty well known – to *young* people.'

'Do you think Ellie knows?' he asked.

'I expect so, yes. I don't suppose she's the first. It's what I said. You can see it right off. Any *woman* could.'

He turned up on odd Thursdays after that, and Digger saw him more often at Bondi Junction in the end than at Keen's Crossing. He began to bring Iris little gifts, as he had Jenny, but Iris, who had none of Jenny's suspicion of him, took the gesture as it was intended and made a fuss over his presents and over him too. He was delighted. The things he gave her he had thought about. You could see that.

Digger never did get used to having him there, but he accepted at last that the flirtations he practised were harmless, at least where Iris was concerned, and that his real reason for coming was the one she had seen on that first occasion: there were times when he had nowhere else to go.

13

Digger was dizzied by the world. He could never, he felt, see it steady enough or at a sufficient distance to comprehend what it was, let alone to act on it. This was a disadvantage; but he had long since come to the conclusion that his perplexity about life, which did not prevent him from living it, was essential to him.

A nailhead. That was clear enough. Round, flanged, with ridges that allowed the hammerhead a grip. The weight of the hammer, too. Driving a nail in, feeling the point go through the soft grain to bite on the last two blows – that was the only action he knew that was simple. Everything else, the moment you really looked at it, developed complications.

Even the least event had lines, all tangled, going back into the past, and beyond that into the *unknown* past, and other lines leading out, also tangled, into the future. Every moment was dense with causes, possibilities, consequences; too many, even in the simplest case, to grasp. Every moment was dense too with lives, all crossing and interconnecting or exerting pressure on one another, and not just human lives either; the narrowest patch of earth at the Crossing, as he had known since he was two years old, was crowded with little centres of activity, visible or invisible, that made up a web so intricate that your mind, if you went into it, was immediately stuck – fierce cannibalistic occasions without number, each one of which could deafen you if you had ears to hear what was going on there. And beyond that were what you could not even call lives or existences: they were mere processes – the slow burning of gases for example in the veins of leaves – that were invisibly and forever changing the state of things; heat, sunlight, electric charges to which everything alive enough responded and held itself erect, hairs and fibres that were very nearly invisible but subtly vibrating, nerve ends touched and stroked.

This was how he saw things unless he deliberately held back and shut himself off.

What staggered him in others, and especially in Vic, was the certainty with which they saw the whole world as a nail to be struck squarely on the head. Yet he suspected at times that Vic did not entirely *believe* in the world. His capacity to deal with it had to do with his conviction that it was there only insofar as he could act on it.

Three or four times a year now Vic went overseas, to Japan, Hong Kong, London. The mineral boom and the listing of Australian shares on the international exchange took his interests out of the country. His nephew Alex had been brought in to run the Australian side. He was a chilly fellow, Alex. Digger heard this from Ellie. He lived on his own in a big old flat at Elizabeth Bay, and Ellie, though she tried, had never got close to him.

Vic came to the Crossing less often now, and when he did come their talk was of a different kind. In recent years their times together had become very easy and sociable, too much so. They had taken one another for granted. But now some of this sociability transferred itself to Bondi Junction, and this allowed their times alone to change. They both felt this, but it was Vic who had managed it, and Digger was surprised yet again, by the talent he had – it was instinctive in him – for getting what he needed.

He had begun to detach himself from things. That was what Digger saw. Or not precisely from things, but from himself. And what this involved was a moving deeper into himself So when they talked now, it was in a quieter mood. What they were exploring was not the interest of difference, which had allowed them to turn everything they knew of one another into a game of surprises, but what they shared.

A lot of this new style of talk was about the years they had spent *up there*. Three years and a half, to be exact. Thirty years ago.

Vic was all questions; shy ones at times, as if it embarrassed him a little that he should have to ask them. After all, it was his life.

Digger's own memory was exceptional, he knew that; but he was surprised just the same to how large an extent Vic had lost all detailed recollection of that period, or had suppressed it or let it go.

The emotion of it was still strong. There was a bitterness in him that he continued to chew over as Digger did not. For Digger it had been one time of his life among others; a time, simply, that had laid hard responsibilities on him, but ones that were too deeply ingrained in his nature now for regret. He accepted them. He made no complaint.

For Vic the injustice that had been done to him was absolute, a thing he could not forgive. Some possibility had been killed in him then, and though he had found others and made what he could of them – that's how he was; that was his nature, his character – that other possibility, the one that had been starved and beaten out of him, seemed especially precious. It belonged to his youth, to some finer and more innocent self than the one he had been left with when he came back.

He could not forgive that. The hurt of it was still with him. But he had deliberately stamped out all memory of the *details*, and it was these now that he wanted to recollect: little individual moments of his own life that only Digger could lead him to. Events, occasions, men – their names, what they had looked like, what happened to them.

Digger thought some of this talk was dangerous. Not to himself – he had lived with it for thirty years on a daily basis; it was woven into the very fabric of his existence, in the tangled lines of what bound him here and led out into the future. But for Vic they were something else, these details. They were what he had broken contact with. And perhaps the ability to survive, in his case, had depended on it – Digger allowed for this sort of difference between them. Making himself the guide now who would lead him back into the immediate presence of it was not a thing Digger felt easy with.

What disturbed him was the way it took him back too. There was something quite different between going over it all with another and the more ordinary business of going over it in his own head.

Looking up briefly, a kind of pain behind his eyes that half-dazzled him, he would see behind the face of this man of fifty, fifty-one, fifty-three, which he knew so well – behind the lines that were thrown like a net over his features, breaking up the skin, and behind the coarsening skin itself with its net of veins – a look that had been, all those years ago, his first real glimpse into the man, the one that had established for him, whether he wanted it or not, their bond with one another and the beginning of a responsibility he had seen, even then, as extending far into the future, and up to the moment they were in now: that candid, guilty-innocent, animal look of the twenty-year-old he had caught eating his rice, who had shown him a kind of wisdom he might not have come to himself. 'Trust me,' that look had said, in the very act of stealing the food out of his mouth.

It had the power still to shake him. He felt a kind of trembling in himself that might have been the last shadow, after so long, of fever – do you ever, once bitten, get over it? – but was really, he knew, not a physical thing at all but another form of emotion. He had never been much good (it was another of his deficiencies) at telling the one from the other.

14

Digger no longer went up to town. He had no heart for it. Town had
been his Thursdays with Iris. To get down off the train at Central and
know he was in a city of three million souls and she was not one of
them made Sydney an alien place. He couldn't breathe the air of it, or
so he felt.

That was in the early days. Later, when his pain lessened, as it did in
time, and he saw things more reasonably, what was the point? He
could have stayed the night with one of the boys, he would have been
welcome enough. He could have gone up for Ellie's sake. But he didn't.
He had not seen, till Iris was gone, how his little morning enjoyments
had only been such because at the end of them he would be catching
the tram (later it had been the bus) to Bondi Junction. Her presence
had underwritten everything, even the city itself, all those millions; his
own presence too, at least in that place. Only much later, when the
children wrote asking why he never came to see them any more, did he
begin to go down once in a while 'to see how they were growing up'
and to walk out to Cooper Park with them.

At the service in the little chapel, the preacher, who had not known
Iris personally, spoke of her easy death (she had died without warning
in her sleep); of her long widowhood, and of the husband, the boys'
father, whose name she still bore, who had been lost so many years ago
in the Islands.

Digger swallowed hard to have all their years together, and so much
affection, and so many events, passed over; but death, he knew, is an
official thing, so are its ceremonies, and there was no public record of
their years together.

She was buried under the name of the man she had in one area of
herself remained faithful to, and though it hurt him a little, Digger
respected that. It was part of a code they had shared. He knew its rules.
A good deal of his affection for her, his admiration too, lay in her
commitment to it.

Nine years she had had with the husband. That was official.

Thirty-four without him. Altogether, if you could count them altogether, forty-three. But twenty-six she had had with *him*. And if you counted the years he had shared with her before they met – not her exactly but the shadow of her that she had stepped into – twenty-nine.

What did all these calculations mean? Digger felt strange sitting there in the pew, one of the chief mourners but anonymous and unofficial, totting up figures that were just figures, when the events of any one day or one moment even might have blazed up and made nothing of them.

The boys were very gentle with him. This was in the informal moments, before and after. Ellie and Vic were also there.

So he no longer went up to town, and it was years now since he had seen Ellie. Instead they had begun a correspondence.

At first it was just little notes – a postcard or two from her business trips with Vic, then at last proper letters.

They were, on Digger's side, longer ones than he had ever written before. He put everything he felt into them, and Ellie wrote back of things, he thought, that she would never have told him face to face. He was surprised what words themselves could do when you gave yourself over to them; as if, in containing the expression of what was felt, they knew what you wanted to say before you did, and the very shape of a sentence, once you started on it, held just in itself the shape of what you needed to express; so it got said without embarrassment, and with no fear of falseness or of saying too much and being misunderstood.

After a time it seemed to them that their correspondence was satisfactory just in itself. To meet again might drive them back from intimacy into a politeness they would regret. But he would have liked to see her; to sit, as they used to do, across a table, and watch the way she used her hands.

He sat down once a week and wrote to Ellie as once a week he had gone up to Bondi Junction and stayed with Iris, and if the thing was not quite the same, there was a continuation of a kind in the regularity of it.

He spoke of Iris. Writing was a way of keeping all that part of his life alive in him – it had in most ways been the happiest part; or rather, of finding in it, as the words brought it back, dimensions he had been only dimly aware of in the daily happening. He wrote in a light mood. They had little code-words and quick half-references that came out of the one thing they shared and could draw on, her father's poems. So the poems too took on a new life in their letters. Odd lines and phrases, worked into what they themselves had to say, kept their old meaning, but acquired, as they used them, a new one, coloured and lit up by *their* feelings now.

One of the things Ellie wrote of was Greg. He had used the money Pa left him to go to Europe, overland via India and Afghanistan. He was in Amsterdam, then in Greece, then he was back home again, but in Melbourne. She knew where he was and kept in touch with him.

So six or seven years passed and Digger had a good bundle of letters. He kept them in a drawer, and sometimes, as he had once done with Iris's letters to Mac, he took them out and read them through. It was a pleasant occupation. What he thought of when he lay them aside, full as they were of memories of Iris and of so much else besides, little things he had in mind to tell Ellie, phrases from the poems, was how full his life had been, and that too he wrote to her since she, and all this business of writing to her, was part of it.

So many letters. Seven years.

He did not realise, as he thought this, that there would be so many more. Till it was eleven years. Then twelve, then thirteen.

15

Vic had come by his driver, Brad, in an unlikely manner.

He used to stop occasionally, when he went for a walk out of his office, at a little coffee shop in an arcade, where he could sit and be quiet with his thoughts.

It wasn't a lively place. It had been left just as it was from the days back in the Fifties when espresso coffee first made its appearance, and a Gaggia machine raising a head of steam, a view of the Bay of Naples, and laminated, kidney-shaped counters with high stools offered the promise that somewhere at least there was a *dolce vita*. He liked it because the only people who came here now were tired-looking women shoppers, and a few muddy-eyed older men who wanted a place where they would not be intimidated by too much style.

Tramps half of them looked, or very nearly. They put three or four spoonfuls of sugar into their coffee and sucked it up noisily, with no loss of dignity. He would settle in a corner and feel invisible, though in fact his expensive clothes made him very conspicuous. The invisibility was in his head, but it worked on people and he was seldom approached.

One day the old fellow behind the counter, who emerged every now and then to wipe the tables down with a damp cloth, came across in his shirt-sleeves and apron and spoke to him. He was in his middle sixties, a rough-looking fellow with a shock of snowy hair.

'You don't recognise me, do you?' he said, and there was a smirk on his face that was very youthful. Vic felt then that he did know him, but couldn't put a name or a place to him.

'Felix,' the man told him. 'I used to work for Needham's. In the old days. On the trucks. With Alf Lees. You remember.'

He did too, and the memory was a sweet one. Since their move up to Turramurra, everything that evoked the old house at Strathfield, and the factory, seemed sweet to him. The man, without waiting to be invited, sat down opposite – it was his place, after all – and said quietly: 'I noticed you comin' in here.'

He shifted the two sauce bottles and the pepper and salt shakers, setting them in a row.

'I've got a favour to ask you,' he said. 'I've got a boy, a good lad really – he's honest, I mean – but he's unsettled. Gives 'is mother a lotta worry. I was wondering if – you know, with your contacts, you could maybe do something for 'im. I know it's a big thing to ask.' It was more words, you could see, than he was used to finding all at the one go.

Vic was impressed by the straightness of him. He wasn't at all obsequious. He was speaking as one man to another, taking for granted an equality between them, given a few million dollars, that Vic was glad to accept. He was speaking too as a father, and that also moved him. So he had taken the boy on as a driver.

He did not like him much. He was a young man who thought a great deal of himself. He was always glancing up to take a look at himself in the rear-vision mirror, and what he saw was a pleasure to him. He wasn't very bright either, but did not know it. He talked too much and a lot of it was rot. But Vic liked the father, Felix, very much, and when he went to have his coffee now the man left the counter, brought a cup of his own, and they would sit together for a time and talk.

He was a sad fellow. He had driven for a big trucking company after he left the factory but had done his back in – that's how he had missed the war. After that he had a newspaper run, out Lidcombe way; then, when he retired, had put his money into the coffee shop. He had married late. There was just the one boy.

'I've done pretty well, considering,' he said, and you could see that it did not occur to him that the man he was speaking to had done so much better. They were very easy with one another. Vic felt that in talking to Felix, though the subject was not mentioned, he was relieving himself a little of what he could not say about Greg. The tie between them was always this difficult business of fathers and sons, though it had never come out in fact that he had one.

What Vic had against Brad was that he had none of his father's fineness of feeling. In his empty-headed, egotistical way he took Vic's acquaintance with his father as a feather in his own cap, referring to it sometimes in a way that was quite out of place and which Vic found offensive, though out of affection for the father he did not mention it.

He had very little use for a driver, preferring, except on special occasions, to take a smaller car. Most often it was Alex Brad drove for. Alex liked to work in the car, and Brad, who was very keen on appearances, felt it gave him too a kind of importance – it was like being in a film – to have someone back there making use of a dictaphone and taking calls; though Vic, of course, was the boss.

Vic was using Brad, and the big car, when he found himself one afternoon at the Cross. He had visitors to entertain, two Japanese with whom he had just signed a sizeable contract, and a Swede. They had eaten at a good Italian place in Darlinghurst, drunk well, and these visitors, especially one of the Japanese, having heard of the Cross, wanted to take a look at it – not, Vic warned them, that there would be much to see at three o'clock in the afternoon. He told Brad he could take a bit of a walk – say, half an hour – and, leaving the car in Kellett Street, they strolled in the sunshine to an outdoor café.

He disliked the Cross and never came here except on occasions like this. Its most recent incarnation, as a playground for American servicemen on R and R from Vietnam, was done with now, gone with the war, but the sleaziness and joyless opportunism of that time had set a standard and the Cross was still living up to it. An odour of tropical despair hung over the place, from battlefields that in those days had been just hours away. The boys coming in in their freshly-laundered Hawaiian shirts had still had the smell of battle fear on them.

The mugs were local now, boys in from the suburbs, football teams from interstate; or they were tourists like the Japs who wanted to see what it was the country produced other than wheat, wool, minerals and a few natural phenomena that were sacred sites to one part of the population and to the rest, if they thought of them at all, a kind of geological Disneyland.

The war was over but the Silver Dollar and the Texas Tavern were still there. So were the strip-joints, the skin-flick movie houses, the pinball arcades, the fast-food shops, the fortune tellers with their little velvet-covered tables and Tarot packs; and at every corner the loungers, the lookers, the dealers in this drug and that – and round behind, in an alley full of garbage, only some of it crammed into plastic bags, the bloody syringes and other evidence, with the bodies themselves on occasion. And on the streets here, in broad daylight, the walking wounded, girls in boots and tights, some of whom were no longer girls either, and some of them not *quite* girls, and in the park around the fountain, or in the bar at the Rex, the boys in T-shirts and parachute pants.

It was all more squalid than it used to be. The big men who lived off it were out of sight. They were, if the newspapers were right, some of Vic's business acquaintances – they did not show up here. But their agents were about, moving their shoulders in the sun, and the whole place had a showy half-innocent, half-corrupt air, as if even the corruption might be a fraud, meant only to deceive and titillate, though that too was a deception.

There was corruption all right. Something of what had been in the heads of those boys who had been shipped down here to get free, for a few days, of terror and carnage, had seeped out and infected everything, so that the proximity of death could, if you had a nose for it, be felt more strongly here than in any other part of the city. It was cheap here, commonplace: and that too, whether they knew it or not, drew people.

The crowds came to stare for a bit at a freakshow, to put their hands, just for a moment or two, and at a price, on something forbidden or dangerous; to watch deals being done while pinballs bounced and set small lights flashing and numbers coming up; to listen to the hot-gospellers promising punishment or immediate cleansing and cure, and watch a lamb kebab turn in its own fat on a spit and boys with floury forearms, in dirty white caps behind steamy windows, knead pizza dough.

They settled at an outside table and ordered coffee. The visitors' eyes were everywhere.

A little way down the street there was a commotion. A ragged looking young man with his head shaved up round the ears and peaks of feathery hair, in heavy boots and a T-shirt and braces and with a little black-and-white terrier at his heels, was clod-hopping about on the pavement playing a mouth-organ. The little dog danced round his heels and yipped. His girl, with her legs sprawled out in front of her on the dirty pavement, sat with her head against the wall.

Three young fellows in leather jackets were tormenting them. The little dog snapped at their heels and one after another they kicked at it. The fellow with the mouth-organ, who had fingerless mittens on his hands, was turning his head away like a child, on the principle that if he did not look at his tormentors they could not be there.

On the pavement was a cap with a few coins on it, and one of the louts leaned down now, took a handful of coins from the cap, stood turning them over in his hand, then distributed them, laughing, to his mates.

The girl swore at them, and when the young man with the mouth-organ did nothing, but kept playing, she began to pummel his legs with her fists. The youths, who had begun to walk off, stopped then and turned back to enjoy the scene, the mouth-organ player playing, the girl punching at him. They laughed. The little dog went after them, but stopped when they threatened, and stood there, barking.

The youth and the girl argued for a moment, then she rolled back against the wall again and he began to dance in his heavy boots, playing a jig now, very wild and shrill, and making little nodding and beckoning signs to the passers-by, who shied away. Finally he stopped playing altogether, leaned down, took up the cap, which he emptied into one hand and set anyhow on his head, and gave a call to the dog, which came running. The girl, scrabbling her legs about on the dirty pavement, got herself up and they moved up the street together to where Vic and the others were.

Vic saw then who it was.

He had not seen him for more than seven years. He looked battered. His hair was bleached, he had an earring. The braces and boots, but something too in the nervous set of his shoulders, made him look like a six-year-old who had suffered at the hands of a crazed or brutal adult. When he came up level with their table he stopped dead, and after a moment, grinned in an inane, rather mischievous way, and Vic saw that his front teeth had been knocked out. He came right up to them and thrust out his cap.

The hand in the fingerless mitten was filthy. The flesh of his forearm, which was bare, was like a fish's belly, bluish-white. Behind him the girl weaved about with her head rolling and her eyes closed. The little black-and-white terrier pranced.

The visitors began to feel in their pockets for change. The Swede, who was very aristocratic and fastidious, was trying to ignore this manifestation of local squalor. He was disgusted, you could see that, and a little scared as well. He could not see what the rules were in this place where begging, he had thought, was unknown.

The Japanese were grinning. They were amused. One of them dropped a five-dollar note into the cap, and Greg raised a finger to his temple in scornful salute.

Vic had not moved. He did not feel humiliated or ashamed before these men. They meant nothing to him. What he felt was a blazing anger, and most of all at the Swede. At the clean-fingered distaste with which he dropped a coin into the cap, as if it, and the arm behind it, had materialised out of nowhere, and what might lie beyond was beneath his notice.

The boy was unabashed. He appeared, with his absent-minded grin and the childish little jerking movements he kept making with his head, to accept no responsibility at all for what was happening, and to have no resistance to it either. The moment sat so lightly upon him that he seemed weightless, and Vic had again a vision of him dancing, clod-hopping about on the pavement like a puppet, but one that was not attached to anything.

'But he is attached to *me*,' he thought, and was struck suddenly with the impulse to stand up and say it aloud, to say it right out, just like that, with whatever dignity he could muster, but if there was none to be had, that would not matter either. To say quite openly, with a heart too bewildered any longer to take refuge in pride, what he was saying already to himself: 'This is the thing I was in panic about, that I knew was on the way and knew I had no power to prevent. Now it is here.'

Bright sunlight played on the table-top and round the mouths of glasses, touched the corners of buildings, swam in windows, lit the highest leaves of the surrounding trees. It was three o'clock in the afternoon. It was not a dream.

He said nothing. Without looking up he began to take out his wallet, and the others watched uncomprehending as before he could open it, the beggar or busker or whatever he was reached out and with a silly little laugh plucked it from him: flipped it open, extracted two, three notes – twenties they might have been, no, fifties! – then, with another laugh, tossed it back.

There was a police station not fifty yards away. It was amazing.

Vic did not once look up. What he could not face, but could see clearly enough, was the look on the boy's face. The *boy* – but he was past thirty. Defiant it would be, but in an indeterminate, rabbity way, as if he was himself being dared by a fellow inside there that he had to watch out for – the one who was high on whatever it was that made his eyes so icy-blue but inward-looking and put the smile at the corner of his mouth.

He stood a moment, looking pleased with himself and fingering the notes. Then, losing confidence, he turned, grabbed the girl, who was swaying about on the pavement, and dragged her off.

The others sat staring. They could not see what it meant, what embarrassing intimacy or bit of odd local behaviour had been revealed to them, and Vic did not bother to explain. He did not bother with them at all. Stumbling to his feet, he took the bill, paid it at the counter inside and they had to set off after him.

They found the car. The driver, with an ice-cream cone in his hand, was walking up and down the pavement keeping an eye on it. Up here he liked to keep a good lookout – he was smart that way.

He twigged immediately that something had gone wrong. When they had dropped the Swede off, then the two Japs, he glanced up enquiringly into the rear-vision mirror, past his own reflection this time. Old Trader Vic (as he called him when he was showing off to his mates) was slumped in the corner against the window. He looked like someone had king-hit him. Brad turned his head so that the old fellow would see something more than just the back of his neck. It was a form of question.

He came back to reality then and asked to be driven to a place Brad had never taken him before, way up beyond Ku-ring-gai Chase to the Hawkesbury, and some bit of a store on the river up there where he had to sit around kicking his heels for ages, and a crazy old girl with no hair practically had offered him a cup of tea, then in the middle of it, for no reason he ever discovered, did her block and started to perform and play rough with him.

16

They were the years now of the *real* boom. What had come before was nothing compared to this. What had been measured in millions was to be measured now in hundreds of millions. No one had seen anything like it.

When Jenny saw Vic on the television these days she sat glum and silent.

It wasn't him that worried her – she *knew* him. She didn't know what he *did*, or any more about him than she ever had, but she had been in the same room with him, her own kitchen, and seen the way he sipped his tea with his eyes looking out over the rim of the cup, and ate a pikelet, and the way the skin wrinkled on the back of his hand. She knew the smell of him too. That wasn't what worried her. What she could not fathom was what he was doing in the world of TV, the News and that. How had he got there? She knew how he had got to the Crossing. Through Digger. But the TV was different.

The moment his name came up and his face appeared in the lighted window there, smiling, assured, with his striped shirts and his brushed hair and the face so bronzed and lifelike, the whole thing lost its credibility for her. She couldn't listen to what they were saying or believe any bit of it. The News! She would go glum and start counting in her head – one, two, three, four – till they took him off.

Vic had always played things close to his chest. All his success had come from his willingness to take responsibility for what he was doing, stay quiet, bear the risks, and keep his nerve. Ma had been his only real confidante. She was so still. He would tell her anything she wanted to know, she had only to ask. Alex he told as little as he could get away with.

He had chosen Alex because he was family, and because he had seen, in a hard-nosed way, that the qualities Alex possessed were the ones he lacked. They were qualities he had no time for in fact – they had all to do with caution, consultation, bookkeeping, accountability – but they were what the times, it seemed, demanded. He had chosen Alex as well because he thought, being family, he would have a kind of ascendency over him.

He had been wrong in this. Alex was stubborn. He held to the code he lived by with a fanaticism Vic found he could neither ignore nor negotiate.

Alex was a company man. Accountability was his gospel. When he spoke it was with all the facts at his fingertips and the approval, always, of a board with whom he had gone over every detail. He could not understand Vic. Or rather, he did understand but could not deal with him.

'He's a dinosaur,' he complained to the few men he could trust not to bear tales. 'It was fine in the old days. It was open slather then. This was Hicksville. He could be a one man show and get away with it. He was brilliant, I agree. But we're in a new phase now. Everything's more complicated. That's what he won't accept. I have to watch him like a goddamn hawk. You've got no idea the tricks he gets up to.'

'So what are you griping about?' Vic would argue when some scheme he had been engaged in was in the open at last and his hand revealed. 'We made money on it, didn't we? Have I ever got us into anything that was a loss? What about that Riverdale business? Who got us into that little pile of pooh?'

He knew Alex was watching him, that he was being humoured – patronised, in fact – and that Alex had a core of supporters, fellows full of *his* sort of ideas who were determined to restrain and thwart him and would one day ease him out. He watched them, and after a time he began to watch outside as well. He had a nose for that, for what was not quite right; a sixth sense that warned him when someone was on his tail. He had played that game himself and knew the signs. When he was sure of what was happening he took action but told no one, acting as he always had done, alone. If Alex was in it, he would be caught out and exposed. If he wasn't, he would be delighted, wouldn't he? – astonished too – that the thing had been seen and forestalled.

It was his big gamble. He needed it. He needed the excitement, and the chance it offered to show, once and for all, what he was worth. When all was ready, fixed and about to go, he would lay his hand down and watch their faces.

He had advisers of his own, of course; you needed them these days. But them too he kept in the dark. It would have been good, he thought, to go over it with Ma. He had no wish to deceive her. But Ma was nearly ninety; still clear-headed but racked with anxieties again that he was afraid to catch.

The one person he could be open with was Digger, he owed him that; and the advantage of Digger was that he offered no arguments. He might have done. There were times, certainly, when he looked doubtful enough. But Digger was out of his element. He did not understand the danger, the beauty of the thing.

So though he tried to stay away, he found himself, as the affair reached its crisis, going back and back to the Crossing, eager to have someone to listen while once again he went over the details of it. It was watertight. No doubt of that. He had considered every eventuality. But he needed to talk it into action, to keep it going where he could best control each movement of it: in his head.

Digger had caught on to one or two things that set him thinking. They had come up in passing, but in a way that caught his ear. One of them had to do with the market's being 'nervous'. He was struck by the word because it had already occurred to him in connection with Vic.

He talked a good deal about how cool he was. He prided himself on that. But what Digger saw was that he was overheated, and he could not judge, since he had never seen him till now under circumstances like these, whether it was normal or not, whether it was or was not to be expected as a by-product of what kept him cool. He would have liked to discuss this with someone, with Ellie for instance; she would know. But the secrecy Vic demanded held him back.

This secret side of things was an agony to him. He wondered how necessary it was outside of Vic's need to impose it. Its effect was to bind them even closer now, as fellow conspirators, but in an area where only Vic knew the rules. He swallowed his doubts, afraid, when so much depended on confidence, and trust, that if he spoke them aloud he might bring about the very thing he wanted to prevent – the upsetting of some balance in Vic that would put him off.

'What's going on?' Jenny wailed. 'What's 'e doin', comin' down here all the time? What does 'e *want*? And don't tell me nothin' again, cos I don't believe it.'

17

Vic stirred and woke. The jolt he felt had taken place in his sleep. For just the space of a breath back there he must have been free of gravity. He came to earth now but the sense of strangeness he felt, of estrangement even, was of being in a body that was not his own. His hand when he lifted it seemed further off and had a new weight at the end of his arm. Or maybe it was still, as they say, asleep. He worked it a little to take off the numbness.

He knew clearly enough where he was. It was the bedroom at Turramurra. But what he was chiefly aware of was not the space he was in but the space that was inside him. Echoes were coming up from it, and it was these that gave him a sense of how vast it might be. Something like a stone had fallen a huge distance in there. From where it touched bottom the sound was still travelling upward, having the power, the unusual one, of belonging to a dream but going on past whatever barrier exists between sleep and wakefulness so that he could still hear it.

What *was* all this? On the one hand the feeling of being lifted free of gravity like a bird, and on the other of an even swifter descent in the opposite direction, a long plummeting and the rush of air around a stone.

And if it wasn't a dream but some purely physical occurrence, why all this business of gravity and stones?

He shifted his body on the bed and lay a while with his eyes open and very still in his head, fixed on the ceiling. A moment later he was asleep.

But at moments during the day, which was otherwise normal, his dream, or the sensations surrounding whatever had happened in there, kept coming back to him. He could not shake them off. For whole minutes at a time there was a luminosity round the edge of everything he looked at or touched, even the most ordinary objects, a coffee-machine, a polystyrene cup.

It was the light out of his dream, in which everything, including his

313

body, had been soaked, he saw now, in a phosphorescence whose stickiness accounted for the heaviness he had felt, and still felt, in his limbs, and accounted too for all this shining. It wasn't at all unpleasant, but it was strange and he was changed by it. He felt a tenderness in himself that was childish since it attached itself to things it was foolish for a grown man to feel so much for. The propelling pencil he took up, for example, and the way it fitted his hand, the sun rings thrown on his desk by a water-glass. 'What is happening?' he wondered.

These moments, which came in waves, were states of acute happiness, but of a kind he had scarcely known before, and there was, so far as he could see, no reason for them. They brought with them a lightness of heart that he associated with youthfulness, with some image he had had once of what it was to be young and in love.

Where did *that* come from? It did not seem like a memory of his own. It was new to him. Yet there was a quality of nostalgia in it too, as if he had broken in on the recollections of another man's life and was as moved by them as by his own. The bursts of happiness came and came, and were so unconnected with any cause he knew of that they might have been the after-effects of a drug.

All this surprised him, but he liked the mood and surrendered to it.

He did all the things he usually did: checked the market reports that had come in overnight from New York, then the Hong Kong and Tokyo prices, then the local ones. Everything was fine, couldn't be better: Cavendish was up two cents, Cathedral steady, Randall's up three. It was going fine, better even than predicted.

For a time he had been anxious that the market might be playing them up. But his advisers, who were áll very clear-headed, sceptical fellows, statistics freaks, not at all star-gazers or voodoo merchants, had assured him that the upward trend was steady and would continue. They were experts. He was paying them in hundreds of thousands for their opinions. It was crazy to do that and not listen to them.

There was a time, a while back, when he would have followed his own hunches, tuning in to the small hairs at the back of his neck. But the market forces these days were too complex for one man to grasp. Even he had to admit that. What happened here was dependent on what they did in Tokyo and New York. You needed advice at every point. Still, it went against the grain with him.

The good thing was, in three or four days now it would be over. They would be out.

Just on eleven, as always, he called Alex. These consultations were ritual. They made them by telephone since they could gauge better that way the little evasions they practised.

Vic joked today, he was in a buoyant mood, and this put Alex on his guard. He was difficult to talk to, Alex, unless you stuck to figures, but he had no suspicion of what was going on, he was certain of that. 'Watch it, Alex,' he said. It was his routine farewell.

He left the office at two to get a breath of air and was surprised to find, when he stepped into the street, that his mood had translated itself to the whole city, and he wondered if it wasn't this that his body had caught wind of, some meteorological occurrence high up in the atmosphere, the first stirring of an air current that had been gathering there and had only now begun to move in over the edge of the continent.

It was mid-October, and balmy. Girls were out in short-sleeved dresses, young fellows carried their jackets over their shoulders, joggers were about. Lemony sunlight made the edges of buildings and low walls luminous. He had a sense of being not only in deep harmony with all this, but maybe even responsible for it. How good he felt.

He dropped in on Felix. He hadn't done that for quite a while now. They had a coffee and talked. Brad was out on his own these days so it was easy for the old man to brag about him. He did it shyly. Brad was in the car-hire business, and was married and doing well.

When he got back to the office he decided, for no reason, to ring Ellie.

'No, nothing's the matter,' he said when she came to the phone at last from somewhere far off in the garden. He felt foolish. He wanted to tell her simply how happy he was, but she would hear that in his voice. It seemed foolish to make so much of it. 'I was just ringing,' he told her, 'that's all.'

At three he called down and had them bring his car up from the parking lot. He would drive up and spend an hour or two (he was still, he felt, on the track his dream had set him on) with Digger, at Keen's Crossing.

Impossible to say when, but at some point in the fifty-kilometre drive the light changed, his mind darkened, and as on other occasions the high state of elation he was in revealed itself as no more than a mood, some condition of mind or body that passed now as quickly as it had appeared, as inexplicably too. His heart tightened, till the cramp in his chest was so painful and his arm so numbed that he could no longer trust himself to keep hold of the wheel. He pulled over on to the rough verge, rested a moment, then turned into a break in the scrub. He sat hunched over the wheel in almost total darkness. 'I should go back,' he thought, and opened the door of the car and got out.

He must have slept or passed out for a moment. In the lapse of consciousness he found himself back in his dream; except that he saw now that it wasn't a dream at all but an actual moment of his boyhood he had come back to. He was in his own nine-year-old body again, standing barefooted in old serge pants and braces, his whole being drawn taut as a bow, at the edge of the dunes, with the day just on the turn and lights coming on all down the shore. One of those occasions when, in the assurance that he had the power to leap out of himself into an imaginable future, he had stood still, and feeling the animal in him crouched, ready to leap, had let himself go with it.

It took off in a long arc. He went with it, and found himself suspended, outside gravity, at the high point, and with the new moment yet to declare itself. But he must have come down that time, *one* of those times, in the wrong life. That was the only way he could explain now the otherness he felt in himself. *The wrong life.* So that everything that had happened to him, from that moment on, all of it, had occurred in another existence from the one he had till then been moving in and was intended for.

Was that possible? Everything?

It was all real, it had happened all right. It had happened to *him*. It was fact. Part of the real happenings of a world that takes note of such things; that records events and enterprises and makes a life of them, and if they are big enough makes history of them. Only none of it had been intended for him, that's what he saw. What had been intended was something quite different, and he had wrenched himself, by sheer willpower, out of the way of it.

In the deepest part of himself he had always known this. He had felt it in the presence of that boy who had appeared each morning to push his big feet into his shoes, and left dirt marks on the collars of his shirts. Later, hanging about the streets and watching with a bad conscience the lines of men waiting for handouts, he had seen quite clearly the gap in the line where he ought to have been, and had wondered when he would have to pay the price for getting away.

Thailand was different. That *was* intended. At that point the two lives somehow crossed. He had seen so clearly, up ahead, that old, white-headed fellow ('The one I am now,' he thought) who had passed clean through him. He had been in the right line that time.

He thought of all those mornings when, still heavy with sleep, he had sat in Meggsie's kitchen feeling for the contours of an existence, some other one, that his body might fit more neatly (more clumsily that is) than the one he was in. Not an easier life. It wouldn't be easier, he was certain of that. But one that was continuous with something in himself that he was afraid of losing contact with yet could not grasp.

Now, once again, he felt that nine-year-old body prepare to leap in him. He took off. He hung a moment free of gravity, and in the long breath in which he was suspended got a glimpse of what it was he was about to fall back into; which was his own life waiting to reclaim him – that other, harsher life that went back to its beginning in his father's life, in his mother's. But gravity was too strong. He could not stay up there long enough to make out the details of it. Once again he felt the force of things take hold and tug him down. And the life he came back into was the one he was in. He took the weight of it again, against his chest, in his belly and groin, and fell with the full force of his body on stones, little sharp-edged ones, and it stayed with him.

Later, when he came back to consciousness, he was surprised to find himself in deep night, with no light anywhere but where the first stars were showing themselves. 'Where is this?' he thought. He was unsure as yet whether it was a place or another condition.

But when he gathered his senses together he was aware of sharp-edged little stones under him, and there was a great climbing edifice of sound as well, though what the creatures were who were making it he could not guess. Frogs? Night crickets?

He sat up a little and looked about, but there was nothing to be seen.

It occurred to him then that he must have got out here by car, but there was no car in sight, and the light was not strong enough to judge directions.

He recalled, because his body did, a period of sharp pain. He still felt the aura of it, not at this point as a physical thing but as a sense of his limbs being not quite returned to him, or not in their solid form. He had difficulty making judgements about things that ought to have been simple. Like where exactly his fingers were. And along with all this were sensations that were unrelated, so far as he could see, to any fact. A softness of spring weather, delicate breezes blowing about on the bare arms of girls, all of which seemed to have nothing at all to do with the weather but to be a movement of his spirit. He was sitting in the middle of nowhere and had no idea which way to move.

The decision was taken out of his hands. Suddenly a new and terrible anguish gripped his heart, or it was a physical agony, he could not tell which, and he was crushed, his cheek to the hard edge of stones that cut his flesh. He was on his side and writhing, pushing himself into the smothering blackness of the night or some other, deeper darkness, which was all he desired now, a sack that he could crawl into and pull over his head, and where he could kick out to the end of his breath.

He must have been crawling. He had come a long distance, pushing himself deeper and deeper into the grass. He lay now in a nest of it that he had made with the working of his limbs, in an agony of spirit that left him breathless.

The sun was up. Big birds were flopping overhead. He rolled his head a little and saw that he was not awake after all. In the dream he was in, his agony, which was something quite separate from him, had taken the shape of a cat with matted fur that was lying just inches from where his outstretched hand was curled. It had the brutal head and overgrown coarse fur of a feral, gone back, after a generation or more, to wildness, and was lying just beyond arm's length and watching him.

But when he blinked and looked closer, it wasn't a phantom, it was real. Its head had been split by the blade of a shovel, maybe an axe, and half its face was sliced away. It had crawled in here to die. It snarled now, its one fierce eye glaring at him; though the sound it made might not have been hostile after all but a plea for aid. Flies were swarming in the rawness of the open wound and the creature used its paw with the savage claws to keep them off.

Vic lay with his head on his extended arm, watching the cat, and the cat lay two yards away in extreme agony.

'I have seen all this before,' he thought, 'many times. I got out of it then. I survived. I always survived. I know about survival.'

But the cat, he saw, was dying. He looked at it. 'Poor bugger,' he thought, 'I'd help you, if I could. I'd put you out of your misery.'

He and the cat looked at one another, quite close like that, for a long time, and the cat went through agonies but did not die. It was suffering, but in what way, he wondered. What sort of consciousness does a cat have? Does a cat have consciousness?

'I'm sorry for you, mate,' he said out loud, and was surprised to hear his own voice.

The cat did not hear, or did not understand. It made no difference to it, one way or the other. It just watched him with its one eye, and he had no idea what it thought.

18

It was ten in the morning. The range was drawing just right, making a good heat, and Jenny was feeling unusually pleased with herself, which in her case meant pleased with the world, the way it settled around her this morning as if she was, for once, just right for it. She was waiting for a batch of scones to come out of the oven.

It was hot but not too hot. October. The yard was dancing a bit where heat came up in waves off a sheet of corrugated iron that Digger had left out there. The leaves of the pepper tree were also dancing. Half a dozen magpies were under the lines. They were excited. Something, some worm or that, or a smaller bird, was *getting it*. *Magpies, Magpies! Watch yer eyes!* They would come diving at your head if you passed too close under their nests. *Watch yer eyes!*

She dreamed at the windowsill, her mind on the yard but also on the oven: the big birds at their business, getting it over with, quick, quick now, Geez, heat dancing up off the iron sheet, and further back in her head, but not too far back, the scones on their tray which were for Digger's morning tea, rising nicely now and going crisp on top then browning. They would be ready in about five minutes. She shifted her heavy bulk on the chair.

When she took them out of the oven she couldn't believe it. And just a minute ago she had been feeling so good! She held the hot tray and stared at what she had done. At what *someone* had done. It's what happens, what always happens, when you start getting too sure of yourself. She couldn't believe it. She stared so long that the tray began to burn her fingers through the worn linen of the teacloth. She cursed and dumped the thing down on the sink, then screwed her mouth up, hugged herself a little and counted, using her finger this time. It was still thirteen. How? How had it happened? She was always that careful. Someone – but who? – must have slipped the extra one in while her back was turned.

So who was it *for*? That was the question. Whose bad luck was it?

And which one of them was it? They were all so alike, all nicely raised and browned. She was good at scones. It was her long suit. There was no way of picking it.

But she had to. It was either that or chuck the whole lot to the bloody magpies, and all the philosophy and practice of sixty-nine years went against it. *Waste not, want not*, that was the rule. If you did waste, then one day you would remember these scones and starve for 'em, and serve you right!

Quite fearful now of making a second error (if it was really her that had made the first one), but trusting too in some agency in herself that would work when she needed it, she squeezed her eyes shut, stretched out her blunt fingers, which were freckled and thickly padded round the nails, and let her palm hover over the scones. Then, when her mind was emptied of all thought, she took one.

Well, it had better be it! She had good reason to believe it was. She could work these tricks when she had to. Only where the hell, she wondered, had her mind been – what had her good sense been doing, *sleeping*? – when she made up that lot of dough in the first place and let the one extra in? *If* she had.

So what now? What should she do with it? Throw it back on the coals?

She looked at the scone sitting there on the sink. Innocent, it looked.

With a little sideways slew of her mouth she took it up rather gingerly, put her shoulder to the screen door and stepped out. The magpies were there, big black-and-white buggers the size of cats. They had already caught sight of her looming at the back door, but didn't let on that they were watching. 'Well,' she thought, this'll fix ya!'

'Here I come,' she sang to herself as she crossed the yard, 'here's yer ol' mate Jenny. You don't know what *I've* got in me hand, do yer, eh? Look at this. Which one of yez is it for? Which one of you greedy buggers is gunna swaller *bad luck*?' She tossed the nicely browned, crisp little scone like a soft stone into the midst of them, and the great black-and-white creatures rolled towards it and flapped and scrabbled, beaks going everywhere, wings too, tearing at one another and squawking.

One of them got it and she watched it gobble the thing down and the others go in under its wings for the crumbs.

'So,' she said, feeling a kind of satisfaction now at playing with such powers, bad luck and the possibility of a choking or worse, and of setting things right as well, getting them back into order again, since that extra scone had definitely been a mistake.

It wasn't *her* fault which one got it. Somebody else would be deciding that. All she'd done was throw the bad luck *to* them, she didn't choose. Greed had chosen. The greediest and strongest of them had got it.

She looked at the big bird, which was preening itself, and chuckled. She knew something the bird did not, 'A cat'll get you now,' she thought, watching it strut. 'A feral. Or some kid with a shanghai. Well, good riddance!' She didn't care. The main thing was, she'd got the bad luck off Digger and herself.

She would have liked to keep a watch on that bird and make sure, only she didn't have the time. She slumped back to the kitchen, and when she saw the tray sitting there, on the edge of the sink, had a sick feeling. Maybe she ought to have tossed the lot out anyway. But if you started that sort of caper, tossing good stuff out just because you were scared and couldn't tell good from bad, you'd be lost. You'd end up tossing everything out.

She'd made a choice. That's what you were supposed to do, make a choice and choose right, by instinct. If you started worrying about mistakes, you'd make one, and if you made a *little* mistake, well eventually you'd make a big one.

That's what had alarmed her so much when she saw that one extra. That it might be the beginning of something.

She was pegging out clothes an hour or so later when she saw the birds making a commotion in the scrub. 'Aha!' she thought. She pinned up the other end of the sheet she was hanging, which billowed and filled with light, and, leaving the remainder in the basket, went off through the grass a little to see what was doing. This would be proof now. The big birds were excited.

But what presented itself when she parted the grass on the over-grown track was not a bird at all but a cat, a big feral, black with reddish lights in its fur, and when it turned on her, snarling, she gave a gasp. Half its face was gone. Someone had sliced it away with the edge of a shovel. Some feller who was sick of having his chooks taken, no doubt. It looked up at her with such a dumb, suffering look, in spite of the snarl, that she was stricken. It was in agony, poor creature.

She turned away to find a rock or something to finish it off, and saw something else. A hand coming out of the grass.

'Jesus,' she thought, 'what a day!'

With her heart beating she pushed the grass aside and a man rolled over and looked right up at her.

It was Vic.

She was in real panic now. Was he poisoned? Had *she* done it? But she'd given that scone to the magpies. She'd seen one of them eat it.

She hung over him, very scared and moaning a little, and his eyes rolled, following her movements, his mouth wet and the tongue moving, but no sound coming from him.

She knelt to loosen his collar, which seemed to be choking him, and the hand grabbed hers and tightened on it. She wrenched her hand loose, jabbering, and when she got it free she had hold of a smooth little stone about the size of a kidney, same colour too, which she thought for a moment he might have sicked up. She stared at it.

About the size, too, of a scone. It was warm.

He rolled over now on his side, drew his legs up like a baby, and lay curled up in the grassy nest he had made by rolling about there.

'What is it?' she said.

The thought of a child, a baby, had softened her.

She took his hand. With her other hand she stroked his face. After a moment she squatted, lifted him a little, and took his head in her arms. She began to rock him, and the cat, opposite, watched with its one eye. He yielded in her arms and she forgot now all that she had against him. She forgave him for it, whatever it was, and she did not even *know* what it was. It didn't matter.

He had his face down between her breasts. She could feel a wetness. She began to weep. She could feel his mouth down there and wished, if that's what he wanted, that she could feed him, but she had no milk. She had had no milk now for more than forty years. They had pumped it out of her with a machine. She had begged and begged them, those nuns, not to take it, and all that night had dreamt of mouths pulling at her, and she didn't care in the end *what* they were, babies or poddy calves or little lambs or what, that were feeding off the rich stuff her body had stored up, which had been meant to feed a *creature*, not to be squeezed out with a machine. And all the time, out there somewhere, her own little baby was going hungry; or if it wasn't, it was being fed some other milk, not the one that had been made for it special in all the world; and for the whole of its life, poor thing, it would know that and feel the loss – that the world had stolen something from it that it would never have. She had looked around wherever she went after that, believing she would recognise the face of that little kid she had had the milk for, and who might be looking for it still.

Forty-three years old he would be now, wherever he was. And now, forty-three years late, *this*.

She hugged his head to her breast, but after a little, when her tears stopped, she eased him off and said gently: 'Listen, listen, Mister. I'm not leaving you. On'y I gotta get Digger, right? Right? Two minutes. Right?'

She got up, and there was still the cat, still with its head rolled towards her. She had to step around it. 'Don't worry,' she told it, 'I haven't forgot. I'll get to you later.'

She began calling Digger under her breath all the way to the yard, and when she was in hearing distance she started shouting for him, and right away he appeared round the corner of the store.

19

Digger was walking with Ellie on a terrace of springy turf, the edge of which fell away into a wild little gully, all reddish boulders and giant ironbarks and angophoras growing straight out of the rock. Behind them was the low, ranch-style house that Vic had built. They had come out with tea mugs in their hands to see the birds that filled the garden as they did the gully below, not observing, since it was barely visible, the point where wild nature became nature tended and organised, except that the garden offered the greater variety of green things spiked or spurred or exploding in dark or dazzling showers and was the more crowded. In the space of just seconds Digger identified blue wrens, noisy mynahs, three Eastern Rosellas, two kinds of honey-eater, all as Ellie in her many descriptions of the place had promised. He had never seen it before but knew every corner of this garden as if it was his own.

Ellie walked with a limp. She had never told him of any illness or injury; he was surprised. This little change in her, and it wasn't, as he saw after a time, the only one, alerted him to how many things in her life their correspondence might not have covered. But all that meant was how much more there was to come.

Her smile was the same, and so, almost at once, was the easiness between them.

She was very calm. Her mother was so distressed, she told him, and there had been so much noise and confusion, that she had to be.

In the evening they had been besieged by reporters. They had clambered all over the drive, banging on the doors, front and back, looming up at windows, making camp with their cameras on the lawn. None of them had shown any sort of consideration, or had the least respect for their privacy or grief, or had thought of the event, so far as she could see, as anything more than News. Ellie, who had always hated this public aspect of their lives, and feared it too, was disgusted. They had had to draw the curtains and sit like prisoners in their own house, and still the banging had gone on, the tapping at windows, the shouted appeals. Then suddenly they had all rushed off again, just packed up in great excitement and were gone. An event of world proportions had intervened, and Vic Curran's death, which on any other day would have been headlines, was reduced to a ten-centimetre column on the front page, with a direction to page three.

As for Albert Keen, phantom dealer in millions, whose rise and fall from nothing to nothing had covered just thirty-one days, you had to go to the financial pages and read between the lines to get a hint of that. It was a story that was lost as yet in the clouds of dust in which a whole ghostly edifice had tottered and come crashing down.

The Needham's Group had been hit, and hit badly. That at least was clear, and there were statements, cautious ones, from Alex and from the managers of two major banks.

'Did you see what the papers are saying?' Ellie asked him.

'Yes,' he admitted. 'But you know the papers.'

'No,' she said, 'it's true.' Digger looked to see how much she knew. Was she testing him? 'He was *doing* something, I don't know what. Alex knows. Something crazy. It wasn't illegal – or not quite, he wouldn't have done anything like that. You know what he was like. But it seems –' Her eye moved out over the layered leaves of the garden, all the different kinds of fronds, and heart-shaped and elongated leaves, and sword-shapes and falls of colour and fiery wheels. 'Alex says we're in trouble. He's out of his mind, poor Alex.'

'It was me,' Digger said abruptly. 'I was in on it. Haven't you heard?' It was a confession. He had no reason to boast of it.

'Yes. Alex told me. But Digger – you don't know anything about these things.'

'It was just the name he was using,' he explained, but it sounded unlikely without Vic to expound the thing and make it real. 'It seems,' he said, 'I'm a ruined man.'

She looked at him then. They both saw the humour of it, and he thought he heard Vic laugh. It was the sort of thing that might have appealed to him.

They walked on for a minute or two.

'Can I come and see you?' Digger asked. 'Or do you want to go on with the letters?'

She thought a moment. 'I don't know,' she said quietly. 'Why don't you *write* and ask me?'

It was too early to say any of the things they would have at last to get round to. Maybe it would be easier in writing.

They sat holding hands for a time, on a bench under the trees, then she said at last: 'Digger, I must go, I've got to see my mother. Do you want me to get you a car for the station?'

'No,' he said. 'Now that I'm a pauper again I'd better get used to walking, don't you reckon?'

The walk to the station was a warm one. It was hot for October. He had to stop and take his hat off for a bit to let his head breathe. From narrow patches of weeds on either side of the asphalt came the smell of dust and grass-seed, mixed in with an acrid but not at all unpleasant odour that showed there were dogs about. One or two of them came trotting past; out on their own affairs, and leaving at points along their route these sharp-smelling traces of their presence, just a few drops each time, as if it was incumbent upon them to mark their passage in this elemental and entirely personal fashion.

Digger liked the way they trotted about so lightly on their claws, with their ears flopping and their noses to the ground. They knew what they were doing, dogs. You could learn something from them. He walked on.

A list had started up in his head. He let it go on. *Burton, Cable, Carwardine, Cooley, Cooper, Crane* . . . The next one was him.

He let the two syllables out and found himself choked a moment. He could hardly go on: *Curran*.

Curran, Victor Charles, one of a list. But they had, after all and despite all, been as close as any two men could be. How had *that* happened?

He got a flash of him as he had appeared, hovering about behind Doug, in those last days before the surrender, and experienced again, and with a force he wouldn't have thought possible, as if time had no meaning at all, the immediate aversion he had felt. No, it was something more hidden than that. A sense of their being, in their deepest natures, inimical to one another; in some part of themselves that was not accessible to view, or to reasoning either, though they were both aware of it, and would trust it too. Except that they had not, not in the long run. What they had done instead, since they could hardly do otherwise, was let the spirit of accident lead them. First the monstrous accident of Mac's killing, then the stranger one of their physical dependence on one another in the coming and going of their fevers, till what was revealed was something stronger even than their first instinctive hostility; unless that had been, from the start, only the negative sign of a deeper affinity. Which they might have missed, and by a long shot too, forty years, if accident had not imposed itself as the true shaper of their lives.

Accident? But what more mysterious force was that the name for in their inadequate language? . . . *Daley, Dannagher, Deeks, Dewhurst, Dixon.*

He walked on. There were shops now, supermarkets with windows covered with cut-price offers for washing powders or mixed fruit, a café with video games where kids were hunched, utterly absorbed, jerking their shoulders from left to right as they swerved past the asteroids, a newsagent's with the headlines outside on wired boards: the collapse on Wall Street, but also Vic's name, just the last one, Curran, in giant letters. In his case that was enough.

Digger stood and looked at it spelled out there, the six letters. It meant one thing on the newsboard and another thing altogether where its two syllables were tucked away, among so many, in his head. Another thing again as he had actually known the man.

He took up the list again where he had left off. *Doig, Dooley, Doone, Durani, Dwyer* . . . It was a long way yet to the end.

20

The child, his broad feet set firmly in the dust, sits on the bottom one of three steps that lead down from the verandah to their front yard.

It is afternoon, and hot. Across the street are other houses just like theirs, weatherboard with red corrugated-iron roofs and picket fences with numbers on the gate. Their number is six, and he is four. Six Marlin Street, and he is Victor Charles Curran, Vic.

They have lived at number six for as long as he can remember. At night people come to play poker. There is noise, smoke, laughter, and he is allowed to bring in the beer bottles in their straw jackets, and when they are empty he carts them out again and puts them with the others on the back porch. Dead marines, they are called.

His mother gets work to do for ladies. She is sitting now just to his left, on a cane chair she has brought from the kitchen. Her work is in her lap and she is very intent upon it, wearing her glasses. Open at her feet is a little cardboard suitcase where she keeps snips of all different shapes and colours.

Sometimes, to keep him quiet when he has no one to play with, she lets him take the pieces out and sort them into their different colours; but today she has given him something more difficult to do. She has given him a needle, wet the end of a piece of thread, and for the last hour, over and over, he has been trying to do this thing he knows is simple yet finds so difficult.

Now and again, just to reassure himself it can be done, he holds the needle up to see the hole more clearly.

If you bring it up close to your eye you can see the sky through it. It is a big hole and holds a lot of blue. Then if you lower it a little you see a whole house there. Jensens', opposite, where Trudy and Jack live.

It's odd, this. You can see a whole house in it, roof and all, but to get just a bit of cotton through is so difficult. He has been trying for a long time, screwing his eye up and setting his jaw, very determined, and the bit of thread which was white when he started is grubby now and getting grubbier. That's because of his hands. He lays the needle down very carefully, then the thread, and rubs his hands against his shorts. Then he tries again. Then he looks through the eye of the needle again.

He sees a truck parking outside Jock Hale's place. He sees two girls, Milly and Jane Benson, swinging on their gate. They are singing something he can't quite hear, and swinging. He sees a boy in grey shorts learning to ride a bike. The bike keeps wobbling and he puts his bare foot down on the bitumen to steady it, then tries again. The boy is about a year older than he is, maybe six, even. It is himself!

He is puzzled by this and looks across at his mother, but she smiles and does not see anything odd in it.

Men begin coming in from the mine. Soon now it will be dark. When he holds the needle up now the eye of it is smoky. It is close to dark in there.

The boy who was learning to ride the bike is riding easily now, he has got the hang of it. He is hardly wobbling at all. He begins to show off, making figures-of-eight in the road, very pleased with himself and laughing. The light will be gone soon and still the thread has not gone through.

He concentrates and holds his hands just so and draws his whole body together.

Soon it will.

Several accounts of the experience of Australian P.O.W.s in Malaya and Thailand provided general information, hints and details for events and moral inspiration for this piece of fiction, chief among them Stan Arneil's *One Man's War*, Sun Books, 1982, Hank Nelson's *P.O.W. Prisoner of War*, ABC Enterprises, 1985 (from Tim Bowden's radio series 'Australians Under Nippon') and *The War Diaries of Weary Dunlop*, E. E. Dunlop, Nelson, 1986. I should also thank the Yaddo Foundation, Saratoga Springs, NY, and the Literature Board of the Australia Council for generous support, and Susan Chace, Joy Lewis and Brett Johnson for their advice and help.

TALKING IT OVER
by Julian Barnes

Through the indelible voices of three narrators—two best friends and the woman they both love—Julian Barnes reconstructs the romantic triangle as a weapon whose edges cut like razor blades.

"An interplay of serious thought and dazzling wit.... It's moving, it's funny, it's frightening...fiction at its best."　　　　*—The New York Times Book Review*

Fiction/Literature/0-679-73687-5/$11.00 (Can. $14.00)

POSSESSION
by A. S. Byatt

An intellectual mystery and a triumphant love story of a pair of young scholars researching the lives of two Victorian poets.

"Gorgeously written...dazzling...a tour de force."

—The New York Times Book Review

Fiction/Literature/0-679-73590-9/$12.00

THE STRANGER
by Albert Camus

Through the story of an ordinary man who unwittingly gets drawn into a senseless murder, Camus explores what he termed "the nakedness of man faced with the absurd."

Fiction/Literature/0-679-72020-0/$8.00

BREAKFAST AT TIFFANY'S
AND THREE STORIES
by Truman Capote

Truman Capote created in Holly Golightly a heroine whose name has entered the American idiom and whose style is now part of the literary landscape. Holly knows that nothing bad can ever happen to you at Tiffany's; her poignancy, wit, and naïveté continue to charm.

Also included in this volume are the stories "House of Flowers," "A Diamond Guitar," and "A Christmas Memory."

"Truman Capote is the most perfect writer of my generation. He writes the best sentences word for word, rhythm upon rhythm."　　　　*—Norman Mailer*

Fiction/Literature/0-679-74565-3/$10.00 (Can. $13.00)

MATING
by Norman Rush

A female American anthropologist of high intellect and grand passion, at loose ends in Botswana, finds love with Nelson Denoon, a charismatic intellectual who is rumored to have founded a utopian society in the Kalahari Desert.

"A complex and moving love story...breathtaking in its cunningly intertwined intellectual sweep and brio...a major novel."   —*Chicago Tribune*

Winner of the National Book Award for Fiction
Fiction/Literature/0-679-73709-X/$12.00 (Can. $15.00)
....

SOPHIE'S CHOICE
by William Styron

A young Southerner who yearns to become a writer befriends Nathan, a tortured, brilliant Jew, and his beautiful lover, Sophie, becoming a witness to their turbulent love-hate affair and to the burdens of Sophie's unbearable secret.

"Styron's most impressive performance.... It belongs on that small shelf reserved for American masterpieces."   —*Washington Post Book World*

Fiction/Literature/0-679-73637-9/$13.00 (Can. $16.50)
....

WATERLAND
by Graham Swift

Set in the bleak Fen country of East Anglia and spanning some 240 years, *Waterland* is "a gothic family saga, a detective story and a philosophical meditation on the nature and uses of history" (*The New York Times*).

"Teems with energy, fertility, violence, madness...demonstrates the irrepressible, wide-ranging talent of this young British writer."

—*Washington Post Book World*

Fiction/Literature/0-679-73979-3/$11.00
....

THE PASSION
by Jeanette Winterson

Intertwining the destinies of two remarkable people—the soldier Henri, for eight years Napoleon's faithful cook, and Villanelle, the red-haired daughter of a Venetian boatman—*The Passion* is "a deeply imagined and beautiful book, often arrestingly so" (*The New York Times Book Review*).

Fiction/Literature/0-679-72437-0/$10.00
....

Available at your local bookstore, or call toll-free to order:
1-800-733-3000 (credit cards only). Prices subject to change.

ALL THE PRETTY HORSES
by Cormac McCarthy

At sixteen, John Grady Cole finds himself at the end of a long line of Texas ranchers, cut off from the only life he has ever imagined for himself. With two companions, he sets off for Mexico on a sometimes idyllic, sometimes comic journey, to a place where dreams are paid for in blood.

"A book of remarkable beauty and strength, the work of a master in perfect command of his medium."   —*Washington Post Book World*

Winner of the National Book Award for Fiction
Fiction/Literature/0-679-74439-8/$12.00 (Can. $16.00)
....

DEATH IN VENICE
AND SEVEN OTHER STORIES
by Thomas Mann

In addition to "Death in Venice" ("A story," Mann said, "of death...of the voluptuousness of doom"), this volume includes "Mario the Magician," "Disorder and Early Sorrow," "A Man and His Dog," "Felix Krull," "The Blood of the Walsungs," "Tristan," and "Tonio Kröger."

Fiction/Literature/0-679-72206-8/$10.00 (Can. $12.50)
....

LOLITA
by Vladimir Nabokov

The famous and controversial novel that tells the story of the aging Humbert Humbert's obsessive, devouring, and doomed passion for the nymphet Dolores Haze.

"The only convincing love story of our century."   —*Vanity Fair*

Fiction/Literature/0-679-72316-1/$9.00 (Can. $11.50)
....

THE ENGLISH PATIENT
by Michael Ondaatje

During the final moments of World War II, four damaged people come together in a deserted Italian villa. As their stories unfold, a complex tapestry of image and emotion, recollection and observation is woven, leaving them inextricably connected by the brutal, improbable circumstances of war.

"It seduces and beguiles us with its many-layered mysteries, its brilliantly taut and lyrical prose, its tender regard for its characters."   —*Newsday*

Winner of the Booker Prize
Fiction/Literature/0-679-74520-3/$11.00
....

INVISIBLE MAN
by Ralph Ellison

This searing record of a black man's journey through contemporary America reveals, in Ralph Ellison's words, "the sheer rhetorical challenge involved in communicating across our barriers of race and religion, class, color and region."

"The greatest American novel in the second half of the twentieth century...the classic representation of American black experience."　　　—R.W. B. Lewis

Fiction/Literature/0-679-72313-7/$10.00 (Can. $12.50)

THE SOUND AND THE FURY
by William Faulkner

The tragedy of the Compson family, featuring some of the most memorable characters in American literature: beautiful, rebellious Caddy; the manchild Benjy; haunted, neurotic Quentin; Jason, the brutal cynic; and Dilsey, their black servant.

"For range of effect, philosophical weight, originality of style, variety of characterization, humor, and tragic intensity, [Faulkner's works] are without equal in our time and country."　　　—Robert Penn Warren

Fiction/Literature/0-679-73224-1/$9.00 (Can. $11.50)

A ROOM WITH A VIEW
by E. M. Forster

Caught up in a world of social snobbery, Lucy Honeychurch breaks from the claustrophobic constraints of her British guardians and takes control of her own fate, finding love with a man whose free spirit reminds her of a "room with a view."

Fiction/Literature/0-679-72476-1/$9.00 (Can. $11.50)

THE REMAINS OF THE DAY
by Kazuo Ishiguro

A profoundly compelling portrait of the perfect English butler and of his fading, insular world in postwar England.

"One of the best books of the year."　　　—*The New York Times Book Review*

Fiction/Literature/0-679-73172-5/$11.00 (Can. $14.00)

THE WOMAN WARRIOR
by Maxine Hong Kingston

"A remarkable book...As an account of growing up female and Chinese-American in California, in a laundry of course, it is anti-nostalgic; it burns the fat right out of the mind. As a dream—of the 'female avenger'—it is dizzying, elemental, a poem turned into a sword."　　　—*The New York Times*

Nonfiction/Literature/0-679-72188-6/$10.00 (Can. $12.50)

VINTAGE INTERNATIONAL

VINTAGE INTERNATIONAL

VINTAGE INTERNATIONAL

VINTAGE INTERNATIONAL

Available at your bookstore or call toll-free to order: 1-800-733-3000.
Credit cards only. Prices subject to change.